# Seagull

# Seagull

# 1

Salih was wide awake long before the early morning cocks. At the first crow he sprang out of bed, splashed a few handfuls of water to his face and slipped away. The household was still asleep and the weaving looms stood silent and sad, like so many corpses drained of blood. Yet the sound of shuttles kept ringing in his head as he walked. In a little while the fishing boats would be putting out to sea. Skipper Temel would be there in his huge blue boat that looked like a bright blue bird. Indeed, that was what the Skipper called her. My own blue bird, he would say with loving pride.

By the time Salih reached the wharf and settled to watch in the hollow of his rock, the first fishing boat was already pulling out. It belonged to Skipper Black Osman who, God knows, had nothing of a skipper about him, with his long neck and red face like a bird of prey. No deck hand would work for him twice and he had the greatest difficulty in finding more than one or two men when he went out to sea. He was enraged with all humanity, as though man had been created solely to annoy him. With Skipper Temel he was not on speaking terms, although they had been neighbours back in their home town of Sürmené on the Black Sea, and their fathers bosom friends.

In the winter and spring, the little port would be crowded with fishing vessels coming from all over the Black Sea, the Marmara and the Dardanelles, and the wharf alive with people and movement.

After Black Osman's boat it was the *Daily Bread* that left the port, and next the bright green *Rose of the Seas*. One by one the fishing vessels throbbed off. Salih counted them and Skipper Temel's was the ninth to leave. The Skipper was as usual wearing a red neckerchief.

The rat-a-pat-pat of the engines died away as the boats receded into the distance and then dropped out of view over the edge of the horizon. A flock of seagulls soared above Outer Isle and billowed down like a white sheet over the blackened earth and the rocks of the island. Bored with the bare smooth expanse before him, the boy fixed his gaze on the gulls, but after a while he tired of this too. He got up and strolled along the shore towards the rolling dunes of Kumtepe, stepping on the fringe of the little waves. The sands were veined and knotted as a board, studded with mussel shells like hairs standing on end, and littered with empty bottles, pine bark, broken jugs and cans. The whole shoreline was blackened with tar as was Outer Isle and the sea smelled of tar too.

A small black coot lay dead on the sand, its head, its lovely tiny head dangling in the water, rippling to and fro with the gentle waves. It looked so sad . . . Salih could not take his eyes off the lifeless bird. Death . . . What was it? Where was it? How could this little coot be dead who only yesterday was diving and splashing gaily in the sea? What kind of thing was death? Where did it come from? Did it have a shape, a form? . . . He picked the dead bird up, scrambled to the top of the rocks, bruising his knees as he did so, and flung it out as far as he could. It sank, then surfaced and remained there floating. The sound of hammering started up from the distant town. Salih was climbing down again, when suddenly he stopped. There, in the hollow of a rock that jutted out into the sea, was a baby seagull, obviously in distress. With beating heart he hurried down to the flat rock. The baby gull's dark yellow bill was gaping, its plumage ruffled. One of its wings was broken and bare of feathers in places. It was cold too and trembling. Salih wrapped it up in his shirt-tail. What beautiful eyes it had! He could watch them forever . . . Suddenly, he shook himself. There he was, mooning, and the poor thing might be dying . . .

What did seagulls eat? Fish of course! Salih was proud to have found the answer so quickly. But what to do about the broken wing? Perhaps the same as with people . . . Perhaps not . . . His grandmother would know, but she was a wretched cross old woman who hated him and the whole world too, and would love to hurt and kill every living thing in sight. But what wonderful healing ointments she made! She could cure a bullet wound in a mere couple of days. The broken wing of a little bird would be child's play for her. She was famous in this small town, and for miles around too, for her healing arts. Even the smugglers, even the armed pirates along these coasts knew that her medicines could restore the dead to life.

How sorry Salih was now! He could kick himself for having done that wicked thing to his grandmother. Even at the time he had regretted it, but now he regretted it a thousand times more. It was a wonder she hadn't died. Then he had wished her to die. Such people, such enemies of all creation, had no business to be alive. 'Let them die!' Salih spat out with venom. Ever since that day, his grandmother had borne him a bitter grudge. Who knows, she was quite capable of strangling him one night in his sleep. Sometimes, sitting at her loom, she would cast a look at Salih that was like a poisonous bullet; it pierced him through and through . . .

And now, because of her, this poor little seagull would die. If Salih hadn't been so nasty to her, she might have given him some of her ointment. She might even have tended the bird's wound herself . . . Surely she would do this now, however much she hated bird and beast and flower. She was so old that at times she forgot to hate, and then her face would become bright as a child's in spite of its web of wrinkles. Perhaps Salih could catch her in one of those moods and wheedle the ointment out of her. Who knows . . .

Was there no one else in this town who knew about birds, who could mend a broken wing? There were such a lot of people, and good souls too, but none to make a healing oint-ment like that purse-faced old woman . . . He felt like casting the moribund bird out to sea as he had done with the coot, but then the coot had been dead and this one was still alive and might be saved . . . He could not resign himself to throw away the pathetic little thing.

'I won't go to that old witch. I'll just leave this bird here . . .'

7

'Oh no, you won't!' he spoke out aloud.

'Oh yes, I will!'

'No, you can't.' Anyone listening from a distance would have thought there were two boys quarrelling down there.

'Who's to say I can't? What's this bird to me?'

'Pish! You can't, you can't! Pish . . .'

Salih thrust his tongue out quickly and the next moment he mimicked an antagonist grimacing, squinting, mocking . . . He was getting angrier and angrier.

'You're afraid of your grandmother, that's what!'

'Why should I be afraid of her?'

'She's going to strangle you . . .'

There was a pause. Salih hung his head. 'Maybe,' he murmured.

'So that's why you've got to give up this seagull for dead.'

'No, I won't. I'll make it well.'

'You can't!'

'The hell I can't!'

'You don't have the guts or you wouldn't have stayed another day in that house.'

The quarrel flared up again, he brandished his fists and spoke hot words that were quite incomprehensible. Just like a Punch and Judy show, Salih laughed to himself. 'Oh, shut up, stinker,' he cried. 'That's enough.'

'You shut up, coward! You're scared of your own grandmother and of everyone else too.'

'Ha-ha! Am I scared of the sea? Am I scared of walking to the lighthouse in the night, and to the heathen graveyard too? And of climbing the highest trees? And of the black-clad pirates of the sea?'

Salih was unaware of it, but the argument with his other self was going on silently now.

Pooh! It's just because you're wetting your pants with fear all the time that you try to go to that graveyard . . . Anyway this bird's going to die . . . Granny . . . Perhaps if I smile at her, kiss her hand . . . Hah, you can kiss her ass if you like, she'll strangle you one night in your sleep with her vicelike fingers . . . Perhaps Bahri could help me, as he did that time with the swans. How many of them had those hunters killed?

Not even for the meat, because you can't eat it . . . And all that blood . . . There! Weren't you frightened out of your wits then? . . . Everyone's afraid of blood . . .

Salih pulled himself up. 'I must be going crazy,' he muttered, 'standing here talking and quarrelling with myself!'

Still muttering he made his way home and stopped at the gate to the yard. With a start he saw that the gull's head was drooping over his right arm. Was it dead? He touched it. No, it was warm. So now he must tackle that goddamn grandmother of his . . . His hand went to the latch and fell back. No, he could not bring himself to open the gate and go in.

'Coward!' the other boy taunted him, springing out of nowhere again. 'Coward! You're the greatest coward in all the world. You can't even go into your own house just because you're so afraid of an old woman!'

'That's what you think! Look, watch me go in . . .'

'You can't!'

'I can!'

'Go then and beg our granny to do something. It's such a beautiful bird.'

'Isn't it now? And once its wing gets well . . .'

'Hooray!' he cried aloud.

At the sound of his own voice Salih came out of his trance and unfastened the gate.

# 2

Today the smell of the sea was everywhere in the little town, a good pungent smell. Screeching seagulls swept over the red-tiled roofs in white cloudlike swarms, soaring up to the hilltop beyond. The houses, white, pink, bright green, haphazardly built, all stood in a row as if tied to a string, on the cliff that rose minaret-high above the beach, and sometimes their shadows would hit the bright, very blue sea below. The sea in these parts was like no other, or so the townspeople asserted, now a smoky coppery mauve, yellow, green, orange, now a very pale milky blue, ash-grey, vaporous . . . It changed colour every hour of day.

On the seaward side of the main street was the blacksmith's shop from which sparks shot out day and night in crackling iron-blue clusters. It was cluttered with old wheels, shining sharp-bladed axes, chains and many other fascinating objects. In the middle was the huge anvil, burnished smooth, with hammers and sledge-hammers all around it. Ismail the blacksmith was a forbidding old man with a white mane of hair tangling into a thick white beard that had never known the cut of scissors. He might have been seventy years old, or eighty, or even ninety. Today, his face was not frowning as usual, his moss-green eyes twinkled like two drops of light under the thick white brows and though his movements were slow and ponderous, his hands and feet seemed to be dancing for joy. Even his apron was fresh and new today, and not the worn frayed leather one he always wore. Blacksmiths need a leather apron to protect them from any leaping flames. Ismail's hands were beautiful too, with long fingers . . . His wrinkled neck was hidden and he was humming a particularly beautiful song today, the Master. Salih listened, entranced.

For how many years had he watched the blacksmith's shop with unblinking eyes, for how many years, from his vantage point under the tall plane tree whose branches spanned the main road to cast their shade over the smithy, had he listened as he played to the birds singing among the leaves and hearing the beat of the smith's hammer over the anvil . . . But today . . . Had the sound ever been as pleasant? . . .

And beyond, the sea stretched far into the distance, boundless, so clean, so clear. Ojakli Island seemed to have sprung from the water this very minute and the square ruined tower on top of it was growing taller like a tree. The sunlight beamed through its empty windows and rippled over the water.

And those gruff fishermen! Even they were smiling today! The fish nets were spread out along the shore or hanging on trees, red, green, purple, white, yellow, brick-red, and thousands of silvery fishes were struggling in their meshes. Deck hands, bent double under their loaded baskets, carried the fish to the middle of the pier and with ecstatic shouts emptied them onto the various heaps. 'Heaven be praised! What a catch!' These taciturn fishermen were even talking today! Today everything was sunny and bright and Salih felt so happy he didn't know what to do.

He made his way down to where the Laz fishing vessels were lined up, bow to bow, stern to stern, moored to the thick wide iron rings on the wharf with orange nylon ropes. All the fishermen wore stiff wide-pleated orange oilskins which gave them an awkward gait. Salih looked about for Skipper Temel. The Skipper owned three boats, all painted blue, one light blue, the other bright blue and the third dark blue, and he had named them all *Skipper Temel.* Skipper Temel I, Skipper Temel II, Skipper Temel III. Each had a green stripe painted across the blue, and on the starboard bow was a deep purple flying fish with long wings and an almost human head like that of a big-eyed girl. The masts were very tall.

The Skipper was lying on the sunny side of the lighthouse, his shoulders propped against the wall and his cap pulled down over his eyes. How well Salih knew that grizzled beard, that wrinkled neck, those blue-flecked hands! As well as he knew the aged blacksmith's hands and face and habits and

11

every corner of his shop . . . For as long as he could remember, just as he had stood near the honeysuckle bush in front of the smithy, unable to take his eyes off the spark-spluttering forge, so he had hung around the wharf by the sun-drenched sea, watching Skipper Temel and his weary salty-faced sailors dragging up the nets full of struggling silvery fish. He knew them both, the Skipper and the blacksmith to the marrow of their bones.

As for the rest of the townspeople Salih had had enough of them. They hated him. Even his parents were sick and tired of his eternal loafing. No one wanted him any more. All those eyes fixed on him, malevolent, deadly . . . But was it really so? Perhaps Salih wished it to be these days . . . For there were times, and he admitted it openly in his arguments with his other self, when he knew people loved him, when all the neighbourhood beamed upon him as he passed through the streets.

In this little town, nearly everyone worked at a loom, even small children, even old men, everyone except Salih, and he would upset himself by imagining what people were saying . . . How could such an idle fellow exist! He had no right to be on this earth. One should give him poison, not food. And think! What if the other children followed his example? That would be the end of this town. Everyone would starve!

Salih was almost eleven. He had a delicate face with huge blue eyes, always wide open, they never blinked. He was tall for his age and very thin, with slim long hands. His dark blue jeans were worn to shreds up to the knees, but his rubber shoes were brand new, with good strong soles. These shoes had excited a lot of gossip in the neighbourhood where it was widely believed that he had stolen them from a tourist. But Salih would never do that . . . True, he had not paid a penny for the shoes, nor for the green T-shirt with the face of a man printed on the front, a kind handsome face, but rather sad. The man wore a beret with a red star right over his forehead. It was a tourist girl who had given him the shirt and only long after she had left the town did Salih begin to wonder who the man with the sad face might be. He kept asking here and there, but no one could give him a straight answer. Many were the days when he retreated to Ojakli Island to tie his shirt by the sleeves around the trunk of an olive tree and stare at this face with the beautiful sad eyes. Who could he be? Why had they printed him on a shirt? Perhaps the tourist girl had done it, perhaps he was her sweetheart or something . . .

Skipper Temel stretched his limbs under the winter sun and scratched himself in his sleep. Further off, crouched on the flat concrete wharf, the sailors were busy repairing their nets, orange blobs bending and straightening among the blues and reds, greens, yellows and whites. How bright everything was today! The fishing vessels, the nets, the fish, the huge plane tree, the clouds, the sea . . . And that briny tang all over the town . . .

On and on Salih sat there, watching the Skipper. He was sleeping like a child, that irascible man who would swear and rant at everyone and everything on earth. But when he woke up . . . Ah, then he would see Salih and be pleased. 'Hey Salih!' he would cry. 'Where've you been all this time? Come, let's get away, you and me. Let's go to that little bay, far from everywhere. Have you got your marbles? Your slingshot, your bird nets?' That's how Skipper Temel spoke with him, Salih . . .

One of the orange-clad deck hands was running up to them, casting an orange reflection over the water. Shouts came from the wharf. 'What's the matter?' the Skipper muttered sleepily. The man stammered something. Skipper Temel rose, hitching up his trousers. He cast a vague glance at Salih and walked away. Salih felt let down. With dragging steps he followed to where the shouting came from.

'Such things can happen,' the Skipper was saying. 'You get about your business and gather up the nets.' His eyes fell on Salih. 'So you've come, eh mate?' he said. 'Give us a hand then.'

'All right,' Salih said grudgingly as he picked up the end of a net.

By the afternoon all the nets had been stacked onto the decks. The fish ponds were still full of live fish, red mullets and goatfish, shining brightly, and the foredeck was packed with bulging-eyed flying gurnards.

When the Skipper was in a good mood he would thrust two fingers into the gills of a huge fish and cast it at Salih. 'Here, Salih,' he would cry, 'catch this!' And Salih would snap up the fish in the air. 'Here's another, Salih!' Never would Salih let the fish slip through his fingers, never. On such days Salih would walk back home on air, as he carried the fish on a string under the envious eyes of the neighbours.

Skipper Temel was angry now. The long greying red hair on his chest rose and fell. His feet thumped loudly on the concrete as he paced the wharf shouting out to right and left.

Then his eyes fell on Salih. All anger gone, he smiled and winked. Leaping into the boat, he seized one of the largest gurnards and threw it quickly at him. Salih was ready. He caught the fish expertly as it glided, flaming through the air. The Skipper threw another, and another. The winged fish streamed out from the blue boat, red flames leaping towards Salih. Soon there was a tall red heap of glassy-eyed fish on the wharf and the cats were gathering around, squatting on their haunches, tails curled up over their shoulders, silent, expectant . . .

The sun rose and set . . . Waves beat at the wharf, high as minarets, seagulls in thousands swept down from the skies over the fish and still the cats did not move. Only once and all together, they flicked their tails with relish and then stood motionless, myriad eyes glowing in the darkness.

And on and on, gliding through the air came the winged red gurnards. And behind them Skipper Temel's genial face. But in the background, always there, was his grandmother's cross fiendish face, watching for a chance to get her hands at Salih's throat . . . Ah, if only Salih hadn't done that wicked thing to her!

And Skipper Temel still slept on in the sun, puffing and blowing, his bushy moustache bobbing up and down, his cap covering his face . . .

'Come, Skipper Salih, have you got your marbles? Let's run away, the two of us.'

'Yes, let's!'

14

'Where shall we go?'

'To that desert island where nobody's ever set foot before . . .'

Who knows, perhaps there are unknown seabirds there, winged horses, giant red ants, sea monsters, talking fish . . . A peach tree . . . Many many trees always in flower, all the year round . . . There, while the whole world is wracked by winter storms and blizzards, those trees will be warmly flowering.

'Let's run away, Skipper!'

'Yes, let's, Salih.'

'Skipper! Skipper Temel! Why don't you wake up? Look, look what I've brought you . . . Listen, I've got something to tell you.'

But the Skipper sleeps on, and the peach tree bursts into bloom in his dream, shedding petals to the ground, pink, mauve, yellow, red . . . Green too, and white and orange and blue . . . Salih stands knee-deep in layers and layers of many-coloured flowers and all about him red-winged, huge-toothed, long-whiskered fish are flying through the air.

'Skipper! Skipper Temel! It's me, Salih! Why don't you wake up? I've got no one else to go to, no one who cares about me but you in all the world . . . Do wake up! But don't be angry, please.'

On the wharf the cats are making away with the red gurnards, each cat dragging its spoil hastily off to some sheltered hollow in the rocks or to the beach, fur standing on end, purring with joy, hunched over the fish, devouring it avidly . . .

'Come on, Skipper Temel, wake up! Listen, me and you, the two of us . . .'

# 3

The seagulls rose and fell in swarms over Outer Isle. Salih knew every nook and cranny of that island for it had always been a haven to him when he was in trouble. He knew all about seagulls too, and about clouds and bees. Who knew as many things as Salih? Who knew about spider holes and swan lakes? Who but Salih?

Skipper Ali never lifted his head from the pile of blue nets he was mending. His hands worked like shuttles. Further away, Skipper Rüstem too was adding to his heap of brick-red nets. Skipper Aslan's nets were stretched in a long bright green line over the concrete. The whole wharf was a gay display of colourful nets. All the fishermen were hawk-nosed and sunken-cheeked, and when they walked their trousers looked like crooked stove pipes. Their bodies were hunched forward, every single one of them, even the younger men.

Mending nets was another of the things Salih could do, and quite expertly too. How and when he had learnt this, he himself did not know. One day, when he was six years old, or was it seven, one early morning when the sea is milky white and the gulls are still asleep, Salih had been sitting in this same spot on Olive Island which the wharf now links to the mainland, when on an impulse he got up and ran down to where the fishermen were mending their nets. Edging up to Skipper Temel he asked for a needle and began, to the great amazement of all the fishermen, to ply it as easily and fault-lessly as the Skipper himself. That evening they had re-warded him with two cases full of mullets and goatfish. He had brought one home and sold the second to Hikmet the fishmonger. And what a lot of money Hikmet had given him! Enough to buy those boots he longed for. Yellow fisher-men's boots with turn-ups, for three nights he'd taken them to bed with him. And then . . . Salih never told anyone what he'd done with those boots afterwards.

It was Salih's habit, come wind come weather, to hurry out to Olive Island the minute he opened his eyes and sit in the hollow of this grey rock. He would remain there until the last of the fishing vessels had set out, watching as they receded further and further over the pale sea, their bright blues and greens, reds and yellows slowly fading, blending with the whiteness of the sea, vanishing over the flat horizon, a frightening thing, for how could it be that suddenly the boats were not there and the sea quite empty? He longed to sail away on one of those broad-keeled boats, with their curved prow and tall masts and high-built cabins. Perhaps if he asked . . . Wasn't Skipper Temel his friend? Didn't he look at him with love in those keen deep-set eyes of his? How gentle his hands were as he plied the wooden needle . . . With what care he passed it through the cold nylon threads of the nets, as though caressing a living thing . . .

Salih was an inveterate gazer. It was as though ever since he could remember he had been given the task of keeping an eye on the whole world. Skipper Temel had even nicknamed him The Gazer. That was long ago, during the first weeks of their friendship. Suddenly the Skipper had stretched out his hand, and what long beautiful fingers he had, and laid it softly on Salih's head. 'Salih the Gazer!' he'd exclaimed. 'That's what you ought to be called. You're an all-seeing eye, that's what you are!'

Salih had always been a wide-eyed little creature, marvelling at everything, putting his whole soul and energy into seeing what he was looking at, staring and staring until he knew it inside out, becoming one with it, whether it was a tree, a bird, a cloud, a fish, a flower, an ant, a human being . . . The plane tree that spread its shade over the blacksmith's shop and the splendidly tall alders beyond it, the many nests crammed with wide-beaked, featherless yellow chicks, stretching their necks to breaking point in the evenings, screeching deafeningly with strange unbirdlike sounds . . . How many days, weeks even, had Salih watched them, standing on the mound opposite? He never knew, just as he never knew how long he had waited on the threshold of the smithy, his eyes glued to the forge, winter or summer, how many months, how many years? He was already there at dawn before the smith even opened his shop, and sometimes fell asleep and woke up in a fright with the clatter of shutters being lifted . . . And there was Dursun the carpenter, who made all those old-fashioned tables and chairs and consoles, always carving a full-blown rose into each piece, always up to his ears in work . . . How Salih loved him, how with dogged persistence he watched this man who had settled in the town from nobody knew where and who, when asked, invariably replied: 'Where would I come from but straight out of that sea yonder,' and follow this with a peal of laughter. The carpenter's shop smelled of trees and gum and paint, and when the timber was being sawed the whole world would be drowned in the odour of pine-wood, the walls, the earth and stones, everything, everyone . . . Salih, too, would smell of pine and even at times feel himself to be a young fir with green shoots growing in the forest . . . This happened if he stared long enough . . . And so he would, forgetting to eat or drink, falling asleep wherever he might be, and his mother would have to go out and find him in the middle of the night to bring him home.

It was like this, by dint of watching, that Salih had imbibed the blacksmith's craft down to the smallest detail. The moment he picked up a welder he would be able to use it or to hammer out an axe, a hatchet or a ploughshare with the greatest of ease. And it was the same for the carpenter's trade too, but Salih had made up his mind. He wanted to be like Skipper Temel. He knew how he had become a skipper and the owner of those three blue boats. The Skipper himself had told him about it. Now, was there anyone who could weave a net as well as Salih? And why did Skipper Temel call him 'skipper' if he wasn't good enough?

But the sea is cold and far away, boundless, frightening. Look how it swallows up all those fishing vessels when they sail away at dawn into its white expanse . . . Oh, they always pop out of the sea's stomach again, but what if once they shouldn't? What if the sea were to drag them down, down into its fathomless depths and never let them go? To tell the truth, Salih was terrified of the sea and for this reason he envied the fishermen. They were like no other people on earth.

'Wake up, Skipper, wake up, do! How can a man sleep at night if he sleeps so long during the day? And I've got business with you too . . . Open your door, merchant-man, open your door . . . My camel be yours, but let me in . . . Come on, Skipper, wake up, do! A man can die of too much sleep!'

The fish nets are flung high over the sea. They sink down very slowly, like huge wings, and emerge again loaded with thousands of fish struggling in the meshes, sparkling in the sun. And down come the seagulls, swooping over the nets, hovering low, wing to wing, hiding the sky from view, screeching madly, striking the sea all together with loud smacks . . . The sea . . . Doctor Yasef's daughter must be somewhere out there, and grandmother's husband, Halil, and big brother Metin's pirates . . . The sea where lurk those coral-horned, emerald-eyed monsters . . .

'Wake up please, Skipper Temel! Aren't you afraid to sleep here like this? Where the sea monsters can come upon you any time . . .'

Their huge emerald eyes aflame . . . Thundering on, cleaving through the waves like a green razor of light . . .

'Look, Skipper, I've got something very important to ask you. Wake up!'

Great breakers are beating at the land, shaking earth and sky, rising foaming white, high above the rocks of Olive Island.

'Oh, why don't you wake up, Skipper? . . .'

# 4

Salih hunted high and low and finally found a reed basket, quite wide and flat, and with a handle too. He lined it with soft fragrant grass and spread a green velvet cloth over it. Here was the perfect bed for his seagull. The bird's feathers were dry now, but still rumpled and it could not hold its head up. Its eyes too were half clouded by a white film and this frightened Salih more than anything else. What if it should die? He looked at his grandmother.

'Perhaps, if I gave it some water . . .' he ventured timidly.

'Well, why don't you?' she grunted.

He fetched a bowl of water and thrust the gull's mouth into it. The bird did not even open its beak. It never moved.

'Here,' his grandmother said, 'take this piece of cotton and wet it, then open its beak and let the water trickle in drop by drop.'

Salih did as he was told. The bird's mouth filled with water. It gulped a few times and swallowed. Its eyes seemed to become brighter. Salih was overjoyed, but there was still the problem of the broken wing that hung down so pitifully.

'Granny,' he blurted out, 'you've got an ointment . . .' He was surprised at his own daring.

'Indeed I have,' she said, 'but it's only for people.'

'Won't it do for birds too?'

'Certainly not,' she said turning up her wrinkled nose disdainfully. Her head was bound tightly in a white kerchief. The lines of her furrowed face were deep-set. 'My ointments are for human beings.'

If there was one thing his grandmother prided herself on it was her healing art. People paid her a lot of money for her ointments. Salih resorted to cunning. 'I know, granny,' he said. 'Who would know better than me that your ointments are the best ever. Why, if you gave them to the doctors, who knows what a fortune you'd get . . . We'd become rich in a day.'

'I'd never give those heathens anything,' she said mulishly.

'Don't, granny. How right you are!'

'Never!' she repeated. 'My ointments will die with me.'

'But isn't that a pity, granny? Look how many people they've saved. If they could save my seagull too now . . .'

'Never!' his grandmother shouted. 'My ointments aren't for birds and beasts. They're hardly enough for human beings as it is.'

Salih fixed his eyes, huge and tearful, on her, trying to put all the love and pleading he could into his gaze. 'Remember, granny, when Fethi broke his arm? In two it was, but you tended it with your ointments and bound it up, and when he came back only a fortnight later his arm was as good as new . . .'

'And so it should be,' she said, pleased. 'My ointments are distilled from the most wholesome plants and flowers that grow in these hills.'

Suddenly, all three looms in the room fell silent, shuttles hanging in mid-air. Salih's mother, Hajer Hanum, was a tall rather handsome, easy-going woman. Now she was incensed. 'For heaven's sake,' she shouted, 'a seagull, of all things, that'll muck up the whole house! This is the last straw. Other children of his age go out to sea and become fishermen. They get apprenticed to smiths and carpenters. They sit at the loom and help weave the cloth. They find a job as a driver's assistant, but this one! All he does is spend his time with seagulls, ants, frogs and other vermin! This open-mouthed simpleton, all he does . . .' She made a move to seize the basket with the intention of throwing it out, but Salih forestalled her. He grabbed it first and fled into the yard.

And to think he'd almost won his grandmother over! What should he do now? He was sure this seagull could be saved. Look how with only a few drops of water it had already opened its eyes. If it could only be made to eat a little . . . Seagulls love fish . . .

His grandmother had followed him out, muttering: 'My

21

ointments are for human beings, not for birds, especially not for dirty seagulls.' She was hunched in two. 'For human beings, d'you hear me?'

'I hear you, granny,' Salih shouted. 'You can go to hell, and your ointments too!'

His mother rushed out. 'You good-for-nothing whelp!' she cried. 'Is that the way to talk to your grandmother? Just wait till I get my hands on you. Just you come home and . . .'

'I'll never come home!' Salih yelled.

'Don't then,' she retorted. 'Get lost!'

Salih ran down the slope to the seaside. He circled the little bay of the Weeping Rock and found a sheltered spot for his basket. Then he tucked up his trousers and waded into the water. The thing now was to catch some fish. A tiny little sprat would do very well to begin with. The baby seagull would be sure to eat that and with a little luck it would soon revive. As for the broken wing, there was no help for it. That mean wretched grandmother of his was doing it on purpose. After all this time she'd never forgiven or even forgotten what he had done to her.

The water was cold. He spotted a shoal of small fish a little further away, but as soon as he made a move they swerved and shot off with incredible speed. Salih stood there and watched them re-form, shedding speckled shadows on the bright sand and pebbles below. Try as he might, he could not catch a single fish. Every now and again he waded out to see how his seagull was faring. It lay in its basket, deathly still, its beak thrust under one wing. Aaah ah, if only he could catch just one little fish . . . But like this, with his bare hands . . . What he needed was a piece of netting, a plastic bag, any old rag. He started off at a run for the town, then stopped short and hurried back, his heart beating wildly. Was he mad? What if a cat should pounce upon his seagull while he was away? And the poor thing unable to fly too! Should he take the basket with him? But what would the fishermen say when they saw him? No, it was impossible. He slumped down on a rock, his head in his hands, and forced himself to think hard. He brought to mind the veterinary, Bearded Haydar Bey, the druggist, Fazil Bey, Doctor Yasef

Effendi . . . Doctor Yasef was even older than his grand-mother, a kind mild man, but it was ages since he'd treated anyone. All he did nowadays was to sit by the seaside from dawn to dusk, his eyes fixed on the sea and the seagulls swarming over Outer Isle. Surely then, he must know what to do with a sick seagull . . . And what about the vet who was said to understand the language of birds and beasts? Why, Salih had even seen him once talking to a crow! Wouldn't he know about seagulls? Should Salih go to him or to Doctor Yasef? But Doctor Yasef sometimes beat the children with his walking stick, though to tell the truth the children teased and plagued him beyond endurance. They would place a sea urchin on his accustomed seat at the seaside and the doctor would sit plump on the urchin and leap up again, howl-ing, whirling round and round, rolling on the ground as though his bottom was on fire. Then they would fall into step with him, fooling and clowning and giving him no peace. Time and again the grown-ups would put the fear of God into their children, so as to make them stay away from the old doctor. And they would, one day, two days . . . On such days the doctor would scan the empty beach anxiously, expectantly, and the children would know that he was miss-ing them. And so they'd return and the screaming and swearing, the brandishing of sticks and the beatings would begin all over again. On those days when the children were forbidden to come to him, Doctor Yasef would cut a sorry figure there, on the beach, lost, empty, dead . . . He wanted the children, oh how he wanted them! Let them pick at his flesh with pincers if they felt like it, but let them come . . .

He would be there right now, in front of those rocks, pick-ing the spines out of his buttocks or just making believe he was doing so, for very often the children would put not a sea urchin, but only a pine-cone for him to sit on, or even nothing at all, and the doctor would jerk and toss and raise hell just the same. One day they'd tried placing a soft feather cushion for him, but the doctor hadn't swallowed that. He'd laughed and waved a friendly hand at them. Sometimes the children would creep up on tiptoe and grab the doctor's spectacles. That was the worst of all. Doctor

Yasef would remain rooted to the spot, turning this way and that, arms outstretched, groping helplessly, until he sank to the ground panting, his wrinkled neck growing longer and longer as though he was breathing his last. Very gently at first he would start pleading with the children. Then gradually he would work himself into a passion and the most unheard-of oaths would fall from his lips. Then he would be sorry, but the children would goad him on until they had him where they wanted. 'Please, Father Yasef,' they'd say, 'tell us that story . . .' Doctor Yasef would strike the ground with his stick three times. 'Come here then, you little whelps,' he'd say affectionately. 'Sit right here, by my cane.' And so they'd crowd around him, handing him back his spectacles, and listen entranced to that deep pleasant voice telling an olden tale of the seas. It was strange, but Salih never remembered a word of what he said, not like Skipper Temel whose every utterance remained engraved in his memory. The other children, too, never recalled the tales the doctor would tell them, but simply listened as though to a foreign song, sad and immemorial.

Struck by an idea, Salih leaped up, stripped off his shirt, knotted the sleeves together and waded back into the water. Thrusting the shirt in he held it drawn out like a fish net. Now the little fishes would come swimming over the shirt and he'd lift it up and lo and behold he'd have bagged dozens of them, a hundred maybe . . .

He waited, thinking of the vet, Bearded Haydar, with his red sullen face, an inveterate drunkard who stank so of *raki* you couldn't go near him. Would he tend this poor baby seagull? Never! Why, he'd roast it alive and eat it. He'd eat anything, even the flesh of a seabird. And the druggist with his gold-rimmed spectacles, of which he wore a different pair each day and whose drugs cost so much people said: Don't buy his prescription and you die of sickness, buy it and you die of hunger. His flabby, almost effeminate face . . . It was said too that he never looked at women . . .

Suddenly, Salih's eyes widened with excitement. He drew up the shirt, delighted to see he had a catch at last. He carried the gleaming fish, still squirming and frisking, to the beach and laid them carefully, one by one over a rock. Then he rushed back to catch some more. His legs were pink from the cold. Shoal after shoal of tiny fishes floated in towards the rocks and the shore, their pinpoint shadows gliding on the sand beneath, then veered swiftly as though struck by lightning. Again and again Salih filled his shirt and carried the fluttering wriggling silvery fish to the rock. Soon he was lost to everything else, wide-open eyes fixed on the sun-drenched sea, watching the play of light and shadow, the shoals of fish darting like bright streaking rays, mingling with the shimmering wavelets, shot through by blinding flashes from the seashells below. He stood motionless, a part of the sea about him, forgetting to catch fish any longer, fascinated by the glistening shoals that kept going and coming like so many luminous rainbows, but brighter, more myriad-coloured than any rainbow he had ever seen.

It was only when a big wave engulfed him that he was jogged out of his trance. He staggered and fell back a step or two, soaked to the skin. A large passenger steamer was sailing by, far out on the sea. He rushed madly to the rocks. The baby seagull had not moved. It lay there, quite still over the green velvet cloth. The little sprats on the rock were dead by now. Salih picked one up and held it to the bird's beak. 'Here,' he said, 'eat this. Look how fresh it is. Open your mouth and eat.' The bird never stirred. Salih waved the fish under its nostrils. 'Look, smell it. See what a good fish it is? Look, if you don't eat you'll die . . . Come on now, eat!' But it was no use. 'Wretched bird!' Salih shouted. 'Idiot! D'you want to die? If you eat this you'll be all right . . .' He tried again and again. 'It's this fish you don't like then,' he said at last. 'All right, I'll catch a live one for you.'

That's it, he thought gleefully. Seagulls always ate their fish up live, as soon as they caught them. Who'd ever seen a seagull eating a dead fish! He grabbed his shirt and was in and out of the water in a trice with a fresh catch, but when he held the wriggling fish to the gull's beak he got no reaction whatever. The fish slipped from his hand and his arms fell to his sides. His eyes went to the cloud of screaming gulls fluttering above the tiny islet that was called Donkey Isle.

25

'So many many seagulls in this world . . . So many . . . Why should it be only my own baby seagull that has to die?'

Unwillingly, he cast a glance at the basket. How sad, how pitiful the bird looked. 'It's dying because of me,' he said. 'Who knows, left to itself, it might have revived.'

Yes, it was his fault. And also his grandmother's, damn her. She hated him and his seagull too. And what about his mother, usually so gentle? What had possessed her? Everyone was against Salih, everyone, even God, or would his seagull have been left to die like this?

He seized one of the fish still twitching on his shirt and forced it down the gull's throat. 'Swallow this,' he muttered. 'Come on now . . .'

The gull's mouth opened and closed three times. Salih couldn't believe his eyes. Had it really swallowed? He felt the bird's throat and realized that the fish had not gone down. It was then that he lost his temper. 'Stupid bird! Fool! Die then, what do I care! Are you the first bird to die in this world?' He snatched up his shirt, scattering the fish all over the rocks. 'So you're being pig-headed, is that so? Well, die then. I don't give a damn. I just felt a little sorry for you, but now I'm going to leave you right here on this rock and it won't be long before a huge wild cat finds you. Huge . . . Hungry . . .' He was making away rapidly when the mangled image of the little seagull rose before his eyes, feathers swirling through the air, bones breaking, crunch crunch, in the sharp savage white teeth. He could not bear it. With beating heart he ran back, dreading to find the cat already there, its jaws at the gull's neck, sucking its blood . . .

But no! Thank God the gull was still safe in its basket. So great was his relief that the whole world seemed bright and beautiful again. His mother, his father, everyone was good and kind, even Vicious Duran who hated children so, that whenever he encountered one he at once lunged at it with contorted face, mouth foaming, eyes bulging, and at this sight the bravest child would quail and take to his heels.

Again Salih felt the gull's throat. The fish was still there. He knelt beside the basket, seized the bird's beak firmly and forced it open. Then quickly he began to stuff fish down its throat. One, two, three . . . At the third fish the seagull stirred. Even its broken wing fluttered, and in one gulp it had swallowed everything. Salih sat back and scanned it eagerly. Surely it would revive now. Oh, how he longed to see it fly, soar up high in the sky . . . Should he try another fish? No, better stop now. Anyway, Salih was tired. Perhaps he should save the rest of them for tomorrow . . . But they'd be stinking by then. He looked at the bees buzzing over the dead fish, their wings quivering brightly. Five of them were wasps, he noted with a start. And then there were honey-bees, yellow-jackets, bumble-bees . . . But what was the name of that fat black almost greenish bee that darted about like lightning, making more noise than all the others put together? . . . Salih was engrossed in the bees now. Alive or dead, how good a bee smells! Breathe in its lovely odour, redolent of many flowers, and a strange soaring feeling comes over you, as though you are flying like a bee yourself . . . As for seagulls, they smell just like the sea, and so do their eggs. If you eat seagull eggs, you can, fried in a pan, it's like swallowing a whole sea, you're up on a wave, tossed here and there, you're walking at the bottom of the sea, you're the sea yourself . . .

One by one Salih picked up all the fish and placed them on the green velvet cloth beside the little gull. Perhaps the smell of fish would bring it around . . . He picked up the basket and started off for the town, his feet flying, walking on air, the salty tang of the sea in his nostrils. Was he going home? Never! Those people there would not rest until they'd killed his poor seagull. No, he was going to Hanifé his big sister, whose husband always fished with hook and line and therefore caught the best, the freshest, most expensive fish on this coast.

'Sleep, my poor sick little seagull,' he said. 'Sleep and don't worry. I'm taking you where you'll be looked after properly.'

The sea below was smooth now, cloudlike. The fat-keeled trawlers were coming into port. Cheerfully Salih waved an arm at them. His hopes were rising with every step he took. 'Who cares if you don't wake up, Skipper Temel! Who cares!'

# 5

His sister greeted him in the yard with a big hug. She was delighted to see him. 'Well Salih?' she said as she stroked his curly golden hair. 'What's new?'

'Is Mustafa home?' Salih asked.

'Yes, he's inside . . . What have you got there?'

'It's a seagull. A poor baby seagull with a broken wing . . .' Salih said piteously.

Hanifé realized that something was up. 'How's everyone at home?' she inquired.

'They're all right,' Salih replied, ready to break into tears.

'Have they done something again to my own dear little brother?'

'Oh sister!' Salih burst out. 'They refused to let me keep this poor wounded little gull in the house. They threw us out, both of us . . . Granny wouldn't let me have a little drop of those ointments she gives to everyone else. They all hate me there, they do! I want to see Mustafa. He's a fisherman. Perhaps he knows about sick seagulls . . .'

'Mustafa!' Hanifé called. 'Look who's here.'

The small yard was planted with roses, marigolds and gillyflowers. Tall narcissus grew in clumps all along the edge of the fence which was hidden under thick honeysuckle shrubs ready to burst into bloom.

Mustafa, a tall, broad-shouldered man, appeared at the door. He smiled with pleasure on seeing Salih. 'Welcome brother,' he cried as he came down the three steps holding out his hand. 'How are you?'

'Don't ask!' Salih said dolefully as he took Mustafa's hand. 'You can see for yourself. It's dying, my little baby seagull. I thought I'd take it home and make it well. Just a broken wing . . . But they threw us out. Mother said a good-for-nothing like me could only bring in a good-for-nothing bird. She flung this basket right out into the yard. My seagull might have been killed . . .'

Mustafa held up the gull's head and examined its wing. His face grew longer and longer. This did not escape Salih's intent eyes. 'Oh Mustafa,' he pleaded, 'is there no hope, no hope at all?'

'Well . . .' Mustafa hesitated. 'One must never lose hope. Look, let's put it somewhere warm and where the cats can't get at it and then we'll see.'

Salih brightened. 'That's true,' he said. 'Cats are the worst enemies of these little birds.'

'We'll think of something to put on this broken wing. We may save it yet.'

'Of course we can!' Salih cried. 'If it was going to die, it would have died long ago.'

Mustafa frowned. 'How long has it been like this?'

'One week,' Salih lied quickly. 'And besides, it's just eaten three huge fish. Really large ones.'

'That's different then,' Mustafa said. 'If this tiny baby seagull's put up such a brave fight, we must help it hold out. We can't let it die.'

'It won't die,' Salih asserted, his eyes shining with hope.

'And if it does, that's no problem. I'm going fishing tomorrow. The islands out there are full of nests. I'll catch another baby gull for you, a good healthy one, not like this and . . .'

'I don't want another gull!' Salih shouted. Then he stopped short, ashamed of himself.

They went inside. In a corner of the room was a heap of old fishing nets. Salih set his basket down over the nets. 'This is a good place,' he said. 'These nets smell of the sea and gulls can't do without the smell of the sea.'

'No indeed . . .' Mustafa stroked his moustache thoughtfully.

'Salih!' Hanifé exclaimed. 'But you're wet through! And I bet you've had nothing to eat either.'

'I was too busy catching fish for my seagull,' Salih said contritely.

'You'll catch your death of cold! My poor brother, so frail, so thin . . . And all for a miserable seagull . . .' Quickly, she

29

stripped him of his clothes and passed one of her husband's shirts over his head. Salih was lost in it. He burst out laughing.

'Your Mustafa's even larger than I thought, sister,' he said.

She was already in the kitchen warming up the soup and bustling about, still muttering to herself. 'Ah, my poor brother . . . All for a miserable seagull . . .'

When the soup was served Salih swallowed it at one gulp. He'd never been so hungry in his life. Then his sister put a plate of stuffed cabbage leaves before him which he gobbled down just as fast. After he had eaten half the *helva*\* which was in the middle of the table, he sat back with a sigh. 'Oooh, but how hungry I was . . . A thousand blessings on your board . . .' Suddenly, he jumped up and rushed to the basket. 'Hey,' he shouted, 'the gull's opened its eyes!'

Mustafa went to see. 'So it has,' he rejoiced. 'It wants to live, Salih. Look, you know what we're going to do?'

'What?'

'First, we'll clean this wing with hydrogen peroxide.'

'Good!'

'And then we'll chew some wheat and bind it to the wound. I've heard that's good for birds.'

'Quick, quick!'

They set to work at once, cleaning the wound with cotton wool steeped in peroxide until it was frothy, then applied the wheat they had chewed diligently. As they bound it up, the bird fluttered once or twice.

'It's going to be all right! Look, look!' they both cried.

It was getting late. Hanifé at a sign from her husband had spread some bedding near the basket. Before lying down Salih cast one last glance at the seagull. It was fast asleep, its head on its wing.

The boy looked up gratefully at Hanifé and Mustafa.

'Your seagull's going to be all right,' she told him. 'In less than a couple of days.'

Salih jumped up and threw his arms round her neck. 'Goodnight,' he said.

\*Helva: a sweet made with sesame oil, cereals, syrup or honey.

30

He was determined not to sleep. No, he must be on the alert and watch how his seagull was faring. But instead, he was fast asleep the minute his head touched the pillow and when he woke up it was broad daylight. He sat up, rubbing his eyes, with a vague feeling that there was something he had forgotten. A warm breeze was blowing in through the window, bearing the scent of narcissus, honeysuckle and roses, and the sunlight cast speckled shadows under the bower in front of the door.

Suddenly he shot up like an arrow. With beating heart he went to the basket and touched the seagull. It was alive. At his touch it even opened an eye.

'I looked after it while you slept,' his sister said. 'Don't worry, your bird's pulled through. It won't die. It even ate all the three fish I gave it before sun-up.'

'No!' Salih was wild with excitement. 'Really? Really?'

'But of course! I wouldn't lie to you, my Salih. It gobbled those fish up so hungrily you'd have thought it was a baby buffalo and not a baby seagull. Come and have some soup.'

The soup was steaming in a bowl on the table. With joy in his heart Salih sat down and plied his wooden spoon. So now his seagull would live! They'd become friends, oh such good friends! He would name it 'Whitebird'. That's what the fishermen in these parts sometimes called the seagulls.

'Sister,' he cried, his eyes shining, 'd'you know what I'm calling my seagull?'

'Nooo . . .'

'Whitebird! And when it grows up, it's going to fly and fly . . .'

'But first you must get some proper medicine for Whitebird. You must see somebody who really understands about birds and their illnesses.'

'Who is there?' Salih said, chastened. 'Nobody cares about these poor seagulls. Everyone wants to kill them. Who can I take it to?'

'I don't know, Salih . . . And listen, there's something else. While you were asleep . . .'

'Mother came, is that so?'

'Exactly. And it seems father flew into one of his rages again and raised the roof at home.'

Salih's eyes filled with tears. 'What does that man want with me, sister? What shall I do? Where can I go? It would be better if me and my seagull died. It's dying anyway and even if it doesn't die, of what use is a seagull with a broken wing that'll never be able to fly? Yes, much better I should throw myself into the sea, together with my poor seagull.'

'Now, what kind of talk is that!' his sister admonished him. 'They were quite naturally concerned about you. I ought to have gone last night to tell them you were here. Mother wants you to come home today.'

Salih went pale. His face crumpled and he bent his head.

At last he looked up with tears in his eyes. 'Sister, Mustafa's a very good man, isn't he?'

'So he is, my dear, the best in the world.'

'Wouldn't he want me to stay here in his house?'

'But of course, darling. Only you see . . .' She sighed. 'Ah, that father of ours . . . He's being difficult. He said to mother, if Salih's not back home by this evening I'll go to that lout of a son-in-law and bring his house down over his ears. As if it isn't enough that my daughter's married a common fisherman, my son too . . .'

'Let him come,' Salih muttered. 'Mustafa can thrash him to pulp, that drunkard, that gambler, that . . .'

'Shh!' His sister put her hand over his mouth.

'Mustafa's so strong he can grab him by the nape and hurl him into the sea from those rocks there, that old dotard . . .'

'Don't call your father a dotard!'

'I will, I will! I'll call him worse than that. Just let Mustafa lay hands on him . . . It's only because he's your father that he doesn't!'

'Salih, you know father. He's quite capable of getting drunk one night and setting fire to this house.'

'I can't go back!' Salih shouted. 'They'll kill this poor little seagull and they'll beat me black and blue. Why can't I stay here, sister? I'll work too, in Mustafa's boat. I know about fishing. You know Skipper Temel, sister? It's from him I've learnt it all . . . Oh please, sister . . .'

'It's not possible, Salih. Mustafa's sore enough at father as it is. And if father comes here picking a new quarrel because of you, there'll be bloodshed, I know.'

'I hope he kills him,' Salih said fervently.

'But what shall I do then, Salih, without Mustafa? They'll hang him.'

Salih was trembling with rage.

'Let him kill father and escape in his boat, beyond the edge of the sea. Look, sister, I know something . . .'

'What's that?'

'You know how ships vanish behind the sea? Well, Skipper Temel's told me, it's not under the sea they disappear. There's another sea beyond, and then still another one. So you see, Mustafa could . . .'

'No, no, Salih. Mustafa's boat is too small. It would sink out there.'

Salih was stricken. 'Oh no, poor Mustafa,' he said. 'His boat mustn't sink. I'll go away . . . All by myself . . . What else can I do?' He kissed his sister, picked up the basket and walked out of the house. Hanifé stood at the door, all the blood drained from her face.

As he passed under the pink roses at the gate Salih looked back. 'Don't worry about me, sister,' he said. 'Say goodbye to Mustafa for me and thank him for having taken care of my bird. I'll never forget how good he's been to me. And don't let him quarrel with father and lose his beautiful boat.'

Hanifé forced herself to be firm. 'You're to go straight home now, Salih,' she said. 'Mother's waiting for you.' Then she turned away, banging the door shut.

'I won't go back, so there!' Salih muttered as he went down the hill. 'I'd rather die. And I shan't come to you any more either, sister. I've no home, no sister, no one. Only Mustafa, but they'll sink his boat if I go to him. Father'll shoot him dead . . . Go back home? Hah! So they kill my Whitebird? So they break my bones? So what if father should raise hell? I'd rather go and live in a cave. I could also ask Skipper Temel to take me on his crew. Or I could be apprenticed to Ismail the blacksmith, or to Dursun the carpenter. Or even be a shepherd up on the hills . . . But what would my seagull eat then? It must have fish . . . Anyway, they can flay me alive before I go back home. I'll find a place where me and my bird can live in peace. Food's no problem, neither for me nor my bird.'

He was getting angrier and angrier as he walked ever more quickly down to the shore.

# 6

Several steep dizzy little paths led from the row of houses on the cliff down to the wide beach below. They were just as difficult to descend as to climb. Salih took the one beneath Chardak, but once on the seaside he did not know what to do next. Even his sister had sent him away. He had to find a place where no one would find him. And what about his poor baby seagull, still too weak to lift its head? Should he leave it to its fate here on this beach? To die, he repeated angrily to himself, to die.

The day was warm, the sea smooth and velvety and very blue. Salih put the basket down and began to skim stones across the water. Soon he was humming a song, perhaps the blacksmith's song, thoroughly engrossed in his game.

It was already long past noon when he remembered his bird.

'I must catch some more fish for the poor thing,' he said wearily. What he needed was a scoop net with a long handle like the one Mustafa used to catch small fish. But his sister had turned him out of the house, so how could he go back and ask for it? Ah, if only Mustafa would come now and take him to his neat honeysuckle-scented home . . . If he could live there, go fishing with him and, when he got tired of that, become apprenticed to the blacksmith or the carpenter, or even sail far off with Skipper Temel . . . But Salih was terrified of what lay beyond the horizon, of that deep well where he saw himself struggling in the dark and being devoured by sharks. No, Salih was only a gazer, it was so much easier to stand and stare . . . That was why people said he was not quite there, possessed, mad even. He knew he wasn't mad at any rate. Only he could not help being fascinated by whatever struck his eye. Things other people would not even notice would hold him spellbound. For the life of him he could not drag himself away until he had wholly exhausted the object of his gaze. And indeed many were the things he had exhausted up to now. But not the sea, never, nor the fish . . . And flowers, and the warmly smelling earth after rain, the wonderful colours of the rainbow, lighting up the whole sky, the myriad stars and the light they shed over the water on certain nights . . . Those were things that he could never tire of, never, never . . . Just like the old blacksmith's forge, Dursun the carpenter's black carved roses, the smell of his shop, and Skipper Temel's blue boats . . .

The scoop net! Salih remembered he'd seen one hanging on the fence of Halim's coffee house. Halim would never let him have it, that he knew, even though it was old and torn, so the only thing to do was to steal it . . . Determined, but filled with dread, he picked up the basket and made straight for the coffee house.

Several men were sitting there smoking their narghilés in the sunshine while Halim bustled about to serve his customers. Salih climbed onto the fence, seized the scoop net and walked away in full view of everyone. Nobody asked him anything, probably thinking the scoop net was his, but Salih's heart was beating madly and, as soon as he could, he broke into a run and ran on until he was safely out of sight among the rocks by the sea.

The little inlet below was teeming with tiny fish. He clambered down and at the first dip he had scooped up quite a number of them. Quickly he began to stuff the fish into the seagull's mouth. This time the bird swallowed quite easily. 'Hurray!' Salih cried. 'It's coming round. It isn't going to die . . .' Again and again the bird swallowed the fish. 'Just let me get its gullet really full and then it'll be able to hold its head up. And then . . .'

Far in the distance, gleaming white under the luminous clouds, a large ship was cleaving through the sea, going eastward. Salih had never seen such a huge one before. Who knows where it was bound for, what kind of people were aboard . . . He sat down and watched, fascinated, as the ship sailed by, growing smaller and smaller, a greyish dot on the horizon, and vanished from sight.

When at last he turned to the basket, his eyes widened in amazement. He bent down, trembling, unable to believe what he saw, but there was no doubt about it. The seagull had raised its head and was gazing about with lively eyes. Oh how it looked! It was actually looking at him, Salih! And though its broken wing lay open over the green velvet cloth, its good one was now well drawn in. Still in a daze, Salih picked up a fish from the scoop net and even as he held it out the bird had snatched it up with a quick jerk of its bill and gobbled it down. Salih gave it another one, then another and soon there were no fish left in the net. Only then did Salih come to his senses. He jumped up with a cry of joy, looked to right and left, but there was no one to be seen. He grabbed the basket and was in the market place without knowing how he could have climbed over the rocks, crossed the sands and gone up the cliff so quickly. The first person he came across was an old man bent over his stick. Salih rushed up to him and kissed his hand.

'Look, uncle, look!' he cried. 'My bird's come to life! Isn't it wonderful?'

The old man was startled. 'Indeed, indeed!' he mumbled. 'Good, very good . . . What kind of a bird can it be?'

But Salih was already away, kissing someone else's hand. 'My bird! Look, it's come to life, look,' he kept repeating. 'And a whole netful of fish it's eaten. See? See its eyes?' Nobody understood what he was talking about. On he went and burst into the smithy. Ismail the blacksmith was beating a red-hot iron on the anvil. He stopped and stared. 'Master, look! Master, it's come to life, see?' Before the Master had even time to look Salih had disappeared. The blacksmith wondered for a second what could have possessed this little boy, usually so silent. Then he shrugged his shoulders and, thrusting the iron into the forge, pulled at the bellows.

Salih was in such a fever of excitement that he could not stand still for a minute. All the town, men and women, old and young, everyone should be sharing his joy and the birds and beasts as well, especially the seagulls. He thought of Skipper Temel, but the wharf was empty. The fishing boats had not yet come in. Suddenly Mustafa flashed on his mind.

He was already halfway to the house when he remembered his resolve never to set foot there again. His eyes strayed to the seagull and his heart overflowed. How well it looked, how full of life, as if it would flap its wings and fly off then and there. Somehow his legs carried him on to Mustafa's house. Hanifé was in the garden. He hesitated, almost surprised to see her, turned away, then back and met her gaze. Hanifé's blue eyes were filled with tears.

'Forgive me, my dear sweet little brother,' she said. 'My lovely golden-hearted Salih . . .' She took him in her arms and kissed him warmly. 'Mustafa was just going out to look for you. Such a dressing-down I got because he thought I'd hurt your feelings . . .'

Mustafa appeared on the threshold. 'Salih!' he exclaimed. 'So there you are! I'm so glad.'

Salih ran up to him. 'Look, Mustafa, look,' he cried, his eyes shining. It was still all like a miracle to him.

They sat right there, on the steps, with the basket in front of them and fixed a rapt gaze on the baby seagull.

'Excellent,' Mustafa said. 'So far so good. The rest is easy. And even if we can't mend that wing . . .'

'It's alive anyway,' Salih said. 'It didn't die and leave me all alone in this world. Never mind if it won't fly . . .' He paused, his clear blue eyes suddenly pensive.

Mustafa picked up the gull and turned it this way and that in his huge calloused hands. 'We'll bind up this wounded wing again and maybe afterwards we can find some good fisherman who knows about birds and their ailments. Fishermen and seagulls can be great pals. Remember Pehlivan? He had a special seagull who'd follow him out to sea and when Pehlivan dropped anchor, the gull would circle overhead, whooping once or twice, then remain quite still, wings outstretched, hovering about the boat, never moving until Pehlivan had brought up his first fish. And however large it might be, Pehlivan would unhook it quickly and fling it high into the air. The gull would swoop down and snap it up, never letting the fish drop into the sea. And afterwards, it would come to perch on the edge of the boat, just where Pehlivan had cast his hook, swallowing hungrily like a human being. One out of every ten fish Pehlivan caught was for his gull, and if he caught less than ten that day, then he'd give them all to the bird. There were days when Pehlivan didn't go out to sea, which can happen to anyone. Say he had other business or was sick or something. On such days you could see that seagull waiting, as though nailed to the sky, watching for Pehlivan all day long, not casting a glance at any other fisherman, not even if a fish was thrown at it. And when darkness fell it would turn away sadly and fly off. And next morning when Pehlivan appeared at last, the gull would spot him from far off. Its wings would start quivering and it would make for the boat at an incredible speed. Pehlivan would greet it with a laugh. "What's all this hurry?" he'd say in a voice brimful with love. "Did you think I wasn't coming again?" At this, the gull would soar up and take its usual position above the boat. Yes indeed, that's how close they were, Pehlivan and his bird . . .'

Suddenly Salih cried out: 'It must fly! It must! Even if it leaves me . . .' He hadn't been listening at all.

Mustafa laid the seagull back into its basket. 'Look here, Salih,' he said, 'have you had anything to eat this noon?'

Salih laughed. He had forgotten all about food. Hanifé rushed inside. She was the kind of woman who nearly always had something cooked and ready in the house. 'Come and eat then,' she called as she laid the table.

When they had finished she sat down hesitantly beside Salih. 'Listen, brother,' she blurted out. 'Mother came again and again, asking after you. Father's very anxious too. He's not angry any longer. So perhaps . . . Of course you can stay here with us as long as you wish, but . . . Perhaps you'd better go home just once . . .' Her lips trembled. What if Salih should take it into his head to run away again?

Mustafa looked troubled. He could not bring himself to look at Salih.

But the boy, his eyes on the seagull, was lost in a blissful dream. They were going to Istanbul together, yes that was it! Salih on foot, the little seagull flying above him, wings stretched wide. Over hill and down vale they went, and

39

along the shore, until they came to Istanbul city and stopped at the foot of the Bosphorus bridge. Salih stepped into the lift that would take them up the giant shafts, but, oh dear, the doors are closing before his seagull can get in! He could see it fluttering around the bridge, terrified, a stranger in this place, searching desperately for Salih, streaking over to the opposite shore, but always, always coming back. The dark shadow of the huge bridge fell over the waters of the Bosphorus. Ships were sailing underneath it, all their lights ablaze. The sea was gilded with myriad lights from the houses on the shore, the passing cars, the stars . . . The seagull darted in and out of the lights, vanishing into the velvety depth of the night sky . . . And now Salih was walking on the bridge. The seagull saw him and with a cry of joy swooped down to stop only an arm's reach over his head, its wings quivering. But Salih had to take the lift again, so he explained carefully to his bird just where it should wait for him, and sure enough it was there, waiting patiently, when he came out! Now Salih and his seagull were going to take a walk around Istanbul. Salih knew the city well. He'd been here often on these boats that sailed from his home keeping close to the coast in order to fish in the Bosphorus. But what was that? There went his seagull, speeding high into the sky, far too high . . .

'Stop, that's enough!' Salih cried aloud. 'Don't start being naughty now . . .'

'What on earth are you talking about, Salih?' Mustafa asked.

Salih came down to earth. 'All right, sister,' he laughed, 'let's go home. Mustafa will think of someone to tend the wounded wing, he will, I know.' And seizing the basket he rushed out.

Hanifé caught up with him at the gate to the yard. Salih had stopped and was listening to the rattle of the three looms that came from inside, his mother, his second sister, his grandmother, weaving away as usual, embroidering the cloth, never letting up.

'Come Salih,' she urged him. 'You'll see how pleased everyone will be to see you.'

40

They went in.

'Look, mother,' Hanifé said. 'Salih's come home! And his bird's much better too. Mustafa said it won't die.'

'It won't die,' Salih repeated, his eyes shining. How beautiful home was today! His mother's back no longer stooping, her wrinkles all smoothed out . . . His sister gazing at him with love . . . His grandmother . . . She hadn't looked at him yet, but had rushed over to the hearth. Surely it was because she intended making one of her salves for his seagull . . .

Just then his father entered the room, a tall imposing figure in his top boots and well-pressed navy blue suit. Salih had always been afraid of his father. Everyone in the town was afraid of Skipper Osman, even policemen and soldiers. But Salih knew that he was not really as brave and strong as he seemed. Once he had caught his father in a moment of stark fear, but he hadn't told anyone, no indeed, for then people would no longer be afraid of him. Besides, his father would kill him. How sternly he was looking at him now!

'What's this I hear, Salih?' he boomed in his deep voice, his gold teeth gleaming. 'So you've run away again to that wormer Mustafa's house, eh?'

Hanifé clung to her father's hands. 'Please don't, father,' she pleaded.

Skipper Osman clinked the large amber beads of his *tesbih*. 'Well, I'm not saying anything, my girl,' he said as he turned and went out.

Salih's head whirled with joy. He had smiled, that stiff unbending man, smiled at him, Salih! How handsome his father was today! What a lion of a man! Everything was bright and beautiful today. Salih skipped up to his mother and kissed her hand. Then he went to the hearth where his grandmother was crouching and flung himself at her neck. 'You'll make that ointment for my bird now, won't you granny? You will, you will, won't you?'

'Is he mad or what, this boy?' the old woman shouted, her tiny eyes starting from their sockets. 'Me, make an ointment for that mucky bird? Just listen to the fool! It's going to die your bird, that's what! Who ever heard of a seagull getting well again once its wing is broken?'

Salih went pale. His hands trembled. He opened his mouth to say something, but the words stuck in his throat.

His grandmother glared at him triumphantly. 'And if it doesn't die of itself, the cats and dogs are going to tear it to pieces. Yes, tonight, they'll pounce on your bird. Each cat will tear off a bit of its flesh. Even the bones they'll devour, crunch crunch. And all the while you'll be fast asleep, hahhah, haaah!'

Salih slept late the next morning. The rattle of the looms had started long ago, but still he tossed there in his bed, mumbling restlessly, 'Skipper! Skipper Temel . . .' This infuriated his grandmother. 'Dog!' she hissed. 'I may be old, but not in my dotage yet to make ointments for mucky birds. It's from that dog, that no-good father of his he's learnt to mock me, to humiliate me. But I'll show them. So my ointment's only good for birds, eh? Why, I've healed countless Beys and Pashas, Sultans even, in my time with this ointment . . . The lords of these seas would come begging at my door and give me one gold coin for just a dram. And you want it for a mere bird? Well, I'm telling you, my son Osman, and that good-for-nothing half-wit offspring of yours, I'm not dead yet, oh no! And after I'm dead my secret will go with me to the grave. To the grave, you dogs!' On and on she muttered as she cast her shuttle with expert speed. No one in all this town could weave as well as she did.

'Mother,' Hajer Hanum attempted to placate her, 'after all, a bird's a living creature too . . .'

The old woman was goaded into a fresh outburst. 'A bird's a bird,' she jabbered incoherently, pale with rage. 'Not a living being, not a being with a soul. You've always been against me, all of you, trying to humiliate me. Ah, it's Osman's fault I've been reduced to this, ah . . .'

When Salih woke up at last the first thing he saw was his bird in the basket beside him. The gull was wide awake, its eyes bright and lively. It had even gathered in its broken wing a little. Salih gazed at it entranced, overcome with fresh joy.

42

'Come and have your breakfast,' his mother called. 'You haven't been eating anything these days. Look how you're worn to the bone. You'll die at this rate.'

'He'll die,' the grandmother shouted.

Salih laughed. Nothing could mar his happiness today. His mother, his father, his sisters were like angels. Even their house, with its low ceiling and ill-lit rooms, always damp and smelling of mildew was different today. He sat down and began devouring the bread, cheese and olives that were set before him. Hajer Hanum could not pour him his tea quickly enough. Never had he had such a good breakfast before. Never, never more would he run away from home. If it wasn't for that grandmother, always angry, cross and scolding . . .

He rose and went into the garden, exploring it as though he had never seen it before, inspecting its every tree and flower, peering under the stones even. Then he went in again and began to prowl about like a cat in a new house. Old pine-wood jars, disused looms, cupboards and closets, carved oak chests, linen cloths, spinning wheels, wooden mortars, coffee mills, ships' logs, bird snares, mousetraps, every object held some happy memory for him. Noon came and he was still prying into every nook and cranny. Nobody paid any attention to him. Taking stock of the home like a new cat was a thing Salih often did.

He had just lifted the lid off one of the huge metalled copper cauldrons when it froze in his hand and his eyes widened. The cauldron was filled to the brim with his old toys, all covered with dust. He shivered and replaced the lid. Memories assailed him that he strove to chase away, dormant, forgotten things, shameful, bold, days and nights of long ago rose before his eyes. He raised the lid again and extended his hand longingly, then snatched it away as from a red-hot iron as soon as it touched one of the toys.

In the end, he closed his eyes and, thrusting his hands into the cauldron, began to rummage through the toys. His hands did not burn, as he had feared, nor did his heart stop . . . Slowly, against his will he caressed each one in turn and laid it into an empty nylon sack. Three horses, one of

43

them larger than the others. He pressed it to his breast. A soft furry bear, a rabbit, a monkey, a fire engine, a tank, a machine-gun, several motorcars . . . A truck . . . His hand shied away and he went on with the other toys. At last only the truck was left, and not only one but several trucks . . . How could he ever touch them again? Steeling himself he picked them up quickly and stuffed them into the sack . . .

# 7

The shops, then as now, were all lined along the main street as though this little town were nothing but a long market place, to which the two mosques, the little square, the breakwater had only been added to give the impression of a town. Even the stiff bluff slopes of Ojakli Island seemed to be just an extension of the market place. On the crest of the island, the ruined tower, with its large empty eyes and mouth, was like an ancient mask. Crows, gulls and starlings, clustered in swarms on the stonework, forming a crown over its bare head. Under the island the sea extended into a huge dark cavern, and on stormy days high foaming waves would gush right out over the walls of the tower. Olive trees grew on this tiny islet and wild rabbits had found their way there, how, it was impossible to tell. And sometimes the towns-people would bring their sheep and goats and leave them to graze there for a while. The ruined tower could be seen first on entering the town, and then closer still, more awesome than ever, on leaving it, its mask staring out with bright wide-open eyes onto the Black Sea, a giant watchman, a keeper of the main. On dark rainy days, when the search lamp of the lighthouse beamed upon it, the tower turned into a giant lifelike head, rearing out of the sea, water streaming down its face.

The children and the old people too would conjure up visions of dreadful dragons in the booming depths of the island's cavern, and indeed on winter nights, when the waves tossed high against the cliff and cascaded down in foaming white boiling masses, it was impossible not to call to mind the first monsters of creation, not to huddle trembling in a warm bed at the thought of those seven-horned, coral-eyed sea serpents that emerged from the far seas, spurting flames as they advanced.

It was a morning such as this, the sky grey and overcast and a strong north wind blowing in from the sea. Great white breakers crashed like thunder against the rocks and hurtled up over the islands. Salih had risen early and wandered about in an idle mood. His hands in his pockets, still half-asleep, he crossed the square and strolled up and down the market place. Everything was as usual, not a new face, nothing. Then he caught sight of Metin walking hurriedly out of the market. His heart leapt and he started after him.

This Metin, big brother Metin, lived next door to Salih's family and there had been a time when his mother and sisters had worked day and night at the loom just as they did in Salih's house, but now they lived like grand ladies, not doing a stroke of work. Ah, when once Allah gives a man the green light . . . Metin had always been a wild youth and, though a good fisherman, one of the best on this Black Sea coast, he frequently got into trouble.

He had fair hair and his eyes were as blue as the sea. But what attracted Salih most were the long pointed moustaches that shone like pure gold. Metin would oil them assiduously with a special unguent that only Salih's grandmother knew the secret of. 'Who can make an unguent like that, who?' she would mutter. 'No one, no one in all the world.' It was her secret, she would never confide it to a living soul. 'Don't then, who cares!' somebody would retort, and she would fly into one of her rages. 'Bursting with jealousy, that's what you are,' she would scream. 'Jealous of Metin's moustache, of my skills. Well, you can all burst to smithereens before I tell you. Never, never . . . Into my grave . . .' And she would too. She'd die before Salih even began to sprout a moustache. What a pity, for Salih was fair and blue-eyed like Metin, and his moustache when he grew up could be just as beautiful. Ah, what a cross contrary-minded grouch she was, his grandmother. Sometimes, Salih would overhear his mother complaining to herself: 'She'll never die, that woman, never! She'll live on and on to plague me all my life, unfortunate creature that I am . . .' How relieved Salih was then. If his grandmother didn't die she'd still be there when his moustache came out. But would she give him her unguent? No, that heartless old witch would deny her own grandson what she gave to any perfect stranger . . .

Metin had a special gait which Salih had tried in vain to imitate. It was clear one had to be grown-up to walk like that. Salih would have to wait. Then, he too would step sideways, the backs of his shoes folded down, knees slightly bent, swinging like a boat at sea. And what about that red kerchief Metin flung negligently over his shoulder? And the black Laz waistcoat he always wore over the striped navy blue trousers and the open-collared shirt? And the jaunty way he sported his cap, well down over his eyes, the visor turned up . . . Yes indeed, Metin was the handsomest youth in town, a daredevil too, with those two large revolvers that never left his side . . .

But Metin was poor, very poor. Who ever heard of a fisherman getting rich? Skipper Temel and all the other fishermen said the same. He who catches fish can never prosper, because he takes a life, no matter if it be only that of a fish. What difference is there between a fish, a bird, an ant, a human being? Where's the fisherman who's ever got a proper potful stewing in his hearth, a decent set of clothes, children he can be proud of? . . .

So it was that one day Metin showed up in the market place, shouting: 'For sale! To the highest bidder! For sale my boat, my nets, all my fishing tackle . . .'

Who wouldn't want to have Metin's boat? She was as fresh and new as a young girl. And those blue nets of his that could be cast two hundred, three hundred fathoms deep? . . . He found a buyer on the spot. Everyone was astounded. Had Metin gone mad? What would he do now for a living? More fools they! Metin knew very well what he was doing. Fishing had never got him anywhere, but now he was going to make money.

How tongues wagged after that! People in this town were such busybodies. But it was all lies what they said, everything . . . Salih should know, for he had hidden in a tree-hollow behind the garden fence in the dead of night and overheard Metin talking with some men who spoke differently, with a Laz intonation. Yes, Salih knew, but he never breathed a word to anyone. Metin had become a smuggler! He would set out to sea with those men secretly, in the night, without even a light to guide the boat, and sail over to Bulgaria, never appearing again for days on end. Salih had even seen the men one early morning and recognized each one by his voice, tall fair men with hawk-like noses and pale shrivelled faces, all so lean that their skin hung from the bones. It was weapons they were smuggling, and cigarettes, American cigarettes, and whisky too. Metin was making millions. He had heaps of smart clothes now and even wore ties, wide flamboyant ties. He let his hair grow like a girl's, because that was the new fashion. Good for him! Let them talk away, those townspeople. What harm was Metin doing? On the contrary, living in constant danger of death made him even more generous than before. No one in this town was as free-handed, as staunch as Metin. He was a bit of a show-off, but who's perfect in this world, and people like Metin had a right to swank a little. After all, he'd been wounded three times in that dangerous new business of his. Three times he'd been snatched from the jaws of death thanks to the salves of Salih's grandmother. So it was no wonder that each time he returned from a journey his first visit was to her. He'd kiss her hand and what presents he'd bring her! Her cross sullen face would break into smiles and she would actually laugh, to everyone's amazement, even Metin's.

Once, Metin and his companions were sailing back home with three whole boatloads of weapons, cigarettes and whisky, when a rival gang of smugglers sprang upon them on the high seas. A blizzard was raging that night, churning the waves into a frenzy and lashing away at them as hard as their enemies' bullets. They had to do something quickly or they would be lost. Come on lads, Metin cried. We're steering right at them. He closed his eyes and put his trust in God. Then came a tremendous crash and there was the enemy boat, a great fourhundred horse-power motorboat, sinking into the angry waves. Of course Metin couldn't let the crew drown. He had them fished out, but two of them died soon after. The other five were warmed up with tea and brandy and their wounds tended to. As for the dead men they cast them overboard without any more ado. They couldn't very well take them ashore and get into trouble with the police . . . But Metin was badly hurt too. Three bullets were lodged in his body and he daren't call a doctor or go to hospital. They would be bound to ask questions. The only person he could turn to was Salih's grandmother and what would take any doctor six months to cure she could cure in a couple of weeks.

And then one day Metin disappeared for good. Night after night Salih would go to bed without undressing, waiting for everyone to be fast asleep before he could slip out to his hollow and keep watch. But no one came, neither Metin nor his friends, until one night he saw shadows gliding silently through the darkness. He tried to count them, but gave up, there were so many. They made no noise, moving as though they were stepping on cotton-wool. One after the other they swung over the fence and squatted on their haunches, swaying up and down, all in a row like birds on a telegraph wire. They lit their cigarettes and one of the men began to talk. Salih strained his ears, but he could not understand a word. The man was speaking Turkish all right, but much too fast and with his cigarette between his lips. He sounded very angry, and so did the other men when they spoke. Suddenly they whipped out their guns which glinted dully in the starlight and, placing them on the ground before them, started chanting something like a very old invocation. They jumped to their feet, swaying, then crouched down again, up and down, again and again, with the special fluttering tremors so characteristic of the Black Sea *horon* dance. How black their clothes were, all of them . . . That was the last thing Salih remembered.

He woke up at the first crowing of the cocks, stiff with cold. There was no one now in Metin's yard, but far out to sea he spotted a tiny pinpoint light moving eastward. Another one followed, then another, all emerging from the steep crags below the lighthouse and sailing away like stars tied to a string. Salih stood watching, his heart throbbing, frozen to the marrow. The sea was a pale milky blue, more immense than ever. The long file of lights trembled, vibrat-

49

ing like a bee's wings and then they were no more to be seen, as though the sea had opened and swallowed them all up. Without knowing how he got there, Salih found himself on the edge of the cliff. He was struck with fear.

'They've killed Metin . . .'

'They're going to kill him! Oh dear . . .'

'But what has Metin done to them?'

'Would Metin ever let himself be killed!'

'Metin's got two guns, not just one . . .'

'And a machine-gun too . . .'

'He'll buy a big ship and deck it with flags and lights. Many lights, thousands and thousands . . . And sail away with all those lights behind him.'

'Where, where? Where to?'

'Whose rifle is that, bursting in the early dawn?'

'Oh dear, they're shooting poor harmless ducks in their sleep . . .'

A pale light is spreading over the shadowy hills and the sky. How white the sea is! A snow-driven frosty waste . . .

'They're going to kill Metin . . . Big brother Metin . . .'

In the old days when Metin went fishing the whole neighbourhood would have a liberal share of his catch. Fires blazed in every hearth. The air filled with smoke that smelled of fish and the sea, a mouth-watering odour . . . The children could not wait. They would grab a half-cooked fish from the embers, rush out of the house followed by oaths and shouts, and make straight for the crags behind the lighthouse. There, with the bread that they had in readiness, they would eat their fish very slowly, savouring each morsel to the full, their mouths and chins dripping with fat and spines. How everyone would look forward to Metin's return in those days, building up their fires in anticipation, the embers glowing already, and when he appeared with his loaded baskets, his trousers swinging about his legs, when they heard the familiar voice ringing out, 'Hey neighbours, what a catch! What a catch today! God's bounty! Enough to feed the whole town.' Then even the sick and the maimed, even the most sorrow-laden would smile and be glad.

'Ah, Metin ah! What if they've killed him?'

Metin would have extended his bounty to the whole town, even to his enemies, but his boat was small, it could only carry that much. All the other people envied their neighbourhood because of Metin. But now that he had been absent these many months, not one person had asked his mother how she was, if she needed anything. Why, in their place Metin would have gone out of his way to be of help. No, people in this neighbourhood were ungrateful wretches, they deserved to be sunk to the depths of the earth. All they did was toil at the looms, rattle-rattle-rattle, from morning to night, and what did it bring them? A mere pittance from the Istanbul shop that bought the cloth. Metin was the only man around here who had any guts in him.

The yawning mouth of the deep, dark cavern under Ojakli Island seemed to open still wider and out sailed a bright white boat with Metin on it . . .

'Oh dear,' Salih said, 'please God those angry men haven't killed him!'

They had scared him, those men, but frightened as he was, he went back to his lookout in the hollow, and a few nights later they came again, with their silent springy gait, and squatted down to wait in Metin's yard. It was a mild night. Spring was in the air, with whiffs of wild flowers drifting from the hills. Now and again, interrupting their monotonous parley, the men raised their faces to the sky, mouths open, like so many birds drinking water. Again Salih fell asleep and was roused only by the crowing cocks. At once, he rushed to the crags beside the lighthouse and looking down the cliff he saw a white horse on the narrow strand below, neck outstretched towards the sea, neighing softly. Salih had seen this horse before. Suddenly, the black-clad men were clambering down the crags, surrounding the white horse, that flashed like lightning in the dark, bounding, kicking, whirling on that narrow strip of sand, until every one of the men had to retreat to the safety of the cliff. Down below the horse flashed once more and hundreds of white gulls rose shrieking into the sky, lighting up the darkness for one brief moment. When all was quiet again, the black-clad men climbed wearily down to their boats and sailed away, a long row of lights like stars upon the sea, one, two, three . . . Salih lost count.

Towards noon it started to rain and the air smelled of flax and cotton and wet earth. Tiny cottony wisps floated through the sky, like the white tufts that poplars shed in early summer. All the people's faces were pallid in this neighbourhood and after a certain age rheumatism afflicted everyone. How could it be otherwise when all the year round they sat in dark corners weaving at the loom, swallowing cotton dust, and on stormy days the Black Sea would spew its foam right into the houses . . . Salih knew this, as he knew all about the bees and rabbits on Ojakli Island, what they ate, how they lived on that tiny islet. Salih the Gazer was curious about every single thing in this world. He even knew who it was had built the strange tower on top of the island! And how proud he was of that! What child, even in the fifth form at school, knew that this tower had first been put up by the Bithynians and then by the Genoese? Pirates they must have been, and Salih could visualize them, hawk-nosed men with long faces and pearl-white teeth, always laughing, their bodies quivering with joy . . . He would let his fancy roam, not only on those people of old, but on many many other things too, and never tell a soul, never. The peach tree, for instance, and the white horse on the strand, Salih would rather die than tell anyone what he knew about them. And about Metin too, and Doctor Yasef and Skipper Temel and Ismail the blacksmith. Salih was a sealed book. Only he had seen that big white ship bathed in sunlight, sailing so smoothly, only he knew where she was going . . . Only he could make friends with the slithering spangle - backed black snake that old sailor had told him about one evening on the beach, as he stroked his fine white beard by the roaring bonfire. And now Salih repeated the story to himself every day, better than the old sailor ever could . . .

One morning, his father and mother found him asleep in the hollow tree by the fence. Somehow he had not woken up at the early crowing of the cocks when the sea is still white. Perhaps those wretched cocks, strutting about conceitedly, flaunting the gaudy red, yellow, green and blue of their long-feathered tails, had simply forgotten to crow that day. Worse luck for Salih, for he was roused to the tune of much slapping and scolding, and when he managed to escape into Metin's yard, he simply stopped short, thunderstruck, oblivious of the blows that rained on his back. Before him was a huge brand-new truck, its body bright blue, its chassis the colour of a pomegranate blossom, as though blooming out of the sea, all painted with green branches and wild roses! And best of all, there at the steering wheel, large as life, was Metin, his curly yellow hair falling over his brow, his moustache brighter, more beautiful than ever!

They dragged him home, washed his face, brushed his clothes and made him swallow some hot soup, but all the time he saw nothing but Metin driving his new truck to Istanbul, raising the dust on the roads, and back home again in an instant. It was noon already when he was allowed to go out again. He made straight for the fence and jumped into Metin's yard. The truck was still there, but Metin had disappeared. Salih squatted down at the foot of a terebinth tree, lost in contemplation of the shining bumpers, the bright fresh paint, the large black wheels with not a speck of mud on them yet . . . How he longed to get into the truck! Who knows how good the new paint smelled inside, like a boat when it is first set to sea. He could easily climb up the terebinth and let himself slide onto the truck, but something held him back, he knew not what.

Suddenly, people were streaming into the yard, men and women, children, old and young, all come to inspect the new truck, touching it, jogging it, sitting in the driver's seat, even sounding the horn . . . And Metin was standing there too, smiling proudly. All the children were having their turn now at getting into the truck, and still Salih crouched there by the trunk of the terebinth, trembling with envy. Why, oh why couldn't he nerve himself to get up and touch the truck too? Why didn't Metin see him and lift him up onto the driver's seat, letting him take the steering wheel in his hands? Ah no, no, God forbid, Salih would never stand it, he would die of joy . . . He came eye to eye with Metin and smiled hopefully, but Metin's gaze had already drifted elsewhere. No, Salih could not risk it again. Quickly, he jumped back over the fence and huddled in his tree hollow. Now he could watch everything through the fence without anyone seeing him at all. Why, there were his father and mother, and his grandmother and sister too! When had they arrived? His father was inspecting the new truck. Round and round he went, with that stiff supercilious air of his, fingering the large beads of his amber *tesbih*, then turned to Metin and patted his shoulder. 'Not bad, my lad, not bad at all,' he said. 'Good luck to you.' He stretched out his hand and touched the blue truck. Salih was shaken to the core. 'Ah,' he thought, trembling, 'I'll never be able to touch it, never!'

How pleased Metin looked! He wasn't saying anything, but his mouth reached to his ears. 'He doesn't know,' Salih wailed to himself. 'Oh he doesn't know they're going to kill him, those men . . .' He jumped up screaming: 'They're going to kill you, kill you!' Then he sank back, terrified at what he had done. But no one paid any attention. People never listened to little children anyway . . . From where he was crouching he could see many feet coming and going about the truck. Some he could tell at once whom they belonged to, others he tried to guess, but when he stood up he could not see the feet. There were three pairs of rawhide boots which he recognized as the woodcutters' who sold firewood in the neighbourhood. Most shoes were much the worse for wear and six persons were barefooted. These were emigrants from the east of the country, all dark-eyed, sad-faced men who earned their living carrying heavy burdens for the town's tradesmen. Their bare feet stepped firmly on the ground, splayed out, well hardened.

Gradually, the feet were thinning out and soon only Metin's elegant brown boots could be seen pacing the yard from one end to the other. There now, Salih knew it! He knew it from those anxious perturbed feet. Metin, big brother Metin was afraid! Those black-clad men . . . What if they came again tonight? Should Salih warn him? On an impulse he swung over the fence, but nothing happened. Metin only gave him a glance and resumed his pacing up and down. Swiftly, Salih vaulted back into his own yard. He was an expert at hurdling, Salih was, a real acrobat.

Now he was leaping back and forth with furious haste, sometimes balancing on the fence on one foot, yelling like Tarzan, rending the air with even stranger wilder shouts, but Metin never turned a hair, so absorbed was he in his thoughts. As a last resort Salih bounded over to the truck. 'They're going to kill you! Kill you!' he shouted desperately. 'Kill you!' Metin had stopped short and was regarding him with sombre eyes. He knows, Salih thought, he knows . . . 'He knows they'll kill him!' He was shouting out loud now. 'He knows they'll kill him . . .' Metin's face paled, his eyes opened wider and wider. Suddenly, Salih was ashamed, and afraid too. He slipped under the truck to the other side and ran for all he was worth down the slope to the beach.

Some boys were gathering seashells there. They would make them into ashtrays, vases and other objects to sell to the tourists. Salih had never liked these boys very much. They were always quarrelling with each other, hankering after what wasn't theirs, gossiping about people's love affairs, whose wife was going to bed with another man, who was cheating whom . . . Only dirty things they knew about. They would spy on the tourists who came in the summer and tell about how they kissed and did other things too . . . And how these boys sponged on them! By the time the season was over every child had new clothes and shoes and all sorts of badges with strange pictures and inscriptions in German and English and other languages nobody had ever heard of.

He drew up to Jemil who was not as bad as the others though his face always wore a bitter moody look. His father, Halo Süleyman, was so poor he had to go barefoot. He came from some far-off mountains where the snow never melts, and day and night he sang interminable songs in Kurdish.

'Hist Jemil! Hist, hist, hist!'

Jemil was hurriedly filling a nylon bag with shells. He paid no heed.

'Jemil, hist! Listen! I've got something to tell you.'

Jemil turned impatiently, but smiled when he saw it was only Salih. 'What's the matter, boy?' he said.

Salih came closer. 'Have you seen it?' he whispered into Jemil's ear as though about to impart a great secret.

'Seen what?'

'Metin's new truck.'

'Is that all? No, I haven't seen it.'

Salih felt let down. He had to explain to Jemil how beautiful this truck was, how important for the whole town. He began to talk, but Jemil had lost interest. 'And there are pirates too,' Salih burst out at last. 'A hundred pirates all dressed in black with guns this size. Every night they come from the sea to Metin's yard and . . . But I'm not telling you any more, so there!'

'Get away with you,' Jemil grumbled. 'I can't stand here listening to fairy tales when I haven't even gathered one bag of shells yet!'

'Fairy tales! So you think this is just a fairy tale?'

'Of course it is. Where can you find pirates these days? Only in films.'

'That's what you think! I've seen them.'

'You have?'

'I have!' It was on the tip of Salih's tongue to tell Jemil about the string of lights on the sea, but he held himself back. How could he make him believe in those lights when he didn't even believe in pirates? 'Metin's a pirate too,' he said.

'Hah! That's a good one.'

'But I swear he is.'

'He's not a pirate, you idiot,' Jemil said. 'He's only a smuggler.'

'Well, that's the same thing. Smugglers were called pirates in the old days.'

'I don't care what they're called . . .'

'Don't then! But those pirates are going to kill Metin one night and I'll be there watching, just as in a film.'

Jemil pricked up his ears. 'Really, truly?' he said. 'Well go on, tell me all about it.'

But now that he had roused the other's curiosity, Salih turned away. 'Just you take a look at that truck,' was the only thing he said.

He must get home, eat and go to bed, so as to be able to slip away when everyone was asleep. How he hated his home . . . Every night, but every single night, his father would come in drunk, lurching this way and that, even when he was sitting at the table, spilling his food all over the place. And his grandmother, never losing a chance to set him against Salih's mother, so that he should beat her, and if not her, one of his sisters or Salih himself. Ah, if it wasn't for the question of having to eat, Salih would never stay another day in this house. He'd much rather live in some cave or other . . .

When he came in dinner was ready. They all sat down. Tonight, his father hadn't beaten anyone, so his grandmother was muttering away crossly under her breath. He wasn't even drunk. He laughed all the time and talked about Metin's new truck. 'Ah,' he said, 'if only fate would give me such a truck! D'you think I'd go on living here?' He slapped Salih's back joyfully. Salih was gratified. This was his father's greatest mark of affection. 'I'd sell this house with the looms and everything, then I'd pack you all into the truck and make straight for Istanbul. There I'd buy a good flat and the truck would keep us in clover for the rest of our lives . . .' On and on he talked, letting his imagination run wild, ignoring his mother's peevish grumbling. Ah, if only his father were always like this, would Salih ever want to run away and live in a cave?

He went to bed at once without undressing and waited impatiently for the others to settle for the night. Who knows if the pirates would not come again, who knows if they wouldn't kill Metin this very night? What if he fell asleep? He sat up, alarmed at the thought and his mother came up to him.

'You're not sneaking out again tonight, are you, Salih?' she said. Then she laughed. 'There now, I knew it! You haven't even taken your clothes off.' She bent down and kissed him tenderly. 'Sleep, my darling. You'll catch your death if you go out in this cold.' Then she tiptoed back to her bed.

His grandmother sat on by the fire, muttering and cough-

57

ing angrily. How could he slip out without her noticing? The blue and red truck rose before his eyes. And suddenly a white horse reared up beside it and the almond trees in the valley burst into bloom. A flurry of butterflies flitted across, like a dark blue wave, followed by an orange cloud. Tiny white mushrooms pierced through the new green grass. A shoal of fish had somehow struck the land and lay there floundering on the sand, at their last gasp. One large fish tossed and pitched, once, twice, and at the third leap it had plunged back into the sea. It was saved! Salih was filled with admiration for this strong fish. The grandmother sighed and wheezed . . . And now he was in an orchard, picking ripe pink peaches and filling his basket. The juicy peaches melted in his mouth. He wasn't stealing them really, Salih would never steal, but people were chasing him. Black-clad men rose from the sea and came after him in hot pursuit. Panting, Salih buried himself under the waist-high peach blossoms that strewed the orchard, and the men searched and searched and could not find him. After they had gone, he struggled in vain to rise, but the blossoms pressed him down with their warm heady smell. He was stifling . . . Then it was his turn to track down the black-clad men. They sprinted over Metin's fence and squatted in a circle round the truck. And there was Metin himself, swaggering above them, hands on hips, a cigarette glowing between his lips . . . And then . . .

He woke up quite early, and what should he see as the mists slowly lifted in the dusk of the morning? Alongside the blue truck was another one, exactly alike, only bright orange. Salih could not believe his eyes. He pinched himself and it hurt, so it must be true. He crept into his tree hollow and fixed his gaze on the orange truck. Why, oh why had he fallen asleep last night? All because that contrary-minded grandmother of his had kept awake, coughing and muttering. Ah, but he knew all about her, and from his mother too. She'd been only twenty-two and Salih's father a ten-day babe when her husband sailed away on that ship, never to be seen again. He'd had his fill of her nagging, the neighbours said. Perhaps she was too full of energy for him.

Anyway, she hadn't looked another man in the face and for nearly forty years now had waited for her handsome husband to return. Every morning she would go out into the garden and gaze far out over the sea. 'Come back to me, Halil, come,' she would say, 'I can't stand it any longer . . .' Even now, she repeated the same thing at least three times a day and, suspecting the others of laughing under their sleeves, she added: 'He'll come, my Halil, you'll see. He'll come to me before I die.' How many looms hadn't she worn out in her life, weaving day after day to bring up all by herself the son he had left her! She was famous on these Black Sea shores for the cloths she wove and the beautiful colours and designs she embroidered on them. But her hard rock-like face, sharp as a razor, never relented, never smiled even. There were moments, though, when murmuring to herself, 'Come back, Halil, oh come, I've had enough,' her face would soften and become tender and warm and full of love. She would weep sometimes too, if there was no one about. Salih had pretended to be asleep once and had caught her at it. 'Come back, Halil, do come back,' she was saying and the tears flowed down her face. 'Come quickly, time is fleeting. Look, even my grandchildren are grown up now and will soon be getting married. What are you tarrying for, Halil, in those foreign lands, far away from home?' And when she caught sight of a passenger ship out at sea, she would stand up on her toes and watch until she saw whether the ship was headed for the port or just passing by. After so many years she could tell even from miles away if it was steering towards the town and she would hurry down to the harbour in a whirlwind of joy and wait there, her eyes bright with expectation and confidence, as though she had received a telegram announcing Halil's arrival. She would scan each passenger in turn caressingly as though seeing Halil himself and after the last of the passengers had gone her face would darken. Climbing back up the slope she would cast one last look back and wave her hand at the ship, almost as if the hope that had died out only a moment ago had sown its seed and was growing imperceptibly within her . . . But woe betide those back home until the next ship

59

came in. She'd give them hell. No, it was impossible she should love anyone, not even her own son and grand-children. As for Halil, Salih's mother vowed that if he hadn't run away she wouldn't have loved him either. She'd have found someone else to wait for and love. Such vixens always crave for what they cannot have. Lay Paradise open before them and they won't have it, but will be hankering for the desert and thorny wastes that are out of reach. If ever Halil chanced to return, Salih's mother said, she wouldn't even recognize him, and if she did she'd still be so furious that she'd raise the roof and drive him away . . .

A sparrow alighted on the orange truck, then started up and flew round its light green chassis.

'I mustn't fall asleep tonight,' Salih said. 'Who knows what might happen? I'll try and sleep during the daytime.'

He went inside. A pleasant pungent smell of burning mountain plants filled the house. His grandmother was at the hearth, stirring something over the embers. In the old days, his mother would recall, when there were still pirates on the seas and outlaws in the mountains, they would come to his grandmother for her salves and ointments. Some-times, they would take her with them into the mountains or out to sea to tend to their wounded and it would be weeks before she returned, always in high spirits and with pouches of gold coins. People gossiped about it and for this reason Salih's father could never look his mother in the face.

He went straight to bed and drew the blanket over his head. If he could only sleep till nightfall, then eat, and then . . .

The looms were clattering away when he woke up. The house smelled good of thyme and resin and marjoram and other herbs. He rose and went out into the garden where he relieved himself at the foot of the mulberry tree. When he came back and sat down before the table, his grandmother stared at him as though she'd forgotten who he was. Then with a look of withering contempt she turned up her nose at him. Salih was stung to the core. Now, what on earth had he done to her that she should treat him like this? Well, he was going to give her tit for tat, that's what. Silently, he began to imitate her, turning up his nose and pursing his face disdainfully, hobbling over to the hearth to make a salve and spilling it all over the place, watching the passengers come out of a ship, his expression changing from hope to despair, shouting, scolding . . . And then, worst of all, he mimicked that time when she had killed the cat who'd eaten one of her chickens. That would get her really mad, Salih thought. How she'd beaten that poor cat and crushed its head, like this, like this . . . The blood, the brains . . . It was so sickening he could not even look . . .

His grandmother let out a piercing shriek and brought her stick down, whack, over his back. Salih only just managed to evade the second blow and rush out of the house. And now his mother and sisters would have to bear the brunt, while she raged and ranted and called them bitches and all kinds of dirty names, on and on, until his father came home. Then she'd take to her bed, tired out, refusing all food, moaning ceaselessly, 'I'm dying, dying, dying . . .' And his father would have no choice but to go hunting for him, bring him back and beat him black and blue in front of her. How she would sit up and gloat, then! She wouldn't even sleep or rest, but weave at the loom, keeping them awake all through the night.

Out in the yard, Salih was simmering. He had to say something to that old hag that would pierce her through the heart. He knew lots of things to drive her mad, but this time it must be a thousand times worse. 'I've got it,' he cried exultantly. He ran up to the door and called inside: 'Granny, granny! Ah, poor granny . . .' He put all the grief he could muster into his voice. 'I've got bad news for you, granny. Ah, I shouldn't tell you, but . . . After all the years you've waited and waited . . . Halil is dead. Quite dead, you know. Father and mother have been keeping it from you all this time . . .' Craning his head through the doorway to see what would happen, he heard a long moan and that was all. But his mother was already after him with a stick. He took to his heels and made for his special hiding-place, a little cave near the shore. What if his grandmother had died of the shock? Would his father in his turn kill him? Or would he hand him over to the police as a murderer?

He waited until it was quite dark before coming out of the cave. How white the waves were in the night, how they crashed and boomed from deep deep down . . . Salih was hungry. He went up to the baker's and bought a big loaf of bread. He had enough money for some *helva* too. Then he sat down to eat on the pavement under a lamp post. The market place was the safest spot for him now. His father could not very well chase him here, in the middle of the market.

When he had finished, he decided to go back and hide in the small terebinth tree in their garden. There was a much larger tree, an olive tree maybe five hundred years old, but his father had once found him there and Salih was not fool enough to be caught again. The terebinth tree was densely foliaged and if he kept quite still nobody would imagine he could be concealed in such a small place. Once there, he could hear weeping and shouting and swearing inside the house and also the crash of breaking crockery. He pricked up his ears and realized his grandmother wasn't dead. After a while he began to feel quite stiff in his cramped position between two branches. He struggled to free himself and fell to the ground all in a heap, but no one had heard him with the din that was going on inside and his father's exasperated puffing and blowing. He ran to the tree hollow. His father must have looked for him there already. He should be quite safe and could watch the trucks while keeping an ear on the house. The noise inside went on, his father's voice rose and fell and Salih's uneasiness increased. What if he should pounce on him in the hollow? There would be no escape, no mercy for him, especially in the night. During the day his father did not beat him so cruelly. He rose and with the nimbleness of a squirrel climbed up the olive tree, settling on the tip of its topmost bough. Even if his father spied him out, he could never reach him here.

Suddenly the noise in the house was cut short and all was quite still. Salih felt as though he had been projected into an endless void and the terrifying thought came to him that if he stayed another moment on this tree he would die. Hurriedly he clambered down and stood facing the house, unable to take another step, his uneasiness growing to bursting point. The silence was complete. Not a bird sang, not an insect creaked. Even the sea, always thundering against the rocks, was hushed. And then an owl hooted, and Salih knew for certain that his grandmother must be dead. If not, why this owl hooting, why this deathlike silence in the house? If they'd gone to bed they would have put the lights out. No, they were awake, all sitting by her deathbed . . . He drew near and stuck his ear to the wall, but not the slightest sound could be heard. 'I've killed her,' he thought. 'I've killed my own grandmother . . .' He could visualize her waxen body lying motionless, not shouting any more, not scolding, not saying a word, and started back as though the wall had seared his ear.

A full moon had risen over the tall mountains in the east and the night was bathed in brightness. The long shadows of the poplar trees stretched out towards the sea. In the moonlight the deathlike stillness was even more frightening. Salih ran down into the valley, then back to the shore behind the lighthouse and on to the Weeping Rock. It was actually weeping in the silence of the night . . . He darted away not knowing where he was going, caught in the web of some dreadful nightmare, repeating over and over again, 'I've killed her, killed her! Killed my own grandmother!' All the good things he knew about her crowded to his mind, all the bad memories were wiped away.

In the end he found himself in the tree hollow, with no thought of hiding now, no fear left in him, just lost in his grief and remorse.

Suddenly he caught his breath. Those black-clad men were pouring into Metin's yard again. One after the other they came and circled the trucks. Then, drawing their long Circassian daggers from their belts, they crouched down and thrust them, glinting, into the ground. Their cigarettes gleamed in the moonlight, as though rimed with frost, and their shadows hit the wall of the house like round balls. At last Metin appeared and stood facing them, very straight, hands on hips, and then he too drew a long dagger from his waist and rammed it into the earth where it flashed and died out.

Salih could take in no more. Something was aching inside him. The angry, shouting men, the glinting daggers brandished in the air, all reached him from very far, muffled by a curtain of thick fog. And instead, before him was a wrinkled corpse swathed in a murky haze, yellowing, elongated, growing longer and longer, and Salih was trying to hoist it onto his back, to carry it away somewhere, but it was too heavy. He could not even drag it by the feet.

For how long had he been sitting here on these steps, leaning against the door? He did not know. He jumped to his feet. Day was dawning. If only the door would open and he would go in . . . He stood shivering, his hands thrust into his shirt, longing to knock, hesitating, with no recollection of what he was doing there, only a vague stirring in his mind of black-clad men and daggers frozen stiff in the earth.

The door was flung open so brusquely that Salih almost toppled over and it all came back to him. Resolutely, ready to face whatever was coming to him, he stepped inside. His father was already upon him, with bloodshot eyes and ruffled moustache, his arm lifted to strike, when his grandmother uttered a cry: 'Don't touch him!' Still purple in the face, muttering angrily, his father lowered his arm. With tears in his eyes, Salih approached the bed and looked at his grandmother's yellowed face. She seemed to be pleading with him, come on child, say it, only you can mend what you've done, only you can save me, come on, say it . . . Salih swallowed. 'Granny,' he said. His voice broke. 'Granny . . .' His grandmother was sitting up, her neck stretched out expectantly. 'Granny . . . Halil isn't dead, you know. I just made it all up to . . . To . . . He'll come back, Granny, for sure.'

There, he'd said it. He shot out of the house, never hearing his grandmother calling after him: 'He'll come, he'll come! Halil will come! I knew you'd made it all up, but I wanted you to say so to me . . .'

A great load had been lifted off Salih's shoulders. His grandmother hadn't died and though she kept to her bed there was nothing much wrong with her. His father had not dealt him more than a passing blow or two in the past few days, and wonder of wonders, one morning just at break of day a third truck was brought into Metin's yard, pink this one, with a yellow chassis. The driver was one of those black-clad men. He had a dagger at his waist and a gun too. Salih stood watching as he jumped out of the front seat while Metin got in and switched on the engine. How pleased Metin looked, how carefully he inspected every inch of the truck! And what do you know, he even noticed Salih and waved to him proudly from that distance!

Three trucks! Three brand new shining trucks! Here was a godsend for Salih. Day and night he stood there while Metin tested all three engines in turn and wiped the headlights, the mirrors, the chassis, the flowers, everything, stepping back afterwards, hands on hips to gaze at his trucks for hours on end, unblinkingly, like a child.

But as time went by, his grandmother still kept to her bed, obstinately refusing to say a word to anyone, her sullen, unsmiling face sourer than ever. Could she be mulling over that incident yet, perhaps really fearing that Halil might be dead? How bitterly Salih regretted what he had done! One day a large white steamer sailed into the harbour and they hastened to bring the grandmother the good news, but to everyone's amazement she never even made a move to get up. 'She's going to die,' Salih's mother said. 'She doesn't believe in Halil's return any more. She can't live long now.'

Yet Salih knew better. His grandmother was going to kill him, Salih. He knew it from the way she looked at him, killing him with her eyes already. It was a good thing that she was too weak to get up. Otherwise, she'd be at Salih's throat one night, strangling him with her vicelike fingers. Salih must be on his guard all the time. He had an enemy now, an enemy to reckon with . . . Every time a ship came in, he ran to give her the good news, but she only closed her eyes and turned away. If only she would get up once, just once, and go down to meet the ship, Salih would be saved. And what if Halil did indeed return? Then there would be no reason left for her to strangle Salih. But after so many years . . . Was it possible? Time and again Salih willed himself to believe it and tried to comfort his grandmother and give her hope, but she only waved him away as though chasing a fly, and with sinking heart Salih would be even more convinced that she was going to strangle him one day. So he spent more and more of his time outside, watching Metin's trucks, listening to the black-clad men. What a lot of things he'd learnt from them! Night after night they came to Metin's yard and Salih would venture out of his tree-hollow and go right up to the other side of the fence to listen better and what he heard could have filled up five books, ten even. But he would die rather than tell anyone. If he ever breathed a word, they'd arrest Metin and sentence him to years and years of prison. And there was someone else too, someone who didn't trust Metin. How Salih longed to see him . . . He was never mentioned by name, but it was clear they all feared him.

One night, Salih had just settled on the topmost branches of the olive tree when he heard the sound of steps, and one of the black-clad men jumped over the fence, probably crushing the flowers, for the scent of honeysuckle suddenly filled the air. After him, the other men poured into the yard and a terrible brawl broke out. Daggers were drawn, guns fired, all in a turmoil of dust and shouting. The whole town was roused, with people jumping from garden to garden, rushing down to the seaside, flowing through the pale blue milky haze of the moonlight. The gendarmes arrived and surrounded Metin's house, shooting away with their long rifles, while the black-clad men took cover behind the trucks and gave back shot for shot. Salih had slipped down the bough and was holding on for dear life to the trunk of the tree, trembling in all his limbs, while bullets whizzed past his ears. A piercing scream was heard above the din, Metin's voice. 'I'm hit, quick comrades . . .' In no time, engines were throbbing away down by the lighthouse. More shots were fired over the sea, and Metin's voice came again from one of the boats. Then all was quiet.

Salih wanted nothing more than to go home and sleep. He was utterly spent. But his grandmother in there . . . What if she came to strangle him when he was fast asleep? His legs

66

dragged him to his hollow and he was asleep the minute he crept into it.

When he woke up the sun was at its noonday height and he was very hungry. He washed his face at the tap in the garden and went in, full of apprehension. But no one said anything to him. His grandmother shot him a black look, that was all. His mother set some food before him. He gulped it down in an instant, brushed the crumbs from his hands and slipped out again, only to stand arrested on the steps. The trucks had gone, all three of them, vanished into thin air, leaving only the imprint of wheels over the reddish earth of Metin's yard . . .

Metin was gone, the trucks had disappeared and the black-clad men did not come any more. The world seemed utterly empty now to Salih. He had absolutely nothing to do. Even his grandmother did not look at him with hate any more. She was slowly becoming her old self again, shouting and scolding and getting up to look at the sea, perhaps preparing to go down to the harbour at the first ship that came sailing in. Or was she just pretending so as to catch him unawares one night and strangle him in his sleep? . . .

Spring had come to the town. The trees and fields, the whole world was in bloom, but still Salih felt a yearning in him that not even the sweet breath of spring could dispel. Down on the rocks he had seen a long trail of blood, all dried up. Metin's blood, he thought, and did not look again. Was Metin dead? There had been no news at all from him since that night. But Salih had heard that motorboats came in the dark from across the sea and unloaded their smuggled cargo into the bays beyond the town and that the trucks then carried the goods to Istanbul, and with the connivance of the gendarmes too.

One morning all the town from seven to seventy thronged to the seashore at the news that cartons of American cigarettes were floating in. Such a huge amount the smugglers had cast overboard that the waves were loaded with them and however many they gathered there were still more. The fishermen had brought out their boats to take them up further out to sea. It was Salih who saw them first. He rushed through the main street with four or five cartons hastily tucked under his arms, shouting: 'Quick, neighbours, run to the shore, the sea's full of American cigarettes.' Then he went straight to his grandmother. 'Here, granny,' he said. 'Look what I've brought you.' His father and mother and sisters all hurried down to the shore and by the end of the day the house was chock-full. His grandmother and father could smoke to their hearts' content. Something like this had happened a year ago, only then it had been shoals of large live fish just hurling themselves onto the shore. The old people explained this by saying that melting snow had got into the fishes' gills, stupefying them to the point of muddling up all their instincts. For days fires had been lit along the shore and the fishes cooked there and then, on the spot, and the wonderful appetizing odour of grilled fish had seeped into the rocks and sands and into the earth itself.

After all the gossip and excitement died down, there was one good thing for Salih. It seemed to him that his grandmother had quite forgiven him. He could even swear that she looked at him with affection as she puffed away at her American cigarettes. Otherwise life was empty. From morning to night he roamed aimlessly along the seashore or in the town market, while all the other children were busy rummaging on the leafy spring trees for birds' nests and chicks, or laying snares with birdlime and nets to catch tiny finger-sized yellow, red, green, brown frail-necked birds. Last year Salih, too, had hunted them down with a slingshot, and not only small birds but eleven large starlings too. He did not care about birds now. Their last pitiful fluttering as they lay dying sickened him. What suffering until he could reach out to wring their necks! And the blood . . . It burned into his hands. Can blood burn you? Well, it did, it burned Salih's hands. And that look in those tiny black beadlike eyes, spinning desperately as the life went out of them . . . Oh, it was past bearing! For no price on earth could one kill birds after having seen that look . . .

So Salih wandered through woods and fields, idle, when only last year he had shared the other children's games.

68

There they were now, setting pin wheels in the stream at the foot of the cliff. These they called watermills. Salih used to make watermills too, cutting and bruising his hands, sometimes with no result at all. Either the wheel refused to turn or it was swept away to the sea. He remembered one that he'd contrived to perfection, but the next morning the stream had carried it away, or perhaps some other boy had made off with it. Now, half-a-dozen watermills were whirling swiftly in the stream, but Salih gave them no more than a passing glance. How could he look at watermills after the events in Metin's yard, after he'd watched those huge bright trucks, and three of them too, day and night? Ah, if only these boys had seen them once, would they be here playing with pin wheels and carts made of twigs and shells?

'I won't kill birds, I won't!' The sound of his own voice shouting out loud startled him. What if somebody had heard him? Wouldn't they think he was touched in the head? 'I'm not sorry for them,' he shouted again. 'Not sorry at all. It's just that I don't care about birds. I don't want to kill them, that's all . . .' He loathed those boys, especially Osman with his bulging ghoulish eyes. Up to thirty birds he'd kill in a day, which he'd pluck and cook over a fire and devour right away. God, how Salih wished the bones of those poor little birds would stick in his throat . . .

Down the wooded valley behind the town, in a shrubby clearing, he came upon another group of boys. The shrubs were in flower and swarming with hundreds of bees of all kinds, which the boys were trying to catch and tie to a string. Salih knew some of them. There was Kaya and Engin, and also Ali, Memet and Babur, who already each had a bee droning away in the air at the end of a string. Most of the bees were yellow-jackets and honeybees, but one small boy held a huge wasp that was buzzing angrily as it plunged and tugged this way and that. Salih was horrified. The boy was so small. What if he got stung? To be stung by a wasp is worse than anything, one prick and he'd be swelling all over, fainting with pain. He ran up to the boy.

'Let it go,' he cried, keeping at a safe distance. 'Quick, that's a wasp! You'll die if it stings you.'

The little boy looked at him quite calmly. 'I know,' he said with pride, 'but I'm used to wasps. They don't sting me.' He drew in the string and caught the madly struggling yellow-striped red wasp with two fingers. 'Stop,' he admonished it. 'That's enough! What's all this noise! You keep quiet now.' And with a pat on its head he strutted off, the wasp now high above him at the end of the string.

Salih was consumed with envy. The boy must be charmed, he thought. Perhaps he had a grandmother who knew of some magic against wasps. Salih's grandmother would know it too, but she'd only glower at him and shout that her spells were not to be wasted on bees and the like. Well, charmed or not, Salih made up his mind. He would catch a larger, more dangerous bee so that these boys and all the town too should be open-mouthed with wonder.

'Have you seen any hornets around here?' he asked one of the boys.

'Hornets!' the boy exclaimed. 'But no one can catch them. They can sting a man to death!'

'Not me! My granny's put a charm on me that protects me against all poisonous stings.'

'Really?' the other boy marvelled. 'Then you must catch a lot of them. Hornets are so huge, so beautiful! And they flash so . . . Look!' He took his hand and led him to a wild rosebush with large pink blossoms. 'Here,' he said, his eyes rolling with fear, 'it's full of hornets here. See? Five of them right there . . .' And he beat a hasty retreat.

Salih was relieved that the boy had gone and would not be watching him. He was beginning to be afraid. What if he got stung and died? How glad his grandmother would be . . . The hornets were whizzing viciously very low over the green grass about the rosebush, glinting under the sun and making more noise than any airplane. It was a hopeless task, and besides he didn't have any string. He was just turning away when he spied the boy he had boasted to, hiding behind a tree. With him were two other boys and they were obviously arguing over his chances, the first boy taking his part, the others sneering.

'Have you got any string?' he called out.

70

'Plenty,' the boy said. 'A whole spool.'

'Well, bring it over here.'

'I can't, not with all those hornets . . .'

With a scornful wave of his hand, Salih went up to him and broke a length of string from the spool. 'Wait here then,' he said, 'and watch me catch one.'

There was no going back now. He took off his cap and, bending low, tiptoed up to the bush. With a sudden spring he clapped the cap right over a group of hornets and paused anxiously. Had he been stung? But no, he felt no pain anywhere. Slowly he lifted a corner of the cap and realized that he hadn't caught anything. Again and again he tried, and at each attempt the buzzing and flashing about him grew angrier and angrier. He was sweating now, no longer afraid, bent on capturing at least one of those infuriated hornets, but they were much too fast and several times he had to crouch close to the ground, hiding his face and hands as they lashed out at him. There now, three huge ones were whirring away round and round, maddened by the chase. It was touch and go. He could not afford to miss. The boys, craning out from behind the tree, had their eyes glued on him. With a sudden swoop he flung himself at the bush. A muffled buzz came from inside the cap. 'I've done it!' he cried triumphantly. How to get the hornet out now, that was the problem, and the answer came to him almost at once. Salih was nothing if not resourceful when in a tight corner. He'd just hold it through the cloth, and then . . . At last he had it. How it squirmed and twisted between his fingers! But he held it firmly so it could not sting him.

'Come here,' he called to the boys. 'You, take the string and loop it up. Don't be afraid, I'm holding this hornet. Now, pass it along here and pull. Carefully now, we don't want to tear its waist in two.' The boy's hands were trembling. 'Good! Now knot it up.' When this was done, he let go of the hornet. It zoomed up wildly. Salih yanked at the string. 'That's enough,' he said. 'Don't go too far.' And without another look at the dumbfounded boys he walked away proudly.

He must go straight to the market place now with that

71

huge savage hornet flying above him. How startled people would be! But first he wanted to have a good look at his catch. He selected a comfortable rock and sat down swinging his legs. Thick clumps of bright blue spurge grew all around the rock and he drew his hornet down onto one of the flowers. But it would not remain still, casting itself this way and that, tugging at the string, whirring furiously, knocking against the rock surface. 'Ah,' Salih cried, 'it's going to kill itself, poor thing.' He ducked in the nick of time as the hornet made a lunge for his face. Missing him, it began to whirl so fast that Salih saw only a black circle above his head. Then the black circle eased up into a hornet again. Its angry buzzing toned down, the tension on the string relaxed and the hornet sank onto a spurge flower. Its wings quivered a little and its tail drooped. Salih noticed that there were three blue circles on its tail, edged with narrow stripes of red. And a little further up three more little circles, yellow this time and very bright. The black part of the tail was almost green and so was its head, so soft, so velvety. The wings were pale blue with thin dark streaks, transparent, brightly glistening. And its eyes, how huge they were, all meshed in an iridescent play of colours, sparkling, changing all the time. He could not have enough of looking at it, trying to impress every detail into his mind's eye, so that for years to come he would always see it there on the blue spurge, quiet now, no longer the stormy hornet of a moment ago, slowly rubbing its eyes with its downy red feet.

Salih looked up at the sun. It was still quite a while before evening and the market place would be teeming with people. He rose and wended his way to the school at the beginning of the main street. There old Alim Agha had his shop where he sold sieves and wooden spoons and ladles and all kinds of baskets. He was a taciturn man, always rushing over to the mosque, sleeves rolled up, ready to perform his ablutions, and now he was sitting there, muttering prayers under his breath and puffing away to exorcise evil spirits. Salih waved his hornet in front of the door, allowing it to soar the full length of the string, then pulled it down until it was almost touching his nose. He talked to it and fooled

72

around, but Alim Agha paid no attention to him at all. Annoyed, he walked off down the street with the hornet buzzing away at the end of the string. The market place was crowded, but people went about their business, not even stopping to wonder how such a small boy could have caught this huge, beautiful, but at the same time terribly venomous hornet. Thoroughly vexed now, he trotted up and down, bumping into people on purpose, but in vain. It was as if hornets, and such a beautiful one at that, were ordinary every-day things for them . . . Even Ismail the blacksmith never once deigned to look up from his anvil. Only some children stopped to stare with huge wide eyes. In the end, tired and discouraged, he sat down in front of the mosque. His hornet must be tired too. How would it live, what would it eat, tied up there at the end of a string? What if it died of hunger? Look how it had settled now on Salih's left arm. It was panting, poor thing. And how good it smelled, of spring and warm sunshine, like all bees do.

It was the hour of the afternoon prayer and devout Moslems were entering the mosque, passing quite close to Salih. He waved his hornet right at them, but nobody seemed to take any notice. Anyway, he was rested now and so was his hornet. He decided to go back to the woods and race this great strong hornet against the other boys' bees.

On the street he fell behind a villager dressed in homespun brown trousers and carrying a bundle at the end of an axe over his shoulder. He was walking very quickly and Salih followed him out of the town. As they went down the valley he spurted forward with his hornet flying contentedly on its string and turned back to look at the man. He had a pleasant face with a red beard and green eyes under thick brows. Salih smiled. 'Uncle,' he said, 'where does this road lead to?'

The man stopped at once and smiled back. 'To Kabakkoz village,' he answered. 'And where are you bound for, wayfarer? What's your name?'

'Salih . . .'

'They call me Big Duran. I'm a woodcutter.' His smile broadened as he caught sight of the hornet. 'That's a nice bee you've got there, Salih. I used to catch them too when I was a child.' Then he looked closer. 'Why, if it isn't a hornet! They're very poisonous, you know. They can sting a man to death or leave him maimed for life.'

'I know,' Salih said proudly. 'But this one's used to me. When I first caught it, that was fifteen days ago, it was ready to swallow me up whole . . .'

'I never even had the nerve to touch one,' Big Duran said, extending his hand tentatively.

'Careful, uncle!' Salih cried. 'It'll sting you.'

The woodcutter looked crestfallen. 'Well, it's a lovely hornet, Salih,' he sighed as he started to walk away.

Summoning up all his courage Salih seized the hornet and waved it after him. 'Goodbye, goodbye,' he called. Several times, the woodcutter turned to look back admiringly as he disappeared into the valley, his axe glinting on his shoulder.

'Hooray!' Salih shouted as he raced on towards the woods. Joy lent him wings and the hornet clung to his back, dazed by the speed. The other boys were no longer there and, besides, he had decided to set his hornet free. Taking his handkerchief from his pocket he grasped the hornet and tried to undo the knot, but like this he risked pulling too hard and severing its slender waist. How many times had it happened before and how strange the bees had been, hovering blindly in the air with their half bodies, unable to find their bearings any longer. At first he had been amused, but then an aching pity had seized him, they were so like crippled human beings . . . What could he do? It was getting dark too. There was nothing for it. He tied the hornet into a corner of his handkerchief, then with his teeth he gnawed at the string as close as he dared, until it broke apart. When he unfolded the handkerchief, the hornet shot up, struck out to right and left, then soared arrow-like high into the sky. Salih followed it with his eyes until it was nothing but a black dot.

After this, time hung heavily on Salih's hands. For days on end he did nothing but sit around the house, listlessly watching the women weaving at the looms and embroidering the cloth. His sisters had a predilection for mauve. The flowers they embroidered were always mauve, with large crown-like petals, and the stalks and buds would be orange. His younger sister was still a child, but Hanifé was growing into a young beauty and it was said that she and Mustafa, the fisherman, met secretly, in spite of the fact that her father detested Mustafa and called him a wastrel, which Salih could not understand, because he liked Mustafa almost as much as Metin. Anyway, he'd never understood that father of his. What did he do all day, leaving the house every morning to return in the middle of the night, swaying drunkenly, more often than not picking a quarrel with the household, raining blows to right and left, while the grandmother looked on gloatingly.

Sometimes, Salih's mother would blow up and pour abuse on her husband, and then all hell would break loose. The grandmother would get on her high horse and start yelling more loudly than anyone. 'What kind of whores are you all? What sort of strumpets have I taken into this house for my son whom I raised like a prince, working myself to the bone so he should have the best of everything . . . Was it for this, that he should be called names by no-good whores?' Everyone would be silenced, but she would rant on and on, rushing out into the garden, howling at the top of her voice, beating her breast, rending her hair, until tired at last she'd drop down at the foot of the olive tree, never anywhere else, and his father, sober now, alarmed and penitent, would pick her up and carry her to bed. She would lie there, her face so pale and drawn that Salih was sure she was dying. But suddenly she'd spring out of bed and, sitting at the loom, would start casting the shuttle briskly, her hands flying, no trace of anger left in her, talking softly, with a good word for each one of them.

Once a week, his father collected the woven and embroidered cloths and took them to the market. Ah, those were the days! What goodies did he not bring back when he returned in the afternoon! For Salih there would always be five large candied apples. A delicious smell of cooking would fill the house and the table would be laid with all sorts of dainties as in any rich Istanbul home. His father would drink at home on those days, and not get drunk but only gay and lighthearted. In the end he would take up his *saz* and play lively tunes and sing merry songs, while the grandmother looked on, lost in some dream-world, her eyes fixed on her son as on a demi-god. And indeed everyone in the town agreed that he was the most generous of men. If only he would not gamble his money away, if only he took up some kind of job . . .

Sometimes, Salih wandered out along the seaside, but all seemed desolate there. He tried making kites. Six beautiful kites he made and flew them for a while, but it wearied him in the end. He let them go, one after the other, high over the sea, and they floated on and on, sinking somewhere far out to the horizon over the blue expanse.

Then for a few days he roamed the hills picking flowers. He filled the house with them, especially those he knew his grandmother liked best, hoping to win her over again, and often he would be rewarded by a flitting smile.

When he passed through the market place he always saw the same people sitting in the coffee houses and shops, never moving, not shifting an inch, simply staring out with unchanging faces as though waiting for some impossible thing to happen. It seemed to Salih they never left their places to eat and drink or even to go to the toilet.

In the yard in front of the mosque was an aged stork that had forgotten how to fly. It nested in the hollow trunk of a plane tree and paced the yard very slowly all day long, with measured steps, quickening sometimes, and stretching its neck out still more. It hardly ate anything. Once Salih caught three frogs which he took to the stork, but it never even looked at them. Salih was angry. It hadn't been easy to catch those frogs. He flung them into the hollow and went away. But next morning he was pleased to see that the stork had gobbled them up.

The truth of the matter was that the disappearance that night of Metin and the three trucks, as if they had never been, had shaken Salih to the core and left indelible scars on him. He kept dreaming up sweet visions of Metin springing out of a boat or driving into town with fifteen brightly coloured motor cars in his wake, yes, it would be cars this time. Oh, how he missed Metin! And the black-clad men too, and the long line of stars they formed over the sea in the night. He had never quite understood what they said, but it was adventure, secret dangerous adventure, a word they used again and again and which transported Salih into an exciting unknown world. Of course he knew this word from the movies too. Adventure was a marvellous place that was reached after triumphing over countless difficulties and of which one could never have enough. That's what Salih had gathered from those long whispered conversations, with the voices now fraught with passion and fear, now eager with prospective joys. Adventure was a land to be attained even at the cost of a lifetime of striving, enchanted, but oh, so out of Salih's reach . . . Adventure was big brother Metin himself . . .

Salih stopped short before the shop window, unable to believe his eyes. He rubbed them and looked again. It was like a dream come true. The same truck, the exact replica of the blue one in Metin's yard, but very small, a toy! And its chassis was the colour of a pomegranate too, with tiny flowers, green and yellow, blue, white, mauve, painted over it.

He crossed to the opposite pavement. From here, he could see the truck better, bright blue like a flower of the sea, that's what Metin used to say . . . He could not take his eyes off it. Here was adventure, real adventure. It was all contained in this blue-flowered truck. The flower of the sea, the blue flower of the sea! Salih's heart sang within him. He sat down on the threshold of a house opposite the shop and gazed on and on, oblivious of the door being opened and shut and of people crossing the pavement or stepping on his feet, so long as they did not obstruct his view of that enchanting truck in the window. The next day he came again, at dawn, and the next and the next. On the fourth day, the night watchman found him curled up on the doorstep, fast asleep, and had to carry him home. On the fifth day, Salih was seized with panic. What if the truck should be sold? Of course it would be! What child could resist having it? He rushed out into the market, dreading to look at the shop window. But no, thank goodness, it was still there. No one had seen it yet. Salih must have it at any price. He had to buy it. But how? How, how? He had no money, no money at all . . .

# 8

A blue radiance glowed far out over the sea, at the confines of the world, but on the beach it was raining. There was no wind and the rain fell very gently, very straight, pockmarking the sands and the smooth surface of the water.

Ships rose over the horizon, as out of a precipice, fishing vessels, pirate barks, and sailed slowly to the shore. Flashes of blue lightning zigzagged through the black clouds above. Under the steep craggy cliff was a cavern whose dark recesses stretched far and deep and whose mouth was large enough to allow tall-masted ships to enter. The men poured out of the ships. They were very wet, but soon a fire was roaring away in the middle of the cave, its flames leaping to the soot-blackened ceiling. Large cauldrons were set over the fire and, beside them, fish and meat, whole sheep and lambs, to roast on spits. A pile of empty tin cans of all colours and sizes was rising in a corner. The food was laid out on the flat rocky surface of the cave and purple wine flowed freely. Cowboys joined the party and bushy-mustachioed bandits. Skipper Temel sat in the place of honour with everyone paying their respects to him, even the Padishah of the Pirates, who wore a sparkling blue precious stone on his breast and had a large ring in one ear. Aladdin came too and the Thief of Baghdad on his flying carpet. Inside that cave was adventure . . . . Ali the Kizilbash arrived, holding his nacre-inlaid *saz*, and everyone stopped talking to give ear to his song. The minstrel's voice travelled to the depths of the cave and boomed back. He sang of great caravans and pirates on the seven seas, of full-eared yellow wheat, of the blessings of this earth, of the four sacred books, all the one God's word. Why these divisions among men? Why these Muslims and non-Muslims? The world is a caravan, here today and gone tomorrow, it is passing by the caravan of good friends, so hail to the brotherhood of all men . . . Outside, blue seagulls fluttered over the sea, their wings glistening dully under the rain.

And now Ismail the blacksmith walked in, carrying his huge bellows on his back and sat down by the fire, and beside him was Dursun the carpenter with his large black carved roses . . . They quaffed the purple wine and in the dim shades of the cavern a rainbow lit up the soot-blackened rocks that shone with millions of tiny sparks, and drove the bats out over the sea. And there was Jemil, Bahri and Kaya, and other boys too, kneeling around the fire! And last of all, big brother Metin appeared at the mouth of the cavern, his two pistols gleaming at the red sash at his waist, a blue-enamelled pocket watch hanging to a thick gold chain, and another watch on his wrist, with gold and diamonds. On his ear was a wide gold ring, just like the pirates. How had he come by that? . . . They all started to their feet on seeing him, even the Padishah of the Pirates. Metin rattled the large beads of his amber *tesbih*.

'Sit down, mates,' he called in a proud voice. His moustache was more resplendent than ever and his golden locks fell over his brow.

They all sat down and tobacco cases were held out to him. He took the one offered by the Padishah of the Pirates, it was of pure gold, and rolled himself a cigarette.

How stately Metin looked, how distant, as though he were a padishah himself! Oh, if the Padishah of the Pirates ever learnt who he really was, the son of Lame Durmush, a mere gardener in the house of an Istanbul businessman! And here they sat, all together, drinking the purple wine . . . The Padishah of the Pirates was a huge man with a long ebony beard and flashing black eyes . . .

Out over the sea the seagulls swooped swiftly this way and that, bright blue under the rain . . .

Once upon a time . . . The Pirate Padishah had many ships and treasures galore, and orchards, and horses, all white, herds and herds of them . . . Automobiles too, aeroplanes, helicopters. Each one of his ships was decked with sails of blue satin and he would send them through the Bosphorus to the Black Sea and the Mediterranean on smuggling expeditions. The gardens of his palace in Istanbul were always bright and sunny, with lakes so wide that the blue-sailed vessels could move about freely on them. And big brother Metin had offered him five blue trucks with pomegranate-red chassis . . . All the potentates of the world stood in awe of the Pirate Padishah. But alas, there was one thing he lacked . . .

The seagulls swirled in thousands, wing to wing, a large shimmering cloud, hurled hither and thither by the tempest, to be cast down at last, a stream of blue, into the shelter of the cavern. Thundering breakers cataracted over the islands and the ships tossed and pitched as their anchors dragged along the bottom of the sea.

Yes indeed, there was one thing he lacked. The Pirate Padishah had no children. He had sent over land and sea for a remedy to this affliction and had tried all sorts of medicines. He asked Skipper Temel's advice and also Salih's grandmother. For forty days and forty nights she brewed an elixir for him out of all the flowers of the hills and for forty days and forty nights the whole town smelled of attar of flowers. The heady smell was everywhere, in the stones and earth, in people's bodies and in their hair, in the birds and animals, even in Metin's trucks.

But in vain . . . The Pirate Padishah still remained childless. He was desperate. His wife was very beautiful. She came from the far-off isle of Serendip* and was the daughter of a fairy pirate king. The world had never seen such a beautiful woman, not even in films. She was real adventure. And now she was dying of grief, for if she did not give birth to a boy the pirates on these seas, the smugglers, the cowboys, the black-clad men, all would be left without a chief when the Pirate Padishah died.

So the Padishah took to the road and travelled far and wide, to the mountains of Ararat and Süphan and the Taurus, to Lake Van, to the famous Chukurova plain, and as far as Zanzibar and Serendip. In Antalya he saw the tongue of the dragon that has been spewing flames from

*Serendip: Ceylon.

under the earth ever since the world began. He went to Urfa and there, on the plain of Haran, ploughing in a field was the Lord Halil Ibrahim* himself, bringing endless fertility at every step he took and beneficial showers whenever he raised his noble gaze to the sky.

'Yours is a difficult case,' the Lord Halil Ibrahim said. He was dressed all in blue robes. His plough and oxen were blue too. And in the distance the arid plain with its thistles and date palms, its huts and paths and people, were bathed in a blue light, steel-blue like melted iron in a smith's forge. 'Very difficult . . .'

'Only you can help me,' the Padishah cried, throwing himself at his feet. 'If help there is.'

The minstrel Kizilbash plucked his *saz*.

'I must sleep,' the Lord Halil Ibrahim said. He unyoked his oxen and laid his head on a clod of earth. 'Wait here until I wake up.'

A great wind sprang up from the desert, shaking the land, and darkness fell. The stars appeared in the sky, millions of huge stars that glowed in the silence of the night, gilding up land and sky.

As dawn broke the Lord Halil Ibrahim, who had sixty-two children and four hundred and seventy-two grandchildren, stirred and broke off a wheat stalk though the wheat was still germinating and it would be months before it was ripe. He sat up and waved the stalk over the desert and in a moment fields of golden-eared wheat stretched before him as far as the eye could see.

'Padishah,' he said, 'it is difficult, but you will have a child. Listen . . . Go to the foot of lofty Mount Erjiyés and there you will come upon a vast orchard filled with every kind of fruit tree, peaches, cherries, plums, almonds, that flower all the year round, blooming with the first ray of the sun and shedding their blossoms at the close of day. In the middle of this orchard you will see a tall apple tree, towering like a mountain above all the others. Now, this tree flowers seven times a day, but it bears fruit only once a year, just one

*Halil Ibrahim: The Patriarch Abraham, an important figure in Islam.

single apple on its topmost bough. You and your wife must stand watch under this tree for a whole year, never batting an eyelid, and the minute the fruit appears you must climb up and pick it, for it ripens and drops all in a flash and then it's of no use. If you can't reach it in time, don't touch the apple on the ground, but wait another year. But if you do, take your knife, I mean your silver dagger, and slice the apple in two. You'll give one half to your wife and eat the other half yourself. Then you'll both undress and lie with each other right there under the tree. No one will see you, for until you're through with that business, the tree will be flowering and shedding its blossoms over you and hiding you from all eyes. That's all, Padishah, and good luck. In nine months and ten days you will be blessed with a bonny boy, who will have a long and happy life. He will shed bounty at every touch of his hand and fill the earth with good things. Go in peace, Padishah.'

The Padishah threw himself down and kissed the ground where the Lord Halil Ibrahim had stepped on, but when he lifted his head he saw only a wisp of white smoke before him. Halil Ibrahim was far in the distance, driving his plough, shouting and prodding the oxen with his goad.

'I know that orchard, my Padishah,' Metin said. 'It lies near Göreme, the land of the Fairy Chimneys. We won't rest or sleep until that fruit appears.'

'But how can we do without sleep?'

'We'll manage,' Metin said.


. . . Seagulls and swans fluttered in the sky, as the hunters' rifles burst out, shot after shot. Last night, while the tempest raged, the restaurant *Our Little Sailboat* was cut off from its moorings and shattered to pieces on the rocks. When day dawned the boat's tables and chairs could be seen floating on the sea and the refrigerator lay right at the bottom. The owner's enemies had done this. Poor man, he suffered a loss of two hundred and fifty thousand liras. Who knows how many years he had washed dishes in other people's restaurants in order to buy this boat and then turn it into that restaurant, so attractive to tourists . . . And all the while the

yacht which the millionnaire Selimoglu used for his contraband business lay in the harbour. Nobody would ever dare
break its chain. People trembled at the very name of
Selimoglu . . .

'Don't worry, Padishah,' Skipper Temel said. 'We'll all keep
watch in turn, you and me, and Metin and Halil
Ibrahim . . .'
'Halil Ibrahim isn't coming.'
'What?' the Skipper cried indignantly. 'He sets us such a
formidable task and then doesn't come to help?'
'He's a saint,' the Padishah replied. 'He can't be expected
to sit up watching trees with me.'
So they set out and came to where Mount Erjiyés reared its
stately pointed peak in the middle of the wide plain, shining
white, like a bride.
They found the orchard at once, a boundless expanse of
flowering trees, overwhelming in its majestic beauty, and
entered through the magic gate. The intoxicating scent of
many flowers assailed them and a shattering brightness that
made them swoon. When they recovered the Padishah
spoke: 'I thought only the bottom of the sea could bloom like
that . . .' he said in amazement.
For three days and three nights they walked through the
flower-laden trees, passing forty streams and forty lakes,
until they reached the heart of the orchard. And there was
the apple tree, so tall it reached right up to the peak of
Erjiyés, like another mountain. It was flowering and shedding its petals before their very eyes, orange petals with a
heady fragrance. The Padishah erected his purple pavilion
at the foot of the tree and the orange petals rained upon it,
but in the morning what should he see! The orange flowers
had been replaced by pink ones, bright pink and of quite a
different shape. 'Look, Metin, look!' he called, struck with
wonder.
Metin came out of his tent. The Padishah had set up a
separate tent for him and one for Skipper Temel, and the
other pirates each had a tent too. 'This is a magic tree,'
Metin said.

'Magic!' the Padishah exclaimed.

'Magic!' Skipper Temel cried.

'Magic, magic!' Salih shouted out aloud, unable to contain himself any longer. Then he stopped, fearing that someone might have heard him.

And in that very instant, the tree shed its pink flowers and put forth silver ones, of pure light! Then yellow and green, mauve, blue, black, white, lilac, a thousand and one colours and shapes. It was as if a strong flowery wind blew them onto the tree, only to sweep them up the next moment to the top of Mount Erjiyés.

'Let's set up the watch,' the Padishah said.

That night the vigil fell to Metin and he saw a wide arc of light cleaving the darkness from behind the mountain and flowing in a dazzling stream towards the tree. On and on it flowed as Metin stood there frozen, and formed spangled leaves on the tree, so brilliant as to be almost invisible. And when day dawned these leaves of light turned blue and the whole orchard, the mountain, the vast plain, all were bathed in a blue radiance.

'Padishah, hey Padishah!' Metin yelled excitedly. 'There's a fruit up there on the tree, right at the very top . . .'

Roused from his sleep the Padishah rushed out, but when he looked he was so dazzled that he cast himself face down. Another look and he would have been blinded. 'I must be quick,' he said when he rose at last.

They tied a black kerchief round his eyes, but even so the light of the fruit burned into them. Without losing any more time he started to climb up the tree, straining every nerve and sinew in order to get to the top before the apple ripened and fell. Bathed in sweat, his hands and feet torn and bleeding, he was almost there when he heard shouts down below. He looked and there was the apple, plunging like a shooting star to the ground where it lay whirling in a coruscating blue radiance.

'Oh dear,' the Padishah cried in dismay. Swiftly he let himself slide down, picked up the apple and slit it in two with the silver dagger at his waist. 'Lady,' he called to his wife. 'Come here quickly and eat this half.'

So they each ate one half of the apple and behold, they were turned into two statues of pure blue light. Only when the tree began to put forth fresh orange flowers did they become themselves again.

'Alas, my Padishah!' Metin wailed. 'Have you forgotten what the Lord Halil Ibrahim told you back on the plain of Haran?'

'Alas!' Skipper Temel said. 'Never to eat the apple if it fell to the ground, but to wait another year . . .'

'Some evil will come of this,' Metin said.

'You've waited these many years for a child,' Skipper Temel said. 'Couldn't you have waited another year?'

'Oh dear, oh dear!' the Padishah lamented. But he could not stop now. He and his wife undressed and lay down under the tree, while the many-coloured fragrant petals screened them from sight, and for three days and three nights they made love.

After this they departed from the magic tree and, leaving the vast orchard and majestic Erjiyés Mountain behind, they came to the palace of the Pirate Padishah which was situated in a valley that ended in a wide bay, beyond the caves and the lighthouse. A large sea-garden surrounded the palace, full of pomegranate trees that tinted the whole valley red in the summer months. And so it came to pass that the Padishah's wife became pregnant. The Padishah was overjoyed. A child at last, and what a child! The Lord Halil Ibrahim had said the whole world would be blessed with plenty the instant he was born, the grain would be twice as tall, the flowers and fruits larger than they had ever been, the honeycombs would overflow with honey and breasts with milk and nobody would be hungry or poor any more. There would be no more tyranny and want. Only death . . .

The day came, and the Padishah's wife was seized with labour pains. Midwife Rose was sent for, the most renowned midwife in pirateland, who had brought into the world all the bravest pirates on these coasts. But this was the first time she was going to assist at the birth of a prince. So it was in the highest spirits that she set about her task. Then the

86

unbelievable happened. It could not be true what she was seeing. She turned pale and trembled of all her limbs, but she could not move an inch. She just stood there frozen, her eyes widening with horror, for instead of a baby's head it was the head of a black snake that protruded from between the mother's legs, its eyes glittering, its tongue flicking out. Suddenly the snake shot out, arrow-like. It stuck its fang into poor Midwife Rose and retreated at once into its mother's womb. Midwife Rose fell down stone dead.

Outside the door the Padishah was growing impatient. At last, hearing no sound at all from the room, he went in and what a sight met his eyes!

'A snake, my Padishah!' his wife moaned. 'A black snake is what I'm giving birth to. It has bitten Midwife Rose and there she lies, dead. I'm afraid it's going to bite me too, and you . . .'

At the moment the snake popped out its head. 'Don't be afraid,' he said. 'Not even a snake would kill his own mother and father. Just find another midwife who'll deliver me.'

The Padishah was relieved, but not for long. 'Alas,' he lamented, 'if only we'd waited another year and not eaten of that fallen fruit! A black snake instead of a son . . .'

But the ways of Providence are inscrutable.

Another renowned midwife was found, the snake bit her too, and a third one as well. Then the Padishah was told of Salih's grandmother who had made a name for herself among the pirates. 'Skipper Temel,' the Padishah said, 'a great disaster has befallen us because we ate of that fallen apple. My lady is giving birth to a snake. If such be our fate, at least let her be delivered and no midwife can do it but that grandmother who brews healing balms.'

'She can indeed,' the Skipper said. 'She'd deliver a dragon too, but she's cunning, that one. She must have got wind of the black snake and how he's killed all those midwives. Who knows where she'll be hiding herself by now?'

'Then what shall we do? How can we get hold of her?'

'Well, Metin lives next door to her . . .'

The Padishah clapped his hands to summon Metin. 'I want you to find that old grandma for me at once,' he ordered. 'I'll give you five, ten trucks if you do. I'll make you vizier of all the pirates, if you like. Only let my son be born, even if he is a snake, for who knows what divine wisdom may be the cause of it.'

'True,' Metin said. 'Anything but that your realms should be without a prince. And who knows, perhaps a snake padishah will prove to be better than a human one . . .'

In less than no time Metin was outside Salih's house. 'Grandmother, grandmother!' he called.

'She's not here,' they told him. 'She's gone away.'

Metin was dismayed. 'But where is she? I've got to find her at once or they'll chop off my head.'

'Oh dear! Who?'

'The Padishah of the Pirates who lives beyond the edge of the sea. He was going to give me thirty-three trucks if I brought her back, all blue, brand-new German makes . . . Where the hell can she have gone to, that old grandma, just when she was going to be of some use?'

'She had an old swain far off on the seas, an aged captain of the pirates with whom she coquetted on and off. When he heard that the Padishah was looking for her, he came and carried her off on his back.'

'Oh dear, oh dear, I'm lost,' Metin wailed.

The Padishah flew into a furious rage at the news. 'I want the old hag here,' he thundered, 'alive or dead.'

In imitation of Salih's grandmother, all the other old women began to run away too, hiding in the mountains or on sea, down wells, in caves, even in Istanbul. Those the Padishah's men managed to catch were brought back, but the snake killed them all and soon there were no more old women to be found.

One morning a woman presented herself at the palace. 'I know somebody who can deliver the prince,' she said.

'Who's that?' the Padishah cried.

'My stepdaughter, Rose Fatma.'

'How will she do it?'

'That I don't know. But she's a witch and can do anything,' the woman replied. In truth, her only aim was to have her stepdaughter killed by the snake.

'If your stepdaughter succeeds, ask anything of me and it shall be yours,' the Padishah promised.

So the stepmother went back home gloating, and began by giving Rose Fatma a good scrubbing-down in the bath. Then she dressed her up in the best finery she could find. Rose Fatma, who had never had such beautiful clothes in her life, was delighted. Her stepmother set her on her way. 'Let's see you deliver the Padishah's son,' she said. 'If you do we'll be saved from poverty.'

Rose Fatma was only a little girl, not more than five or six. How could she know to what her stepmother was sending her? 'Of course I will, mother,' she said. 'And bring you back pots of money from the Padishah. A whole coffer-full . . .' Singing a gay song she walked down to the seaside where the Padishah's boat would be waiting for her. Just then she heard a voice calling out, 'Rose Fatma, Rose Fatma!' She stopped and listened. 'Do you know where you're going?'

'Of course I do,' she replied. 'I'm going to help the Padishah's wife who's having a child.'

'But it isn't a child, Rose Fatma, it's a snake she's giving birth to, that'll sting you to death as it did all the other mid-wives.'

'Oh dear, what shall I do?' Rose Fatma wailed. 'My step-mother will beat me black and blue if I don't go. She'll kill me.'

As she said these words a shepherd appeared before her. He had a long white beard and held a pipe in his hand. 'Wait Rose Fatma,' he said and, sitting on a rock, he began to play the pipe. He played so beautifully that the very earth and stones vibrated at the sound. Then he laid his pipe aside and spoke. 'I'm a shepherd, Rose Fatma,' he said. 'I have one single goat that I lead with this pipe. Just now I've sent it to the top of those crags. Go up the mountain and try to catch it. If you do, take this pail and milk it. If you don't then there's no help for it. That snake will sting you to death.'

The mountain was steep and craggy and swathed in blue. Rose Fatma stood at its foot and gazed up. There, on its topmost crag she saw a red goat flashing like a flame. 'Come goat, come!' she called. 'Come and let me milk you, for if not that snake will sting me to death.' Again and again she called to it, but the goat never moved. It just stood there as though part of the crag itself. Suddenly, she heard the faint notes of a pipe. As the sound increased a bright blue cloud sailed through the sky and came to settle on the peak of the mountain, hiding the goat from view. Almost in the same instant she looked down and saw the goat right beside her. She embraced it and began to milk. When the pail was full to the brim, she let the goat go and in one bound it was back on the summit of the blue-glowing mountain.

The shepherd greeted her with a long pomegranate branch bearing many flowers, and on the ground was a cage also woven out of pomegranate branches. How pleased he was on seeing the pail full to the brim! 'Snakes, even princely snakes, can never resist my red goat's milk. It would draw them out of the very pit of hell. Now listen to me carefully. Take this pomegranate branch and on no account are you to let go of it. This cage here, you will carry into the room where the lady is giving birth. Look, there's a little door here. You'll stretch the mother's legs wide and place the pail between them. Come prince, come and see what I've brought you, you'll repeat three times, and the snake will hurl himself on the milk and lap it up hungrily. The world is a lovely place after all, he'll say when he's had his fill, and at that moment you'll strike the pomegranate branch to the floor three times, and say to him very loudly, get in, get into this cage this minute. The snake will slide in and you'll quickly close the door and never open it again, even though he begs you to, for if you do he'll bite you and you'll die. Do you understand?'

'Oh yes,' Rose Fatma replied. She heaved the cage over her back and with the pail in one hand and the pome-granate branch in the other she made for the palace where the Padishah was waiting on tenterhooks. When he saw her come in with rosy blooming cheeks, he was seized with pity. She was such a pretty little girl, how could he let the snake kill her? 'I've changed my mind, child,' he said. 'I don't want

90

you to bring my son, that black snake, into the world. You're too pretty and I'd be sorry if something happened to you.'

'But I must,' she insisted. 'He's not a snake, he's a prince and he must be born.'

Nothing the Padishah said could dissuade her. 'All right then, I wash my hands of you,' he declared and opened the door to his wife's room. 'Here, Lady, I've brought you a midget of a midwife.'

Rose Fatma followed the shepherd's instructions to the letter. And indeed, after she had called out three times, 'Come prince, come and see what I've brought you,' the snake slithered out to the milk and eagerly lapped it up. She struck the pomegranate branch to the floor and that huge glistening black snake entered the cage like a lamb. Only when she had closed the door did the snake realize what had happened. It cast itself from one side of the cage to the other, begging to be let out and making such a noise that Rose Fatma became quite angry.

'Be quiet,' she said sternly, striking the pomegranate branch to the ground three times. 'Be quiet, prince.'

The snake was silent after that and the Padishah beside himself with joy. 'Ask of me whatever you wish and it shall be yours,' he said to the girl. But she only bowed her head . . .

And way in the distance, beyond the seas, at the far end of the earth, a blue radiance glowed and died out.

# 9

It was no use asking his father for money. He would not give him a farthing. As for his mother and sisters they were never allowed to keep any. All they earned went to the father who squandered it at will. Where on earth was Salih to find some money now? Without knowing how it came about, he found himself inside the shop, facing a man with a black trimmed beard and a beret on his head. This was the moneylender Haji* Nusret who was such a devout Moslem that he'd made the *haj* five times and had even married his daughter to an Arab, a lazy creature who spent his days drinking away his father-in-law's money. Haji Nusret's dull jaundiced face never smiled. His glassy eyes seemed to bear a grudge against all the world and they were staring fixedly at Salih now. He became more and more flustered. His mouth was so dry he could not utter a word, but just stood rooted there with the figure of Haji Nusret looming huge and awe-inspiring above him. Suddenly Haji Nusret's deep guttural voice boomed out: 'Well, child, what do you want?'

Salih lifted his head and saw only two frowning brows. He longed to rush out of the shop, away from it all, but he had to know the price of the toy truck or he would die. He forced himself to speak. 'That . . .' Something stuck in his throat. He swallowed and tried again. 'That truck . . .' The words came out more easily now. 'Blue . . . In the window . . . How much?' Bathed in sweat, his eyes burning, he saw everything through a haze.

Haji Nusret's white teeth gleamed in the ebony beard and his glassy eyes glazed still more as he measured Salih up and down. 'It costs a lot,' he said. 'Too much for you, boy.'

Salih felt crushed, but he stood his ground. 'You just tell me the price, uncle,' he said assuming a confident air.

*Haji: a Muslim who has made the pilgrimage to Mecca.

'One hundred and fifty liras,' Haji Nusret said in a quelling tone. 'One hundred and fifty,' he repeated stressing each syllable. 'A worker brought it back from Germany. You couldn't buy it for five hundred liras in Istanbul. It's no ordinary toy. If you wind it up with this key here, it'll work like any real truck.'

'All right,' Salih murmured. 'I'll buy it anyway.' Had Haji Nusret heard him? All Salih knew was that he was out of the shop and sitting again on the threshold of the house across the street, lost in contemplation of the blue truck. 'I must find the money, I must,' he kept saying to himself. Then he saw Haji Nusret standing in the doorway, a mocking look on his face, actually laughing in his beard. 'I'll buy that truck, I will,' Salih vowed. 'I'll show you.' He dashed down the street and only stopped when he reached the smithy.

Crouching at the foot of the honeysuckle fence opposite, he began to watch the blacksmith, who was alone, welding something over the anvil. His last apprentice had run away. It was not easy to keep up with the Master's requirements . . . He would be in the smithy at dawn and keep on until late into the night. 'You've got to work so much,' Salih had heard him say many a time, 'that Azrael will never have the chance to take your soul away.' And he would laugh proudly showing all his white teeth. He was rich too and owned a lot of houses and orchards. The townspeople never tired of reckoning his daily earnings. But to his apprentices he never paid more than thirty liras a day, and that to the really skilled ones. A beginner would not get more than ten liras. Ismail the blacksmith had his principles and would rather go without help for years than to break them.

There were boys who, like Salih, would sit at the foot of the honeysuckle fence day after day, a year, two years, watching the forge, and from the moment they came the blacksmith would size them up. Some disappeared after a month or two, never to return. The blacksmith knew it would be so at the first glance, as he knew those who would make good smiths in time, and he was never wrong. These he would cherish and caress with his eyes as he would a beautiful flower. The boys would feel the warmth, the secret

93

love with which he smiled at them every morning and there was nothing they would not do for him. And then, one day, maybe two or three years later, the Master would select one of them and summon him to the forge. The boy would obey without hesitation and, seizing the bellows would blow it so hard that the whole place would be filled with sparks. The Master would not object to this flood of sparks on the first day, in fact he never spoke to his new apprentice, for they knew each other too well by now.

On the second day the boy would plunge into work, taking up whatever the Master had in hand, welding and beating the iron as though he had done it all his life. And one of the first things he would fashion would be a knife for himself or perhaps, if he came from the villages, an old-style lighter for his father or uncle back home. And then one day, six months or a year later, the apprentice would leave without a word. The smith was never surprised. He had learnt to predict the very minute at which this would happen. All his apprentices made straight for Istanbul where they found good jobs in machine-shops and factories, and whenever they visited their home town the first person they went to was the smith. He was really proud of them, of the skills he had taught countless young boys. But if one of them returned and asked to work for him again he would never take him back. It had been the same with his own son, who'd watched from the honeysuckle fence for three years before his father signalled to him to come in. But he too had left like the others, without a word of goodbye. Now he owned a large foundry in Istanbul. The smith had refused ever to speak to him again, nobody knew why. How could he explain? . . .

The smith's craft is a holy craft, and so it has been since days of yore. The patron saint of smiths is the Prophet David, may peace be upon him, who was as skilled with his hands as he was gifted with his tongue. Magic hands he had, that could grip the red-hot iron without ever getting burned. One day his wife, who was very beautiful, said to him: Tell me, oh David, does your skill on the forge come from me or from you? From me, answered David, and his

94

wife broke the spell, so that when he tried to take the burning iron from the coals his hand stuck to it. He was not angry with her. A smith can never be angry. His is a work of love and patience. Only thus can he melt mountains of iron and create something. Only the well-tempered iron, white-hot from the forge, can be fashioned by beating. Only with well-tempered love can a man become a good smith.

Ismail drew a long lump of white-hot iron from the forge and began pounding it, grunting at each stroke. When it was quite flat and turning red again, he thrust it back over the coals and grasped the bellows. Salih's eyes were fixed on his huge, handsome hands as though he expected a miracle from them. They seemed to be detached from his body, working of their own accord, as their owner talked with the people who happened to drop in at the smithy.

The Prophet David had a beautiful voice and he was the first to sing to an instrument. It began with his beating on the anvil. He would strike up a song to the rhythm of the hammer, and the blending of the two was so harmonious that all the people of the desert would gather around to listen. The first musical instrument ever was therefore the hammer and anvil. And after his wife had undone the magic of his hands, he invented the tongs. A dog was lying asleep in the forge, its front legs crossed before him, and that gave him the idea. He hammered out two long rods of iron and joined them together, and so he did not have to use his hands any more.

Ismail the blacksmith was proud of his ancestry. He came from a long line of smiths which, he boasted, went right back to the Prophet David himself, and he was convinced that his descendants would uphold the tradition till kingdom come, for God would never let men go without smiths, neither in war nor in peace. Smiths lived very long too. In Ismail's family not one of them had died before the age of ninety. He remembered his grandfather and his great-grandfather too, working on this very anvil before him. And when evening fell he would start humming to the rhythm of the hammer, just like his forefather the Prophet David, the immemorial song of metalworkers, and people would crowd around as in olden times, fascinated, their hearts lifting in love and friendship, washed clean of all evil and guile, cruelty and foulness, in the glowing sparks of the Master's forge.

Suddenly, Salih leaped up from his place under the honeysuckle fence and sprinted over to Haji Nusret's shop. What if the truck had been sold? What if someone had bought it for his dirty snivelling son while he had been away? Breathless, he stopped before the window and almost cried with relief. It was still there, blooming like a fresh magic flower among the dusty objects in the shop.

However much he thought, he had nowhere to turn to. No one but the blacksmith . . .

He had watched him long enough, stamping his every move and gesture into his mind . . . Surely now the Master would call him, like he had so many others before . . . Salih would jump to it and blow the bellows until the shop and the whole market too would be aglow with sparks. And then . . .

Master, he'd say, I need one hundred and fifty liras. You can cut it from my wages afterwards. Otherwise, I can't be your apprentice and you know how long I've waited here at your door. Ever since I first opened my eyes . . . You'll see how well I can make axes, swords, daggers, ploughshares, hunting rifles . . . And engrave them too . . . So, if you don't want to lose me, give me the money . . . Oh Master, I need it so badly . . . Why don't you call me, Master? I may be thin and small, but you'll see how I can blow that bellows, how I can wield that hammer and beat the white-hot iron on the anvil . . .

Salih picked at the honeysuckle flowers and crushed them between his fingers. They smelled even more strongly than before. He waited, his heart in his mouth, for the blacksmith to lift his head. They would come eye to eye and he would summon Salih and give him the hundred and fifty liras. How pleased the Master would be when Salih returned with the truck, wound it up and let it run by itself on the floor of the smithy! Passers-by would stop to stare in amazement and all the children would flock in too. His father and mother, the whole family would hear of it. His father would want to touch this wonderful truck that went by itself with no one to drive it. But . . . Stop, the blacksmith would thunder, you can't do that . . . How angry his father would be . . . What d'you mean, isn't it my own son's truck? . . . But who can withstand the Master? His father would take himself away, long-faced.

Salih could not remember how he went home that evening, what he ate and did, when he slept. The next morning found him glued to the shop window. How brightly the blue truck glowed in the first rays of the sun . . . Haji Nusret opened the shop and went in, muttering prayers and breathing superstitiously all over the place. Salih summoned up all his courage and tried again.

'Uncle, that truck in the window . . .'

'I told you it's too dear for you!'

'May I look at it? Touch it a little?'

'Certainly not!'

'Just with the tip of my finger . . .'

'Bring the money and then you can touch it with both hands and your whole body too . . .'

Salih rushed out, tripped and fell head over heels on the pavement. His knee was bleeding and he could still hear Haji Nusret's grating voice. 'One hundred and fifty liras! Then you can touch the truck as much as you like . . .'

'Oh God,' Salih prayed, when he was sitting again under the honeysuckle fence, 'please don't let that truck be sold today. Don't let any other boy see my truck, please God! Not for another three days at least . . .'

The blacksmith caught sight of him and his pleasant face clouded. Laying aside the hammer he came out and took hold of his knee. 'It's bleeding a lot,' he said. 'What happened?'

Salih ground his teeth. 'I fell,' he said in a moan. 'It hurts so much . . .'

'Wait a minute.' The smith went inside and came back with some cotton and gauze and a bottle. The gash was quite a deep one. Deftly he cleaned and dressed it. Salih cried out in pain. 'Come now,' the smith laughed. 'It's nothing. It'll stop bleeding right away.'

Alas, Salih had forgotten to look him in the eye . . .
'Master,' he murmured, but the smith was already at the
bellows, shrouded in a blaze of sparks.

The sun was pleasantly warm and a gentle breeze carried
the smell of the sea to where Salih was sitting, waiting for the
Master to look at him again. Should he pray to God and ask
him to do it? But no, he had already asked him to watch
over his truck for three days. God had more important
things to do than to concern himself with Salih all the time.
He might even get angry and stop guarding the truck . . .

Night fell and sparks swirled from the door, windows and
chimney of the forge into the darkness. The smith was humming a song to the beat of his hammer, lost to the world. It
was nearly midnight when he stopped at last. He stretched
his limbs and Salih heard his bones cracking. The iron
sizzled in the water, while the smith removed his apron and
sprinkled water over the embers. He took his coat from its
peg, put it on and lifted his hands in prayer. 'Thank you, my
God, for giving me strength to work this day, and grant me
strength tomorrow and for many days yet.' The clatter of the
iron shutters sounded loudly through the town. The smith
fastened the padlock and walked off, slightly bent, but with
rapid steps, up the slope that led to his house.

'Perhaps it'll be tomorrow that he'll call me,' Salih
thought as he rose and crossed the empty market place to
Haji Nusret's shop. The toy truck was only dimly visible in
the darkness.

For three whole days Salih waited in front of the smithy,
rushing again and again to Haji Nusret's shop to see if the
truck hadn't been sold in the meantime. He even tried
touching it once, but Haji Nusret lost his temper. 'Are you
making fun of me, you little brat?' he roared, and seizing a
stick he chased him out of the shop.

Salih had never felt so humiliated in his life and his hopes
sank to zero. Only God had not let him down in this business
and had kept the truck from being sold. He vowed to himself
to sacrifice three cocks to him in a sacred place. He'd do
that, yes, even if he had to wait until he was eighty. God
should have no doubt about it.

That night he could not sleep at all, as he racked his brains for a way to find the hundred and fifty liras. His grandmother . . . Everyone knew that she had bags of money hidden away somewhere, and gold too, but she never let anyone have an inkling of where they were, not even her own son. She kept it for the day when Halil would return. If Salih hadn't said that wicked thing to her, if he'd only fed her hopes, maybe she'd have bought him the truck. What if he tried to find her hoard? The very thought jogged him into terror. To steal! It's a good thing I don't know where it is, he thought, and tried to wipe the very idea from his mind.

The next morning he made his way forlornly to the market place. The truck was still there, in the window. Then he met Haji Nusret's eyes and turned away. That dark baleful gaze pierced him to the core.

It was a warm spring day. The whole town was bathed in a bright lilting light, the trees in flower and humming with bees, the sea smooth and calm, as though flowering too. Salih passed back and forth in front of the carpenter's shop, gazing thoughtfully at the carpenter who was working inside. It was market day in the town and the streets overflowed with people. He threaded his way among them, staring into their eyes, hoping against hope that something would happen. After a while he had forgotten even what he was hoping for . . . And then it was evening and he turned back desperately to the carpenter's.

'Uncle,' he cried, bursting into the workshop, 'take me as your apprentice. I really know the work, I do, I do! I can help you a lot. I can carve out roses for you every day, small ones . . . Or big ones too if you like, black, mauve . . . Just give me a hundred and fifty liras now so I can buy that truck and run it here. You'll love it too, it's such a beautiful truck . . .'

The carpenter's eyes widened.

'Master . . .' Salih said again, a cry of utter despair. The carpenter shivered and turned back to the walnut board on which he was chiselling the petals of a rose.

Salih's feet dragged him back to the truck. It was gleaming blue behind the window pane. 'Thank you, God,' he breathed, 'thank you for guarding my truck. I'll sacrifice those cocks for you, never fear. You've been so good to me. It's my fault if I failed. You can let it be sold now, if you like. Surely you've better things to do than take care of a toy truck . . .' But here he faltered. What if something turned up tonight? What if Metin came back? What if he found his grandmother's hoard? After all, he would only take a hundred and fifty liras and never touch the rest . . . 'Please, God,' he said, 'only a few days more . . .'

At home, for the first time in days he ate with appetite. His father was not there, and as soon as he finished he rose to go out again.

'Where are you going?' his mother asked.

'Just to look around. I heard in the market that Metin's come back.'

'You stay right here! That smuggler's not coming back so soon. They've probably killed him.'

'No one can kill Metin,' Salih retorted defiantly as he stalked out of the door.

'What shall I tell your father?' his mother called after him. 'He's been complaining that he hasn't seen you for days . . .'

Salih did not answer. In the darkness he made his way to the hollow tree and settled there to wait for Metin. But after a while his thoughts strayed again to his grandmother's treasure. Where could she have hidden it? He'd seen an embroidered silk purse in her hands recently, chinking with coins . . . Perhaps she kept her money right under her seat at the loom . . . Or was it in that chiming chest of hers? It was a very ancient walnut chest embossed with flowers, whose lock chimed when she opened it. Salih would beg to have it opened again just to hear the sound of the chimes, but she would never do so. The inside of the chest smelled so good too, of lavender and mint and wild apple . . . Yes, that was where the money must be. Now he understood why the lock had been made to chime. As a protection against thieves like Salih . . . And the key to the chest was always tied to her waist . . .

If only Metin were to come now! He would stroke Salih's

100

hair very gently and his hand would smell of tobacco and brine. 'Hallo, Salih,' he'd say. 'How are things?'

'All right,' Salih would reply, but he'd remain standing there and Metin would realize something was wrong. 'What's up, Salih, at this hour of the night?' And Salih, his heart beating, would pour out the whole story, down to the last detail. 'If you hadn't come,' he'd say in the end, 'I was going to open my granny's chiming-chest and steal her money to buy that truck. It's a good thing you came and saved me from becoming a thief.'

How glad Metin would be! 'It's a good thing indeed! How could anyone take that money she scrimped and saved for Halil's return?'

Salih felt suddenly sorry for his grandmother. To think he had been on the point of robbing her, after he'd done that other wicked thing to her already . . .

And then Metin would say: 'Quick, let's go and get that truck right away.'

'No, no,' Salih would demur. 'We can wait till morning. Anyway, the shop's closed.'

But Metin would be too worked up to wait. 'I'll wake that low-down Haji Nusret up and make him open it. Just let him refuse, I'll blow his brains out with this gun here, the dirty scoundrel. Don't I know why he became a *haji* that one? Just to throw dust into people's eyes and suck them dry.' Salih remembered having heard Metin say this once . . . 'So he bought that truck from a worker returning from Germany, eh, the old hypocrite? The truth is he got it off the dead body of a sailor killed on a smuggling expedition who was bringing it back to gladden his little son. Well, I'll take it away from him. Just watch!'

Suddenly the night was all in a turmoil. Watchmen's whistles blared out, peal after peal, mingling with shouts and the booming of the sea, and Salih found himself on the shore, not even knowing how he had got there. All he remembered was that he had strayed into Metin's yard to see if the traces of truck wheels were still there when he heard a noise that prompted him to jump into the next garden where a dog had attacked him as he fled through the brambles. Thoroughly shaken, his legs bleeding, he crept back home and into bed.

It was a restless sleep for him, full of dreams which he could not recall. He woke up very early, but as he prepared to rise he met his grandmother's eyes and quickly drew the blanket over his head again. Oh dear, it was clear that she knew everything . . . The sun rose to the height of a minaret and still Salih dared not get up, though he longed to have a look at his truck.

'Salih,' his mother called, 'what's the matter with you? You never stayed in bed this late before.' She drew back the blanket. 'Look at you! All this gadding about will be the death of you. Now, go and wash your face and come and have a proper breakfast.'

Salih went to the outhouse in the garden and relieved himself as he hadn't done in days. He felt hungry. What can I do, he said to himself as he buttoned up his trousers, if it's sold, it's sold. At least it'll keep me from becoming a thief . . .

A rich breakfast such as he had never seen was ready for him, honey, butter, eggs . . . He sat there staring. Instead of spending so much on food, couldn't they have bought him that truck?

His mother brought him some tea. 'Come on, Salih, eat,' she said sternly. She sounded so angry that he complied. Quickly, he stuffed down his food, without looking anyone in the face, especially his grandmother, and made his escape.

Once in the market place he stopped by the wide plane tree from where he could see just one half of Haji Nusret's shop window. His clear blue eyes wide as saucers, he strained his neck towards the shop, unable to take another step.

The suspense was unbearable. Shake yourself, Salih. Come to your senses . . . Closing his eyes he sprang forward. He was there, still not daring to look, feeling that his heart would stop if he did. When at last he opened his eyes and saw the truck in its old place, brighter, bluer than ever, he gasped out: 'Thank you, God, oh thank you!' He must find his grandmother's money this very night or he would die.

102

After all, the world was full of thieves. Wasn't Metin himself
a thief of sorts? . . .

That evening he made straight for his grandmother who
was bent over her loom, sorting out threads from the bob-
bin. He crouched down and met her eyes and held them
until she turned away shouting: 'What's wrong with this
boy? Is he mad or what?'

That decided it. The truck would be his in the morning.
He ate a good meal and slipped away to his hollow tree.
Metin might still turn up this night, and why not? He'd been
away for months and when he came there'd be no need for
his grandmother's gold. He started up at the sound of
footsteps and stuck his eye to a crack in the fence. It was a
woman, all dressed in black. With a swaying gait she walked
up to Metin's house. The door opened as of itself and she
glided in. This must be his sweetheart, Salih rejoiced, he's
going to meet her here. He began to rehearse what he was
going to tell Metin, repeating to himself all the conversation
of the night before.

The first cocks crowed, and still nothing happened. The
night had grown damp and Salih felt cold. He stretched his
limbs until they cracked, and peed in a long steaming squirt
at the foot of the tree. How strange the trees and houses
looked in the moonlight . . . A sudden reasonless fear
gripped him and he flung himself at the door. He managed
to open it without making a sound and, slipping in, he stood
by the large earthenware jar at the entrance, listening to the
breathing inside. They were all fast asleep. His eyes grew accustomed to the darkness and he made out his grandmother's bed which was always spread on the ground beside
her loom. The keys were fastened to the belt of her dress
which she thrust under her pillow. He tiptoed up and
stealthily, without so much as a rustle, pulled out the dress.
Should he untie the keys or take them together with the belt?
Take the belt, of course. That would be easier. He crawled
to the chest, felt for the hole in the lock and inserted the key.
His heart was thumping so loudly now that he paused, certain that his grandmother must have heard him. But no, she
was breathing regularly, deep in sleep. Slowly he turned the

key. The lock emitted a chiming sound and almost in the same instant a scream rent the air. Salih flew to his bed and drew the blanket over his head.

His grandmother had switched on the light. 'Thieves! Burglars . . .' She was shaking all over, beating her breast, whirling this way and that. 'Thieves! They've stolen my money, they've opened my chest! Thieves, thieves . . .'

Hajer Hanum hurried up. 'What is it, mother, what's happened?'

'Thieves, my daughter . . . They've broken open my chest and made away with all my money,' the grandmother moaned casting herself down. 'They've killed me. I'm dying. Water!'

Salih could no longer pretend to be asleep. He sat up, rubbing his eyes and staring dazedly about him.

Hajer Hanum was holding a glass of water to the grandmother's mouth. Then she put the glass down and went to the chest. 'Mother!' she exclaimed. 'Look, the key's on the lock.'

'Don't touch it,' the grandmother shrieked as she pushed Hajer Hanum aside. Kneeling before the chest, she turned the key. The lock chimed twice and she lifted the lid. After rummaging inside for a while she came up with a fat embroidered purse. 'Thank God!' she breathed. 'Oh thank you, God.' Gently she laid the purse back and closed the lid. But when she locked the chest there were three distinct chimes. At this she looked searchingly at all the faces about her. Her eyes rested on Salih. 'Thief! Thief!' she burst out in an awful voice.

Struck with terror, Salih jumped in his bed.

'Don't shout so, mother,' Hajer Hanum said. 'Look, you've scared the child out of his wits. I saw the thief run out of the door. He was a tall huge man . . .'

But the grandmother was not listening. Her eyes fixed on Salih, she kept repeating: 'Thief, thief, thief! Don't I know who's the thief?'

'Granny,' his sisters said, 'we saw him too. Why, he was tall as a poplar.'

The grandmother tied the belt to her waist and lay down

with the keys beneath her body, but even in bed her tongue did not stop. 'Thieves, miserable little thieves! I know who you are, never fear.'

Everyone in the house knew who the thief was . . .

Early next morning Salih crept out of bed and went down to the beach, there he washed his face with sea water.

That day he simply could not bring himself to go to Haji Nusret's shop. In the evening when he came home his mother cast him an angry look, but she said nothing. His sisters seemed bewildered. His grandmother, on the other hand, was in an unusually good mood, talking about the old days, even laughing. But when her eyes rested on Salih, they flashed malevolently and her whole expression changed, if only for an instant.

Salih was afraid. He wanted to run away, but where could he go? As soon as he had finished his meal, he fled to his bed and cowered under the bedclothes. Several times in his sleep he started up, screaming, 'thief, thief.' His mother made him lie down again.

When he woke up in the morning he heard his father pacing up and down in the small sitting-room. Whenever he did this so early in the morning, it augured well for the next couple of weeks. He would stay at home, not once going out to drink or gamble. He would not abuse and beat them, but would make himself useful about the house, repairing the looms, weeding and planting the garden, painting the walls, even earning some money by weaving nets for the fishermen.

Now he would begin to speak and Salih knew exactly what he was going to say. So did the whole family, and the neighbours as well.

Up and down, up and down, ever more quickly, and suddenly he stopped and laughed. 'Look at me,' he cried. 'Just look at me! What have I done with my life? But I'm going to make a new start. I'll work. I'll try to be a man. Last night at the coffee house I was talking with some young people who are studying in Istanbul and have dedicated their lives to the working people. How ashamed they made me! To exploit other people, they said, even a few, even one, is base and disgusting, unworthy of a human being, just as bad as

America's exploiting the world. And here I've been, exploiting others all my life. My mother first, and then my wife and daughters. And worse still, allowing them to be exploited by Istanbul merchants, letting them weave and embroider day after day, an eye-straining labour, and to earn what? Only two hundred and fifty liras a week, while the merchant makes two thousand five hundred! Why can't we stop this? A whole town, children and all, toiling away to fill the pockets of half a dozen Istanbul merchants! From now on I'm going to work like a slave and not exploit anyone any longer. But then others will be exploiting me, and these young students, that the police and military are chasing and killing all the time, they say it's just as despicable to let yourself be exploited and not do something about it. Listen to me, if any of those youths come to this house running from the police, you're to keep them well hidden and never turn them over. They've taught me something, that it's better to be exploited and then to rise up against those who exploit you. If a man does that he'll go straight to God's heavenly Paradise . . . Salih! My only son Salih . . . I haven't even been able to send him to school! When he grows up I want him to be like those young men. If the police torture him, if he meets his death, let it be like them, fighting against tyranny and oppression . . . Ah, it's difficult to be a real human being . . . It means to work like you all do, putting your heart and soul into it. And then what happens? I come along and take the sweat of your brow, the light of your eyes and spend it on drink and gambling, I, I, I . . . Ah, why are men so alone, so cruel, so selfish, so joyless, such thieves? All these years I've been robbing you! Robbing you of your eyes and hands and love, and you never complained . . . But I'll make up for it, I'll find a job, I'll work like all of you. To work means to live. The iron axe is all the brighter for use. Look at old Ismail the blacksmith. Why doesn't he die? As for me, at this rate I won't last another year. Work is the only thing that makes a man . . .'

At this point he would dash into the garden and start digging. In no time the earth was turned upside down, reddish, unctuous, yielding a pleasant pungent odour, which he breathed in long and deep. And afterwards for as long as he was in the house he would not remain idle one minute, silent, at peace with himself, smiling lovingly at all and one, never uttering a cross word, so that the whole household took on an air of festivity and gladness. All through the year, the family would long for these days which invariably recurred in the spring. Like a bright flowering tree he would be, the father. Big brother Metin, all the others Salih had hitherto admired were forgotten. He wanted to be just like his father when he grew up.

But this happy state only lasted two or three weeks at the most. One morning the father would suddenly stop whatever he was doing and remain motionless, eyes glazed and fixed in the distance, then, in feverish haste he would don his good suit and make straight for Abdi's tavern. 'Quick, Abdi, quick!' he would moan. 'Hurry, I'm dying.' And Abdi, who was familiar with his customer's ways, would spread the table in a jiffy. The first glass would be seized with trembling hands and downed at one gulp. He'd sigh with relief and his eyes would begin to shine. 'I've been working, my friends,' he'd tell the other customers. 'I've earned this. Oh how good it is to drink after a good bout of work!' And he'd proceed to his next glass.

Salih was happy. What a lucky thing that his father should be in a good mood these days. Who knows, perhaps he'd get used to working this time and not give it all up as usual. Then maybe he'd buy Salih his blue truck . . . But what if it was sold in the meantime? His heart twinged. He didn't want to think of his truck today. Perhaps if he didn't, other people wouldn't too. It would be forgotten there, in the shop window.

He breakfasted very slowly and stood for a while staring at his thin lank figure in the old mirror that hung beside the door. Help me, God, he prayed. I mustn't see that truck today. He walked out, telling himself that after all it was only a small toy that he'd be sure to tire of when he'd played with it a couple of days. But a voice inside him rose up at the thought. Ah, would I ever tire of that truck if it was mine? Don't I know? Would I ever let it go, like the hornet, in one day? . . . Then the defeated voice spoke again. Who cares, let it be sold then, it's not even a nice colour . . . Even as he said these words he repented. And when he raised his head, there before him in its place in the window was the truck, its blue and red blooming like spring flowers. Salih laughed for joy. He began to skip and run to and fro in front of the shop. Then he zoomed over to the blacksmith's. 'Zizzzt,' he shouted as he capered and clowned in a way he'd never have dared to do before. Now he didn't care. He'd die rather than be an apprentice to the smith. The Master was staring at him. 'Zizzt, zizzzt . . .' Salih darted off to the carpenter and began his clowning all over again, making faces, pulling his tongue. Then he rushed over to Haji Nusret's. Of course the truck was still there! How could it be sold? How could any one of the poor folk in this town pay one hundred and fifty liras for a toy?

Salih felt tired. He walked past the houses that topped the cliff and sat down on the steps leading down to the lifeboat station and observation towers on the shore. Strange mad thoughts chased through his head. The beat of the smith's hammer sounded ever more loudly in his ears. He was half asleep and numb all over when he saw the trawlers coming into view over the horizon. The day was drawing to a close and long shadows fell on the shore. Something stirred in him, some forgotten thing full of hope and promise. He rose and went down to the wharf.

Accompanied by swarms of gulls the trawlers were entering the harbour which was crowded with town children and trucks, big and small, trying to back in as near along the shore as possible. It was a good year for fish. Crates and crates full of them went straight into the trucks which carried them to the fish market in Istanbul. The five or six man crew of a boat were not enough to handle all the transport, so the children rushed in to help, knowing that they would be rewarded with generous amounts of fish to take home in their nylon bags. Salih had often done this and earned large quantities of fish which he'd shared with the neighbours too. He'd never thought of selling them before. But now he would. What a wonderful idea! He'd earn enough money to buy the truck, all by himself without being obliged to big brother Metin or anyone else. He ran past the old boathouse onto the jetty where the boats were unloading their cargo. Hurrying up to Skipper Temel's boat, he jumped on board and set to work at once. Five or six boys were there before him. They passed the crates from one to the other and into the waiting truck. Hooray, Skipper Temel must have caught more than three hundred cratefuls of fish today, turbots, red mullets, goatfish, whitings, deep-sea fish, all gleaming under the crude electric lamplight.

Salih was sweating, but in a short while they had emptied the first of Skipper Temel's three boats and had passed on to the second. As they were finishing with the third, Skipper Temel called out: 'Stop now, mates. Bring me that crate over there.' It was full to the brim with shining red mullets. 'That one too . . .'

Six whole cratefuls of red mullets and goatfish he lumped together on the deck. He looked at the tired sweating boys affectionately and his eyes rested on Salih. He had noticed how Salih had worked today, with machine-like swiftness. Anyway, the Skipper always gave Salih a substantial portion, even when he hadn't worked so hard. It was his catch after all, to dispense with as he fancied.

There was a time when big brother Metin too had worked for Skipper Temel. They had sailed in the warm waters of the south, far away. It was only for the last couple of years that Skipper Temel had taken up fishing on the Black Sea shores. He was an old salt, in his element on the high seas, catching thousands of dolphins and selling the oil for huge sums. That's how he had bought those three large fishing vessels. Not so very long ago these seas teemed with dolphins that gambolled and raced alongside the boats. Salih had heard that dolphins were clever creatures, almost human. Once, sitting on the rocks behind the lighthouse, he'd seen a school of them in the distance, tracing wide arcs through the air, but they'd vanished in a flash. And last year the news had reached Skipper Temel that a dolphin had been observed in the Bosphorus. 'Eh mates,' he'd said, 'this remaining dolphin's mine by right,' and indeed, after chasing it for a week, he'd caught it. That's how he was, the Skipper. Eyes like radar he had. He'd gaze over the sea and know by its colour, its smell, its waves, just where the fish was and at what depth too. Metin used to call him Radar-Eye Temel . . .

'You there, mate, come here.' The Skipper was pointing at Salih, laughing, the corners of his eyes, his copper face crinkling up. 'Where's your bag?'

Salih was dismayed. He didn't have one.

'Hey mates,' the Skipper shouted. 'Get me a big bag for this young sailor, one that won't burst.' They brought him a large nylon bag with a picture of Leander's Tower printed on it. Skipper Temel bent down and carefully selected Salih's share from the heap. 'Here you are, sailor,' he said. 'Fill it up.'

The bag was so heavy that Salih could barely lift it. As he made his way home, his head was seething. How was he going to sell his fish tomorrow? Would he be able to cry like Arab Nevzat, the fisherman, 'Fiiish! Gifts of the sea. Fiiish! Alive, alive-oh . . .' Arab Nevzat had a powerful voice and stiff, very bushy moustaches. Salih could never shout like him since he had no moustache . . .

The call to evening prayer sounded as he entered the house.

'Look!' his mother exclaimed. 'My laddie's brought us some fish. All by himself he's earned it, my little darling, by the sweat of his brow . . .'

Three neighbour women were sitting on the sofa near his grandmother, fanning themselves with the corners of their white headcloths and telling their beads. In a little while they would begin their endless *namaz* prayers. The grandmother shot Salih a venomous look, but quickly hid it under a vague smile.

'And he'll give some to the neighbours too, my generous boy,' Hajer Hanum went on. 'He's got so much . . .'

'No, I won't, not this time,' Salih said. He flushed to the roots of his hair. 'And we shan't eat any either. I'm going to sell this fish tomorrow and earn some money.'

Hajer Hanum was taken aback, but tried not to show it.

'Now, isn't that splendid?' she said. 'My little boy's a grown man now, earning money and all. Good for him! Let him sell his fish and then he'll buy nice things for his mother.'

'I won't buy anything for anyone,' Salih said. He kept his voice very low on purpose and she did not hear him.

'Come,' she said. 'Let's empty the fish over here or they'll spoil in that nylon bag by morning.' She took the bag from Salih's hands. 'Oh dear, but it's so heavy! How could you have carried it all the way from the wharf, my poor darling?' A large saucepan was not enough to contain the fish. She had to get another, and another.

Salih was filled with pride. Even his grandmother's malevolent glare could not disturb him. He knew what her eyes were saying. 'So you're thinking to make money yourself, eh, little goddamn brat, now you couldn't pinch my gold? Let's see you get anything for that stinking fish of yours, discarded by some fisherman and which you picked up God knows where . . .'

'Fresh as daisies they are, my fishes,' Salih shouted out loud suddenly. 'They were still alive and tossing in the bag as I brought them home. You'll see how I'll sell them tomorrow and get pots of money, pots!' His voice rose. 'My fish are fresh as daisies, still alive!' He was screaming now, the veins in his thin neck swelling. 'And nobody'll be able to kill me, nobody!'

The women held their prayers. Everyone froze. His mother swept him up in her arms. 'Who'd want to kill you, who'd dare touch a hair of your head with your father here to protect you? Wouldn't he make mincemeat of them, wouldn't he?'

The grandmother growled and all eyes turned to her. Had she given herself away? Hurriedly, in a loud voice, she took up her prayers again.

Salih turned away and slowly munched at the food his mother laid before him.

The next morning he woke up in an exhilarated frame of mind. He washed and swallowed his breakfast in haste. His mother had found a wooden fish tray for him, painted bright green and she had arranged the bright red fish in neat rows upon it. 'It's much too heavy,' she said worriedly, but Salih was already outside.

How was he to cry his wares? What price should he ask? And what about the bargaining side of it? His feet slowed down and he decided to try the lower streets of the town, where people did not know him.

The first house he came to was a decrepit wooden structure, its boards and window frames cracked and its buff paint faded and flaking. Only the windows of this poor home were alive and cheerful. The turquoise calico curtains, printed with tiny flowers of many colours, at once caught Salih's eye. How he longed to remain there and stare at them to his heart's content! But he had work to do. 'Fish,' he called out. His voice sounded strange to him. Nothing stirred in the house. The street, too, was quite deserted. The mild spring sun shone over the weathered cobblestones, in between which grew tufts of grass and small white and yellow daisies. A warm whiff of honeysuckle wafted to his nostrils and he was reminded suddenly of the smithy. Tears rose to his eyes. 'Ah, Master,' he murmured, 'to think I've come to this when I could have been working for you . . . To be selling fish in the streets, not even shouting properly . . .' At that moment he turned and saw the cats swinging after him, tails on end. 'Fiiish,' he cried out with renewed confidence, and this time his voice was loud and strong, almost like Arab Nevzat's. 'Cheap fresh fish!' More and more cats materialized with lifted tails and tensed whiskers, tabby cats, yellow cats, snow-white cats, grey cats, tortoiseshell cats, black cats . . . And the more they came, the more Salih's spirits rose. Up and down the street he strutted, shouting at the top of his voice. No one appeared, but Salih hardly noticed, so proud was he of his performance, just like Arab Nevzat with all those cats behind him and his voice at the exact pitch. 'Fiiish! Fresh as daisies! Alive, alive-oh! Flowers of the high seas, fresh fiiish . . .' He was not even aware of passing into the next street, and the next. There was now an army of cats in his wake, scrambling over each other for the front places, but always perfectly silent.

Towards noon a woman poked her head out of the window

of a wooden house. 'Hey you, fisher boy! Come here . . .' she called.

It took some time for Salih to realize she was talking to him. 'Co-o-o-ming!' he shouted joyfully.

The woman had huge breasts that sagged over the window sill. 'What's the price of your fish, little boy?' she asked.

Salih was caught off his guard. He blushed scarlet, tried to say something, but his head was quite empty.

'Child, I'm asking you how much you want for your fish.'

In a panic, Salih began to stammer, but before he could answer, a dishevelled woman was yelling from the window of the house across the street. 'For heaven's sake, Zehra Hanum, don't you go buying fish from these boys. I got some yesterday and they'd all gone bad. I had to throw them away.'

'Go away, boy,' the woman at the window said. 'I've changed my mind.'

His head whirling, his legs weaving into each other Salih walked off. He could hear the women laughing after him. All the windows along the street seemed to be full of huge-breasted cackling women. What kind of women were they, laughing their heads off like whores? In Salih's neighbourhood if a woman laughed like that, especially at a little boy selling fish, her husband would tear her tongue out . . .

On the verge of tears he hurried into another street. How mournful the neat rows of lovely red spangly fish looked in the wooden tray where his mother had so carefully arranged them! 'Stupid women,' he muttered. 'Would rotten fish have eyes shining so brightly? Why, they wouldn't be red any longer either! Stupid ignorant women . . . Why should I care what they say?' With a glance at his cat followers, he pressed down the narrow street, shouting with renewed vigour: 'Fiiish, fresh as roses, my fish!' This pleased him. It was his very own invention. So, on he went through the streets, absorbed in finding new words to praise his fish and with a multitude of cats of every variety close on his heels. There was a white one that Salih particularly fancied, snow-white, with long fur and sparkling green eyes. And would you believe it, a large *blue* cat too, yes indeed . . .

113

It was only as day was drawing to a close that Salih realized he hadn't sold a single fish. 'They just won't buy from
children,' he tried to convince himself. But he knew there
was another reason. If he really wanted to, he could still sell
all this load before sundown and return home with pocket-
fuls of money. He was dead tired, though. He remembered
having run for his life with all those cats racing after him,
when some women had wanted to buy the fish. What if they
too laughed at him like the others? What if they told him his
fish stank? He simply could not face it. He'd die if such a
thing happened again.

What was he to do now? Should he take the fish home?
How his grandmother would gloat at him. And the others?
His mother? His father? What a clod, they'd say, at his age,
not to be able to sell a trayful of fish . . . His arms were
aching so, the tray would be dropping from his hands any
moment now. He looked back despondently at the flock of
cats. They were tired too, downcast now, their tails drooping, their faces glum. Salih felt hurt. Only the white cat
smiled at him. Don't worry, it said, how can anyone sell fish
the very first time? There's a period of apprenticeship for
everything. 'Of course,' Salih said, 'how right you are!' All at
once a bright thought came to him. 'Come along, cats,' he
cried triumphantly as he hurried down the hill to the sea.
"Follow me! Fresh fiiish! Lords of the oceans! Flowers of the
seas!' His voice rang out clear and joyful. 'The springtime of
the seas . . .' That was a good one he'd just thought up. All
the freshness, the scents, the flowers of springtime in his
fish . . .

They passed through the little wood and came to the
shore. Salih sank down on a rock. 'Come here, cats, come,
come!' he called. 'I'm going to give you a treat. Such a treat,
you'll remember it all your life.'

The first fish would be for the white cat. He tossed it
deftly, but before the white cat could make a move, a huge
ogre with ruffled fur and scratched face, well-seasoned to
the fight for life, leaped forward and snapped it up in the
air. It was only at the fifth throw that the white cat got its
fish and began to eat it daintily, so daintily that if Salih

114

hadn't hastened to throw fish after fish to the other cats they would have snatched that one too from its jaws.

As he went on casting his fish this way and that, trying to throw them at the less nimble ones, more and more cats materialized out of the blue. He could never have imagined there were so many cats in this town.

The sun had set when he threw his last fish. 'That's all, cats,' he said. 'Look!' And he showed them the empty wooden tray.

# 10

The blue vortex whirled on and on towards the shore and stopped there, sparkling under the moon like a column of light. Blue-winged boats floated in the distance and a blue dragon surged from the sea, coral-eyed. The lighthouse beamed wetly in the rain. Black-clad men rushed to the tower on top of the island, shooting their guns, and lit a huge fire over the rocks. The flames reached as high as the lighthouse, illuminating the blue sailing boats, and in the reddish glare they shed over the blue night, flights of storks, cranes and swans swam past and faded away. An old woman was weeping on the shore. 'Come back to me, come,' she cried. 'It's been so long . . .' A shepherd sat playing his pipe to his red goat that stood on the peak of the crags. A boy ran barefoot along the beach, shouting: 'He's dead! Dead, so there! Dead and won't come back any more . . .' And, whoosh, he was swallowed up at one gulp by that coral-eyed dragon. Another boy came running up, shouting, and the dragon devoured him too, and another, and another. Seven boys he gobbled down in one instant . . .

. . . And one day earth and sky and sea, even the palace of the Pirate Padishah began to tremble. The roofs of the palace, the crags all around it were black with twittering swallows huddling together in alarm, as they always do on feeling the coming of an earthquake.

'What's happening?' the Padishah cried.

'It's the prince, your majesty,' they told him, 'plunging and tossing in his cage. I'm getting bored, he says, shut up here all the time. Let me out or I'll do something terrible . . .'

The Padishah was alarmed, and well he might be! The snake prince had now grown as large as a dragon.

'He wants to go out into the garden, your majesty. Let my father find some friends for me, he says, so I can play with them in the royal gardens.'

'He's right,' the Padishah said. 'My son, a prince, can't live all his life in a pomegranate branch cage just because he happened to be born a snake . . .'

At this, the grand vizier cried out: 'Let my son be the first to make friends with the prince!'

'Nothing could be fitter, esteemed grand vizier,' the Padishah approved.

The grand vizier's son, a meek boy with long eyelashes, was brought to the royal gardens where the cage had been placed. They opened the door of the cage and the snake prince slithered out. He was now nearly five yards long, a huge black snake whose spangled skin shimmered in the sunlight. He flowed straight to where the grand vizier's son was standing under a terebinth tree, holding a nylon bag full of coloured marbles. At the sight of the snake prince the boy's eyes widened. He went pale and began to tremble like a leaf. The snake drew nearer, while the Padishah and the grand vizier sat on their thrones, waiting for the two children to start playing together. Suddenly, the vizier's son flapped his arms wildly and bolted, screaming, towards the sea, but the snake flew after him and barred his way. At that the boy cast himself on the ground, bawling and kicking. The snake stood by, staring at him. 'Come on, get up,' he exhorted the boy. 'They've only just let me out of that cage where I was getting bored stiff. Please don't be afraid of me . . .'

'I'm afraid,' the other quavered. 'Go away.'

'But you mustn't be afraid, brother. I'm not like I seem to be. And I know some lovely games, snake games, bird games, royal games . . . Games to play with flowers and fish, bees, people, trucks . . . I'll teach you. And dances too . . . Come, get up, do!'

'I can't. I'd die of fright.'

'But why? I'm just a boy like you.'

'You? A boy?'

'Of course.'

'You're not a boy. You . . . You're a huge snake!'

'I may look like a snake, but I'm really a boy. Would a snake ever be able to speak like I do?'

117

'He would if he's a king snake . . .'

How could the snake prince convince him? He begged and pleaded, promising to show him wonders no human being had ever seen before, the land of the fairies, the magic gardens of Mount Erjiyés, the paradise of the sea, fathoms deep, way beyond the seven oceans, but the other only cowered closer to the ground, quaking in all his limbs. 'I don't want to,' he wailed. 'I don't want to be friends with a snake . . .'

The snake prince was desperate. Here at last was a boy of his age, but he didn't want to play with him. 'I'll give you a pomegranate branch with red flowers that'll carry you to whatever place you fancy in the twinkling of an eye.'

'I don't want it.'

'I'll give you a magic ring. When you rub it a huge negro will appear, one lip in the sky, the other hanging to the earth. Wish me a wish, he'll say . . .'

'No, no, no!'

'The remedy for death . . .'

'Go away!'

'You don't want even the remedy for death?'

'I don't want anything from you. You're a snake.'

At his wits' end the snake prince glided up and gently licked the boy's hand. At this the boy gave one leap into the air and fell back, stone dead. The snake prince burst into tears. 'But why did you die, brother?' he wept. 'What have I done to make you die?'

The Padishah was distressed. 'Don't cry, my son,' he comforted him, keeping at a safe distance all the while, 'I'll find better, stouter comrades for you.'

'He was a good boy,' the snake prince moaned. 'But why was he so afraid?'

'What can we do, it's fate,' the Padishah said. 'People are such weaklings . . .'

Next it was the first vizier's son who was chosen to play with the snake prince, but as soon as he laid eyes on him, he fled and, before the prince had time to intercept him, he had jumped over the cliff and lay dead on the sands below.

The son of another vizier was found, a brave boy, this

one, who actually played three days with the snake prince, but on the fourth day he too was found dead on the topmost branch of a tree. So it came to pass that there were no more boys left in the land, because some fathers longed for their sons to make friends with the son of the Padishah even at the price of death, and others spirited them out of the country for fear the Padishah would set eyes on them.

And all the while the snake prince was growing up, disconsolate, lonely, friendless . . .

. . . The trawlers came in from the sea. It was evening. Fires were lit on the shore and purple wine flowed in plenty. There was singing and dancing, and large bass, breams and sturgeons were broiled over the embers. Clouds of fish-smelling smoke swirled over the beach . . .

'Why don't we go?' Salih suggested.

'Why not?' Bahri said.

'What a splendid idea,' Jemil cried.

'Only, we won't do like the other boys,' Bahri said. 'We'll go secretly and watch this snake boy. Let's find out what kind of a joker he is.'

'Yes, let's,' Salih said. 'Who cares if he's a padishah's son?'

'Who cares?' Jemil said. 'Besides we're not fool enough to go into his garden. Let him come to us. It's only in his palace, near his Padishah father that he can do all those wild things.'

'Yes, and as soon as he's outside his magic spell will be broken,' Salih said. 'My granny said so.'

They came to the mouth of the cave, which was the gate to the palace of the Pirate Padishah. Nobody for hundreds and hundreds of years had ever had the courage to enter this cave and get to the palace. Bahri produced an enormous torch that beamed for a mile ahead. Where had he found it? Now, what did that matter? What if he *had* pilfered it from the sailors? It wasn't the end of the world. And anyway had those lazy sailors ever had the idea of pointing their torch into this cave?

They emerged into a blue moonlit night and went on, leaping over blueing brooks and springs and violet-scented bushes, their feet sinking into the soft spring earth. As the

119

east brightened they came to a wide garden full of many flowers. At the end of the garden was a huge gilded gate, high as a hill, all carved in marble and wood, with birds and fishes and dragons, an awesome sight, but the three children soon overcame their fear . . . Besides, they had their reed hobby-horses with them and as the space in front of the gate was temptingly flat, they decided to race them. Five times they raced and each time Bahri came first. His hobby-horse was really beautiful. He had walked a whole day to get his reed from the distant marshes. It was a long thick purplish reed, whereas Salih's was just an ordinary garden reed and Jemil's a makeshift thing obtained from some fisherman's tackle. Of course Bahri would win.

But Jemil was angry. 'You're cheating,' he accused Bahri. 'How can you come first every time?'

'See here,' Bahri protested. 'My horse . . .'

'It's a mangy horse!'

'Mangy yourself!' Bahri retorted, giving him a kick. And now they were at it, fighting tooth and nail, while Salih stood by watching. It never crossed his mind to try and separate them. All at once a loud burst of laughter was heard, and peal after peal rang through the air.

'Stop!' Salih cried, his eyes widening. 'Look! Look who's on the wall, laughing at us.'

It was the snake prince, huge and black, and his forked red tongue was pointing at them gleefully.

Bahri was furious. He walked up to the wall and stood there, his hands in his trouser pockets. 'What are you laughing at us for, you wretched snake?' he said. 'Who cares if your father's the king of the pirates? What if he does own five factories, two yachts, five Plymouth cars? D'you take yourself for God that you go and bite all those children to death? Why are you laughing at us? We're fighting like men, not biting poor children treacherously. Come off that wall, you son of a bitch, and let me show you what's what.'

'I'll come if you don't fight,' the snake prince replied, 'I hate fighting. And besides, I never bit those boys.'

'Then how did they die?'

'They died of fear.'

Bahri ran back to Salih and Jemil. 'What shall we do?' he said.

'Let's lure him here and kill him with our knives. Think how many boys' lives we'll be saving . . .'

'All right,' Salih said. But he was trembling already.

'Hey, snake boy,' Bahri called. 'You see we're not afraid of you. Come down to us here.'

'So you'll all three plunge your knives into me? Certainly not!'

'How did you know we'd do that?'

'Because I heard you.'

The three boys retreated behind a plane tree. 'We won't kill him,' Bahri said. 'Let's talk to him. He may be a good boy after all, this snake. But first I must have a good fight with him and teach him a lesson.'

'All right,' Jemil said. 'You talk to him, and fight him too if you like. I'll keep at a safe distance.'

'So will I,' Salih said.

'I don't mind,' Bahri said. 'Well, I'm calling him now. Hey, snake boy!'

The snake sprang up, straight and black on top of the wall, tall as a poplar. 'I'm coming,' he cried joyfully as he slipped down. He hurried up to them, frisking and gambolling like a clown, but the children, suddenly seized with panic, took to their heels.

'Don't run away,' the snake cried after them. 'Please stay and play with me. What are you afraid of? You're three against one. And on top of that you've got arms and legs and everything, while I have nothing at all. Why, oh why are human beings such cowards?'

Bahri stopped dead, clenching his fists. 'Take that back, snake boy! Who's running away? Stand firm, here I come.'

The others turned back too. The snake was waiting for them, bolt upright on his tail.

'Who's a coward?' Bahri challenged him. 'Say that again, you snake, son of a snake.'

'Look, Bahri brother,' the snake said. 'I've heard what a staunch brave person you are. I want to be friends with you.'

'Then take back what you said . . .'

121

Salih and Jemil held their breaths.

'I do, I do!' the snake boy exclaimed.

'Come here,' Bahri ordered. The snake was beside him at one leap. 'On your guard! We're going to fight here, the two of us. But no tricks, mind you, no snake biting.'

'No,' the snake said. 'And no knives either.'

'Just fist to fist . . .'

'But I haven't got any fists!'

'Well, that can't be helped,' Bahri said, and dealt him such a blow that the snake's head hit the ground and rebounded. Again and again Bahri hit him, until the snake was quite dazed and cowering on the ground. Now Bahri started kicking him.

'Stop, Bahri,' the snake boy pleaded. 'That's enough. You're strong because you're a human being.'

'I won't stop,' Bahri shouted in a frenzy. 'I'm going to crush you to avenge all those boys you killed.'

'But I told you I didn't kill them!' The snake was getting angry. His whole body to the tip of his tail turned a fiery red. Bahri took fright, but it was too late. The snake retreated, drew himself into a huge red ball, then shot through the air and struck at Bahri who fell flat to the ground, sprawled out like a frog. 'I'm going to kill you, you wicked boy, kill you!' the snake howled, beside himself, glowing like a live coal. Again and again he hit out at Bahri who never moved. Then he caught sight of Salih and Jemil shaking like leaves in the wind and made a lunge for them. Salih escaped into the pomegranate garden, but Jemil fell before the onslaught, screaming and squirming on the ground.

It was a good thing Salih remembered about the pomegranate magic. He'd just heard about it somewhere . . . Quickly, he slashed off a flowering branch with the knife he carried at his waist and rushed back to save his friends. 'Stop, snake!' he cried, hitting him three times with the branch. 'Leave off this minute!'

The snake quailed, no longer red, but a sickly blueish black. 'Don't kill me,' he pleaded. 'I'll do anything you wish.'

'All right,' Salih said. 'But first we must tend to Bahri and Jemil. Look how they're bleeding.'

'Don't worry about them,' the snake boy said. 'I'll cure their wounds. But don't you want anything from me?'

'There is something . . .'

'I'll give you anything you wish for.'

Salih leaned to his ear and whispered.

The snake boy threw his head back and laughed. He was bright blue now, a real son of a king, royal blue, sea blue . . . 'Ohhooo Salih, is that all you want? Why, I'll get you a thousand of those tomorrow if you like!'

Salih was pleased. 'Now we must revive my friends,' he said.

The snake boy, that is the blue prince, took a large pomegranate flower in his mouth and brushed it over the bodies of the two boys and there they were, on their feet again, as though nothing had ever happened. The first thing Bahri did was to strike a stunning blow at the snake prince.

'Stop,' Salih cried, as Bahri seized a large stone to crush the snake's head. 'You can't do that. He's our brother now. He didn't kill you.'

So the three boys carried the snake into the pomegranate garden and sprinkled water over his face. And when he came to they embraced each other and began to play together. Bahri made a hobby-horse for the prince out of a very long thick purple reed and the prince rode right out over the sea and back. 'Never in my life have I seen a flying horse like this one,' he marvelled.

'I make very good horses,' Bahri said proudly.

Jemil was looking worried.

'What's the matter?' they asked him.

'It's all right for you,' he replied. 'But they're waiting for me at home. I'm supposed to bring back seashells so we can make them into ashtrays and vases and sell them to the tourists. Otherwise, we'll all go hungry . . .'

They were sorry for Jemil! So they lost no time in rushing to the seaside and collecting bagfuls of the most beautiful shells they could find. After that they could play as much as they liked, and so they did, till nightfall. The snake prince was beside himself with joy. He had never played human games before, poor thing . . . But suddenly he stopped. 'My father, the Pirate Padishah, will be looking for me now,' he said. 'He'll throw a fit if he can't find me. I'm his only son, you know . . . Only, wait a minute.' He flowed into the pomegranate garden and returned soon after with three wonderfully fragrant luminous blue flowers. 'Eat these,' he told the boys. 'You'll feel all the odours of sky and earth, of the stars and the seas coursing through your veins. Everything will be bright and beautiful for you every moment of your lives. You'll be like Skipper Temel, who's always happy. My father had given him one of these flowers.'

It was a dizzying enchanting sensation. Wrapped in a blue radiance, they closed their eyes and floated on air.

'Bahri, wake up!' Salih cried at last.

Jemil was sprinting home, carrying three nylon bags full to bursting with seashells.

# 11

Summoning his last remaining strength, Salih trudged back
up the cliff to the market place. His whole body ached
unbearably and he longed to go home and sleep. But he
couldn't. Oh no! Not once had the thought of his truck left
him as he wended through the streets with his heavy load of
fish. At any moment it might catch the eye of some boy or
other who would make his father buy it for him. What
matter, he tried to tell himself, I'll never be able to buy it,
what matter if it's sold or not? But he could not help it. He
must go and see. He must make sure.

And there the truck was, still in its place in the window!
'I'll buy it, I will,' Salih vowed with renewed faith. 'I'll find a
way . . .'

He was dead tired when he came home. Not a word of
what was said to him did he hear, nor did he know if he ate
or not. An army of cats swam about him, golden eyes glowing in the night, thousands and thousands . . .

The next morning he woke up so early that even his
grandmother was still asleep. As always, the first thing that
came to his mind was the truck. He tried to drive the image
away, to think of other things, of Skipper Temel, the fishing
boats, the thousands of blue-shimmering fish struggling in
the nets, glowing golden-red under the sun, phosphorescent
in the dusk of the evening, the Skipper's neck, cord-like . . .
The carpenter, Doctor Yasef, the blacksmith, the fragrant
honeysuckle, the itinerant yogurt vendors, the wood-sellers
from the villages, he called them all to mind. He even dwelt
on his grandmother, who hardly ever moved from her loom
all the year round, ate her meals there, the rattle of her
shuttle varying with her thoughts. Oh yes, Salih knew just
what was passing through her mind by the way she shot the
yarn, by the sound and speed of the shuttle. He could
discern when the longing for Halil overcame her. The

125

shuttle would come and go like a rippling brook, almost silently, as though afraid to make a sound, and the grand-mother's face would be transfigured, beautiful even. Sometimes her hand would stay for a while, and when she began again it was in an entirely different tone, sad and subdued. But these last days the shuttle held a menacing note and Salih was afraid. The grandmother was having bad thoughts and it could only be against him, Salih . . .

That day he would not go to Haji Nusret's shop. What was the use? He directed his steps to the woods. They were quite empty at this early hour. Ah, if only he could find just one other boy . . . Then he caught sight of Bahri in a hollow overgrown with wild rose bushes. Bahri was about his age, but tall and broad-shouldered, with huge strong hands, and all the children hereabouts were afraid of him. Salih had always avoided him like the plague up to now. But today something galvanized him into action. Bahri was busy playing with bees. He'd strung up quite a number of them and tied the strings to the bushes where the bees were buzzing away furiously. And whirling round and round unsteadily with sad weird sounds were a dozen or so bees whose tails Bahri had snipped off and who were unable to find their bearings any more.

Salih drew near, caught Bahri's eye and made a face at him. Bahri stared. 'Listen,' Salih said, 'that sister of yours, she's the greatest whore in all the neighbourhood . . .' Quickly he drew back and only just avoided Bahri's fist. They came to grips and began to fight like Kilkenny cats. On and on they fought until they were too tired even to swear at each other. But how to stop without losing face? Their eyes searched the road for someone to come and separate them, as they dealt a few last feeble blows at one another. No one came and, too spent to lift their arms now, they fell back.

'Let's stop . . .' one of them said, or perhaps they both said it at the same time.

Torn and bleeding, their backs sore with welts as though lashed by a whip, they sat up, panting, and faced each other. Then Bahri winked and smiled. 'Come Salih,' he said. 'Let's go and wash. Your face is a mess.'

'So's yours,' Salih said, winking back.

Hand in hand they walked to the shore and waded in, knee-deep. When they returned to the wood, Bahri's bees were still tugging furiously at their strings, while the mutilated bees gyrated blindly up and down like a wave-tossed ship. Salih looked at them, then at Bahri and lowered his eyes.

'All right, Salih,' Bahri said. 'Help me free these bees.'

'Oh yes, let's,' Salih cried eagerly.

Together they untied the strings and watched the bees shoot away, arrow-like, and vanish from sight.

'I'm sorry about these tailless bees,' Bahri said. 'They look like people without legs, paralyzed, don't they, poor things?'

'That's true,' Salih said.

'Why do we do this? As though it's amusing to watch them fly about, blind and helpless . . .'

'It isn't at all.'

'We should have taken our shirts off,' Bahri commented. 'Won't your people spank you when they see you've torn your shirt?'

'No, they won't,' Salih said. 'And you?'

'Who cares if they do . . .' And they separated in the market place.

Salih rushed home and quickly changed his shirt. Deaf to his mother's scolding, he hurried out again and, with a premonition of disaster, made straight for Haji Nusret's shop. The window was empty. The truck had disappeared! His head whirling, Salih sank to the pavement.

Haji Nusret was standing in front of the shop, laughing at him . . . Salih tried to pull himself together. He got up, clinging to the wall, his legs trembling.

'It's sold,' Haji Nusret said. 'The lawyer Osman Ferman bought it for his son. But don't be so sad, child. I've ordered many toys from Germany. There'll be plenty of those trucks soon . . .'

Salih heard nothing more. Osman Ferman! The name was a magic key to his goal . . .

The lawyer Osman Ferman had his office right there, in

the market place. Salih found it without losing time. Osman Ferman was inside. He could see him through the window, scratching a shiny bald pate with a pencil, his double chin puffed out, and talking importantly to some villagers who sat around respectfully, hands on knees. Osman Ferman's face was screwed up as if in pain, almost tearful. Then suddenly it changed. He laughed bitterly and shouted at the peasants. Salih could hear him even from where he was hiding behind the plane tree. The peasants said nothing. And after a while they took their leave humbly and walked out with faltering steps. Once outside, they all burst out talking at once, arguing at the top of their voices. But Osman Ferman paid no more attention to them. His hands were flying through a file in front of him. He leapt to his feet, rushed to a cabinet and rummaged through the shelves and drawers. Obviously he had lost something of great importance, for he sweated profusely and even looked under the table and all over the floor. Finally, he snatched up his hat and, banging the door behind him, he made off at a running pace in the direction of the higher quarter of the town. Salih followed and watched him charge through the open gate of a garden into a house. Some time later he emerged again, mopping his brow and sighing with relief.

This was it. Salih must wait now until Osman Ferman's son came out with the truck. He settled on a heap of stones, well out of sight behind a thick terebinth tree and fixed his eyes on the house. It stood in the middle of a neglected garden and had been newly painted and repaired. The six windows were closed and there was no sign of life inside. The only sound to be heard was the twittering of a flock of starlings that had alighted on the wide white marble steps leading to the front door.

It was well into the afternoon before a boy appeared at the top of the marble steps, and sure enough, there was the truck, Salih's truck, behind him. Salih felt as though his heart would stop beating. The bastard, he fumed, he's tied my truck to the end of a string, like a dog! He doesn't even know how to wind it up . . . Good for Haji Nusret, Allah's own servant! He'd stood up for Salih and not shown this bastard boy how to wind the truck . . . Still, Salih was consumed with envy. He longed to jump at the boy's throat and beat him black and blue for daring to touch his truck. Then a wave of despair swept over him. He crouched low on the heap of stones, paralyzed, while the boy passed quite near him, the truck trailing on the ground, in the mud, those beautiful wheels all caked in mud . . .

He had large hazel eyes and a good face, but with a bored, lonely expression. He was well-dressed and combed slick, and even wore a red tie over his white shirt. Salih had never seen a boy wear a tie before. His shoes were brand new too, but he stepped in the dirt carelessly. What did such boys know of the value of beautiful things . . . Look at the way he was treating Salih's wonderful truck!

The boy walked up to the road, then turned back and went up the stairs, dragging the truck after him like a dead cat. It banged against the steps and Salih was terrified it would break. The boy had stopped at the top of the stairs, his arms hanging, bored to death. He spat a few times, tugged at his penis, looked up at the clear blue sky and stuck his tongue out at some seagulls whirling in the distance. Then to Salih's indignation he stuck his tongue out at the truck and, worse still, dealt it a resounding kick. It was too much. Salih closed his eyes. He got up quickly and walked away, almost sobbing. Suddenly he remembered Bahri. He must go to him. Together they might think of something. Two heads are always better than one.

He found Bahri on the bottom step of his home, absorbed in making a toy called 'Camel' out of willow shoots. Three fingers of his left hand were bound with bloodstained rags. He looked pleased to see Salih and made him sit on the step beside him. Salih poured out his story.

'And he stuck his tongue out at my truck!' he repeated again and again, red with vexation. 'He spat on it and kicked it too, many many times.'

'Don't you worry,' Bahri said at last. 'We'll get that truck from him as easily as taking candy from a baby. Come on, let's go. And if we find the slightest scratch on it, we'll beat him till he begs for mercy.'

'Oh yes,' Salih cried, his spirits rising.

'We'll stick our tongues out at him too . . .'

'Both of us!'

'And spit on him . . . Now, I'm going to get my marbles. They'll come in useful, you'll see . . .'

The boy was sitting on the steps, his face cupped in his hands, brooding and muttering to himself. The truck lay neglected by his side. Bahri and Salih selected a dry open space under the terebinth tree, in good view of the house, and dividing the marbles between themselves, began to play. The new glass marbles, inlaid with red, blue, yellow and green, sparkled with a thousand and one colours under the sun. Bahri was the best marble player in the town and he was soon well on the way to bagging all Salih's marbles. Poor Salih, his mind was not on the game. His eyes kept straying to the blue truck. The boy had now taken off his shoes and was counting his toes. He pressed his naked feet into the mud and stared at the imprint as though he had just un-covered something very important. Then he stamped it out, scolding at the top of his voice, heaped it with stones and, putting on his shoes, kicked at the stones and pulled horrible faces. All the while he never once had a glance to spare for the truck. This infuriated Salih and suddenly he picked a quarrel with Bahri.

'You're cheating!' he yelled.

'I'm not! I'm an expert at this game, my boy, so I'm win-ning. You're just green . . .'

'You don't say!'

'The hell I do! Keep your eyes open and see if I'm cheating.'

'I won't play with you,' Salih shouted. 'You're spoiling a good game.'

The boy had pricked up his ears at the sound of the quarrel. He took a few hesitant steps towards them. Bahri was quick to seize this chance. 'Don't play then,' he flashed back. 'As though I can't find someone else! Who wouldn't want to play marbles?' He looked pointedly at the boy. 'I'll play with him there . . . Hey, you! Don't stand gaping at us. Come along and play. We won't eat you.'

The boy cast a wary glance at the house. There was no one at the windows. He shot forward and stood timidly sizing up the other two boys.

'D'you know how to play marbles?' Bahri asked him.

'Oh yes,' the boy said eagerly.

Salih stepped up to him. 'Take my marbles if you like. I don't want to play with that cheat.'

'I've got my own marbles,' the boy said, his face brightening for the first time. He dashed into the house and was back in an instant with a bag full of marbles of every size and colour.

'No tricks now,' Bahri warned him. 'Like this fellow here.' He pointed to Salih.

'Oh no,' the boy smiled. They started to play and at the first go the boy snapped up three of Bahri's marbles.

'Zizzzt!' Salih scoffed. 'Who's the expert now?'

'We've not even started yet,' Bahri retorted. 'Just you wait and see.'

'I'll play with that truck in the meantime,' Salih said, trembling already, unable to look at the boy, nor at Bahri. He darted into the garden. The truck was his at last. His hands burned, but really burned as he touched it. The boy had paid no attention to him at all. He was utterly absorbed in the game, delighted to find someone to play with. These marbles had been brought to him from Germany by his doctor uncle. His father and elder sister had indulged him a little. Then he had been left to himself and, after a while, bored with playing alone, he had cast them aside. If only he could be certain no one would spot him from the house and shout at him to come in . . . He had not a thought for the truck, nor for Salih, who was making stealthily for the street, his heart pounding as though it would pierce his chest.

It was only when he turned the corner that Salih thought of taking off his jacket and wrapping the truck up in it. Then he took to his heels. How he reached the mouth of the old pirate cave on the shore, he never knew. With tremulous hands he caressed his truck and set to washing it and picking out the dirt lodged in its wheels. He wiped and polished it

with his jacket and laid it on a rock under the sun. How it
flashed and glinted! Like the lighthouse lantern, only more
blue, brighter even, bathing the sea and sands in a deep
blue radiance . . .

He heard a faint sound and sat up, ready to fly. The
police! It must be the police. In all this excitement he had
not given a thought to Bahri and the boy. Now, he saw it all,
as in a film. The boy must have missed the truck and raised
a clamour. There was the gardener now, rushing up brandishing a pair of shears. He'd taken the situation in at a
glance and pounced on Bahri who was gathering up his
marbles. Run Bahri, run! Too late. Such a blow the
gardener struck that Bahri saw stars. But he put up a fight
though blood spurted out of his mouth and nose. The boy
had thrown himself on the ground, howling. 'I want my
truck,' he sobbed. 'My truck!' His mother, his sisters, his
grandmother, everyone had poured out of the house. Word
was sent to Osman Ferman and he'd come over at full speed
and started questioning Bahri.

'Where's the truck?'

'That boy took it.'

'What boy?'

'I don't know him. He's a friend of your son's. They were
playing here, under this tree.'

'It's a lie!' the boy shrieked. 'They came here together. I
*saw* them.' His face stained with tears, his beautiful clothes
soiled with mud . . .

'Truss him up and take him straight to the police station!
They'll know how to make him confess there . . .'

But Bahri stands firm. He won't talk. He's a real man.
They clamp a tube to his mouth and pump air into him. He
swells and swells, large as a barrel, huge, bursting . . .
'Who's taken that truck?' Bahri can hardly speak. 'I . . .
I . . . don't know . . .' Poor Bahri! Salih was on the verge of
tears. Hold on, Bahri, don't tell them . . . Now they're giving him electric shocks . . . Once Salih had only just grazed a
live electric wire and it had hurled him to the ground. So it
was with Bahri . . . Again and again he hit the floor and the
walls. His mouth all twisted, foaming . . . They tied the wire

to his penis, just like Salih had heard his father tell they did to those students, the ones he daren't even name . . .

'Stop!' Bahri moaned. 'Don't kill me.'

'Then speak! Who is it?' the stern-faced police officer said.

'Salih . . .'

'Oh, that one? We know him.' And turning to the boy's father: 'I'll get hold of that Salih in no time and recover the truck for you, sir. I'll hang him up by his penis, I will. And this Bahri, I'm going to send him to jail. That'll teach him to make friends with thieves . . .'

'At once, at once!' Osman Ferman was shouting as he mopped his brow. 'Five hundred and fifty liras I paid for that truck. Five hundred . . .'

'Certainly, sir, at once . . .' All the policemen stood at attention, cringing before the lawyer.

'You call yourselves policemen? Why, this country's infested with thieves, unlivable! And now they've started stealing our children's toys!' On and on he ranted, while the policemen combed the town in search of Salih. They asked for him at home, and the grandmother started muttering and growling and never stopped . . .

Salih rushed to the top of the crags and scanned the path that led to the town. There was no one to be seen. He clambered down again and stroked his truck. Oh, how it burned his hands . . .

133

# 12

Skipper Temel, the other fishermen and some old women sat in front of the cave, weaving a giant fish net with cords as thick as a finger. In the distance, on the smooth calm sea the Pirate Padishah's ship rode at anchor, all sails lowered.

A caique made of pure gold was brought out and the Pirate Padishah appeared on deck, holding his sceptre that Dursun the carpenter had carved for him out of the blackest ebony. It was topped by a magnificent blue-flashing pearl, large as a fist, found in the depths of the seven seas. The Padishah's face, strangely enough, his whole person, was the exact replica of Skipper Temel's. Dress him up in the Skipper's clothes and set him to weave a fish net and everybody, including his own wife, would swear this was no Padishah, but the Skipper, large as life. And the Skipper, arrayed in the Padishah's apparel, could if he liked penetrate into the queen's own alcove . . .

The Padishah stepped into the golden caique and seventy-two sailors grasped the oars, rowing him swiftly on, heave-ho, heave-ho, heave-ho, to where Skipper Temel was weaving his net. The Skipper rose to greet him.

'Isn't that net ready yet, Skipper?' the Padishah asked.

'Almost,' the Skipper replied. 'We've been working day and night, as you see. And anyway, we agreed on forty days . . .'

'That's true. You've still got plenty of time and this is a very big net. But what is it for?'

'Ah, that I can't tell you yet, my Padishah.'

The Padishah cast his gold-braided purple cape over his shoulders and sat on a rock to watch the weavers.

The prince had grown up now, still a snake, but a huge one. His coat was very black and glossy, almost blue, and his forked tongue a bright red. All day long he wandered about the pomegranate garden, hunting birds up the trees and playing all kinds of snake games to while away the time. But at night sleep would not come to him. He hurled himself this way and that, bellowing madly, in quest of something, but what, he himself did not know . . . Something he needed badly . . . Could not do without . . . He lashed out furiously at whoever drew near him, lunging at the trees even, twirling himself round the trunks and making the thickest tree shake like a steel wire.

'The prince is getting out of hand,' the grand vizier said to the Padishah. 'He's a young man now and should get married.'

'Yes, but who would marry his daughter to a fierce snake like that?' The Padishah dared not ask, 'would you' . . .

The grand vizier understood. 'Who wouldn't give his daughter to the son of the one and only pirate king of the seven seas, even if he is a snake? My daughter's at your service if he likes her.'

'No,' the Padishah said. 'The prince has already killed your son. I don't want your only daughter to die as well, nor those of my other viziers. Let's think of someone else, but someone worthy of a padishah's son.'

So they put their heads together.

There was a gentleman from Istanbul, called Mustafa Kaval, who used to come to this little town in the summer. He was the owner of the Kaval Holding Company and had built himself a villa on the crags with a vast garden that ran right down to the sea. He had three daughters and two sons. The family would arrive in large limousines and they never talked with the townsfolk. The girls were tall and beautiful, with carefully dyed hair and their guests rich foreigners, speaking French and English and German. All night through, their mansion rang with the sound of dancing, drinking and feasting. Mustafa Kaval had also bought up all the best land to be had in these parts. He'd got it for a song from the townspeople and now it was worth millions. But he never had enough and was busily acquiring more and more land along the Black Sea coast. His chief concern was his daughters' future and that was why he worked so hard to amass fortunes. Ah, but he didn't know what Providence had in store for him! The Padishah and his grand vizier, after much deliberation, decided on Mustafa Kaval's eldest daughter, Gülderen, as a wife for the snake prince.

'It's a splendid choice,' the grand vizier said. 'He owns thirty-six factories and a hundred and twenty agencies. His fortune amounts to one billion liras, to say nothing of the dollars he's stored in foreign banks. Twenty years ago he was only a petty grocer in Ankara. Then he secured a leg-up from the government and he was on his way. Soon, it was the Americans who adopted him and furthered his business. Now he's got the whole of Turkey at his beck and call.'

'Who told you all this?' the Padishah asked.

'Skipper Temel did. He says Mustafa Kaval is a proper rogue who's made his fortune by all sorts of crooked ways.'

'But he's even richer than I am,' the Padishah said glumly. 'He could easily buy up all my vessels and palaces and treasures.'

'That wouldn't make Skipper Temel respect him any the more.'

'But would Mustafa Kaval give his daughter to a snake?'

'He'd jump at the chance. His kind would give anything to be related to royalty. It's the only thing they cannot buy, for all their money.'

So a delegation composed of Ali Jengiz Köse, Keloglan*, Ismail the blacksmith, Doctor Yasef and the druggist Fazil Bey, and flanked by fifteen black-clad pirates, was sent to Mustafa Kaval to ask for his daughter's hand. He went wild with joy. 'I'll make my son-in-law general manager of my bank,' he shouted. 'Like they do in Europe. Here, people of noble stock don't work in banks, but in Europe they even sweep the banks . . .'

Ali Jengiz Köse soon put him in his place. 'Our Padishah's not one of those European kings, you know,' he said sternly, 'nor is he the son of an upstart army sergeant like the Shah of Iran. Our Padishah is lord and master of all the pirates on the seven seas, d'you understand?'

'Yes, yes,' Mustafa Kaval mumbled, chastened. 'I'm sorry.'

*Ali Jengiz Köse and Keloglan are popular heroes in several Anatolian folktales.

'Neither you, nor your daughter are to see the prince until the wedding day, and she only in the nuptial chamber. Now, do you, by Allah's will and with the Prophet's blessing, agree to give your daughter to the Padishah's son?'

'I . . . I do,' Mustafa Kaval stammered.

'Then let the wedding festivities start in three days' time.'

'All right,' Mustafa Kaval agreed, very much awed.

The festivities were held both in the town and in the Padishah's palace. All that counted in Istanbul's high society were invited. They came decked in furs and jewels and the little town teemed with expensive cars. Whisky flowed like water and shots were fired all through the night to mark the occasion. Three government ministers were among the guests and one of them was said to be the head of the clandestine gang who kept killing university students. Thirty-four armed bodyguards accompanied him wherever he went.

And suddenly the rumour was all over the town: the prince was a snake!

'Who isn't a snake nowadays?' Mustafa Kaval sneered. 'Everybody's biting everybody else. But our snake's the chief of all snakes. Nobody can bite him.'

Gülderen was thrilled. 'What if he is a snake? He's a prince, isn't he? And besides, I'll be the first woman in the world to have a snake for a husband. *Intéressant, n'est-ce pas, mes amis?*'

Her high society friends were quite envious.

So the bridal night came and the bride was transported in a satin-sailed vessel across the sea to the Pirate Padishah's palace, where the snake prince awaited her with fervent eagerness, promising himself to be very careful and not frighten her. He felt his manhood rise within him, and when snakes are enamoured they become just like well-tempered steel.

The bridal chamber was decked in gold and silver-embroidered silks and the bride lay on a goose-feather bed, arrayed in a pink nightgown. When the snake prince saw her he liked her so much that he turned red as a live coal from tip to toe. 'Don't be afraid of me, my princess,' he said quickly. 'I won't hurt you. I may look like a snake, but I'm a man really.' His voice was soft and tender, but it was impossible not to tremble at the sight of his awesome frame. 'Shall I come to you?'

'All right,' Gülderen assented. She took off her nightgown without embarrassment and waited for him, quite naked. Flame-red now, the snake flowed towards her and entered between her parted legs. This gave Gülderen much pleasure, but the snake, beside himself with burning desire, was holding her ever more closely. 'Stop, my prince,' she gasped, 'you're too strong. You'll kill me.' It was no use. The snake prince tightened his embrace, quivering in a paroxysm of ecstasy. But when he came to, what should he see! Gülderen had died! Sorrow-stricken, he carried her to the shore and tried to revive her. He had enjoyed making love to Gülderen. It must be said that Gülderen had a lot of experience with men. She could give them more pleasure than that German tourist girl who, last summer, had lain with all and sundry in the crags and caves around the town. Why, there wasn't a young man in Istanbul who hadn't gone to bed with Gülderen! Poor snake prince, what did he know of the doings of high society girls? He sat there on the shore, grieving, ready to stab himself with a huge dagger. But the Pirate Padishah stopped him.

'Don't kill yourself just for a girl, my son,' he pleaded. 'I'll get you another wife tomorrow. Istanbul city is full of merchants who've got beautiful daughters and there's nothing they wouldn't do to have them married to a padishah's son.'

'Really, father?' the prince asked, starting up on the tip of his tail in eagerness.

'Of course! Don't give it another thought,' the Padishah assured him.

Many more daughters of rich merchants were brought to the snake prince as brides, but he was too passionate and squeezed them all to death. He was so ashamed afterwards, he could not look anyone in the face any more.

The Padishah was desperate. 'What can I do for you, my son?' he cried. 'Here I am, the supreme king of these seven seas, yet powerless to find a remedy to my only son's need.'

'It's not your fault, father,' the snake prince said. 'I was just born a snake.'

'But it *is* my fault. It's because I was too impatient to wait that you were born like this.'

'Well, what's done is done,' the snake prince comforted him. 'But there *is* something you can do now and that's to find my boyhood friends.'

'Friends?' the Padishah exclaimed. 'I didn't know about that. Who are they? Jinns or *peris* or what?'

'They're human beings, father. And the best and bravest in the world. If anything can be done for me, they'll be the ones to do it.'

'Well!' the Padishah marvelled. 'Tell me who they are and I'll have them brought here at once.'

'Wait a minute! You can't summon them just like that. A hundred padishahs like you couldn't force them to come against their will.'

'Then what shall we do?'

'We'll try sending one of your clever pirates to them with my greetings. Perhaps they might accept to come then.'

'What d'you mean, accept!' the Padishah roared.

'Father, you don't know them,' the prince said. 'Even as a child one of them beat me to a jelly and wasn't at all afraid of me.'

'But who are they? Where do they live?'

'Their names are Salih, Jemil and Bahri. Everyone knows them in the town. They may be married by now and have families and children . . . Who knows . . .'

'Well, I'll do my best.'

The Padishah's men found Salih first. Salih was a married man and the father of two boys. His wife was the daughter of Skipper Temel, a fair-haired, blue-eyed beauty . . . Salih owned seven large fishing vessels, all brand new and painted blue, and seven trucks too, also blue, that he drove every day over the bridge to Istanbul to sell his fish. He'd made good, and he'd bought seven toy trucks for each of his sons, all of them blue . . .

Jemil was a *hamal** in the market place. All day long he

---

*Hamal: a porter in the Middle East.

toted heavy loads on the pack-saddle over his back. He had seven sons who gathered shells by the seashore to make vases and ashtrays which they sold to the tourists. They had to, poor things, for Jemil could hardly feed them all with his earnings as a *hamal*.

As for Bahri, he'd ended up in jail, just as everyone had predicted. He'd killed Osman Ferman's son, though no one had been able to find out why . . . He'd broken open Salih's grandmother's chest too . . . And he'd stuck a knife into Haji Nusret, after setting fire to his shop. Haji Nusret was maimed for life, paralyzed on the right side, and the rest of him trembled like a leaf in the wind . . .

'All right, we'll come,' Salih said. 'But first Bahri must be released. He's in the Sagmaljilar Prison in Istanbul.'

'That's easy,' the Padishah's chief pirate said. 'We'll have him here this very evening.'

'And Jemil's very poor,' Salih continued. 'One day without work, and his children will go hungry.'

'That's no problem,' the pirate said. 'I'll give him a hand-ful of gold right away.'

The first thing Bahri did when he arrived in town was to administer a sound thrashing to the druggist and the carpenter. The police never dared interfere for they knew that it was the Padishah who'd got him out of prison.

Jemil was overcome with joy at the sight of so much gold. Without waiting a minute he bought a plot of land by the lighthouse and laid the foundations for a villa.

On the second day, Salih, Jemil and Bahri set out for the palace, guided by the Padishah's pirates. The prince met them halfway and embraced them with tears in his eyes. That night a great feast was held in their honour. The food and drink came from the seven seas, so wonderful that even Mustafa Kaval's fare was nothing to it. Afterwards, forty virgins took them to the *hamam**, bathed them with scented soap and dried them too, all three of them. They slept that night on feather beds smelling of ambrosia, of soap, of sun-shine . . .

*Hamam: Turkish bath.

The next morning the prince greeted them in the big audience hall of the palace. 'I've asked you here, my friends, because I'm in terrible trouble,' he said. 'You must have heard about it, how each time I want to take a wife she dies on our wedding night. I must find a wife who's as strong as I am.'

'That's not so easy,' Salih said.

'Not easy at all,' the others concurred.

'Alas,' the prince wailed. 'Then there's nothing left for me but to kill myself.'

'Save him!' the Padishah implored. 'Aren't you his childhood friends? He already tried to kill himself once and I stopped him. Save him.'

'All right,' Salih said. 'But grant us three days.'

'You can have three days and three weeks too if you like!'

They left the palace and returned to the town.

It was a difficult problem they were facing. How to find a woman for the snake prince whom he would not kill when he made love to her? They squatted in the yard of Salih's house, under the olive tree, swaying on their haunches and smoking cigarettes. Skipper Temel was staying in Salih's house now, but he had grown very old. 'What's up, my lads?' he asked. 'Is there something wrong?'

Bahri sighed. The Skipper squatted down beside them, leaning his aged frame against the tree, and heard them out.

'Well!' he said, scratching his head. There was a long silence while the Skipper cracked his fingers one by one. 'These snakes that are half-human are something to reckon with,' he mused. 'Long ago half the human beings were snakes and half human . . . Half were bulls, the other half human. The same with goats, with horses . . . It's only recently that human beings have taken on an entirely human form. But then they discarded their human qualities and came to grief. Yes,' he cried, working himself up, 'men have become quite inhuman in our age. Now, your snake prince did what was right when his father, the Padishah of the seven seas, stooped to taking the daughter of that merchant, Mustafa Kaval, as a wife for him. He bit her to

141

death. Yes indeed . . . Half giants, half men . . .
Behemoths . . . Half eagles, half men, half lions, half . . .'
On and on he rambled, and only stopped at the elephants.
It was easy to put a human head on an elephant, but when it
came to an elephant's head . . . Where was the body that
could support it? 'That snake prince of yours is better than
all human beings put together,' the Skipper declared. 'Don't
worry, I'll find a wife that's right for him and they'll have
children half human, half snake. That's how it should be,
closer to nature. That'll save men from being such
degenerate moneygrubbers. Now, go and tell the Padishah
to send me a good quantity of thick nylon cords. Blue they
should be . . .'

But the Padishah was standing at the gate, listening.
'What are you going to do with those cords?' he asked.

'A large strong fish net, my Padishah.'

'What for?'

'Don't ask too much, Padishah,' the Skipper roared.

'I'm sorry,' the Padishah said anxiously. 'You'll get your
cords at once. As many as you wish, and all blue.'

'I want your largest vessel to be put at my disposal.'

'Certainly.'

'You'll grant me forty days . . .'

'Anything you say, Skipper Temel . . .'

The next morning the whole wharf was covered with piles
and piles of blue nylon cording. Skipper Temel's mouth
reached to his ears. 'Now we can get going,' he declared. He
gathered about him as many expert weavers as he could find
and they set to work.

The Padishah sat there watching. He ate Skipper Temel's
fish soup and listened to Kiziloglu singing his beautiful old
songs. And the Skipper told him of ancient times and of men
that were also snakes and lions, tigers and eagles . . . How
surprised the Padishah was! 'Then I'm glad my son was born
a snake,' he said. 'People that are half snake, or half tiger,
or half eagle must surely be closer to the essential roots, isn't
that so, Skipper Temel?'

'Indeed it is,' the Skipper answered.

And one morning when the Padishah came again the

wharf was empty! Skipper Temel had heaped the fish net onto the royal ship and sailed away beyond the seven seas to the Seven Blue Isles, where everything was blue, the birds, the fish, the cats, all living things, and the sun and moon too, and the flowers and clouds and streams . . .

The Skipper knelt under a lofty blue tree and prayed for a whole day. Then he boarded the ship and sailed to where the sun was setting. There, he spread his net over the smooth unruffled sea and set to wait. The moon rose, shedding a blue light everywhere, and suddenly they heard a long anguished scream that echoed far and wide. The sea shook and the net strained to snapping point.

'Draw it in, my lads,' Skipper Temel ordered. All night long the deck hands pulled, and when dawn came they saw a creature leap up, entangled in the nets, like a blue streak of lightning, and splash back again. 'Quick pull! More quickly . . .'

The sun rose and there in the nets, almost fainting with exhaustion, was a long-haired blue-eyed mermaid, a real beauty, though her body from the waist down was that of a fish and covered with blue scales.

'Why have you caught me, Skipper Temel?' she moaned. 'It can't be for yourself. You've had your day. I'd willingly have been a wife to you in your youth. Let me go, for I want no one else.'

'Come, come, my little mermaid. You'll see what joy, what pride is in store for you . . .'

The mermaid begged and implored, but she could not get another word out of him.

This time the snake prince's wedding festivities were held all over the Black Sea and other maritime lands, but no one could find out who the bride was. It was the mermaid herself, and she was staying in Salih's house, where his wife, Skipper Temel's daughter, was taking good care of her.

'Don't be afraid of the prince even though he's a snake,' Salih told her. 'He's a good lad and won't bite you. He never bit anyone. All those other girls simply died of fear . . . Besides, I'm going to tell you a secret and you won't need to be afraid at all. On the wedding night when he says, undress, you'll say, you undress first. That'll make him very angry and he'll turn bright red and become dangerous. But I'm giving you this pomegranate branch, it's his talisman . . . You'll strike the ground three times and cry: Whoa! He'll be quiet as a lamb then, that great snake, and obey you at once. There'll be a fire burning away in the fireplace and, as soon as he's undressed, you'll seize his skin . . .'

The day came and the street along Salih's house was lined with cars and trucks, all decorated with flowers. The port was full of sailing-boats, yachts and ships, and cars and boats all began to hoot their horns and klaxons, while women who'd come from the palace of the fairies arrayed the bride in her finery and dressed her hair. Finally, she was set on a white horse and sent to the Pirate Padishah's palace.

A bright fire was burning in the grate, as the mermaid waited in the bridal chamber, carefully concealing the pomegranate branch under her skirt. And then the door opened and the snake prince appeared, his coral eyes glittering, his forked tongue stuck out. At this sight, the mermaid lost her nerve and rushed to the window. 'Stop,' an awful voice sounded. 'Stay where you are and undress.'

But the mermaid had regained her senses by now. She turned and saw that the snake was standing straight on his tail, like a pillar of fire. 'You undress, you!' she cried desperately. 'At once . . .' And she quickly produced the pomegranate branch from under her skirt and hit the ground three times, shouting, 'Whoa!'

The snake prince stopped short. 'Oh dear,' he said, 'Salih, you've given me away. You told her about that pomegranate branch!'

'What if he did?' the mermaid challenged him. 'Undress at once or . . .'

'Wait, don't hit me or you'll kill me! Stop!' the prince cried in fear. 'Look, I'm shedding my skin.'

And what should the mermaid see! In place of the black snake, there stood a handsome young man, more beautiful even than big brother Metin. The mermaid fell in love with him at first sight. She rushed up and, snatching the snake

144

skin from his hands, cast it straight into the flames of the fireplace where it was burnt to ashes in an instant. Now the prince could never turn into a snake again . . .

'Will you undress too?' he said to the mermaid.

She complied willingly. The Prince lifted her in his arms and took her to the bridal bed, where all their desires were fulfilled.

As dawn broke the mermaid went to sleep. The prince rose and took the pomegranate branch from under her pillow. 'Let it bloom,' he whispered, and so it did, in an instant. Then he threw the flowering branch into the fire.

# 13

Two shadows were coming this way along Kumbaba beach. Policemen! Salih knew it at once, for only policemen walked in pairs like that. They must have tracked him here. He had to hide the toy truck and the only safe place was the pirate cave. Salih had always been terrified of entering it, but so was everyone else in this town. If he could only brave it now . . . Just a little way inside . . . Not all the policemen in the world, not even generals would dare go into that long dark fearsome cave . . . Clutching his truck he faced the mouth of the cave, but it grew darker as he looked, a gaping blackness that panted from the very depths of the earth. He tucked the truck behind a stone and clambered up the rocks, hoping against hope that the two men would turn back. But no, they were drawing nearer and nearer. Rushing down, he seized the truck and closed his eyes. When he opened them he was at the mouth of the cave, on the edge of darkness. Quickly he shut them again and dragged himself forward, his heart pounding. Groping for the wall on his right, he laid the truck down carefully. It was exactly seven steps to the entrance. He counted them to be sure he would find the place again. Then he took to his heels. 'Now let them come!' he gloated as he ran towards the lighthouse. 'Let me see them penetrate that cave! They'd die of fright.'

Should he go home now or hide somewhere else? Of one thing he was sure. The police would never get a word out of him, not if they plugged electric current to his penis, not if they pumped air into him, not if they killed him even. And one night he'd board Skipper Temel's boat and sail away for Istanbul, with the truck in his arms.

The marble game was in full swing when Salih escaped with the truck. Bahri had seen him make his getaway. As for the boy, he was quite absorbed in the game. He had been winning steadily, but half an hour after Salih's disappearance, everything changed, and it was not long before Bahri had bagged all his marbles. The boy had taken his defeat in good spirit. 'Come again Bahri, won't you,' he said. 'I've got many more marbles and lots of toys too.'

'I'll come,' Bahri promised. But he felt a twinge of pity for the boy. 'Look, you can have half the marbles you lost back, if you like.'

'Oh no!' the boy cried happily. 'My uncle from Istanbul always brings me so many.'

Bahri couldn't help himself. The devil prompted him to spring the question: 'Where's the boy who was playing with your truck?'

'I don't know,' the boy said, not grasping what the other was driving at.

'Who is he?'

'I don't know.'

'Don't you see he's stolen your truck?' Bahri said, exasperated.

'Let him,' the boy laughed. 'It wasn't working properly anyway. My father's getting me a new one with headlights you can switch on and all. He's going to Istanbul tomorrow just for that. He'll bring me a helicopter too, that can fly of itself, and perhaps an airplane. When you come to play marbles again, we can fly them together if you like.'

Bahri thought for a moment, then suddenly spat in the boy's face and dealt him a hard kick. But the boy, his eyes wide and frozen, only stared at him. It was unbearable. 'Come on, let's fight,' Bahri cried. He put down his bag of marbles and held up his fists.

'I don't want to,' the boy said. 'It's not nice to fight.'

'Aren't you a man?' Bahri challenged him. 'Men must fight.'

'But I've never fought before . . .' The boy was almost in tears.

'There's nothing doing with you,' Bahri said contemptuously. 'You're not even worth your salt.'

'My father doesn't allow me to fight,' the boy said defensively.

'Fathers don't have anything to say in boys' fights,' Bahri bridled.

The boy gaped at him as at some strange creature and bolted into the house.

'Then I won't come back,' Bahri shouted after him, 'though you may have all the marbles in the world, you poor ninny!'

He hitched up his trousers, grabbed the marbles and walked off, whistling derisively.

The lighthouse was a broad ancient edifice, painted with black and white stripes. The townspeople were proud of it and boasted that its beams could pierce the darkness far out beyond the seven seas. Many a child had spent sleepless nights watching the houses and hills, the trees and the sea pass through its brilliant shaft of light, especially the lofty plane tree at the crossroads whose branches spread even longer when illuminated, all filigreed in light . . .

It was well onto midnight before Salih could bring himself to go home, and this after much hesitation and coming and going. Eight times he'd crept up the mound behind the house to listen for the sound of policemen, but had fled, even more frightened at the deathlike silence inside, to hide again among the crags behind the lighthouse. In the end he stopped rooted before the gate, unable to lift his hand and open it, his heart beating loudly. He coughed a few times, but nobody seemed to hear. Then he broke into a song, and sang on, quite forgetting what he was doing there. His mother's voice roused him. 'Salih, my darling! Wherever have you been? I was worried sick.'

'We were just playing with some boys near the lighthouse and forgot about the time. I ran back as quickly as I could . . .'

'But wasn't it you singing outside then? It sounded like your voice, but much stronger, so I said, this can't be Salih.'

'It was me,' Salih said proudly, following his mother inside. But he was still uneasy. 'Mother,' he blurted out, 'did anyone come here today, big people . . . Policemen?'

148

'Why no!' his mother said. 'What's the matter? Have you been up to something?'

'No, no, of course not,' Salih said hurriedly. 'Some policemen were looking for Metin and I just wondered if they'd come here to ask.'

'Well, no one came here,' she said without the slightest suspicion, 'Except a boy who brought you a bag of those things, what d'you call them? Never mind,' she went on with a sudden smile. 'Look what I've cooked for you, Salih.' She lifted the lid of the pan and a delicious smell of mint mingled with garlic, yogurt and butter filled the air.

'*Manti**,' Salih cried. '*Manti*! I'm dying of hunger. I'll eat and eat until my tummy's like a drum.'

'Eat as much as you like. I've made such a lot . . .' She sighed. 'I thought your father might be coming tonight, but he hasn't.'

Salih felt light as a bird and was asleep the instant his head touched the pillow.

The next morning he rose early. The sea was pale and smooth and the trawlers had not yet left the pier. Quickly, he splashed a little water on his face and made for the cave, his feet flying over the stones and rocks, not a bit afraid now to enter the dark hole. He wrapped the truck in his jacket and rushed back home. 'Mother, look!' he cried. 'Isn't it just like Metin's big truck that they took away?'

Hajer Hanum stared. She bent over the truck and touched it doubtfully. 'It's beautiful, very beautiful,' she said. 'But where did you get it?'

Salih was flustered, but only for a moment. 'Big brother Metin gave it to me,' he said. 'It comes from Germany. Look!' He wound it up, wondering whether it would work, and set it down. The truck started off, pitter-patter, and only stopped when it struck the wall. He turned it round. How it gleamed and flashed, bright blue in the sunlight that poured through the window! Salih could never have enough of playing with it. Again and again he wound it up and watched as it ran from wall to wall, its sound drowned now

*Manti: a kind of ravioli prepared with ground meat and yogurt.

149

in the rattle of the weaving looms. If only he could take it out . . . How the other children would marvel! And not only the children, but the grown-ups too . . . He longed for night to fall. He could go out into the garden then, or even into the street. Anyway, he told himself, trucks always carry their loads at night. One corner of the street would be the town. The small terebinth would do quite nicely for the lofty plane tree in the market place, while the other end of the street would be Istanbul. And the Bosphorus Bridge? . . . He had to think of a really good place for it. Ah, if only he could go out in the daylight . . . Then he'd make a bridge over the little canal below the town . . . No matter, he was still wonderfully happy, as he had never been before. He kissed the blue truck again and again and hugged it to his breast.

As soon as it was dusk he went out into the garden and played with it until he felt tired. He sat down on the steps and the boy's sad face rose before his eyes. A tame lamb tied to his mother's apron-strings . . . What had he done when he'd found out his truck was missing? How he must have cried his heart out all through the night, his eyes red, his pillow wet with tears . . . Well, serve him right, sticking his tongue out at a harmless little truck, spitting on it, kicking it . . . And in front of another boy too, to whom it ought to have belonged in the first place . . . Who knows how angry the boy's father, that bald Osman Ferman must have been! What a thrashing he must have dealt his son . . . Salih could visualize the boy howling, his clothes torn, blood all over his face, matting his hair . . . Oh dear . . . Perhaps he ought to return the truck, throw it into the garden . . . The very idea made him shudder. Whatever would he do without it? Still, he pitied the boy. Who wouldn't pity someone who let such a beautiful thing be taken away from him?

He rose and took his truck into the street. It was dark now, but the blue and pomegranate red gleamed even more alluringly in the starlight. Near the end of the street where Istanbul would be, he built a bridge with some tiles and a long narrow board, and underneath he placed an almond branch in flower. This was the sea. And indeed, from a distance, and after the moon dawned the almond flowers seemed to flow like white-capped waves. He could not tire of taking his truck from the town at one end of the street to Istanbul at the other. His mother discovered him late after midnight, fast asleep by the little bridge, his truck held tightly in his arms.

For days afterwards Salih did not move from the house, except to play in the street after dark. When he did go out at last he met Bahri running up the street.

'Hey Salih!' Bahri cried seizing his hand. 'Come and see something.' And he led him straight to Haji Nusret's shop. The window was crammed with all sorts of toys, dolls, animals, helicopters, airplanes, tanks . . . Salih was taken aback, but relieved to see there was not a single truck, blue or otherwise, not even the smallest motorcar.

'All ours,' Bahri said.

'Ours,' Salih winked. With sudden shame he remembered he had not even looked at the marbles Bahri had brought him. 'We'll take our marbles and go there every day . . .'

'Like the last time!' Bahri said jubilantly.

The very next morning they were outside the boy's garden, under the large terebinth tree, but the boy was nowhere to be seen. Salih was just beginning to think that his father must have beaten the life out of him, when he appeared on the steps holding a large bear. Bahri and Salih quickly embarked on a noisy game of marbles, watching him out of the corner of their eyes. The boy drew near, smiling eagerly, and jingled the bear's bell. The others pretended not to hear. The boy hesitated, then his voice came out almost in a shriek. 'Can't I play too? I've been on the look-out for you all this time . . .'

Bahri straightened up. 'Well, here we are,' he said and held out his hand. The boy took it timidly, then turned to Salih and shook hands with him too. Salih could not bring himself to look him in the face.

'Wait,' the boy said. 'I'll get my marbles.' He was back in an instant with a large red bag of marbles which he emptied under the terebinth tree. Bahri was gloating in anticipation. He had never seen such large iridescent marbles before. They began to play, while Salih inched over to the bear. He picked it up and stroked its soft fur . . . Before turning the street corner, he looked back uncertainly, but the others were completely engrossed in their game, especially Bahri who was surprised to see that the boy had become quite an expert now and was actually winning once every three throws. He tried to cheat, but the boy stood up and looked him firmly in the eye. 'I'm ready to fight if you want to,' he said in a low voice.

Bahri laughed. 'All right,' he said. 'We'll fight. But first, let's finish this game. You're playing all right now.'

The sun was setting when they heard a loud imperative woman's voice. 'Sakip, Sakiiip! Where on earth have you got to?' It was the boy's mother. Sakip swept his marbles into the bag. 'I'm here. Coming!' he called as he started to run. Then he looked back pleadingly. 'You'll come again tomorrow, won't you Bahri? And bring your friend too.'

'All right,' Bahri said, as he swaggered off, a whistle on his lips.

After this Bahri and Salih teamed together to steal every toy they fancied not only from Sakip, but from other children as well, and so expert had they become that no one ever caught them at it. But all good things come to an end, and a melancholy end it was for Salih.

It was Bahri who brought the unthinkable news. They rushed to the market place and Salih could not believe his eyes. Not only Haji Nusret's, but all the shop windows were crammed with toys of every description, the grocers, the hairdressers, the hardware store, the electrician's, the radio and television repair shop . . . Even the baker had displayed half a dozen toys among his loaves. And the restaurants had hung dolls and other toys like grapes at their windows. But what cut Salih to the heart was the sight of countless trucks, just like his own, blue with pomegranate red chassis. Every single snotty boy seemed to be carrying one, every snotty boy . . . His own blue truck, his very very own . . .

And when he went back home, there was his father with no less than seven blue toy trucks! 'These are for you,' he told Salih, twirling his moustache proudly. 'It's not only Metin can buy toys for my little boy.'

Trying hard to look pleased, Salih gathered up the trucks and went into the next room where he threw them among his other toys.

'Doesn't a man kiss his father who's brought him such toys?' his father called, very much pleased with himself.

Salih threw himself at his neck, then his legs weaving he went out and sat on the doorstep until his mother called him in.

For days afterwards the whole town went through some kind of delirium. Not only children, but grown-ups too were to be seen all over the place, playing with toys. Men in the coffee shops cast away their gambling cards, and instead raced their sons' toy trucks against each other, placing bets on them too . . . On Salih's blue and pomegranate red trucks . . .

There had always been a thriving contraband trade on the Black Sea coast. Sometimes it would be hundreds of cases of whisky that a villager would hit upon in a cave by the shore. Or a shepherd up in the hills would find cartons of American cigarettes carefully concealed in sacks in some deserted sheepfold. Or it would be boxes of guns abandoned on the beach. Once a Laz fishing vessel was spotted adrift without its crew. It turned out to be carrying a cargo of medicine bottles. Nobody knew what the bottles contained, so they were of no use to anyone and therefore left there in the moored boat. Not many days later, bottles and ship had vanished into thin air.

As for the toys . . . One night seven large fishing vessels drew ashore, and out of the first one a well-dressed handsome man descended, accompanied by three others. They talked for a while in whispers and then made straight for Haji Nusret's house, which must have been quite familiar to them. Haji Nusret had seen the boats and the door opened even before they had time to press the bell.

The well-dressed man conferred with Haji Nusret for a long while.

'Don't you worry,' Haji Nusret assured him. 'We can still retail them to shopkeepers here . . .'

'I don't want any profit,' the man said. 'After having been

hoodwinked in this way . . .'

'But we can make a great profit on this,' Haji Nusret said. 'It's a good thing they put these toys in instead of those other goods. Nobody will ever suspect they're contraband. Who ever heard of smuggling toys before? This will bring in a lot of money, my valued friend.'

The man shook his head doubtfully. 'You get me out of this fix, Haji Nusret Bey, and keep all the profit. Just let me have my initial capital back.'

That very night the toys were carried to a safe place and later distributed to the shops. 'They'll sell,' Haji Nusret repeated. 'With the summer coming . . . And the tourists . . . Besides, they've come to us dirt-cheap. We'll make a fortune.'

After that, the word toy never crossed Salih's lips again. His toys lay there forgotten, as though such things did not exist, had never been . . .

# 14

So many years later the blue truck still seared his hands. He fastened the sack of toys securely and heaved it onto his back. Then he picked up the basket with the seagull and went out.

The crags behind the lighthouse dropped in a sheer precipice down to the sea and the tall Black Sea breakers seemed small and far away from above. Salih stopped right on the edge of the cliff and, after settling his seagull in a safe nook, took the first toy out of the sack. It was a tank. Quickly, he cast it over the cliff and watched it vanish under a white crest. He could not help himself. One after the other, the toys went down. The sea was afloat with toys, soon carried away by the waves. The blue truck, his very own, he instinctively left for last. He held it to his breast and caressed it tremblingly, moved by long-forgotten memories of bitter pain and warm loving joy. The seagull's bright gaze roused him. He closed his eyes so tightly that they hurt and hurled the truck out to sea with all his strength. He heard the splash as it fell. When he opened his eyes again the truck was drifting away into the distance, gleaming blue as it used to, long ago, sparkling and flashing like lightning over the sea. He turned away, grabbed his seagull and, without another look, ran by the back road all the way to the opposite end of the town.

Hurrying down to the beach, he took the seagull from its basket and plunged its head into the water. 'Drink, my poor wounded little bird,' he said. 'You need it so . . .' How could he have left the seagull without water for so long? It was a good thing it hadn't died of thirst . . . He kept its head under the water a little, drew it back and dipped it again. There was no danger of its drowning. Seabirds were used to plunging and, indeed, the bird's beak moved as if it were swallowing each time he brought it up again. He let it float by itself for a while. Then it occurred to him that, though its wing was broken, it was full of life now and might swim off. 'How difficult it is to take care of these seabirds!' he fretted. He lifted it back to the beach, but the seagull fixed such a long-ing gaze on the sea that Salih had an idea. A pond! He must make it large and deep so his seagull would have the illusion of being at sea. Only until its wing was cured, and then . . . Seabirds would never stay away from the sea, not if you tied them to the land. Besides, it would be cruel to imprison a bird used to roam freely over the wide rolling boundless seas . . . But this one's right wing was broken, just at the tip. If he couldn't find some bonesetter to put it right, it might never be able to fly, never be whole again, only a crippled thing, a half-creature, not even a seagull any more, but some odd bird locked to the land, far from its native seas, almost like some wretched chicken. The very thought revolted Salih. He'd rather it was dead. He'd rather . . .

With an eye on his bird, he was carrying huge boulders he could barely lift and building a wall far enough along the shore for the water to be knee-deep, so the seagull should not yearn for the open sea. As though it could ever stop yearning . . . Look how sad its eyes were even now as it looked at the sea. It was heart-rending. Salih vowed to himself that by hook or by crook he'd cure his bird. In the meantime he'd get it to grow accustomed to him, Salih. He'd hold it to his breast and make him like the human smell. Skipper Temel said that once a bird gets to love the smell of a human being then it will never leave him. And so it is with all other animals, lions, tigers, snakes, any wild animal you can think of. They become tame and mild as lambs once they get used to the smell of a human being.

The little gull itself had a fine fresh smell like the sea in spring, warm and heady, a scent that drifts to you at break of day when the sea is still milky white, that lifts your heart in wave after wave of pure delight as a gentle breeze rolls the first tiny wavelets to the shore. And the sea, the sands and rocks, the fish, the flowers, people, everything on earth, ugly or beautiful, become a thousand times more beautiful. You are at one with the rising sun, reborn, the unblemished human being again, glad in the knowledge of starting afresh, in concert with a new Creation, washed clean of all selfish thoughts, lost in the ineffable bliss of being at one with the great world. If only men could taste this wonderful feeling all the time, as in childhood . . . Little children can rejoice in nature's eternal renewal. They are still close to it, not yet severed from it . . .

The warm spring-sea smell of his little seagull sent Salih into raptures. He wanted to give thanks, but to what he did not know. For the world was so full of bad things, the never-ending intrigues of the townsfolk, always plotting and scheming against each other, all for money, all for their own self-interest . . . The way they beat the children, scolded them, spurned them . . . And the hunters with their big guns, killing the green-crested wild ducks and the white gracile swans that came from far-off lands, flapping their wide white wings in slow rhythm, their long white necks outstretched, homing for the calm blue waters of the little lake formed by the stream before it flowed on to the sea . . . The town children would hide among the rushes, holding their breaths, entranced by these timid birds, the languid motions of their long white necks, their white reflections on the blue waters, a dreamlike beauty, the whitest of whites since the world was created. But suddenly this vision of beauty would be shattered, never to be recovered, never to be attained again, drowned in cruel red blood. The burst of a gun, and before their eyes a swan floundering in the water . . . The other swans winging away, slowly, unhurriedly . . . A volley of shots, and two more swans drop, whirling, into the lake. With savage joy, the hunters send their dogs after them or row up in boats to bag their prey, while the children who so cherished the magic of the swans, turn away silently, broken, defeated. And always, in his dreams Salih sees the snow-white swans turning red, coral-red, with their own blood . . . Salih who had wanted to be a swan himself, a baby swan, just like his friend Selim, the son of that poor Kurd . . . Selim, killed only a year ago by Yusuf, the son of Mustafa Kaval, owner of Kaval Holding . . . Selim had not even been on the street when Yusuf's car drove up.

157

He was walking along the pavement, absorbed in his thoughts. All the others, seeing Yusuf bearing down at full speed, had from long experience retreated into the first shop or doorway they could reach, but the boy was unaware of the coming car. Such insolence infuriated Yusuf. He stepped on the gas and swung onto the pavement, straight at Selim. He never even stopped to look back at the mangled mass he left behind, but drove on at the same mad speed to his father's villa on top of the cliff. Yusuf's cars were always new and fast, the latest makes. When he came slashing through the town streets, the wooden houses and shops rattled at his passing, and he always had a girl with him, never the same, now a blonde, now a redhead, or a brunette. His face was hard and cold. When the police came to the villa, he sent them packing. 'Dead, is he?' he said. 'Well, I can't help that.'

'But the child was on the pavement . . .'

'He had no business to be,' Yusuf retorted, slamming the door in their faces.

Yusuf was not even arrested. The whole town knew he had hit Selim deliberately, and could testify to it, but it would have been no use. The laws of the land did not apply to the likes of Yusuf. There was no law for them, not as yet. And so, Yusuf went on driving his car at whirlwind speed through the town and no one dared to say a word. No one except Selim's father, Halo Shamdin. He wanted justice done, but he had six younger children and the struggle to keep them fed was a hard one. He applied to the police, to the prosecutor, to the authorities in Istanbul. People pitied him, even the police, but could not help deriding his futile efforts. 'Go to the United Nations, Halo Shamdin,' they said. 'The Turkish Republic will never get the better of Yusuf's father.' And added, chewing a pencil and shaking their heads, 'Sorry, Halo Shamdin, but you're just beating the air. Look around you. Every day young men, university students in the prime of life are killed in bloody incidents all over the place. The police, the state, everyone knows who's responsible. Yet what happens? Now, you go about your business, Halo Shamdin, before you get into real trouble.

Look, you've got six young ones to see to . . .'

And one morning Halo Shamdin was found lying in the market place, beaten to a jelly. Some said it was Yusuf himself who had done it, others his father's men from Istanbul, though eyewitnesses swore it was the police who'd drawn a sack over his head and given him a good dressing-down at the police station. Halo Shamdin never mentioned his son's name or Yusuf's again. He hardly ever spoke now, a man consumed with frustrated anger and grief, he who had always made the market place ring with laughter at his stories. Salih could not bear to look at his face after Selim's death. It made him want to sob his heart out, just like he and the other children could not bring themselves to go to the swan-lake any more and see those lovely necks sagging lifeless on the water. But secretly, between themselves, they vowed to set fire to the villa one day, and with Yusuf in it too, and from that day onward invisible hands systematically despoiled the wide gardens around the villa, leaving not a single rose or flower on its stem . . .

The pond was ready now. Salih took the seagull from the sand and set it on the water. It wallowed a little at first, then seemed to take to its new surroundings. Salih stroked it softly. 'That's my brave little gull,' he said. 'And now I'm going to catch some good fat fish for you. Hooray!'

He retrieved the scoop net from where he had hidden it and, tucking up his trousers, he waded in. The sea was smooth as blue satin. He plunged the net over a shoal of tiny fish that were darting right in front of him. The fish sparkled blue and red in the net as he ran back to the pond. 'Here,' he said, 'eat these. Live fish just as you like them . . .' The bird swallowed hungrily and its gullet filled and swelled. How beautiful it was! More beautiful even than a swan . . . Besides he had never held a swan like this, so close to his breast, never been friends with one and felt the warmth of its body.

Now the little gull was swimming contentedly in the pond, stretching its neck and gazing around with bright eyes, that were sometimes blue, sometimes green, mauve, jet black . . . Its back was a smoky cloudlike white, darkening in the middle, but turning white as snow underneath. Two black spots marked the tip of its two tail feathers. Its feet were orange and its little bill a blackish red. On its sound left wing Salih counted twenty-eight pinions. The first was shorter than the second, black halfway, then white. The second pinion, the longest, was quite black, the third paler, while the fourth and fifth had even less black and the sixth only a tiny black speck at the tip. The rest of the pinions were pure white and grew shorter towards the body. The right wing was the same, only the fourth and fifth pinions were broken, with a deep gash at the joint where the white bone was laid bare.

There was nothing for it. He must beg his grandmother again. Who knows, perhaps . . . If he was very cunning and spoke to her tenderly, she might yet relent and make an ointment for his poor seagull. He took the bird from the pond, dried it with his handkerchief, put it back into the basket and walked home, pondering on what he was going to say.

The weaving looms were rattling away when he went in. He gave ear to his grandmother's loom. From long experience he could tell by its sound what mood she was in. The shuttle came and went absently, as of itself, with easy smoothness, and Salih knew that she was thinking of Halil, that she was in a mellow reminiscent vein. It was just the right moment to tackle her. He planted himself before the looms and laughed loudly. Everyone stared at him, hands arrested. He stopped and tears filled his eyes. 'Look at this poor baby bird,' he said mournfully. 'Doomed to die . . . Isn't it a pity, mother?'

'Poor thing,' Hajer Hanum said with a glance at the grandmother. 'Haven't you found some ointment yet to make it well?'

'Not a chance!' Salih said. 'No one cares about a poor bird. Why you little bastard, they say, we can't get medicines for the people round here who are dying like flies of sickness and dirt, and you want an ointment for a miserable bird! . . . And they chase me out, swearing at me and at my family too. Yes, all my family . . .' He looked at

160

his grandmother. She was casting her shuttle again and the sound was growing ominous. Salih was alarmed. 'A tiny little bird . . . Even if it isn't human, it breathes and eats and drinks just like us. Its eyes are so lively and it knows its friends. When it sees me, it beats its one good wing and stumbles up with such joy . . . Doesn't it, mother?' He looked pleadingly at her.

'Indeed it does, my darling.' She knew what Salih was driving at. 'Birds, animals, all living things were created by Allah, so there can be no difference for Him between a bird and a human being . . .'

'No difference at all!' Salih cried excitedly. His grandmother's shuttle hesitated and toned down. He must press his point. 'A bird needs to be helped more than a human being. No one ever helps birds. I saw a sick coot the other day, all alone on the beach, no one to befriend it, no mother, no father. Its beak opened once or twice, seeking something, and then it dropped and died. Now, if it wasn't for me, this little seagull would be dead by now. Only a little while ago I came upon Mufti Effendi near the lighthouse and he caressed my seagull, it's so lovely, you see, everyone in the market place says so. He asked me what was the matter with it and I told him about the broken wing and how everybody was mocking me because I wanted to make it well. Tsk-tsk, he said, how cruel people have become . . . And its wings like clouds too . . . Tsk-tsk! Sure, the hand that makes an ointment for this bird will be blessed . . . And Mufti Effendi should know for he's a holy man and talks with the Forty Saints on Thursday nights. Whaaat? I'm lying? Why should I lie? All the town knows it's so . . .'

'Zirrrt, zirto, zirrrt zirto,' the shuttle mocked him. 'Who ever heard of a young mufti like that becoming a saint? Holy men who converse with the Holy Forties have long white beards. You're mixing him up with Alim Hoja who could silence a tempestuous raging sea with a wave of his hand . . .'

'But he's a mufti. He studied in Egypt . . .'

The shuttle shot forward. 'It's a lie, a lie! Zirrrt zirto, zirrrt zirto . . .'

'It isn't a lie!' Salih yelled. 'And he said that people who

161

cure birds go straight to Paradise and those who don't, who let them die . . . They go to Hell!'

The shuttle rattled back and forth so angrily that Salih realized he was making a hash of things. Whatever could he say to mollify her?

'Granny,' he blurted out, 'don't the Forty Holies wear robes of white just like the seagulls?'

'A lie!' the grandmother shouted, holding the shuttle. 'The Forty Holies all have green turbans.'

'Sorry, granny, you're quite right . . . And Mufti Effendi said . . . It's Alim Hoja who told him so. He said that swans are the favourite birds of the Forty Holies . . .' The shuttle had started again, less angry now. 'And seagulls are their next best favourite. He said . . . The holy green-turbaned Alim Hoja said that . . . There was this person headed straight for the gates of Hell, when a bird appeared before her, all green to the tip of its wings. Stop, the bird said, why have they sent you here? Come with me. And it led her instead to the door of Paradise. Don't you recognize me, it said, don't you remember how there, on earth, you made an ointment for my wing and cured it? Now I'm repaying you, I'm saving you from an eternity in Hell . . . The bird flapped its wings and a powerful gust swept the old woman into the heart of Paradise. How she rejoiced! If only I'd cured more birds down there, she kept saying . . . On earth, that vale of tears . . .'

Salih wasn't even paying attention to the shuttle now. He began to talk about the swans, how the children would watch in silence, entranced, their love making on the deep blue lake, how the grown-ups, mean and envious, killed them all one by one . . . It was Ismail the blacksmith who said that God must have made men blind, mad, to kill two creatures who were making love. There was a time, he said, when people too, oh a long long time ago, knew how to love like the birds, the snakes, all the other creatures of this earth, to love just for the sake of it. But afterwards Allah punished them. They forgot how to love, purely, selflessly. And now they killed any creature they saw making love, and if they didn't it wasn't for lack of wanting to do so . . . Salih

162

remembered the smith, angry, raging, saying these things and beating furiously at the red-hot iron on the anvil. He tried to convey them to his grandmother, but got more and more mixed up. Still, he plodded on, hoping for some miracle. 'Why do you kill them, you cowards? What have you to gain from it? Blood makes men mad, hungry for more blood . . .' These were the smith's very words. He had repeated them so often that Salih knew them by heart. 'Can you ever, by killing those mating swans, recover what you lost thousands and thousands of years ago? The power to love . . . No, you can only kill, because you are jealous of their love making. You want to kill love itself . . .' Salih did not understand all the smith said, but he shared his bitterness, his dream of a distant lost paradise, and knew that was the reason why the smith was apart from other men and gave himself wholly to the shaping of red-hot iron in that spark-filled forge . . .

On and on Salih spoke, like an old time storyteller, sitting down now, caressing the soft feathers of his seagull, his eyes closed. Only one swan left, out of so many . . . Swans always go in pairs. The one was shot, the other left all alone, while its mate whirled down, a bloodstained mass, into the lake. So pitiless men were . . .

Salih clenched his teeth. 'But we shall go to Paradise,' he said. 'Because . . .'

Before sunrise, before the hunters were even out of bed, the children would make for the lake where the swans were still asleep, their heads thrust into their wings. They would not wake them up. Not until the hunters came into view . . . Kazim was watching out from the top of a tall plane tree and when the children heard his sad song, 'My lion, my Kazim, is lying there, his silken hair all bathed in blood,' they knew that the hunters were approaching with their murderous guns . . . Then a loud noise would wake the echoes round the lake, wild shouts, the banging of drums and cans. Startled out of their sleep, the swans would glide away and slowly take wing. But it was not long before the grown-ups discovered what the children were up to. They beat them, shut them up in their houses, frightened them. The children did not give up, but . . . The swans were doomed . . .

Salih leapt to his feet. 'And this poor seagull will die too!' he shouted.

His grandmother stared, her eyes widening.

'It will die. Its wing will rot if an ointment isn't found for it. And whoever has that ointment and doesn't give it to my bird will never have a single wish come true, never!'

There was a wavering look on his grandmother's face. The shuttle, too, seemed to hesitate. It was now or never. But he had to find the right words or all was lost. He began to play with his seagull, fooling and clowning, and soon he realized that his grandmother was smiling, actually laughing at him, her lips thinning out like paper, her eyes lost in a maze of little wrinkles, laughing strangely, like somebody unused to laughter. Now, he thought, now . . .

'Granny,' he said in his sweetest, most appealing voice, 'my dear good granny, please make an ointment for my little bird. You'll go to Paradise for it. My bird will snatch you from the gates of Hell and take you straight to Paradise . . .' The smile was freezing on her face now. He had to say that thing so she'd be really frightened and give in. 'You know what Alim Hoja said, granny? If somebody who can make ointments won't do it for a little bird, won't cure its wounded wing, then . . . Then the man she's waiting for will never come . . . He'll . . . On the boat that brings him here, he'll . . . He'll die!'

The grandmother's face turned yellow, then poison-green. Her lips trembled. Her mouth opened and shut as though her breath was failing. Then she exploded. 'I'll wring that bird's neck, I will,' she screamed, beside herself with rage. 'And yours too, never fear. You've killed me, you misbegotten brat of that bastard son of mine, you've killed me! Just you wait, I'll wring the necks of both of you yet . . .'

Salih grabbed the basket and fled. He was thoroughly frightened at what he had done. His grandmother's eyes had pierced him to the heart. He felt them in his back like two wounds. 'She's going to kill us,' he said. 'And if not me, my seagull. She'll wring its neck while I'm asleep, in the night . . . .'

He made his way down to the beach and sat down to wait until it was quite dark. Then he'd set the seagull out to sea, without seeing its eyes looking at him . . .

The waves were lapping gently at the shore. He rose, numb all over, cold and wet to the bone, took the seagull in his arms and stroked it gently. He had to do it, had to let it go here, on this little wavelet . . . If not, his grandmother would kill it this very night . . . Its snow-white breast all stained with blood . . .

He set it down, let go, and in the next instant gathered it up again, his heart thumping madly. He could not do it, that was all . . . The seagull had become a part of him, he could never let it go.

Suddenly, he recalled the pond. Why, what could be better! It was getting on for midnight and after he had watched the seagull swimming up and down, safe in its pond, he wended his way back home. But the minute he opened the gate, he turned back and ran. What if something had happened? What if the seagull? . . .

It was still there. He saw its small dark shade floating on the pond, seized it and held it to his breast, almost choking it. Then he put the bird into its basket and rushed away as though some awful thing was at his heels. It was only when he had shut and bolted the garden gate behind him that he felt safe. He sat down, panting, on the steps. How long he remained there, half-asleep, he never knew. His mother's voice roused him. 'Why Salih! Whatever are you doing there on those cold steps? You'll catch your death. Come on in . . .'

'I can't.'

'Come in, I say!'

'No! She . . . She'll kill me, and my seagull too.'

'Don't say such things.'

'I saw her eyes,' Salih said. 'That's how they were, ready to kill . . .'

The early morning cocks were crowing by the time she could persuade him to come inside. 'All right,' he said. 'But promise you won't sleep. You'll watch over me and my seagull.'

'I promise.'

'If ever she kills my seagull, I'll go away never to return, just like her Halil.'

'I won't let her. Just let me see her touch you or your seagull! I've had about enough of her . . .'

They went in. Salih placed the seagull between his bed and the wall. 'Mother,' he pleaded, 'dear mother, you won't fall asleep, will you, and let her kill us both?'

She stroked his hair and he fell asleep from utter exhaustion, conscious yet, in a dream, of a soft hand caressing his head. A tear dropped from his mother's eyes over his forehead, but he never felt it.

# 15

Salih had been waiting in front of the little tavern since noon. The seagull was beside him in its basket, quite frisky now, opening and closing its wings, even the wounded one, tasting the joy of living again, of having eaten its fill.

In the summer months, the children would gather gulls eggs on the steep crags of Outer Isle and Ojakli Island and sell them to fanciers. Bearded Haydar, the vet, was one of those. He could tell at a glance whether an egg was fresh or not and, if he laid hands on a new-laid one he went wild with joy. There and then, he'd break it open, sniff it blissfully and down it at one go. 'Ah, this is life!' he'd exclaim, wiping his bushy moustache with the back of his hand. 'It's all the seas of the world I've swallowed with that one gull's egg. All the seas of the world are coursing in my veins. Ah life! Life in all its plenitude . . .'

He was in the tavern now and showing no sign of getting up and going home. Before him was a large bottle of wine, half empty, and he was talking to a man, asleep with his head on the table. Once in a while the man grunted and lifted a bleary gaze at him. This acted as a spur for Bearded Haydar. 'Yes, my friend, indeed you're quite right,' he would say and hurry on more quickly than before, shaking the man awake whenever his head fell back onto the table. 'This sorrow is going to kill you. Sorrow can destroy a man and it's killing me here, in this godforsaken town. All my studies, all those schools . . . The highest degrees in the sciences of men and animals . . . To end up in this town! Why did I come here? Why did I stay here? It wasn't for the love of a woman, oh no, it was for love of nature, of the sea, of seagulls and their eggs . . . And now I'm dying of sorrow . . . Listen, my friend, everything's dead in me, love, all human feeling. I'm sick of things, sick of everyone. I must kill myself, today, tonight . . . Why should I live, for

167

whom, for what reason? To drag out this miserable existence? Listen, my friend, let this be my last will and testament to you. After I'm dead, throw yourself into the sea and put an end to your life too, the best of ends, at one with the sea! What a beautiful death!' He grabbed the man's hair. 'D'you hear me? My last will and testament . . . You'll kill yourself at sea, d'you understand?' He shook him sharply. 'D'you understand?'

The man opened his eyes and stared blankly. 'Yes, yes, yes,' he mumbled. 'I understand.' And his head fell back onto the table.

'Well, I hope you do,' Bearded Haydar panted. 'How I'd like to die at sea too! To become a part of the immortal sea, immortal . . . But I'm afraid, my friend. I'm afraid of the sea.' He was shouting suddenly. His voice could be heard all over the market place. 'Afraid! Afraid . . . Too bad, but I'll have to kill myself in the forest. One day they'll find me gone . . . Who? Someone will surely notice I'm missing. They'll look for me and find me hanging on a tall tree. Not at sea, ah, not at sea . . .'

Salih's hair stood on end. What he'd gathered from all this talk was that the two men inside were bent on taking their lives. The one was going to drown himself, that was sure, but Bearded Haydar was still hesitating, undecided on the kind of death he should choose. What if Salih went to him now, before he killed himself, this man who'd studied all about birds and beasts, and said to him: Look, you love seagull eggs and anyway you'll find a way to kill yourself today. Won't you do a last good deed before you die and mend this baby seagull's wing? If you do, who knows, Allah may give you the courage to kill yourself at sea. You wouldn't be at all afraid and would drown yourself right where it's very deep . . .

The bottle was almost empty now, but Bearded Haydar rambled on, though his tongue seemed to have thickened in his mouth. 'A man can have about enough of it all. Hey, my friend, wake up! I'm saying a man can get bored to death in this town, not larger than the palm of my hand. The same sky, the same earth, the same sea with the same white waves, the sun rising there, in the same place every day, the trees never moving, the flowers returning each spring, always, always, never any different . . . And we? Waking, drinking, sleeping, and beginning again the next day and the next and the next . . .' He grabbed the other's hair again. 'Isn't that so?'

'Yes, yes,' the man said, his head dropping, but Bearded Haydar would not let it go. 'Tell me, tell me!' he yelled. 'What can a man do in such a world but kill himself? What?'

'Yes, yes . . . Kill himself,' the other moaned as he fell asleep once more.

Bearded Haydar got up and blundered to the door, knocking against chairs and tables. He stood in the doorway like a bird holding on with its talons to a sharp crag, its wings fighting against the wind. Suddenly he laughed and stuck out his tongue. Salih looked behind him. There was no one. It was at him that Bearded Haydar had stuck out his tongue. Salih did the same and also thumbed his nose, which Haydar promptly reciprocated. Encouraged, Salih crept up to the door where the vet was tottering more dangerously than ever. 'Look at this bird,' he said as loudly as he dared. 'Look, it's a wounded seagull . . .'

Bearded Haydar was trying to focus his gaze. Clutching the door-jamb, he carefully negotiated the three steps and placed his hand heavily on Salih's shoulder. 'Who are you?' he said. 'Where d'you come from, friend, and where are you going?'

'I'm Salih. They told me you know all about birds and their ailments. This gull's got a broken wing, so I came to you for some medicine.'

The vet bent down to look, reeling this way and that and making Salih reel too. Then he leaned back against the wall and laughed until the tears ran down his face.

After a while he started to walk away, taking a few stumbling steps, then stopping to regain his balance. Salih followed him step by step to the gate of his house and into the yard. Bearded Haydar's face lit up at the sight of an old stunted olive tree with only a few leafless branches on its trunk. He made straight for it and relieved himself. As he was buttoning up his trousers, his face took on a hunted expression. He looked about him in alarm and his eyes rested on Salih.

'Forgive me, effendi,' he said, bowing to the ground. 'It's just a habit of mine to urinate each evening in this same spot. Only I didn't realize it was still day . . . I'm sorry, very sorry.' He took a few cautious steps toward Salih. 'You've been following me, effendi. Did I seem to be doing anything suspicious? Let me assure you, effendi, that I committed suicide the very day I was appointed to this town, twenty-seven years ago. Like a stone at the bottom of a well I've been ever since. Thirty years without any political activity whatsoever . . . We belong to a lost generation, effendi, born dead, dead already when we die . . . Ah, but you *have* been following me, effendi! Please go on. It's such an honour for a suicide of thirty years to feel he's important once more. After such an honour I must go inside and blow my brains out . . . But I pity my wife . . . My children too, but my wife most of all . . . She's had to suffer so much from me. It's not easy to carry on your shoulders for thirty years a man who's committed suicide. And a drunken one at that . . .' He drew nearer to Salih and looked fixedly into his eyes. 'A great honour, effendi, you've conferred on me. You've brought me to life after all these years . . . Just as in my student days, when the police used to follow me . . . Ah, what a time it was in Ankara then! All for equality, justice, brotherhood . . . Do you know Dr Hikmet, effendi? Of course you do, who doesn't? He died only recently in Yugoslavia, and in the presence of Comrade Tito himself . . .' He was talking himself into a fever. Salih hardly understood what he was saying. All he knew was that this man had decided to blow his brains out the minute he entered the house.

Suddenly, Bearded Haydar seized Salih's hand and kissed it noisily. 'Thank you, thank you,' he said with tears in his eyes. 'You've made me so happy, so happy . . .' And he plunged into the house, banging the door. The walls rattled and a woman's scream rent the air. Bearded Haydar was howling too: 'Whores, harlots! You've destroyed me. You're all in league in this ignorant town to ruin me. I'll kill you, kill you! See this gun here? And afterwards, I'll hold it to my own mouth and shoot myself . . .'

Whack, came the sound of blows raining inside and shrieks from the woman. There was a crash of something breaking and Salih held his breath, waiting for the blast of a gun. Then the door was flung open and he saw a woman rush out, dishevelled, almost naked in a torn green nightgown. He ran after her. 'He's going to kill himself,' he cried. 'Blow his brains out tonight. He said so to me . . .'

The woman stopped and looked back at Salih. 'Don't worry, child,' she said softly. 'It's been like this for thirty years. I'm just getting out of his way not to get beaten too much.'

How strange! She sounded almost amused. Could this be the same woman who'd been screaming for her life only a minute ago? She smiled at Salih and disappeared into a neighbouring house.

After a while Bearded Haydar appeared on the threshold, as though nothing had happened. He had combed his hair and straightened his tie, and even changed his soiled trousers for a freshly-pressed pair. He stared at Salih pleasantly enough. Then he saw the seagull in its basket and laughed.

'Its wing is broken,' Salih said. 'Remember?'

Bearded Haydar peered at the bird and ran a finger over its broken wing. His face changed and wrinkled up as though trying to recall something, but it was no use. 'There's nothing doing with this bird,' he snapped at last with a look of hatred at Salih. 'It'll die. Wounded gulls can't live. Never!' He staggered off, his legs weaving into each other, muttering under his breath. 'Why can't I kill myself, why? I've never been able to do anything, anything . . .'

The truth was that Bearded Haydar in all his twenty-seven years in this town had never tended to a single animal. He wouldn't even look at the sick horses, donkeys or goats that were brought to him. Official letters from the administration in Ankara were usually left unanswered, unless some friend obliged, just to save him from further trouble.

Quivering with indignation Salih dashed down the slope

171

after him. 'Stop,' he said, his voice strangling. 'Look, this bird's full of life. How can you say it'll die?'

Bearded Haydar glared at him. 'I say it'll die, and that's that, my greenhorn!'

'You know nothing about it,' Salih challenged him. 'It would have died long ago if it was going to die . . .'

'That's neither here nor there,' the vet retorted. 'Once wounded, they always die.'

Salih was at a loss, but not for long. 'You killed yourself thirty years ago,' he flung at him. 'What does a dead man know about a live bird?'

It was Haydar's turn to be baffled. He blinked and cast around, swaying backward and forward as though looking for help. 'Hee-hee-hee!' He forced a laugh. 'I'm not really dead. It's inside me, I'm dead, inside . . .'

Salih took the seagull in his hands and held it out to him. 'Then look! Look at it! Does it seem to be dying?'

But Bearded Haydar felt he couldn't retract now. 'It'll die,' he repeated stubbornly. 'It'll die . . .'

Salih eyed him with scorn. 'Go fuck yourself!' he cried. 'A maniac, that's what you are!' He settled his seagull back into its basket and stalked away. 'And you call yourself a vet! Go fuck yourself!'

Everybody, old and young, in this town knew all there was to know about Doctor Yasef, the old Jewish doctor who'd come here as a young man of twenty-five and never left again. After settling in the run-down wooden mansion up on the hill near the windmills, he had sent for his aged father, a famous doctor in Istanbul, to live with him, together with his mother and two sisters. Then he had married a Greek girl from the town, a graduate of the American College in Istanbul. They had one daughter, but by the time she attained the age of ten, his wife had run off to America, taking the child along with her. Ever since that day she would write one letter a year to the doctor. The letter always came in April and was full of words of love. To tell the truth, Doctor Yasef was perfectly happy with this arrangement. That one single letter kept him content the whole year round and, by the middle of March, he was already preparing himself for it. Every day he would wash and dress up meticulously in elegant suits, starched shirts and bright ties, and with barely suppressed excitement, would direct his steps to the post office. The whole town would hold its breath in expectation and share his joy when the letter arrived at last. As for the doctor, he would shut himself up in his house, not to be seen for days afterwards. Then, one early morning, he would emerge and walk pensively to the seaside, where he would remain standing, wrapped in thought, until the evening shadows fell. Then slowly, with infinite care he'd take the letter out of his pocket and begin to tear it up, making the pieces smaller and smaller and casting them all into the sea, down to the last tiny scrap.

The doctor had carried on his practice until ten years ago, tending to the townsfolk and villagers hereabouts, accepting whatever remuneration they were willing to make, money, eggs, chickens, honey, grain, and never exacting a penny from those who couldn't pay. It was said that he had inherited quite a fortune from his father, including houses and apartments in Istanbul. His two sisters had never married and kept house for him. They looked after the garden and read a lot, and at every hour of the day one could hear the sad strains of a piano coming from the mansion.

The doctor had very fixed habits, and Salih knew them very well as did everyone else. His first visit on leaving his house was to the druggist, Fazil Bey, whose pharmacy was open so early that, indeed, some people believed he never closed shop at all. He could be seen at all hours, sitting at a table with a microscope, a balance and little mortars, fussing about with herbs and flowers and powders. If anybody came in with a prescription, he screwed up his face, left the table with an ill grace to get the drug and return to his herbs as quickly as he could. But he would always brighten up at the arrival every morning of the doctor. 'I'm getting nearer now, doctor,' he would cry joyfully. 'It won't be long before I find it.'

All the year round old people from the mountain villages gathered unusual herbs and flowers to sell to him, and Fazil

Bey would sort them out, classify them and pore over them for days. If he should chance upon some kind he'd never seen before, he would rush over to the doctor, wild with excitement. 'I've got it, doctor, got it,' he'd shout, and the two would put their heads together to try and unravel the mysteries of their new find.

Salih had trailed after the doctor to the pharmacy. Surely, out of so many drugs something could be found for his seagull's wing . . .

Fazil Bey and the doctor were deep in a long argument over a strange plant that resembled the comb of a cock. With trembling hands they snipped off a piece, sniffed at it, tasted it with the tip of their tongues and then pounded it in a mortar. Outside, white-bearded, slant-eyed villagers sat about on the pavement with baskets and saddle bags full of herbs, waiting with long-accustomed patience for the two to finish their discussion. The druggist's white smock was spick and span. He changed it every day. His gold-rimmed spectacles rested on the tip of his nose.

'We'll find it, doctor,' he said, sniffing at the crushed flower in the mortar. 'If it isn't this one, it's the other. There are such a variety of medicinal herbs, infinite really. Why, mother nature yields forth a new one every day, breeding, fertilizing all the time, thousands and thousands.'

'How right you are!' Doctor Yasef said, as he rose to go. 'If nature were to stop breeding new kinds and only repeated itself, everything would die out. Nature never repeats itself. It creates again and again infinitely.'

Fazil Bey's face paled, the spectacles on the tip of his nose trembled and his long wrinkled neck twitched. 'But we'll find it, I'm sure we will, sure!' he blurted out quickly, as though something was eluding his grasp. 'Tomorrow I'll have analyzed this plant and I'll give you the result.'

'Thank you, my dear sir.'

'Not at all . . . Pleasure . . . It's all for the good of mankind.'

The doctor walked to the door, leaning on his cane, his sparse beard bobbing at the end of his chin, and Fazil Bey accompanied him, still talking. 'We'll find it, my honoured friend. It's been fifty years now . . . And look! See what a lot of fresh herbs these people have brought me!' He hurried over to an old man, who looked well over eighty and was squatting at the foot of the wall. 'What have you got for me?' he asked eagerly.

The old man's face broke into a smile. 'Such a flower I've brought you, Bey!' he said, very pleased with himself. 'I haven't seen the like in all my life.'

Fazil Bey drew him up by the hand and embraced him.

The doctor's route after this led him to the honey dealer, Faik Effendi, who raised bees, and there the two of them would sit awhile talking to the bees. This, Salih could swear to, and it was as if the bees answered them too.

Salih was beginning to lose patience. 'A bunch of crazy people, that's what I'm dealing with,' he muttered to himself. If it wasn't for the sake of this poor little wounded bird, he wouldn't have taken a second look at them. Crazy fools . . .

After the bee man it was the baker, Resul Agha, the doctor went to. And then, just at the call to the noonday prayer, he walked over to the lighthouse and sat on his accustomed rock, the one that was shaped like an armchair, talking away without a break to himself and to whoever came his way.

This was Salih's chance. He settled on a rock opposite the doctor, who greeted him politely and went on with what he was saying. 'Such a lot of wars I've seen . . . Cannonballs hurtling right past me, but I wasn't afraid there at Chanakkalé, though we hadn't yet heard of the Gazi, Mustafa Kemal Pasha. I fought in the Balkan wars too and on the Caucasian front. Ninety thousand men we lost there, devoured by lice, exterminated by typhus, frozen to death . . . Our Fazil Bey must be a little crazy. Have you ever had the honour of meeting him, sir? . . . I have a daughter, a small child like you, sir. And this little daughter has had six babies by now . . .' He began to laugh, his beard trembling, but there was something sad, almost tearful in his laughter. 'Strange, isn't it, sir? My daughter's in America, you know. My wife too. Every year they write to me, inviting me to join them. How can I leave you all, leave my home and country, and go there?' He sprang up and brandished his stick angrily at the sea. 'I can't! I'd die the minute I got there. Can a fish live out of water? . . . Don't you believe Fazil Bey, my dear sir, he's an idealist, a great romantic. If nature were to repeat itself, everything would inexorably wear out into nothingness. Have I made myself clear, dear sir? Look at us, can we ever re-live a single day that is past? The rose that blooms again each year is not the same as last year's, though it may seem the same to us. See that wave lapping at the shore, it'll only come once, never again. Eternity is a great illusion, sir, and our friend Fazil Bey a great romantic . . . Therefore America . . . Do you think my daughter will come to see me? Because I don't want to go anywhere away from here. I'm afraid to. As you will have noticed, sir, I've grown old, and the Lord's will be done sooner or later. I love life, my dear sir . . . If she wants to see her father, why doesn't she come herself? She's my daughter, yes, but at the same time she isn't. She never lived with me that I should regard her as my daughter. Then what is it, why do I welcome those letters I get each year? For the pleasure of having something to wait for . . . And it cannot have escaped your attention, dear sir, that the whole town expects those letters with even more eagerness than me. Now, Jerrah* Ali, the magician, there's a man for you! A real creator. Do you know him?' He riveted his clear blue eyes on Salih and repeated insistently: 'You know him? Jerrah Ali . . .'

Salih seized on this pause in the doctor's unending discourse. 'Yes, yes, I know him,' he said quickly. 'But doctor . . .'

'Yes, my dear sir?'

Salih loved the way the doctor kept calling him 'sir'. It made him feel so confident. 'Have you seen this seagull?'

The doctor rose and bent over the basket Salih was holding out. 'Very pretty, my dear sir. Beautiful birds, these seagulls, and friendly to men too, the little rascals.'

*Jerrah: surgeon

'This one's got a broken wing.'

'Oh dear, dear, dear! That's bad . . .'

'Why don't you examine it? You can cure it, you who worked wonders during the war . . .'

Doctor Yasef changed his spectacles, took the baby seagull in his hands and inspected it with meticulous care. He looked at its eyes, fingered its gullet, put his ear to its heart and listened. But when he lifted its wing, he shook his head dolefully, as though faced with a desperate case. 'I'm sorry, sir. What a pity! Quite regrettable . . . Such a lovely bird. But there are two creatures on earth that can never recover from a wound.'

'Which are they?' Salih shouted.

'Don't get excited, sir, please calm yourself. I know this is going to be painful for you, but it's the law of nature. The snake is one. It cannot renew its cells after a wound. And the seagull is the other.'

Salih glared at the doctor. 'D'you mean to tell me that this bird here is going to die?'

Doctor Yasef's beard trembled. His hands flew as he replaced the seagull in its basket and slumped wearily onto his rock.

'Is it going to die? Is it? Is it?' Salih kept repeating. 'Isn't there anything we can do?'

The doctor was silent, his face brightening and falling in turn. It was obvious he was trying hard to find something, and Salih began to pity him.

'Hah!' the doctor exclaimed at last. 'I've got it . . . Fazil Bey's herbs . . . They've never been of any use, not in fifty years . . . But perhaps . . .' He laid his chin on the knob of his cane and closed his eyes. The hairs of his beard stood out like spines. 'Perhaps among those herbs there's one that might cure this seagull's wing. Are gulls and snakes alike? Ah, old age! I can't remember . . . Yes, Fazil Bey's herbs . . . Who knows?'

'Of course, there must be!' Salih cried. 'Many many good herbs . . .'

'But Fazil Bey is a very touchy person. He'd take it ill if I asked him. The best thing is to tackle him yourself when he's in a good mood. In the morning . . .'

'Yes, yes,' Salih shouted excitedly. 'He even laughs sometimes. I've seen him laughing just like you and me. I can ask him then.'

'Well, I wish you every success, my dear sir.'

His hopes buoyed up again, Salih looked gratefully at the old doctor. He must do something to thank him, something . . . Suddenly it came to him. He seized the doctor's hand, kissed it three times and touched it to his forehead. 'Doctor,' he said, and hesitated. Should he? . . . He cleared his throat. 'Doctor, if ever those boys do anything to you again . . . Those boys who . . . You know . . . Just let me see them. I'll make them sorry they were ever born. We'll beat the life out of them, Bahri and I.'

The doctor's face grew anxious. 'Please, sir,' he begged. 'They're my friends. I entreat you, please don't do anything to them.'

'Very well,' Salih said. 'I won't if you don't want me to.' But he felt terribly ashamed of himself. Unable to face the doctor another minute, he turned and ran all the way to the market without another look behind him.

The next morning he rose very early and, after feeding his seagull at the seaside, took up his observation post outside the pharmacy. Doctor Yasef had come and gone, and they had winked at each other in secret complicity. A few villagers were waiting too on the pavement with baskets and sacks from which emanated the fresh smell of mountain plants. As the morning progressed Fazil Bey began to brighten up. Now and then he tasted a herb or flower which he was pounding in a mortar and an ineffable look of gladness spread over his face. After a while, as he was sniffing at a flower, he gave a laugh of sheer delight. Salih saw his eyes, moss-green, full of kindness . . . He decided the moment had come and went in.

'Uncle,' he began.

Fazil Bey absent-mindedly held out his hand for a prescription. Then, as nothing came he looked up and saw Salih. The boy's insistent gaze fixed on him ever since early morning, had disturbed him, mocked him, made him feel small, useless . . . At the sight of him there before him in the pharmacy, he lost his temper and seized the broomstick at his side.

'Out!' he yelled. 'Out with you, miserable brat!'

Salih was not quick enough to escape the blow. He only just avoided falling down with the basket and all, and killing his seagull.

'Like leeches, they are these brats, like sticky leeches!' Fazil Bey was foaming at the mouth. 'Where have they sprung from, these impudent whippersnappers? What has this town come to?' He lunged out of the pharmacy. 'Look at him, still standing there!' he screamed. 'Look at those eyes, as though he wants to kill me . . .'

Salih turned away slowly, walked past the school and sank onto the steps that led down to the shore. He was almost in tears, but there was still Jerrah Ali, the magician . . .

Jerrah Ali was very old and wise to the ways of this world. Everyone in this town, young and old, had heard tell of his exploits. Long ago, he had been in the habit of walking on a tightrope stretched between Ojakli Island and Olive Island, always choosing a sunny day in April for his stunt. The town would be roused early in the morning to the sound of drums and fifes and pour down to the shore, where Jerrah Ali would be pacing up and down at the foot of the ruined tower on Ojakli Island like a purebred making ready for the race. He was very handsome then, a tall fair man, and very proud of his prowesses too. When the crowd was large enough, he would climb up a ladder to the tightrope, fling his arms out like wings and run quickly across to the other island, a distance of a hundred and fifty to two hundred metres, turn around and walk back in slow tempo this time. Afterwards, until the close of day, he would perform all kinds of acrobatics on the tightrope, standing on one foot, somersaulting, walking on his hands, his legs opening and closing in the air like a pair of scissors, inventing new feats every fresh year, which he displayed first to his own townsfolk. It brought him luck. The rest of the year he toured the country, going as far as Arabia and other neighbouring lands, to make money, but that one spring day in April was set aside for his home town, and indeed it was a day of festivity for all. Ali the magician had many other tricks up his sleeve too, like producing doves from his nose, swallowing flaming swords, stepping barefoot over red-hot coals, winding a boa snake round his neck and thrusting his hand right down its throat . . . All this, and countless other marvels, Ali had learnt when he was a prisoner of war in India. It was said that he could shut himself up in a deep grave and remain there without breathing for forty days. Also there was the magic bonnet he had managed to steal from his Indian master. When he wore it, he became invisible and could travel to wherever he wished in the twinkling of an eye . . .

In time, Ali grew to be very rich. He bought up land and property in the town and all along the Black Sea coast. He had one son called Sultan. No one had ever seen his wife, nor even Sultan in his childhood. He suddenly appeared one day, out of nowhere, a grown-up handsome young man.

Ah, Ali the magician could have been the richest man in all of Turkey, but for that evil day when the passion for treasure hunting seized him and he sold his lands and houses to go seeking up hill and down vale for long-lost treasures. In the end, when that final blow hit him, he was still rich, with half-a-dozen houses and some land and even those three bays all his own, but nothing like he could have been. Yet, when he embarked on this venture he was full of confidence in his powers of divination and thought he could win over the gods and jinns and supernatural spirits to his cause. Think of it, treasures immeasurable that had belonged to the wealthy Croesus, to Alexander the Great, to King Darius, and to untold kings and potentates, buried in the ground, useless, when so many people on this earth lived in want and poverty . . .

For three years he shut himself up in his house with history books and read and read until he felt he would go crazy if he did not start out at once. Who could blame him? Fourteen thousand ancient cities still lay unexcavated all over Anatolia, and what cities! From Anavarza, to Tarsus, to Misis, Castabala, Hattushah, Troy, Sardis, each one of them crammed with tombs, mausoleums, shrines and who knows what roomfuls of treasures . . .

For a full twenty-five years he pursued his quest, aided by seven companions, digging and delving into tells, unearthing gold coins, ancient statues, precious stones that he smuggled out of the country with the collusion of a German, five Americans and two Englishmen. But they were badly duped by the German who gave them forged dollars in exchange for thirty-six Hittite, Phrygian and Greek statues of inestimable value. It was a good thing that Ali had the dollars checked before using them or they would have been in real trouble. After this, they often had to melt the gold and silver objects they found in order to sell them, because one way or another these illicit antique dealers always found a means of cheating them.

But nothing could discourage Ali. He was thoroughly bewitched by these old cities, the tombstones, the shrines, and lived among them as though they were his own town, making heartfelt offerings to the Hittite tempest god in the ruined shrines just like any citizen of the time and dressing up like the Greek, Hittite, Roman or Phrygian statues he encountered. On Nemrud Mountain, King Antiochus was his closest companion, and everywhere in those ancient sites, at Yazilikaya, Karatepe, Hattushah, Sakchagöz, Gözlükule, Kültepe, he had friends, statues, reliefs, inscriptions that he loved. He had grown to regard himself as the last monarch of all these kingdoms dead and gone. So immersed was he in the past that he even imagined himself married at times, or in love with old-time queens and goddesses.

The digging would always be done at night, in secret. Sometimes, Ali would take his son, Sultan, along, for the youth had grown even more fascinated with the quest than his father, devouring in a few years all the history and archaeology books he could lay hands on.

One of the places that interested Ali most was Nurhak Mountain in the Chukurova, for it was there, Ali was certain, that Cleopatra's treasure must lie buried. The Egyptian Queen had brought it along with her when she sailed over to Tarsus in her gold-embossed ships to meet her lover, and had stored it away in the palace he built for her on Nurhak Mountain. And when she died there in the Chukurova, her lover had buried her in a sumptuous underground vault on that same mountain. But there were so many ruins on Nurhak . . . Any one of them could be Cleopatra's castle. Poor Ali tried them all and, though he never found Cleopatra's treasure, he was lucky enough to unearth three Hittite statues which he sold to an American colonel at the Injirlik Air Base for a goodly sum in dollars, and genuine ones too.

At Divrigi, in the province of Sivas, stands the copper mountain that King Solomon had mined in times of yore. The imprint of his foot can still be seen on a copper rock, and beside it that of Belkis, the Queen of Sheba . . . For many long years Ali explored this mountain, searching for King Solomon's fabulous treasure, made even richer by the gifts the Queen of Sheba had brought. The mountain, reddish, tinged with green in places, exuding an odour of burnt ammoniac, smoked day and night, smouldering as though from some perpetual fire. And there were nights when it glowed like a mass of incandescent coals, shooting blinding sparks into the darkness. Ali and his companions would cast themselves down, prostrate in worship, until the brightness passed away. This, they had learnt to do from the peasants of the region.

Ali had discovered an ancient manuscript inscribed on deerskin, full of information about the mountain and its history, and in it were three maps, all three showing the exact location of the treasure. But the writing was in Armenian, so Ali had his old friend Agop Süleymanian* read it out to him. Now, Agop Süleymanian had an irrefutable theory that he was a descendant of King Solomon and that his ancestor's treasure must be buried somewhere here, on this mountain, in the old Armenian homeland of Divrigi. The treasure for him would be palpable proof of his theory. He would not touch a single gold coin of it, he promised. All would go to Ali, who deserved it for his life-long exertions to

*Süleymanian: Süleyman is the Turkish form of Solomon and *ian* is a suffix in most Armenian family names.

bring to light the historic values of Anatolia. 'Indeed I do,' Ali would boast. 'Think how many old bones have passed through my hands, the bones and skulls of kings and queens and goddesses, of Cleopatra, Alexander the Great, Hattushil, Midas, Mithridates, Hadrianus . . .'

The copper mountain was bare of all vegetation but for three tall trees on its very crest, which nobody dared touch even, for fear of being caught in a spell. A bright spring sprouted beneath these trees. According to the deerskin manuscript, the treasure lay seven paces below the tree to the east. Dig into the copper rock there, it said, seventeen metres down, and you will uncover the entrance to a passage, on the right wall of which seven hands, three times the size of an ordinary hand, are engraved. Do not touch them, but work your way down the passage and ninety-nine paces further, you will come upon thirty-three green serpents on the stone floor. Lift up the first serpent and you will see the mouth to a well wrought with pearl and coral and jade. At the bottom of the well is a palace, the like of which has never been seen. Forty spacious rooms, thirty of them filled with gold, diamonds, rubies, all the rarest gems of this earth. But a dragon guards this treasure. It must be killed before you can reach the treasure. For this, you shall recite the ancient Armenian prayer, ten thousand years old . . .

Now, Agop Süleymanian knew this prayer, but he dared not break the age-old proscription and reveal it to anyone. Only the Grand Rabbi could teach this prayer to Ali. He was the only person who, though not Armenian, knew the words and would not be cursed if he taught them to others . . .

All these things Ali did, but it was labour in vain. Sixty-six wells he found, and descended into the bowels of the earth at the cost of the lives of nine of his companions. Many prayers were read, verses from the Koran, from Christian, Jewish, Armenian, Yezidi liturgies, but the doors to the treasure of King Solomon would not open for him. He even had a book of prayers sent to him by the King of Abyssinia, for who knew whether the Queen of Sheba might not have put some kind of Abyssinian spell on the treasure. For seven days and seven nights he knelt at the foot of the mountain and recited all those prayers. But when they struck their picks and mattocks again, the copper mountain only resounded emptily, boom, boom, boom . . .

In the end Ali lost hope and with aching heart he gave up the search.

But not Sultan, his son. He persisted. For years he attacked the copper mountain with pickaxes, dynamite, bombs, splintering, smashing, tearing it apart, hoping against hope, making of his very hopelessness his strength. At last he, too, fled in despair, but the mountain would not let him go. It pursued him wherever he went, a red smouldering mass vomiting its poisonous green, sounding deafeningly even in his sleep, boom, boom, boom . . . In Priam's celebrated Troy, in Croesus's Sardis, on Antiochus's Nemrud Mountain, in the Lord Abraham's Urfa, wherever Sultan sought refuge, the mountain tracked him down, boom boom boom, even in the Land of Canaan, boom boom boom . . . It gave him no peace until it had dragged him back again to Divrigi.

Sultan was all alone now. He slept on the mountain's crest under the three lofty plane trees by the brightly bubbling spring. And King Solomon appeared to him in a dream, holding the Queen of Sheba by the hand, and at last revealed the magic words to him. After this, Sultan started again with renewed fervour. He found many hands of gold, many serpents, and came upon the well, wrought in pearl and coral and jade. The doors to the forty rooms of the palace opened wide before him and he saw the glittering treasure, the gold, the rubies, the precious stones . . . But when he stretched his hand out to them, they receded and the doors closed down again. Instead, a seven-headed green dragon stood before him with seven flickering tongues of flame. Seven times it lashed its tail at the mountainside. The hollow copper mountain shook and boomed, seven times.

'Oh son of man,' the dragon spoke to him, 'give up your quest! This treasure is not for the times you live in. Solomon, the King of Kings, has hidden it away for a day when men will no longer be wicked and cruel, another age of gold.

This world is too full of evil and violence. I cannot let you have the treasure.' And so saying, it lashed its tail at the mountain again, three times, and vanished.

So Sultan went up to the spring on the summit. He washed and cleansed himself. Then with a strong rope he hanged himself on a branch of the central one of the three plane trees. As he gave up the ghost, the mountain throbbed and shook for seven days and its angry booming was heard as far as Sivas city and the great bazaar in Kayseri.

Jerrah Ali, the magician, heard it too and hastened back to Divrigi, only to find Sultan swinging at the end of the rope. 'Too late, too late,' he lamented. 'What have I done! Dead, my only son . . . All because of me. Immolated to the copper mountain . . .' He brought him back home, and with great keening and ritual prayers buried him on a hilltop near the town. Everyone mourned for Sultan and the tale of his adventures was told and retold until it became a legend.

Salih had heard it from Ismail the blacksmith, from Skipper Temel and countless others. His feet flew as he climbed the hill to the magician's house, a two-storied wooden structure, its wood blackened by time, its white curtains always tightly drawn. The garden was planted with fruit trees, plums, cherries, peaches, all in full bloom, humming with bees under the warm spring sun. He peeped through the wooden fence, and there was Jerrah Ali himself, half naked, his long white beard reaching to his wrinkled belly, wearing only a pair of blue trousers tucked up to the knees and a red kerchief knotted loosely round his neck. With wild gesticulations, talking aloud to himself, he paced the grass-grown stones of the garden path, stopping now and again, frozen in his tracks to glare balefully at earth and sky.

How was Salih to tackle this barrel of rumbling wrath? He was still hesitating when he saw Jerrah Ali making for a cherry tree where a large swarm of bees had settled on a bough, blanketing all the flowers. The magician began to seize the bees by the handful and cast them up into the air. Not until he had cleaned up the whole bough did he stop and the bees never stung him at all! Salih was enchanted. So the magician was so powerful he could even cast his spell on

bees! Forgetting his fear, he climbed over the fence and
faced Jerrah Ali eagerly, the basket with the seagull as
always in his hand.

Jerrah Ali showed no surprise. 'Hello!' he laughed and his
white beard shook over his chest. 'What's this? Who are
you?'

'I'm Salih . . . And you are Jerrah Ali the magician, aren't
you?'

'That's right.'

'They say you own twenty times a thousand old cities . . .
With the title-deeds too . . .'

'Yes, but without the title-deeds.'

'And the copper mountain?'

'Yes . . .'

'And you can bring back the dead to life?'

Jerrah Ali was silent.

'And fly like a bird in the sky?' Salih was trembling of all
his limbs now.

'Don't be afraid,' Jerrah Ali said. 'You sound like a good
sensible boy and if you want the truth, flying's one thing I
cannot do.'

'But the whole town says that you do.'

'I know. Only people like to exaggerate sometimes.' The
magician tugged at his beard. 'Why have you come here?' he
asked suddenly.

'My seagull . . . Its wing is broken and no one could mend
it in this town, no one. Fazil Bey just chased me away. Everyone says you can cure it.' Salih looked up with pleading eyes.
'Doctor Yasef sent me to you with his compliments. We all
know about your son and grieved for him, me and Bahri and
Jemil . . . It was such a pity . . . If only the mountain hadn't
closed up against him that one time . . . The snake prince,
too, grieved for him . . . If only . . .'

The magician's beard trembled. 'Do you love that bird so
much?'

'Very, very much,' Salih shouted.

'Let me have a look then.' Jerrah Ali picked up the gull
and stroked it before lifting the wounded wing. His face
changed slowly as he looked at Salih and back again at the

186

wing. It was just like that he had been glaring at earth and sky a while ago. He began to mutter to himself too, but Salih could not make out a word of what he was saying. Then it came out quite clearly. 'This bird can't ever fly again. This seagull will die . . . It will die . . .'

Salih's ears rang, boom boom, like the copper mountain. His head whirled and his eyes went black. He grabbed the bird from Jerrah Ali's hands and fled blindly down to the sea.

And there he sat, his head in his hands, and in front of him the seagull in its basket was looking at him with bright trusting eyes, lifting its good wing up, longing to fly . . .

# 16

Look here, snake prince, what kind of a man are you? Think of all this boy's done for you. Helped you to be born, made old Skipper Temel find you a wife from way over the seven seas . . . Why don't you lend him a helping hand when he's in trouble, you, the lord of the seas and the snakes? Shame on you snake prince. Salih's got only one friend in all the world, his seagull, and its wing is broken. Salih took it to Jerrah Ali, but even he, who brings the dead back to life, could do nothing for it. It'll die, he said . . . If it dies, Salih will die of grief too . . . Nonsense, why should Salih die because of a mere seagull? . . . He will, he will, you don't know Salih, he'd die for an ant even, if that ant was his friend . . . Don't cry, Salih! What's there to cry about?

'My seagull will die . . .'

'It won't die,' the snake prince said.

'You were a snake. How did you turn into a man?'

'I was human before being turned into a snake. All creatures are human in this world, wolves, ants, flowers, reeds, horses, donkeys, elephants . . . Even the one-horned rhinoceros. Even the stones of the earth, the stars of the sky.'

'And the birds? The birds?'

'They too are human,' the snake prince said. 'And the bees . . . I myself was a bee once and Salih caught me and tied me to a string. I was so frightened he would kill me, but he set me free . . .'

'Then my seagull is human too.'

'Of course it is! Just like I was a snake and became human, and my wife, a mermaid, half a fish really, became human . . .'

'My seagull will turn into a human being too?'

'Why not?'

'But Salih is so alone, so helpless . . . And that grandmother, she's going to strangle him to death . . . And wring his baby seagull's neck too. Oh, it's too too horrible . . . Poor Salih, all alone in this world . . . Not even his mother, not even his sister . . . Mustafa's all right, but what can he do? Ah, Salih is surrounded by monsters in this town, everyone hates him. Poor miserable Salih . . .'

'Poor Salih,' the snake prince sighed. Then he clenched his fists. 'I've got half a mind to become a snake again and rain snakes upon them all.'

'No, no, don't do that! Salih wouldn't want that of you.'

'It wasn't good being a snake,' the prince admitted. 'I would have died of boredom if Salih hadn't come to my rescue . . . But how else can I punish those people who are being so cruel to my Salih?'

'Think of something, please! Salih's in really bad trouble and no one's been of any help, not even Bahri and Jemil, not Doctor Yasef, nor Ismail the blacksmith . . . And that grandmother . . . Her hands like a vice . . . Fifty years of throwing that shuttle have made them so strong she could crush a piece of iron with her bare hands. Let alone poor Salih's thin neck . . .'

'I *will* be a snake again!' the prince shouted. 'A red, flame-spitting snake. I'll pour down from the sky, spring from the earth, flow in from the sea . . . I'll surround this town . . . Speak, I'll say, what have you got against this harmless chit of a child . . . Just wait and see what I'm going to do to you. The town is encircled by snakes. Not one of you can escape . . . What? The anti-missile base up there? Hah-hah-ha! What can the colonel there do against so many snakes? He's no taller than a dwarf anyway. And besides, my snakes can become invisible if they want to. Yes, invisible, and come to bite you all, d'you understand me, stupid townsfolk? Not Doctor Yasef, no, no, that kind doctor who says "sir" to little boys. Snakes would never bite him, nor Skipper Temel, nor Ismail the blacksmith. Snakes aren't like human beings, they know a good man when they see one.'

'No, prince, you won't be a snake again. Salih will never allow it, never . . .'

Salih had been burning with fever, delirious for the past two days after being so badly beaten up by those youths, Behchet, the son of the Albanian gardener, and Nihat, the son of Bosnian Hüsnü . . . The Circassian's son had joined them too, and the three of them had broken his bones.

What had Salih done? He hadn't the slightest idea.

It was on Saturday that Behchet had caught him in the courtyard of the mosque. Salih was making his seagull swim in the fountain's pool when Behchet grabbed him by the shoulder. 'Bastard! Traitor!' he howled and slapped him hard on both cheeks. Salih fell to the ground. Three times Behchet hauled him up, slapping him again and again. Salih's nose was bleeding and he was terrified that this monster would also kill his seagull. Then Behchet thrust Salih's head under the fountain and washed away the blood. 'Let me see you like this once more,' he panted. 'Just let me! You'll be killed like those students in Ankara.'

'But I haven't done anything!' Salih protested, his nose still bleeding profusely.

Behchet seized his shirt and tugged it violently. 'And this?' he said. 'What's this shirt you're wearing?'

'What's wrong with it?'

'D'you know whose picture this is?'

'It's the tourist girl's sweetheart. That German girl who gave me this shirt . . . I didn't steal it or anything. Why should I do that? She gave it to me. With her sweetheart's picture . . .'

'Her sweetheart?' Behchet was taken aback now.

'Of course! Who else?' Salih said, drawing his nose. 'Why have you beaten me like this?'

'We're commandos,' Behchet said. 'It's our duty. We get orders and we beat and kill. Are you sure this is the German girl's sweetheart?'

'How can I know? She said so.'

'This looks like someone else to me. We'll investigate and woe to you if you're lying.'

'Why should I lie?' Salih cried indignantly. But he was relieved this wrathful commando had not seen his seagull.

On Monday, Behchet and Nihat found him at the seaside. The son of the Circassian was with them too.

'Come here, you,' Behchet commanded. 'You're in for it.' He took a photograph out of his pocket and the three of them compared it with the picture on the shirt. 'It's the same man!' he exclaimed. 'We've caught him red-handed. Their network's infiltrated even into our town . . .'

After putting a few questions to him, they went away without another word. Again they had not noticed the seagull swimming in its pond by the beach.

On Friday the commandos pounced upon him in the valley, threw him down, wrenched the shirt off his back and, with a pair of nail scissors, proceeded to gouge the eyes of the portrait, very slowly and with great enjoyment, passing on to the red star on the beret, then to the neck of the man. Salih lay there watching. He had loved that handsome bearded man with the kind eyes and the star on his forehead, and there he was now, blood gushing out of his eyes, and mouth and ears, falling on the earth, drip drip drip . . . After they had diligently cut the shirt to shreds, the commandos tackled Salih about the German tourist girl again. But this time Salih had learnt his lesson. He kept saying he didn't know anything.

'So you won't speak, eh?'

'Stinking little rat! A traitor to his country . . .'

'Whose portrait was it? Speak!'

'I d . . . d . . . don't know.'

'Then why do you wear that shirt?'

Salih had no answer to this.

'Look, if you tell us the truth . . .'

'But I don't know . . .'

They tried everything, threats, good words, promises of money. We're Turks, they said, the real guardians of this fatherland. We'll kill all those who aren't pure Turks like us . . . But they could not get a word out of Salih. Obviously, they were dealing with a well-trained militant . . .

'Just you wait then,' Behchet said. 'See how I'll make you talk!'

'The snake must be crushed when it's still young.'

'He deserves to die!' the Circassian exclaimed. 'Betraying

191

his blood-brothers. Going around the town with that picture on his breast . . . Making subversive propaganda . . .'

'Stuff this handkerchief into his mouth, one of you,' Behchet ordered. 'We'll show the son-of-a-bitch what kind of Turks we are.'

'Glorious Turks,' Nihat said. 'Not like these microbes, these whelps of the Russians. We'll kill every one of them soon. Just let our great leader give the word.' He was trying to force the handkerchief into Salih's mouth. Salih bit him three times before he could succeed. 'A rabid dog, that's what he is, the bastard!' Nihat's hand was bleeding.

'We'll show him!' They fell upon him with blows and fists, pulled his hair, struck him to the ground, threw him at each other like a ball. After an hour of this, Behchet took the handkerchief from Salih's mouth. 'Who's that man?' he asked.

'The girl's brother . . .'

'Why, you son-of-a-bitch!' He dealt him a kick. Salih sprawled to the ground. They picked him up again. 'Who is it, who?'

Salih racked his brains. Who on earth could that bearded man be? 'Her father,' he ventured hopefully. 'That girl's father. She told me so, but I forgot.'

'Why, you little whelp!' A slap on the face brought him down again, and again they drew him up. 'Who?'

Salih thought hard. 'A smuggler! A smuggler!' he cried suddenly.

'What smuggler? Are you trying to fool us, dog?'

'I'm not, I swear it. That man is a friend of big brother Metin, our neighbour, you know, who smuggles American cigarettes. It's Metin who gave me that shirt.'

Once more they fell upon him, forgetting to gag him this time, and to escape the blows Salih kept screaming out whatever came to his head. 'Her lover . . . Cousin . . . Something . . . Her gigolo . . . A commando . . . Pirate . . .'

At last they left him there and, retiring under a tree, put their heads together in a long important parley. Then Nihat came and prodded him with his foot. 'Up you get,' he said. 'Up!'

'Confess,' Behchet said. 'Wasn't he a bandit?'

'Of course, of course! A bandit!' Salih shouted.

'A guerilla,' Nihat amended.

'Yes, yes, a guerilla,' Salih said quickly. Whatever that might be . . .

'A South American guerilla,' the Circassian added, proud of his knowledge. 'Our people liquidated him three or four years ago, that traitor.'

'That's how you'll end up too,' Behchet said in a paternal manner, 'if you start meddling with such matters at your age. Come now.' He took him by one arm while the Circassian took the other and they led him off towards the town. The seagull was left behind in its basket at the foot of a plane tree. Salih forgot his sores, his aching body, he forgot his fears. What if some dog or cat discovered the seagull and tore it to pieces? Or the children . . . They'd wring its neck, if only to steal the basket.

'Please let me go, big brothers,' he pleaded. He'd agreed with all they said, that the man was a dead bandit, killed long ago, what more did they want? But the more he begged the better pleased the commandos seemed to be. Begging and pleading they dragged him to the police station.

'What!' the Laz police officer laughed. 'Is this our hero? This, the renegade bastard? Well, we'll give him a taste of our donkey's paradise this night, just to teach him to carry that bandit's picture on his breast all through the town.'

They locked Salih up in a dark dank cell, stinking of urine and dirt. He vomited three times. Towards morning, when his father came to fetch him, he was utterly spent. 'My seagull . . .' he whispered. 'My seagull . . . Down in the valley . . .' These were the only words he managed to utter, but his father understood what he meant. He took him up on his back and carried him to the valley. The seagull was there at the foot of the plane tree, just where he had left it, and the sight put new life into him. 'Put me down, father,' he said. 'I can walk now.'

But once at home, he took to his bed and lay there, burning with fever, utterly delirious. 'My seagull!' he kept screaming. 'The commandos are eating my seagull . . . My

193

grandmother's eating my seagull . . . Quick, Skipper Temel, the commandos are killing me! Help, quick, snake prince . . .' He would jump up, only to fall back, half-conscious, all in a sweat. His father brought a doctor several times. He was given all sorts of medicines. Even his grand-mother hovered about, making herbal potions for him to drink.

The fever abated after three days, leaving Salih very weak and passing blood. Still, he recuperated rapidly. But he was loath to leave his bed and did everything he could to make his temperature rise again, secretly slipping out at night so as to catch a good cold this time. The thing was that every-one was pampering him. His mother cooked stuffed cabbage leaves for him every day and any other food he happened to fancy. But best of all, no one said anything against his seagull. He could keep it beside him in his bed as much as he liked. The bird was now so used to him that it would not stay one minute in its basket, but made straight for Salih's bed. Every day, his brother-in-law Mustafa brought it more fish than it could eat, all fresh and alive from his day's catch. The seagull was gathering flesh. It was plumper, bigger. Ah, if only that wing did not hang down so piteously . . . How proudly it strutted around the house . . . True it was dirtying up the whole place, but no one dared voice the slightest objection because Salih was so ill. But afterwards, when he was well again, they'd be sure to get even with that shitty bird . . . That was why Salih had no intention of get-ting better.

Besides, whenever he brought to mind his beating at the hands of those commandos and the way the police had treated him, all his bones began to ache. His wounds seemed to bleed again and his temperature rose. He was devoured by a growing thirst for revenge. Just let him grow up a little and he would show them all. But he had to do something to those monsters now, he must! He could not wait to grow up. His father was no help at all. 'Don't ever wear such shirts again, son,' he kept saying to him. 'Even if the tourists offer you one, stay away from it. They're dangerous. Now, that man on your shirt, he's an adventurer, a propaganda man,

God knows what. I got into trouble too because of that shirt. They kept me at the police station in a cell for a whole day and night. It was a close shave, I can tell you. For heaven's sake, son, don't ever wear any of those shirts again.' It was clear that those commandos had terrorized his father, and the whole town too. It was also clear that the man on the shirt was a good man, while the commandos, the police were the worst of monsters. Salih, when he grew up, would join this bandit's gang. He would make Bahri and Jemil join too and together they would give hell to those bullying commandos, to the police, to the whole town. And to Mustafa Kaval's son too . . . And Bearded Haydar . . . All those others . . . He would get his own back on them.

'So that's what happened, snake prince . . . They beat Salih to within an inch of his life. Just because of some man's picture, a man he'd never even heard about . . . And you sit there doing nothing! Think of all Salih did for you when you were in trouble. Here he is now, pissing blood, and nobody to take his revenge . . . And big brother Metin's gone too. D'you think he's dead, snake prince?'

'Metin?' The prince laughed. 'Of course he isn't. He's got nine lives that one.'

'How can Salih show his face in this town again after being beaten so, humiliated, insulted? How can he live without taking his revenge on those three commandos?'

'We have to think,' the snake prince said. 'I'll ask the pirates . . .'

The town was swathed in a dense fog, white, impenetrable. From the sea, beyond the fog came the rattling of anchors being lowered. All at once, a cry rose from somewhere near the mosque. 'They're coming! The pirates are attacking the town!'

Here they come, the prince's followers, hundreds of them, with Metin at their head, and the prince too, all holding automatic rifles.

'I want the whole town to gather in this square,' Metin ordered. 'Everyone from seven to seventy.' No sooner said than done. 'Now,' Metin said. 'I want Behchet the Alba-

195

nian, Nihat the Bosnian, and their Circassian friend.' The
pirates dragged them out of the crowd. 'Bring those policemen too!'

The snake prince stood watching sternly, his hands on his
hips. Suddenly a pigeon alighted on the branch of the plane
tree and the prince's face paled, his hands trembled . . .

'Come here, Salih,' Metin said. And Salih came forward,
still walking shakily because he was only just up from his
sick-bed. 'Are these the ones who beat you to within an inch
of your life and made you pass blood?'

'They're the ones,' Salih said.

'All right then. First, you spit on them, one after the
other, in front of the whole town.'

Salih filled his mouth with all the spittle he could muster
and spat on each one in turn with a resounding noise.

'Now for the policemen,' Metin said. 'Everyone in this
town has suffered at their hands. I don't want to see a piece
of them left.'

An angry roar rose from the crowd as they closed in on the
policemen and the brutal commandos. There was a great
tumult, the dust rose in clouds. Screaming, shrieking, weeping . . .

'Thank you, my prince. What can you not do if you want
to . . . You can save my seagull, cure its broken wing so it
can fly again. Otherwise Salih will die of grief.'

'But what can I do?' the prince exclaimed. 'Isn't there
anyone in all this town who can deal with a broken wing that
you come to me?'

'No one. They say that a seagull with a broken wing is
doomed to die, that the wing can never be mended.'

'Well then, couldn't Salih get himself another bird? I'll
send him an eagle and let him cast that seagull into the sea.'

'Never!'

'A falcon . . .'

'No.'

'A peacock.'

'No.'

'A nightingale, a canary, a goldfinch.'

'No.'

'A parrot, green and yellow and red . . . Or blue, a bright shimmering blue, and who can speak too.'

'No.'

'For heaven's sake, what's so special about that seagull?'

'Nothing special, except that it is Salih's friend, that its eyes are so bright and lively, that it will not sleep anywhere except in Salih's arms . . .'

'I see,' the prince said. 'That's different. Let me think. Where can we find some ointment that'll cure a seagull's broken wing?'

'Where? Where else but in the magic garden of Erjiyés Mountain? Weren't you conceived there? All the flowers will talk to you. They'll tell you what sickness they're good for, as they did to Lokman the Physician.'

'You're quite right,' the prince said. 'I'll set out first thing tomorrow.'

'And don't forget to bring back the flower that is the cure for death. Life is sweet. It's such a pity to die.'

'It is indeed. I'll bring that back too while I'm about it.'

'A little bit for Salih . . . Don't let poor Salih die.'

'Oh no! he must live and live . . .'

'A little bit for you . . . And for the mermaid.'

'Yes, she's been a good wife to me,' the prince said.

'A little bit for Metin . . . And also for Skipper Temel.'

'Certainly. They deserve to live till kingdom come.'

'A little bit for Ismail the blacksmith . . .'

'That's enough. This isn't water from a public fountain, this is the cure for death, the flower of life that men have been seeking for a hundred thousand years!'

'Lokman the Physician found it.'

'Nonsense,' the prince said. 'Would a man lose the flower of life once he found it? Just see if I'll let it go. Even Azrael will never take it away from me.'

'A little bit for Salih's seagull? . . .'

'Seagulls don't want immortality. No other creature but man wants it. The others don't know what it is. Only man knows, only man wants to live for ever.'

'For ever, snake prince!'

197

# 17

The seagull still rambled contentedly about the house, messing up the floor and rugs, and Salih still kept to his bed and might have remained there any length of time but for that event which made his heart hop and changed everything. Who was it brought the news? His mother? His father? Or that beautiful, warm, loving elder sister of his who hadn't left his side all through his illness? Without stopping to dress, Salih rushed to the porch and stood there open-mouthed. This was a dream come true! Three brand-new trucks were parked in the yard to Metin's house, and the first one was blue, shimmering brightly under the spring sun . . . A wealth of colour flitted before his eyes, blues and yellows, greens and reds, mingling with the red bloom of the pomegranate tree, the flowering trellis over the door and the strong scent of sweet basil that grew knee-high in the garden.

In a dither, he rushed back and got dressed.

'Where are you going?' his mother cried. 'Not out? You'll catch cold again . . .'

'I'm quite well now,' Salih replied. Suddenly he looked down and saw the seagull pattering at his heels. In his excitement he had forgotten all about it. How could he! But his faithful seagull hadn't forgotten him . . . Who was it had said there was one bird which never could get used to the human being and that was the seabird? Was it the blacksmith or Skipper Temel? It must be one or the other. Who else knew or cared about such things? Well, here was this broken-winged seagull, deeply attached to him now, gazing at him as lovingly as his dearest elder sister . . . He took a turn about the garden just to test it and it followed him like a pet dog. He opened the gate and went out into the street. The seagull came too. The trucks wiped from his mind now, he ran all the way to the lighthouse and when he looked back he could not believe his eyes. The seagull was making straight for him! He waited and it drew up at his feet, opening its wings, trying to jump into his arms, but, oh the pity of it! That broken wing . . . He picked it up and thrust it gently under his shirt, shivering pleasantly at the feel of the moist smooth feathers on his skin. Then putting it down he clambered down the cliff, holding on to the yellow sun-drenched broom, and there, on the sands, by the sunny sparkling sea, he and his seagull walked together, he in front, the seagull behind, until they came to the place where he had concealed the scoop net. The sea was very smooth with shoals of tiny fish frisking in and out of it like popcorn and Salih came up at once with a glittering blue mass that he set before his seagull. How hungrily it swallowed them up, five, ten at a time! Again and again Salih cast the scoop net. The seagull ate up everything. Its gullet was swollen almost to its own size. Surely these seagulls must be the most gluttonous creatures on earth!

'Now, that's enough,' Salih said. 'You'll burst. We'll come again tomorrow.'

Only then did he remember the trucks. Quickly, he picked up the bird and hurried back home. From the porch he could see Metin standing in the yard, one hand on his hip, the other scratching his head thoughtfully. His moustache drooped as it had never done before and he looked troubled. Salih did not hesitate. He jumped over the fence and went straight up to him.

'Welcome back, big brother,' he said, holding out his hand.

Metin took it. 'Hello,' he said. 'Who are you?'

'I'm Salih, from next door.'

'Not Osman's son? How you've grown!' Metin laughed and clapped his hand to Salih's shoulder. 'Why, you're a big lad now!'

'So I am,' Salih said, pleased. 'Listen, big brother, I wanted to tell you that you needn't worry about those men, those adventurers who sat around swinging like storks in your yard and plunging their daggers into the ground. They haven't come once since you went away . . . Everyone but I thought the pirates had killed you . . . I knew that nobody could kill you, not all the pirates and smugglers and adventurers in the world . . . Isn't that so, big brother?' He looked earnestly at Metin.

'Of course!' Metin laughed. 'But why should anyone want to kill me?'

Salih was upset. 'It's only that . . . These adventurers . . .' He stammered. 'The ones with the daggers . . . Always talking, chatter-chatter-chatter, and no one understanding a word of what they were saying . . . These aren't the old trucks, are they, the ones those men took away? There was a blue one, just like this. And every snotty boy had one too then . . . Blue, blue, blue, every snotty boy . . .'

Metin stared. 'What on earth are you talking about, Salih?'

Salih blanched. He cast about and suddenly saw his seagull right there at his feet. 'Look, big brother,' he cried. 'You see this baby seagull? It talks to me like a friend and follows me everywhere like a dog . . . Tell me, are these the same trucks?'

Metin had begun to enjoy this. Salih's quaint ways had shaken him out of his blue mood. 'These trucks are brand new, Salih. As for those men with the daggers, they'll never be able to take them away from me again.'

'May I get into one?' Salih asked, trembling with eagerness.

'But of course! And if you wish, you can drive it too when you grow up. The blue one or the . . .'

'The blue, the blue!' Salih cried. 'The blue's mine.'

'That's a deal,' Metin said.

Salih went up to the truck and stood there, wondering how he could ever climb into it. His head hardly reached to the huge wheels.

'Shall I help you in?' Metin asked.

'Yes, please,' Salih said.

Metin heaved him onto the seat. Salih felt as though he had wings now. 'Metin . . .' he said.

'Yes, Salih?'

'Could I have my seagull too with me? It's a clever bird

and won't dirty your truck.'

'All right,' Metin said. He picked up the bird, caressed it and handed it over to Salih. 'I've got to go somewhere now, Salih. You stay here and play as much as you like.' And he walked off towards the lighthouse.

How could Salih ever have enough of playing in this truck! He even found a way to get off and up into the other two trucks, opening and closing the doors, sitting at the wheel, and carrying his seagull along with him.

It was well into the afternoon when Metin returned, but Salih was still playing about in the blue truck, blissfully absorbed. Metin stopped and watched. Salih's happiness had made him happy too.

'Well, Salih?' he said at last. 'Have you had fun?'

'Oh yes! They're such beautiful, beautiful trucks. I love them. If I could only learn to drive them too . . .'

'You will. I'll teach you.'

'Really?'

'Why shouldn't I?'

Salih lowered himself out of the truck, carefully cradling the seagull. He put it down, took Metin's hand and drew him under the pomegranate tree in a corner of the yard. 'Listen, big brother,' he whispered fearfully. 'Listen to what I'm going to tell you.' His deep blue eyes were fixed earnestly on Metin's face, pleading a little, humbled, crushed . . . 'You know the Albanian's son Behchet and Bosnian Nihat? And the Circassian . . . What's his name?'

'Idris,' Metin said.

'Well, those three. They beat me and beat me . . . God, what a beating they gave me! And then they took me to the police station where I was thrown into a pond and beaten again. And I said to them . . . I said, just wait till Metin comes home, you'll see. And Behchet said, we're commandos, we'll beat you and your Metin until you both piss blood. And I said to them, no one can touch a hair of Metin's head, neither you nor even the snake prince. Isn't that so, big brother?'

'No, of course not,' Metin said proudly.

'And then they cursed and swore at you. At your lovely

201

moustache . . . And I said . . . And because I said it, they fell on me again and beat me to pulp . . . I said, Metin's moustache shines like the sun because he rubs it with a secret ointment my grandmother makes for him out of the flowers and herbs of all the hills around here. And they said, let that shitty Metin of yours try and come near us and we'll break his bones too. We're commandos . . . Even my father didn't dare say a word to them and scolded me instead. Only the snake prince . . .' He hesitated. Should he tell Metin about the snake prince? . . .

'What's all this about a snake, Salih? Are you afraid to tell me?'

'The snake? It's just . . . If you can't get the better of those commandos then I'll have my snake bite them . . . Though he's a man now . . .'

'Who's a man?'

'The snake.'

Metin burst out laughing and Salih blushed to the roots of his hair.

'But tell me Salih, why did they beat you?'

'Because of the shirt the tourist girl gave me last summer, with the picture of a man on it, smiling, with a beard and moustache just as beautiful as yours and a star on his forehead . . .'

'Who was that?'

'The tourist girl's something . . . Her sweetheart.'

'Oh, I see. And did they beat you just because of that shirt?'

'Yes . . . But I didn't steal it . . . And they said this man on the shirt looks like that bastard smuggler Metin, so that's why you stole it. You're a thief and so's Metin . . . So they beat me and swore at you. Look, be very careful and don't show yourself around these days.'

'But why?'

'Because they're three and they've got the police with them too. Listen, let me whisper it in your ear . . .' Metin bent down. 'Don't ever go to the market place and if you do, keep your hand on your gun. They said to me, we'll kill that Metin of yours, the minute he returns and take away his trucks too . . . So you see!'

Metin straightened up. 'Yes, I see . . .'

Salih grasped his hand. 'Look, you don't believe I stole that shirt, do you?'

'Of course not.'

'And even if I did, what business is it of theirs?'

'What indeed, the dogs . . .'

Again, Salih's wide blue gaze dwelt adoringly on Metin. 'You will kill them, won't you, before they kill us?' he blurted out. 'You will, won't you? If you don't I'll have to tell my snake and he'll be so angry he'll destroy the whole town. Wouldn't it be a pity for our town? . . .'

'Wait a minute, Salih!' Metin laughed. 'I've only just come back. Let me get the feel of the town. Besides, it's not so easy to kill a man.'

'It is, it is!' Salih shouted. 'Don't be afraid. I'll kill them too when I'm grown up.'

'Look here, have a little patience. What's the hurry?'

A sudden misgiving seized Salih. Was Metin making fun of him? Hardly knowing what he was doing, he jumped back into his own yard and hid behind the old olive tree. He was ashamed of himself. How could he have rambled on like that, and about the snake prince too? Who knows what Metin must have thought of him? He bent over and looked through a crack in the fence. Metin seemed angry, talking to himself, gesticulating. This reassured Salih. If Metin was angry . . . 'He'll kill them!' he shouted out loud. 'Big brother Metin will kill them all.' Metin's face brightened and he looked up eagerly at the sound of Salih's voice.

His hopes rising again, Salih seized the seagull which had been lying beside him and crept into the house. 'Big brother Metin is going to kill them,' he announced with conviction. 'He made me sit in his new truck too. Don't be afraid, Salih, he said. There's no need for the snake prince either. I'll settle their account . . . Metin's going to kill them!'

'Hush!' his mother said, clapping her hand to his mouth. 'One doesn't say such things aloud.'

Salih cast a wary glance at his grandmother and lowered his voice. 'He said he'd kill them. He said, you just have a little patience, Salih . . .'

'Aren't you hungry, Salih?'

'I'm dying of hunger! And so is my seagull . . . And you know what big brother Metin said?' He looked pointedly at his grandmother. 'He said this seagull of yours is cleverer than a human being. I've brought you herbs from beyond the seven seas to cure its broken wing. Let those wretched . . . Those . . .' He lowered his voice. 'Let those old hags do what they will. He gave me a dagger too, with a poisonous tip . . . It's the snake that gave him the poison, because now he was turned into a man he didn't need it any more. And Metin put the poison on the tip of the dagger. So if anyone does anything to my seagull, I'll . . . Metin told me to . . . I'll plant this dagger into her stomach.'

'What dagger? Where is it?' his mother cried in alarm.

'I won't say! Just let them touch my seagull, just let them . . . I'll spill their blood.'

The grandmother's shuttle froze in her hand, her eyes glazed. Then she flung it at the loom with all the force of her anger. 'I'll show you poisoned daggers, you little bastard,' she screamed. 'I'll take that poisoned dagger and stick it into your mother's you know where!' The shuttle came and went so fast it was almost invisible.

'Come and eat, Salih,' his mother called.

Salih sat down to his soup. 'Big brother Metin,' he began and then he laughed. He laughed and laughed and the more he laughed the more furiously the shuttle shot back and forth.

The white horse emerged from far beyond the sea, as though galloping along a dusty road. But where was the snake prince? The horse was riderless . . . And why was it coming across the sea? . . . Salih waited on the shore where wild roses bloomed, large, dewy, with bees asleep all over them, their wings stuck stiffly to their backs.

The horse drew up beside Salih. Without warning, it seized him by the teeth, threw him onto its back and galloped on towards the mist-swathed purpling hills. In the dawning light the fields flew beneath him, blue, shimmering like the waves of the sea. A golden breeze touched his face, the sun rose, and Erjiyés Mountain reared up before him, majestic, towering in the middle of the plain, milky white, its crest bathed in sunlight, glittering brightly against the deep blue sky. And the blue grew bluer and deeper, and Erjiyés whiter and brighter than the sun itself.

The magic garden of Erjiyés . . . A seething luxuriant riot of flowers and bees, butterflies, birds, insects . . .

Salih closed his eyes. 'Take me back . . .' he said. Those scents . . . The stars, the plants, the glistening-shelled beetles . . . Salih's head whirled, his ears throbbed, thousands of blue pinpoints of light danced before his eyes. 'Take me back. My seagull . . . I left it behind, there by the sea.'

A voice sounded in the distance. 'Look! Look at the peak of beautiful Mount Erjiyés. There's your seagull!'

Salih lifted his head. The seagull was flying high up in the sky. But was it his? His very own seagull? . . . 'My seagull can't fly. Its wing is broken . . .'

A peal of laughter from the distant voice. 'Can't you recognize your own bird?'

'Of course I can.'

'Well, here it is then.'

The seagull materialized on the horse's mane. Salih could not believe his eyes. The wing was healed, the bones firmly knit together, the wound closed. He leaped for joy and fell to the ground. The horse picked him up, but Salih fell again and again. At last, clinging to its mane, he cried: 'Take me back, back to my town . . .'

The shuttles rattled incessantly at the weaving looms . . .

The snake prince was standing at the foot of the magic tree whose branches reached to the peak of Erjiyés Mountain and spread the whole plain over, laden with orange flowers, aglow in the early dawn. Soon the flowers faded and fell, and the bare boughs bloomed mauve, then golden yellow. Endlessly the tree shed its flowers and blossomed again. But the snake prince waited for the three fruits the tree would yield from the essence of all those flowers, one to bind broken bones, one against all kinds of sickness and the third, the fruit of life.

A luminous green cloud enveloped the tree and when it lifted there were green flowers everywhere. A blue cloud followed it and large blue flowers tinted the slopes of Erjiyés bright blue. Only for an instant, and then the tree was pink, bathing the mountain in a pink glow. But when the white cloud came, even Erjiyés dissolved in the dazzling brilliance. The fruit of life is a radiant flame, invisible to the human eye.

A pigeon alighted on one of the boughs. It was trembling with anger. 'Let all the boughs I settle on wither, Bahtiyar,' it shrieked. That was the snake prince's real name, Bahtiyar ...

And the bough dried up at once ...

'What do you want of me, Hopdiyar?' the prince asked. That particular pigeon's name was Hopdiyar ...

But the pigeon only flew to another bough. 'Let all the boughs I settle on wither,' it repeated. And that bough dried up too, and so did the other boughs and the tree was left all bare and sere, while the prince stood by watching helplessly.

'Let the skies I fly through spill to the earth, Bahtiyar,' the angry pigeon went on. And the skies cracked and splintered to shivers. Blue fragments rained down endlessly until nothing was left.

'Let the mountains I wing to dissolve, Bahtiyar.' And Erjiyés, Aladag, Hassandag simply melted away.

'Let the earth I land on rot, Bahtiyar.' And even the ground under the prince's feet crumbled into dust.

The snake prince leaped onto his white horse and galloped off. On the way he met Salih. The horse picked him up with its teeth and sat him behind the prince.

On Ojakli Island, the pigeon perched on an olive branch, laughing. All of a sudden, it turned itself into Salih's grandmother. And then it was Behchet the Albanian, Nihat the Bosnian, the boy Sakip, Haji Nusret, one after the other, and a pigeon again, laughing, laughing. 'Let that seagull's wing rot,' it shrieked. 'The seagull is a bird of the sea,' Skipper Temel said, 'your curses are powerless against it.' How the pigeon laughed! All the birds and bees, snakes and people, the tourists gathered on the shore stared. 'Let the seas over which I fly ebb away, Bahtiyar, Bahtiyar,' it said and darted straight at the sea. Skipper Temel had the fright of his life. But the sea did not dry up. The pigeon winged back to the tree. 'Let the boughs I perch on wither, Bahtiyar, Bahtiyar,' it cried. But again nothing happened. 'Let the heavens rain down that I wing about,' the pigeon insisted, but the sky remained firm. The pigeon flew back to the bough, laughing, laughing so much that it burst in two and dropped at the foot of the tree.

Skipper Temel clapped his hands in relief. 'Eh, mates,' he said, 'that's another one we've got rid of.'

# 18

Ever since Metin's return Salih had kept a strict watch on all his movements. There were two men who came to his yard every night at midnight . . . The first had a golden tooth that gleamed in the moonlight. He was very tall and thin and quite bald. The other was broad-shouldered, always sniffing avidly at the scents of the night, his nostrils opening wide.

Metin would get into the blue truck and start the engine. His companions followed in the other two. They would drive out of the town, taking an unused path along the cliff down to the bay, where the Laz fishing vessels would be waiting, all lights extinguished. Silently, swiftly, their cargo would be transferred to the trucks.

Salih would slip unseen into the blue truck, crouching in a corner until it stopped in the bay, then glide out and hide behind the bushes.

And one night the black-clad men spilled into Metin's yard again. They crouched down in a circle and planted their daggers into the ground. Metin came out and faced them, his gun gleaming in his hand. 'We have to get rid of the Colonel,' he said. 'He's no use at all to us and besides, he takes more than half our earnings.'

One of the black-clad men rose. 'But we all fear him,' he objected in a low voice. 'He'll be coming any minute now. Who's to tell him we don't want him any more?'

Metin was silent.

Salih's heart almost stopped beating. He had seen the Colonel one night in the bay, a harsh man giving stern orders to the sailors who were unloading cases of guns and ammunition.

'I will,' Metin said at last. 'But his men will kill me if you don't stand up for me. What d'you say? Speak!'

'Speak,' Salih muttered to himself. From his perch on the

olive tree, he had a good view of the whole yard.

The black-clad men never uttered a word.

There was a light tap on the garden gate. Metin ran to open it and the Colonel entered, accompanied by three armed men. The black-clad men all leapt to their feet.

'Sit down,' the Colonel said. 'And now, what's this I hear? Is it true you want to go on without me?'

There was a deathly silence. Salih held his breath. Only the sound of the distant sea could be heard.

'Well?' the Colonel pursued. 'Who doesn't want me? And why? Haven't I made millionaires of you all? Down-and-out beggars you were, each one of you, before I took you into my ring! Now speak, who doesn't want me?'

Metin stepped forward, his head held high. 'I, for one, my Colonel,' he declared. 'Because you are simply exploiting us. We risk our lives every day and though we're forty we get only one share while you get the other share all to yourself. Is that fair?'

'Yes, it is,' the Colonel affirmed.

'It isn't! And these men think so too. Only they're afraid to say so.'

'And you? Aren't you afraid?' the Colonel mocked.

'I am not, Colonel. I'm a simple fisherman. I wouldn't compromise even to save my life. Death is the last call, there's nothing beyond it.'

The Colonel's laughter ran through the night. 'We'll see,' he said sharply, turning to the black-clad men. 'Take your daggers and get up,' he ordered.

They all obeyed him at once.

'Now, you and you and you . . .' The Colonel pointed to three men. 'Get into those trucks and drive away. They're mine.'

Salih nearly fell off the tree. He clung desperately to the branch.

Metin stepped up to the trucks. He lifted his gun. 'Get off those trucks if you value your lives,' he said. The men clambered down.

'So!' the Colonel said. 'You're appropriating what's mine? We'll settle accounts later. Come on, lads, let's go.'

The black-clad men followed him, as well as his three bodyguards.

'Cowards!' Metin shouted. 'So you're leaving me? Cowards!'

'And with all those daggers too,' Salih said aloud. 'You're not men. Cowards, cowards . . .'

Metin must have heard something for he looked about him warily and searched the grounds and the trucks. Reassured, he fell to pacing up and down, muttering under his breath: 'Cowards, cowards . . .'

Three long shadows fell in front of the open gate and three men entered the yard.

'You've come just in time,' Metin greeted them. 'The Colonel's going to kill me. And all the Lazes have lost their nerve and gone over to his side.'

Salih almost fell again at the shock. One of the men was none other than his father! They retreated into a corner of the house and, laying down their guns, began to converse in whispers. Salih climbed down and crept nearer to the fence, but he could not catch a word of what they were saying. It was almost morning when they rose. 'All right,' Osman, Salih's father said. 'That Colonel will have to reckon with us.'

'He thinks the whole Black Sea is his by right,' Metin declared. 'But the sea belongs to everyone. We've got just as much a right to do our smuggling here as he has.'

'And so we shall,' Osman said stoutly. 'We'll become rich too, by the sweat of our brow.'

'We must,' Metin said. 'It's a matter of life and death now. Either him or us.'

That day, Salih's father slept like a log till nightfall. And after this he was never at home again. He had joined the pirates. Every night he came to Metin in secret with half-a-dozen other men and they held long parleys. The black-clad men were following them but they were unaware of it. How could Salih warn them? What would his father do if he learnt his own son had been watching him night after night?

And all this time the seagull's wing was rotting away. And Salih's grandmother kept looking at him with those threatening eyes. I'll strangle you, they said. I'll strangle that seagull of yours, sure as fate. How long have I got to live anyway? I'll go straight to Paradise for having rid the world of a heathen like you . . . And it was not only with her eyes that she said these things. One day, Salih was sitting in a corner petting his seagull when he heard her mutter quite clearly: 'Limb of Satan, you've killed him, you Salih, you've killed my Halil. And if I don't kill you in turn and your seagull as well, then my name's not Dilber . . .' This was the first time Salih had heard her name. He turned and their eyes met. The grandmother's tiny eyes, smothered in wrinkles, were full of hate. He felt them in his heart like a lead bullet and fear seized him. Sooner or later I'll strangle you, they said inexorably, sooner or later, and that mucky bird too . . . Salih's eyes pleaded with her, asked her forgiveness. He'd committed a great error. He'd said Halil was dead. Would Halil ever die? . . . My grandfather . . . I'm his grandson, aren't I, granny? Granny Dilber . . . He smiled and this sent the grandmother into a fresh fit of fury. But he could not help himself.

This silent conflict had been going on for days. Salih's every move, to the lift of an eyebrow, the way he called to his seagull and caressed it, the way he ate and drank, proclaimed 'Halil's dead, Halil's dead'. He had even made up a song that stuck to his tongue day and night:

> Dilber, Dilber, my own Dilber,
> Dead and gone, your precious Halil,
> Dilber, Dilber, withered Dilber,
> Halil's gone, and you forsaken.

And what's more, his grandmother had heard him. At first she'd been struck dumb. But the second time she'd flown into a wild rage and fainted away.

And now every time she cast her shuttle, it rattled out unspeakable curses and invectives at Salih, who gave back as good as he got. But his uneasiness and fear grew . . .

The Pirate Padishah sailed into the cave in a golden ship. He was attired in silver robes and the aigrette on his turban

211

was held by a huge glittering precious stone. The snake prince, too, was very handsome. He looked just like the prince in the film Ali Baba and the Forty Thieves. All the pirates kissed the ground before them, all but Skipper Temel. The Padishah took his seat on a golden throne. The prince had a throne too, studded with pink pearls, emeralds and rubies. Salih had seen a photograph of just such a throne on a calendar. At the prince's waist was a dagger with an emerald as large as a fist on its handle. Only last week Salih had seen the same one in a film in which gangsters had stolen it from Topkapi Palace. That day Salih had taken his seagull to the cinema with him. He had hidden it in his shirt and when the lights went out he'd brought it out and together they had watched the film without anyone having the slightest suspicion he had the bird with him.

'Get up!' the Padishah ordered the man who was bowing low before him. 'Who are you?'

'I'm Osman,' Salih's father said.

'What Osman?'

Salih's father faltered. 'No one really . . . Just an Osman . . .'

'What does that mean?' the Padishah said sternly. 'What Osman are you that you take the liberty to come here?'

Skipper Temel stepped forward. 'They call him Dilber's Osman, my Padishah. His mother is that Dilber so well-known by all the pirates on these seas. You knew her too, I'm sure, when you were young.' The Skipper gave an arch smile.

'Indeed I did!' the Padishah said, mollified. 'So this is her son, eh?'

Osman prostrated himself again and kissed the ground three times.

The prince had been looking at him intently. 'Are you our Salih's father by any chance?' he asked. How like a blue snake he looked . . .

'I am, I am!' Osman rejoiced. 'But how is it you know Salih?'

The Pirate Padishah answered him. 'Salih is my son's

212

childhood friend. And very dear to us too.'

It was the prince's turn. 'But you haven't been at all good to Salih,' he said. 'You beat him, and your mother's going to kill him and his seagull too. Now I warn you, if anything happens to Salih, I'll take you beyond the seven seas and nail you to a tree where a bird will come and pick your flesh day by day . . .'

'So it's like this?' the Padishah roared. 'They're not treating our Salih well, eh?'

'But I love Salih, I do,' Osman wailed. 'Only I didn't know he had a prince for a friend . . .'

The prince laughed and stroked his beard. Did the snake prince have a beard? Now, wait a minute . . . No, no, of course he hadn't! The prince rubbed his chin. 'Salih's not one to boast of his friendship with a prince,' he said. 'I owe my life to him, everything. If it hadn't been for him . . . But Salih wouldn't tell a soul about this. As for me, what have I done for Salih, after all he's done for me? I haven't even been able to find some medicine for his wounded seagull.'

'Osman,' the Padishah said, 'I've decided that you shall work for me. Just because you're Salih's father I'll make you rich, a millionaire, so rich you can buy Mustafa Kaval's villa if you like.'

'But what shall we do about the seagull's wing?' the prince said. 'If it can't be cured Salih will die of grief.'

'He'll die,' Osman said sadly.

'Yes, he'll die,' Metin said.

'What a shame!' the Padishah said.

For days now Salih had been turning over a new plan in his mind, a last chance to melt his grandmother's hard heart. He would take that long Circassian dagger of his father's and stand before her, the dagger in one hand, the seagull in the other. 'Here you are, granny,' he'd say, 'you can cut its throat if you like, and then plunge the dagger into my heart.' Over and over again he lived through the scene, his grandmother seizing the dagger, Salih lying at her feet in a pool of blood, the seagull casting itself over him with horrible shrieks of grief . . .

It was but a fantasy, yet Salih avoided the house as much as he could. He ate his meals at his sister's and only went home to sleep, carefully concealing the seagull under the blanket and the Circassian dagger under his pillow.

One day he was idling along the shore, his seagull at his heels, when turning round he saw it floating away on the waves. He could not swim after it. The spring sea was too cold, the waves too high. He stood there helplessly and at that moment a group of boys rushed up with whoops of joy, clapping their hands and raising hell in order to drive the seagull still further away. They had been watching Salih for days now, envious of this pet seagull that followed him faithfully wherever he went.

'Idiots!' Salih cried disdainfully. 'My seagull swims out like that every day to its friends, the other seagulls. Then it comes back to me. I wouldn't have let it go if it didn't . . .'

The boys kept up their wild capering along the sea. One of them had got hold of a tin can and was banging away with all his might. Another blew shrilly on a whistle. The rest hooted and caterwauled, while the startled seagull drifted off, turned the point of the bay and disappeared.

Salih had never expected this. What was he to do? His arms fell to his sides, but suddenly he turned and attacked the boy nearest to him. He struck him down, then the next, and a third . . . But soon they banded together, and when they had finished with him his nose was bleeding and his shirt was in shreds. 'I'll show you!' he screamed after them. 'Just you wait!'

These birds! There was no trusting them. Look at this one, whom he'd fed and cared for so long . . . The minute it felt a little stronger, it went and left him! How was he to face Doctor Yasef now, and the others? What would he say when they asked after his seagull? And his grandmother! She would dance for joy at the news that his pet was lost.

The shore was muddy with tar carried on the waves in tiny bubbles all the way from the high sea. Salih's feet and hands were smeared black as he tried to wash the blood off his face. How empty he felt, how dark and hopeless everything had become. Death must be like this, he thought. He began

214

to shout at the top of his voice. Again and again he called to his seagull, rushing up and down the shore like a mad creature. The sun was setting. What if some sea monster came to pounce on his poor baby seagull now? It had no wings to fly away . . .

'Oh you stupid bird, oh oh oh . . .'

He stopped, wet to the skin from running in the water and even swimming a little way out too. Then he broke into a run. There was still one slim hope . . . He ran all the way to the wharf. 'Skipper Temel!' he cried breathlessly as he jumped into his boat.

The Skipper was broiling savoury sausages over the coals of a brazier and greasy appetizing fumes spread through the whole boat. He started in alarm at the sight of Salih. 'What's wrong, boy? What's happened to you?'

'My seagull . . .' Salih panted. 'Oh Skipper, it's gone! Out there on the sea with its broken wing, where a monster will come and devour it . . . A huge monster . . . All the other gulls can fly and escape, but not mine, not mine . . . That monster will swallow it up.'

'Now then, Skipper Salih, sit down a minute and get your breath.'

'No, no,' Salih cried, turning round and round in the boat. 'I can't. Look, it's out there. There among those seagulls . . . There! And the monster's coming, it's coming, Skipper! Quick, Skipper . . .'

The Skipper laid a hand on his shoulder. 'Calm yourself, lad,' he said. 'We'll find a way to save your seagull.'

Salih blanched and trembled. 'Please Skipper, please, now! Now! Look, the monster, the monster . . .' The words spilled from his mouth in a shriek of pure terror.

'Hey mates!' the Skipper called to his men on the wharf. 'Listen, there's a seagull over there . . .' He pointed to the headland in the distance. 'It's got a broken wing. Row out at once and bring it back.' He looked at Salih. 'Hurry now, you must get there before the monster comes.'

There was a hoot of laughter from the men.

'Quick!' Salih cried. 'Come on!' And he jumped into the rowing boat that would have capsized if the sailors had not held it just in time.

Skipper Temel laughed, showing his snow-white teeth. 'All right,' he said. 'Skipper Salih is going with you. You're to do exactly as he tells you.'

The men seized the oars and rowed off with might and main. 'Quickly, more quickly,' Salih cried as he clung to the bows, his neck strained forward as though it would snap. 'Quick, before the monster comes.' The men hove to, making the boat fly, and still it seemed to Salih as though they were just marking time. 'Quicker, quicker!' he shouted.

As the boat approached, all the seagulls took wing in a swarm. Only a small shadow was left on the sea. 'There! There it is, there,' Salih screamed, reaching out perilously. Someone held him back. They rowed up and one of the men gathered up the seagull and handed it to Salih, who clutched it to his breast and did not move again.

They carried him, motionless but trembling, into the fishing boat.

'Light the stove, men,' Skipper Temel ordered. 'This skipper's so wet and cold he'll catch his death.' He undressed the boy and wrapped him in a warm blanket. For a long time, Salih remained there shivering and trembling, his teeth chattering, but holding on to the seagull for dear life. The Skipper forced hot tea into his mouth, and it was only after he had drunk nine cups that his shaking stopped. He fell asleep out of sheer exhaustion.

'Let him sleep,' the Skipper said. 'Who knows what secret troubles he had that he should adore this bird so much.' He sighed. 'Poor child! Ah, children have terrible cares we don't know of, but joys too . . .'

Salih did not sleep long. He awoke with a start and only remembered where he was on knocking his head against the cabin door.

'Awake so soon, mate!' the Skipper exclaimed. 'Why, your clothes aren't even dry yet!'

'It doesn't matter,' Salih said, hugging his bird tightly. Then, realizing he was naked he slipped back under the blanket.

'Why don't you have a bite with us? We can talk a little.'

216

'All right,' Salih said.

They put a plastic bowl of piping hot lentil soup before him and then a plate of potato stew. Salih ate up everything hungrily. He thought he'd never had anything so tasty before in his life.

The men had dried his clothes before the stove. He put them on quickly.

'Another cup of tea, Skipper Salih?'

'Yes, please.'

'Nice bird you've got there . . .'

Suddenly Salih broke into tears.

'What's the matter, lad?' the Skipper said in alarm. 'Tell me, what is it?'

'My seagull will die,' Salih sobbed. 'Its wing is broken.' He wept unrestrainedly and nothing the Skipper could say to console him was of any avail.

'Let him weep,' the Skipper said at last. 'It'll do him good to get it out of his system, poor little chap.'

Outside, the spring night was cold, but perfectly clear and cloudless, a deep blue, with the stars teeming in the sky and the sea.

When Skipper Temel went in again he found Salih calmer. He was stroking his seagull thoughtfully. 'Your bird won't die, lad,' he said. 'Its wing will heal, and in less than a week it'll be flying like any other bird. Come to me early in the morning and I'll make an ointment for it . . .'

Salih leaped up and seized the Skipper's hands. Again and again he kissed them as though he would never let them go.

# 19

Skipper Temel set aside all his usual occupations and gave himself up wholly to the task of curing the seagull's wing. He prepared several different ointments and dressed the wound with fine strips of bandage and matchsticks cut in two or three pieces.

'There now, Skipper Salih,' he said. 'Your bird's going to be all right. It'll fly like any other normal seagull, you'll see. Come back in a few days and we'll take that bandage off. And then . . .'

'And then . . .' Salih pointed to the sky. 'Up it'll go, as high as the moon.'

'And beyond the sky too . . .' The Skipper was delighted.

They sat side by side on the rocks of Olive Island under the spring sun, not talking now, watching the little seagull as it trotted up and down before them. Skipper Temel took a deep breath from the cigarette he had carefully rolled.

'It must be hungry,' Salih said after a while. 'Let me go and catch some fish for it. The wound will heal more quickly if it eats properly, won't it?'

'That's right, lad,' the Skipper said. 'Go, but don't forget us.'

'As if I ever, ever could!' Salih replied fervently.

Kind, wonderful Skipper Temel, the best in all the world . . . If only Salih could have been his son, his mate, his apprentice . . . What was there so special about being a smith? And besides, that Ismail was always cross and grouchy. If Salih had gone to him with his bird, he wouldn't have stopped to give them a second look. But the Skipper, with his soft caressing, loving eyes . . . He'd sacrificed three whole days' work, he hadn't even gone out fishing, just for a little seagull! Salih would a thousand times rather be a mate on the Skipper's boat than apprentice to the smith. Ah, if only it had been Skipper Temel who worked the smithy, and not that crusty, unapproachable Ismail, who'd be much better off on a boat, vanishing beyond the horizon into the sea's dark abyss, never to return. But who knows, perhaps Skipper Temel would have been just as black and glowering as Ismail if he worked in the smithy. Because the smith's craft is a difficult and holy one . . . Had anyone ever seen a smith with kind smiling eyes like the Skipper's, clear as the sky?

The sun had set and dusk was creeping up over the sea. A blusterous south wind shook earth and sea to the very foundations of the houses lined up on the cliff and of the concrete wharf built over the rocks. But in spite of the wind Salih caught very many fishes for his seagull. It never seemed to have enough. Its gullet swelled until it touched the ground and it waddled like a duck, hardly able to carry its own weight.

The sea was only just paling when Salih woke up the next morning. He inspected his gull's bandaged wing, then made straight for the wharf, with the gull running after him. Skipper Temel had started up his engines and was preparing to set out to sea.

'Skipper! Skipper Temel!' Salih shouted.

'Who's that?' The Skipper's voice rose above the throb of the engines as from a well.

'It's Skipper Salih,' a sailor called down to him.

The Skipper emerged at once from the hold. 'Well, mate?' he smiled.

'I've come for you to open my seagull's bandage,' Salih shouted.

The Skipper roared with laughter. 'Why Salih, it was only yesterday we bound it up! The bones can't knit so quickly. Have a little patience, do! Goodbye now.' He gave an order and the boat took out to sea. Salih stood waving on the wharf until it had turned the lighthouse.

That night, Salih took up his accustomed post on top of the olive tree. His father was the first to come to Metin's yard. He was followed by another very tall man. Then Metin appeared, accompanied by five men whom Salih had already seen before. They all crouched in the shadow of the honeysuckle fence and talked in whispers. At the first crow of the early cocks they started up and vanished between the houses. Salih felt an uneasy foreboding. This night there was something ominous. He climbed down the tree and went out into the street with his seagull at his heels, and sure enough three shadows were stealthily approaching Metin's house. He had only just time to throw himself behind a bramble bush. The seagull was left in the middle of the street, staring about stupidly. Oh dear, if only it would fly at last and he could have some peace . . . The men crept up to the door and drew their guns.

'Metin?' the first one called. 'Come out, Metin, we've got something important to tell you . . .'

A woman's voice answered them, Metin's mother. 'Metin's not at home . . .'

'Where can we find him then?'

'How do I know?' The voice was frightened now. 'He never tells anyone where he goes.'

The men hesitated, then slowly went out of the yard. They stopped to look back at the trucks. 'I'm sorry for Metin,' the first one, who was the tallest, said.

'He's a brave chap,' the second one said. 'These trucks are his by right.' The man had very long arms that seemed even longer in the moonlight.

The third man was slightly hunchbacked, with a very long face. 'What can we do?' he said. 'It's the Colonel's orders. We have to obey.'

They made their way down the valley and stopped under a pear tree in full bloom, so loaded with flowers that boughs and trunk were hidden away and it stood there like a giant flower, gleaming white in the moonlight, its pungent scent reaching right up to the road above. The men crouched down and lit cigarettes. Gliding like a snake, Salih drew nearer and hid under a wild rose bush. He was trembling all over.

'Think of it,' the hunchbacked man said. 'Metin's our friend and yet we have to kill him . . .'

'It's so strange,' the tall man said, 'when only yesterday we were like brothers . . .'

'Well, we have to,' the long-armed one said. 'It's either Metin or our daily bread.'

'But how are we to kill him?' the hunchbacked one said. 'He's nowhere to be found.'

'We'll have to watch the house.'

'He may have run off somewhere . . .'

'Then we must find him wherever he is, because if we don't . . .'

'The Colonel will settle our account instead.'

'If Metin's got wind of this . . .'

'He'll have slipped away and the devil himself couldn't find him again.'

'But the Colonel would! Even in hell he would . . .'

'Metin's formed a new gang with some Black Sea bandits . . .'

'It's clear now who double-crossed the Colonel in that business of the toys.'

'Fobbed off all those toys on him, instead of television sets, radios and computers . . .'

'The Colonel will never rest until he's had him killed. He'll find him even if he flees to the other end of the earth.'

'We must find him first,' the tall man said, 'and kill him. Who knows how the Colonel will reward us?' He laughed gleefully. They all lit fresh cigarettes.

Salih's heart was in his mouth. If it wasn't for the seagull who had crept into his shirt, he would have died of fright.

'We must go back and watch the house,' the tall man said after a while.

They rose and started up the hill, their cigarettes glowing in the darkness.

A cool breeze touched Salih's face, carrying the salty tang of the sea, of fish and seabirds. He could hear the sound of the waves. 'They're going to kill Metin!' he spoke out aloud. 'Kill Metin!'

The men stopped in their tracks and looked around suspiciously. The shrilling of crickets filled the night, and the clatter of amorous tortoises. Right before Salih's nose, a tiny tortoise was being prodded on by a very large one that kept trying to mount it.

The men retraced their steps to the pear tree, plainly disturbed now.

'I heard something. I can't be mistaken.'

'So did I. It was a voice . . .'

'Someone's been following us.'

'Let's have a look around. Maybe Metin knows . . . Maybe he's trying to kill us before we kill him . . .'

Three guns flashed suddenly in the moonlight. 'Come on! Let's not just stand here all together. This might be a trap, some trick of Metin's . . .'

They started a search, the tall man down the valley towards the sea, the hunchback up the hill, and the long-armed one in the vicinity of the pear tree. Salih could see his long arms almost touching the ground, his feet stepping warily as though he expected to be attacked any moment. Five times he bent over the wild rose bush where Salih was hiding. Salih held his breath. The bush was thickly overgrown with briars and the man did not see him.

Some time passed, and the other two returned. They all crouched down again and lit their cigarettes.

'It was a man, for sure,' the long-armed one said.

'Yes,' the tall man concurred. 'I heard him too, shouting out loud. It's going to be difficult to kill Metin. At this rate, it looks as if he will be killing us.'

'I've got good ears,' the long-armed one boasted. 'I can hear the buzzing of a fly a seven-day journey away. He said it five times too: help, they're killing Metin . . .'

'Oh, come on!' the tall man protested. 'You're overdoing it.'

'Overdoing it, am I? Well, if it isn't from that far, I can still hear better than any of you. Overdoing it! Well, what are we waiting for here? We haven't found Metin's man. Let's go and wait by his house at least.'

They threw their cigarettes away and marched off towards the road, stopping under the row of poplars to let a night truck rumble past. Salih jumped out of the bush, coughed three times as loudly as he could and shouted: 'Nobody can kill Metin, nobody!' His voice echoed back from the crags of the island opposite. The men stopped in their tracks, then rushed back and began to search the wood. For more than an hour they beat through the bushes, leaving no stone unturned, then slowly retraced their steps towards the road. Again a voice held them nailed to the spot. 'Nobody can kill Metin! Nobody can kill him, nobody!' The men cast themselves flat on the ground. Salih did the same, and for a long time they all lay quite still, not making a sound. The moon had passed its apex and was sinking to the west over the sea, when Salih saw the men start up and take to their heels.

For five days Salih waited, on the look-out every night, and on the sixth day the men came again. This time they made for the lighthouse and sat on the crags to the north. Just as they were lighting their cigarettes, Salih shouted out again. The men crouched low behind the rocks, then scurried away, bent in two, struck with fear.

After this, Salih played with them for nights on end, in the woods, under the lighthouse, in the old Greek graveyard, around the lifeboat station and even in the boathouse, dodging around the boats, thrilled to be making fools of these people who wanted to kill big brother Metin. And once he'd even mocked the Colonel himself, who had set more than a dozen men after him, in vain. How could they find Salih when he squeezed himself into some hole, shrinking to half his size? Another time they came to the bay with police dogs. Salih had the fright of his life, but he glided swiftly along the beach, jumped into a boat and rowed away. The dogs were left barking on the shore and no one suspected a thing. They must have thought he was just a fisher boy in his boat. How mad the Colonel had been when even his dogs had not been able to track down the person who'd been shouting 'Good for Metin' all these nights!

Every evening Salih waited on the wharf for Skipper Temel's boat to return.

'Skipper . . . Aren't you going to open my seagull's bandage?'

'How long is it now, mate?'

'Fifteen days . . . '

'Let's wait a little longer, Skipper Salih . . . '

On top of all his worries was the gnawing thought that he should warn Metin of what was threatening him. But he dreaded being rebuffed and always put it off. Until one night he saw those huge automatic weapons in the men's hands . . .

The next morning Metin was sitting under the trellised bower near the honeysuckle fence, a pink rose in his ear, legs crossed, contentedly sipping a cup of coffee. Salih dropped before him like a ball and stood there sweating, flushing to the roots of his hair. He forced himself to speak. 'Three men . . .' he stammered. 'Every night . . . In the woods, the lighthouse . . . The lifeboat station . . . Their guns are this size . . . The Colonel's dogs . . .' Metin could not make out what he was saying and burst out laughing. The more he laughed the more incoherent Salih became. 'They're going to kill you,' he burst out at last. 'Kill you! Three men. Ten, twenty . . .' But Metin only laughed still more.

Salih jumped back over the fence, grabbed his seagull and stalked off towards the wharf, Metin's laughter still ringing in his ears.

It was a clear sunny day. He sat down to wait, for surely, with the sea so smooth, Skipper Temel would not return before evening. The seagull's bandage must be opened that very day. Salih could not bear this suspense any longer.

But the fishermen must have had an exceptionally good catch for they came in much earlier than usual, and Skipper Temel was among the first. Salih paced up and down the wharf while the boats drew alongside. Should he tell the Skipper that Metin was in danger? What if he too laughed at him like Metin had done? Everyone laughed at little children. Well then, serve Metin right! Let them kill him . . . He saw him lying dead, one golden lock stained red with blood, and his heart ached. Metin must not die! But what could he do?

The many young boys who worked on the boats began jumping out onto the wharf, their oilskins smelly and covered with scales. How proud they looked to have been working like grown men, tired but happy, their hands rough and shiny and larger than normal from plucking fish out of the nets. The decks were crammed with crates of fish, glistening coral-red Black Sea mullets, yellow-eyed . . . Turbots, gurnards, whitings . . .

Skipper Temel, vigorous, limber, jumped out, his large hawk-nose, his broad forehead sunburned and gleaming. 'Hello, Skipper Salih!' he called. 'How's your seagull?'

'How could it be?' Salih said bitterly. 'With its wing bound up since God knows how long . . .'

The Skipper smiled. 'All right, we'll unbind it now and hope for the best.' He sat down on a bollard, took the bird on his lap, carefully unwound the bandage and passed his fingers over the wing. Then he laughed in sheer delight. 'Look Salih! Feel it too. The bones are quite joined now and the wound's healed. My ointments have worked wonders.' He rose, held the bird up in the air and let it go. For the first time, the seagull opened its two wings and alighted easily on the wharf. Its eyes flicked back and forth from Salih to the Skipper in pure astonishment.

'Will it really be able to fly?' Salih asked in an awed voice.

'Certainly,' the Skipper said. 'Only you've fed it so much, it'll be hard at first. Just look at it! It's as fat as a goose. It'll learn to fly, yes, slowly at first, and then one day it'll take wing for good.'

'You mean it'll never come back again?' Salih asked anxiously.

'Well, seagulls are like that,' the Skipper said. 'They love the sea more than human beings. But don't worry, your seagull will always know you. It'll come back to you often.'

Salih's face cleared. Laughing with glee, he ran back home. 'Mother, mother look!' he cried. 'My seagull's cured! The broken wing's healed! And in a couple of days it'll be able to fly.'

The grandmother's shuttle quickened angrily. It came and went like the crack of a whip . . . It'll die! That broken-winged gull will die! As for that Laz skipper, he was always a trickster, even in his youth. *His* ointments cure a broken wing? Hah, let him use them to close his wife's crotch! Hah-ha, that seagull will die. It never never will fly again . . .

'My seagull's going to fly! Yes, it will, and no later than

tomorrow! Skipper Temel's the best, the richest of all the fishermen around here. He's got a villa like Mustafa Kaval's in Istanbul and six apartment buildings too. And a fleet of fifteen fishing vessels, all blue . . . And today he's caught so many fish, he said he'd get ten thousand liras for them!'

Zirto zirt, zirto zirt, went the shuttle. Who ever heard of a fisherman getting rich! Clickety-clack, clickety-clack . . .

'Of course Skipper Temel is rich! The whole of Istanbul buys its fish from him. He's such a good man, light flows from his face . . .'

The shuttle flew into a passion.

'And those dead, frog-eyed, spider-faced old hags can burst with rage, but my seagull's going to fly! To fly!'

The shuttle whirred on the loom, only a furious grey streak now . . . *You* burst, *you* die! You . . . You . . . It stopped suddenly, breathless, quivering . . .

Salih laughed, oh how he laughed! He went into gales of laughter as he stroked and kissed the seagull. 'Good for you, my little bird! You didn't die, and tomorrow you'll fly again, won't you?' He lowered his voice and winked at the bird. 'You'll soar right up into the sky over the garden and come back to me and that Dilber Jilber will burst with rage . . . Dilber Jilber, ha-ha, Dilber Jilber . . .'

The shuttle flushed crimson as though it would suffer a stroke . . . I'll strangle you, strangle you both! I'll wring your necks! The shuttle rattled back and forth with cold fury now. Salih could hear it all quite clearly. Clack-clack-clack, I'll wring your necks, I'll gouge your eyes out . . . I'll put that bird in the mincer and make mincemeat of it . . .

Salih's mother and sister were watching, aghast. They had never seen the grandmother so angry. Suddenly everything stopped. There was a deathly silence that seemed as though it would never be broken, not for a thousand years. Salih was petrified, while his mother rushed to the grandmother. 'Don't, my good mother!' she cried, seizing the old woman's hand and holding it to her breast. 'Please don't do anything to him. He's my only son, your only grandson. Forgive him, he's just a child . . .'

The grandmother's hand snapped back vehemently and

the shuttle shot at the loom again, lightning-like, vomiting all its pent-up rancour.

Salih grabbed his seagull and fled.

Down by the shore there was no one, not even Jemil gathering shells. He put the seagull down on the sand and stretched himself flat on his stomach. Soon Skipper Temel would be going away to Istanbul, as he did every year. These fishermen would come to the little fishing port in the winter, from the Marmara coast, from the Aegean, from Istanbul, and all through winter and spring their boats would put to sea in the early dawn and return at sunset with clouds of seagulls in their wake. The day's catch would be unloaded into the waiting trucks at incredible speed by the boys of the town and the trucks would roar away, all headlights on, for the fish market in Istanbul. But at the first breath of summer the fishermen would start to leave one after the other, and one fine morning the townspeople would find the harbour quite empty. It was as if all life had departed from it and from the whole town too.

Salih knew exactly when Skipper Temel would leave. Every morning, he counted the days on his fingers. The year before he had gone eleven days later than the others . . . Salih raised his head, his clear blue eyes filled with tears. 'Please God,' he prayed, 'make him stay another month, so he can see this bird fly. How glad he'll be, when it's he who cured its wing . . .' He rose, picked up the seagull and cast it as high in the air as he could. The bird spread its wings and floated down gently over the sand. Again and again he threw it up and once it actually flapped its wings a few times before alighting. It had grown so large and fat that it would need a lot of practice before it would fly. Salih must train it patiently for days and days.

'Ah,' he sighed, 'if only it would fly, if only . . .'

At home, he could think of nothing else now. 'If only it would fly . . . Mother, wouldn't it be wonderful if it flew?'

'Of course it'll fly, my darling,' his mother replied every time. 'Such a beautiful bird too . . .' And Salih would jump for joy, kissing his mother and his seagull again and again.

'Sister! Sister Hanifé, if only it would fly! High up into the sky, and come back to me . . . Who knows, who knows what will happen then? Isn't that so, sister?'

'It'll fly, of course it will, my darling sweet little brother. What bird doesn't fly?' How beautiful she was, his sister, with her swan-like neck, her large blue eyes . . . She and Haji Nusret's daughter were the most beautiful women in town. Everyone said so . . .

'This bird will fly, my friend,' her husband Mustafa assured him, as he inspected the wing, a little shamefacedly, sorry he could not have cured it himself. 'It'll fly to the other end of the sky and come back to you.'

Everyone, everyone was sure his bird would fly. But what would happen then? Skipper Temel knew, though he would not tell. Soon, soon, mate, was the only thing he said, it'll fly soon, you'll see. Ah, he was a deep one . . . Something was bound to happen when it flew at last, something . . . Salih visualized it streaking through the dark blue of the star-laden night sky, pure white, like a ray of light, flitting over Outer Isle, a radiant white blaze . . . All the other seagulls were but black spots in the night, Salih knew that of course. Only his seagull was different, so white that it would illuminate the darkness of the night. How amazed the other seagulls would be! That whiteness, that brightness . . .

'Oh, if only it would fly at last . . . If only . . .'

Three times Doctor Yasef changed his glasses as he examined the seagull. 'A miracle, my dear sir!' he marvelled. 'A wonder of nature! I always believed a seagull with a broken wing was bound to die. But that valuable captain of the seas, our brother Temel, has cured it with his skilled intervention. Why, if Fazil Bey saw this bird . . . That miracle-working ointment . . .'

'Never!' Salih shouted. 'I'd never show my bird to that disgusting man!'

'Now now, don't let's get irritated, dearest sir,' the doctor pleaded, straining his neck, his trembling hands grasping the ivory and silver knob of his cane. 'This is a scientific service to all humanity. Fazil Bey may seem a hard man, but his heart is good. Please don't be irritated, dear sir . . . I was at Chanakkalé and at Sarikamish too where so many many men were launched into eternity . . . Yes, my dear sir, ninety thousand men alone at Sarikamish . . . Before my very eyes . . . Devoured by lice, frozen in the snow, a prey to the wolves . . . I'm a doctor, sir. Such things break my heart. Figure it, dear sir, ninety thousand human beings, and we doctors unable to help. It made you want to die too, but I couldn't do it . . . Instead I came to this town, and very glad I am to have done so, for I've met you, a gentleman, a model of a human being. You've made me so happy, dear sir, with your attachment to this little bird . . . The English, sir, name it *seagull*. The French *mouette*, and the Russians *chaïka* . . . For months now you have been striving to make it well . . . And I've seen this, I who have also witnessed the death of ninety thousand men in only a few days . . . Do you realize the contradiction in my life? Ninety thousand dead on the one hand, and on the other a human being like you, Mr Salih, ready to give his life for a broken-winged bird . . . Please mark my words, dear sir . . .'

Salih listened, entranced. He did not understand half of what the doctor was talking about, but what he did understand warmed his heart. He knew the doctor loved him and his voice sounded to him like some old forgotten song. 'Ah, if only it would fly, if only . . .'

'But of course it will fly,' Doctor Yasef assured him. 'The wound has healed, the bones have joined. There's no reason why it shouldn't fly. But it'll always come back to you. These seabirds love human beings, especially kind ones like you. That's my personal observation here on this coast, Mr Salih, my dearest sir. If my memory doesn't fail me, your name is Salih, isn't it?'

'Yes . . . Salih . . .'

If it wasn't for that wretched grandmother, everything would have been so perfect . . . The minute Salih entered the house, her shuttle began to speak. Clickety-clack, clickety-clack . . . That bird will die, and even if it doesn't it'll never fly, never! Clack-clack . . . Who ever saw a broken-winged bird fly? If it had been at all possible wouldn't I have tended to it for the sake of my dear loving grandson? Clickety-clickety-clack, it mocked, and Salih trembled with rage. Clackety-clack, that dotard cure a wound? That mangy Skipper? Hah-hah-ha! Three times he was wounded, that fool, and it was this Dilber here dressed those dirty wounds of his with her own hands . . . Clackety-clack . . . That seagull will never fly, never! Clack-clack . . . And if it does, it's only a wild bird, it'll never come back, never! Clickety-clickety-clack!

Those words . . . Those looks . . . Salih kept away from home as much as he could, just to avoid them.

# 20

Salih's father, Osman, made his appearance one day, dressed to the nines in brand-new clothes and even wearing a tie. His shoes were new too, brightly polished, and with the toes more pointed even than Metin's. His well-pressed dark blue suit still smelled of the factory and the tailor's. His shirt was yellow and he had a mauve-dotted red handkerchief in his breast pocket.

He burst into the house in a whirl of excitement. 'Come out all of you,' he shouted. 'Come and see what this Osman's done who's been living off your backs all these years! You too, mother, quick, quick!' And he rushed out again.

A red truck stood at the garden gate and the first thing in it that struck the eye was a tall pink refrigerator.

'Bring it in,' Osman ordered.

'Bring it in . . .' the grandmother repeated joyfully. 'My son! My own son, my Osman!' Her eyes rested triumphantly on Salih and his mother in turn.

Half a dozen men carried the refrigerator into the house. 'Here, here,' Osman said. Who knows how many long years he had dreamed of where he would put the refrigerator when he bought it . . . He bent down and fixed the plug into the jack. The refrigerator started off with a loud throb, then settled down to a gentle vibration.

Osman watched it for a while, arms akimbo. 'It works,' he said.

'It works,' Salih echoed, arms akimbo like his father.

After this, the men brought in a television set, a vacuum cleaner, a washing machine, a marvellous gas range, large and bright orange, an electric grill, and a whole lot of tableware, forks, knives, spoons, carafes . . . And last of all they carried in five suitcases. Osman drew a fat wad of bank-notes from his pocket, paid the men and sent them away. Then he placed a suitcase in front of each one of the family.

Salih's was the smallest. It was red. The largest was the mother's, yellow. His sister's suitcase was blue. As for the grandmother's it was very long and narrow and its colour was green, which means 'heart's desire'. This was Osman's last prayer for his mother. The old woman's eyes filled with tears. 'My son, my son,' she murmured again and again.

Salih was the first to open his suitcase. 'Mother! Mother, look!' he cried in a sudden transport of delight. He drew out a red shirt, pomegranate-red, and with the picture of a flying seagull printed on it too. His mother held it up to his breast. 'It's beautiful,' she sighed. 'Beautiful . . . And how well it'll suit my darling, my precious heart . . .' She gazed at her husband with love flowing from her eyes, her whole face transfigured, younger now, her wrinkles wiped away, lovely . . .

Osman stood by savouring his family's happiness, speechless with emotion, a smile on his face that would remain there all his life.

The shirt slipped from Salih's fingers. He crept up to his father and laid his head on his leg. Osman picked him up in his arms, kissed him on both cheeks and carried him back to the suitcase.

Salih bent down again and came up with another shirt, blue, with the picture of a rearing horse . . . A third shirt with boys and girls playing under a tree in full bloom . . . At every fresh object, he lifted a grateful gaze to his father. Two pairs of trousers, long ones too . . . Three jackets, a linen one for the summer, the second a dark mauve velvet, and the other brick-coloured . . . Three pairs of shoes, socks, underwear . . . Pencils, books . . . His father had thought of everything. A small transistor radio, like a toy . . . And a tiny round jingle bell . . . Salih looked up questioningly. His father's smile broadened. 'That,' he said, pointing to the seagull, 'is for your bird. Hunters always tie bells to their birds so they shouldn't be lost.'

Salih jumped up and embraced his father's legs passionately.

The grandmother had taken her suitcase into another room. Salih's mother was looking through her presents in hushed wonder. At last she turned to her husband with adoring eyes. 'Thank you, Osman,' was all she said. Salih's sister, the silent one, always meekly weaving and embroidering, was weeping secretly, her head bent over her suitcase.

'Tonight,' Osman announced, 'we'll be dining out. I'm taking you all to the casino. Some famous singers from Istanbul will be performing, Ali Riza Binboga, Shenay, Nilüfer. The whole town will be there and I've booked a table right at the front, beside that of the *Kaymakam* and the Mayor. Come on, I want you all dressed up smart. Be quick! You too, mother,' he called inside.

They were soon ready. The grandmother had not touched any of the new clothes her son had brought her. Instead, she wore her old cherished satin gown, and had bound a silver-threaded green scarf over her head.

First, Salih tied the little bell to his seagull's foot and watched it swing and jingle as the bird moved about the house. Then he dressed up in his new clothes and comtemplated himself in the mirror. His curly hair was difficult to manage. He pulled a long lock over his forehead in the fashion of big brother Metin. His father had bought him three handkerchiefs too. He chose the red one and his mother folded it neatly into his breast pocket, the same as his father's.

When they went out into the yard in their new clothes that still smelled clean of naphtaline, a brand-new ivory-coloured Mercedes was waiting at the gate.

'I've come, brother, as you said,' the driver said.

Osman opened the door and handed his mother in first, then his wife and daughter. Just as Salih was getting in he heard the seagull's bell. 'What's that?' he said.

'If I leave it behind the cat will get it,' Salih said. 'But if you don't want it . . .'

Osman roared with laughter. 'Bring it along then, Salih,' he said. 'Let's take our seagull to the casino too.'

It was past midnight when they left the casino. Salih's seagull had been perfectly happy, but the grandmother had cast it virulent looks, and at Salih too, terrible, deathly . . . The seagull had loved the singing, and also the little girl at the next table with a blue ribbon in her hair, the Mayor's daughter, so much so that it had flapped its wings and tried to fly over to her. Salih only just managed to hold it back on his lap. The Mayor had fixed an ox-like stare on the seagull and Salih had been terrified he would say something. Still, it was a beautiful evening. How splendid his father had looked, and the colours and lights and the singers dressed like the daughters of a fairy king! And best of all, his seagull had been with him and had enjoyed the music and songs too.

The next morning the grandmother woke up very early. There were still some stars in the slowly brightening sky. She called to her daughter-in-law. 'Daughter,' she said, 'the things that happened yesterday . . . I've never seen the like before in this house. Wasn't it a beautiful evening, last night?'

'Oh yes, mother,' Hajer Hanum cried fervently. 'So very beautiful . . .'

'The food isn't so good at that casino, though.'

'Well, it didn't really matter . . .'

'Daughter, something tells me . . .' She stopped and gazed unseeingly towards the sea. 'My heart tells me that . . .' Suddenly her voice rang out, full of hope. 'Halil will come!'

'He'll come, mother,' Hajer Hanum said, carried away by the old woman's faith. 'He'll come, our father Halil . . .'

'I saw him in a dream,' the grandmother said. 'Just as on the day he left, with his bright curly moustache and the black tassel on his fez swinging down to his neck. He was smiling, as he always smiled, a dimple in his chin . . . Why ever did he go away, daughter? All these years when he came to me in my dreams I didn't ask him. I couldn't, because in the dream we were together, we had never parted . . . You can't ask somebody who is there why he has gone, can you?'

'No, of course not . . .'

'He was sitting on a green throne . . . It was in a long ship that looked like a white seabird. The ship sailed into port, glittering with lights . . . Then a boy ran up with a sling in his hand, and one by one he shot at the ship's bulbs, so that it got darker and darker. I was trying to strangle the boy, but his seagull attacked me . . . And Halil cried, stop, and protected the boy who went on putting out the lights until the whole world went dark. Then Halil called out to me, Dilber, I'm coming, wait for me. I can't bear it any longer, Dilber, I'm coming back . . .'

'He'll come, mother.'

Salih had woken up and was straining his ears to hear what all the whispering was about.

'He'll come, my good daughter, and no later than next Sunday, on the ship that's due that day. He told me so in my dream. My heart, too, tells me . . .' She paused to think. 'And Osman too must know his father is coming. Look at all the things he's bought us, the places he's taken us to . . . Now my daughter, you must help me make ready. I must henna my hair and hands too. Henna has hallowing properties . . .'

'Of course, mother. You're quite right . . .'

'Osman must have got a presage from Allah that his father was coming. That's why he brought me all those beautiful clothes, the velvet gown, the patent leather shoes, the green stockings, the Lahore shawl, the silk scarves . . . Why should he do this just when this boat is coming on Sunday, Osman who never bought me a thing in his life? Isn't that so, daughter?'

In the following days the grandmother spruced herself up so, that she looked thirty years younger. And when the Black Sea ship entered the port that Sunday, gliding gracefully through the sea like a slim white seagull, the grandmother was there in the same place where she had stood for forty years, her neck strained towards the disembarking passengers, scanning each one from top to toe. Until the very last passenger had descended . . . Then she looked at the ship with empty eyes and slowly sank to the ground. They lifted her up and carried her back home.

Salih stood on the wharf and watched the ship weigh anchor. This time he had really believed Halil would turn up. Everyone had shared the grandmother's conviction that he would come back at last. But he hadn't . . . What if he *had* been on the ship, just about to come out, but had turned back at the sight of the grandmother, of her mean old face? What if he were hiding now, going back on the departing ship? Poor Halil! He would never see his son, his grandchildren, just because of that wretched old witch! Poor lonely Halil . . .

He walked off towards Kumbaba beach, the seagull struggling in his arms, opening its wings, trying to fly, its little eyes spinning madly. What if it took itself off and never returned, like Halil . . . But why should it do such a thing? Hadn't Salih been good to it, even taking it to the casino? What seagull had ever been taken to a casino at night, and heard Ali Riza Binboga singing too? . . .

He put it down. The seagull stood for a while on the sand, its left eye cocked to the sky, then padded quickly along the shore, one foot in the water, its imprint on the wet sand, the little bell jingling gaily. He hurried after it. Three times it opened its wings and lifted itself in the air as high as Salih and, each time it alighted, it fixed a strange meaningful gaze on Salih. Suddenly, it took wing, rose up into the sky and glided swiftly across the sea towards the lighthouse. Salih followed it with his eyes until it vanished beyond Outer Isle beneath three luminous billowing white clouds.

Salih was left all alone on the shore, trembling. Then he heard the tinkling of a bell, and there was the seagull, floating out of the white clouds, coming towards him, settling at his feet!

'Aaaa,' he murmured, 'but why has nothing happened at all?' Even the beat of his heart had not quickened. On the cliff the row of houses stood just the same, their glowing windowpanes reflected in the sea below. And the seagull was quite still, its bell silent now, its wings hanging, as though startled at what it had just done.

But in a miracle . . . Hundreds and thousands of seagulls, screeching, clamouring . . . Ships, all lights ablaze . . . Strange things coming out of the dark depths of the seas . . . Tall foaming whitecaps, drowning the islands, shaking the land . . . Sea monsters, a great wind, thunder and lightning, bursts of rain . . . A ferment of sea creatures . . . And frogs

236

and tortoises and red and green snakes . . . And in the
fishing nets, rows and rows of red, green, blue trucks . . . As
Skipper Temel struggles to draw them in . . . Fish and
airplanes all entangled . . .

Salih opened his eyes. Only the smooth sunny sea and
sheets of dozing seagulls spread upon it . . . Nothing else. A
deep silence, echoing through the emptiness. He rubbed his
eyes and looked again at his seagull, at the town houses, at
the sea. Everything was just the same, in its place. Nothing
had happened, nothing at all . . . His seagull had flown,
flown right over the sea . . . Only that, nothing else . . .

He grabbed the bird and streaked back home.

'Mother, mother!' he shouted, his eyes wide. 'My bird has
flown!'

Without stopping, he sprinted on to his sister's. 'Sister!' he
called already from the gate. 'My bird! It's flown at last!' She
stared as though trying to collect her wits. Mustafa came
out, laughing.

Salih dashed off to the smithy. 'Master Ismail, Master! My
bird has flown, it's flown . . .' The sparks flew all about
them. 'Indeed!' the Master said, but Salih did not wait to
hear more. He went to the carpenter, to Doctor Yasef, to
Bahri, to Jemil. Five times he ran down to the wharf, but
Skipper Temel had not yet come in. 'It's too bad, too bad,'
he repeated to himself.

He put his bird down on the beach and began to whirl
round and round like a dervish until he dropped down half
in a faint. As soon as he recovered his breath he sprinted
into the valley, clambered up a tree and began to strip it of
leaves and flowers. It was a large tree, but Salih never gave
up until all the branches were bare. With bleeding hands he
hurried to the shore and plunged into the water up to the
neck. He found the scoop net and caught so many fish that
even his seagull was not able to eat them all. Up and down
he went, from the cliffs to the sea, over the sands, slipping,
falling, his mouth full of sand, his seagull's bell jingling
furiously, his new clothes caked with mud and sand. He
plunged the seagull six times into the water and the bird was
more startled than ever. Salih even had a fight with the

snake prince, a fight in good earnest. And after that he made for the sheltered grove where Mahmut Alaybey kept his bees. There were fourteen hives. He opened them all and the bees buzzed out in swarms, clustering over the trees and bushes and as far as the eaves of the houses. Salih got stung too. His hands were quite swollen. Mahmut Alaybey came rushing up like a madman when he realized what was happening. It was a good thing he did not see Salih or he would have broken his bones.

But Salih was already away, up in the trees, searching for storks' nests. He counted eighteen and climbed up to all of them, not really knowing what he was looking for. He collected shells for Jemil and pelted stones at the sea. Tired of that he mounted the water-carrier Mestan's donkey and rode it all the way to the pine wood and back. Three times he fell off the donkey, almost crushing his bird, who fluttered off in the nick of time. He found some fish nets near the lighthouse, green and yellow and brown, whose he neither knew nor cared, and flung them over the water, only to gather them up again. He toiled on like this until he sank down, his head whirling, still hoping in his heart for something, some miracle, but what, he did not know. With empty eyes, he sat on there, Salih the Gazer, staring at his seagull as it flew back and forth to Outer Isle, its little bell jingling . . . Salih the Gazer . . . Gaze, Salih . . . He peered into the bird's eyes. They were the same as ever . . . Exhausted, he dragged himself to the foot of the lighthouse, leaned back against the wall and closed his eyes. The seagull settled on his shoulder, tickling his neck with its cool bill, and still Salih did not open his eyes, utterly benumbed, bereft of all feeling, unable to rejoice, laugh, hope, or even weep and wait. He just lay there at the foot of the lighthouse like the cast-off slough of a snake.

The sound of engines roused him at last. He looked up and saw Skipper Temel's three boats chugging in, followed by the others, and above them a huge whirling cloud of gulls. Once again the seagull flew towards the gulls and came back to him. Salih gave it a cold glance and slowly made his way along the wharf to where Skipper Temel's boat was moored.

The Skipper stepped onto the wharf, tired, his back a little bent, and saw Salih sitting on a rock, his chin cupped in his hands, looking thoroughly run-down. 'What's up, Skipper Salih?' he called.

Salih rose reluctantly and dragged himself forward. 'Nothing really, Skipper,' he murmured, on the edge of tears.

Skipper Temel drew near and stroked his head. 'Now then, tell me,' he said. 'Has anything happened?'

Salih fixed his clear blue gaze on the Skipper. 'My seagull . . .' he blurted out. 'It . . . It flew.'

'What!' the Skipper exclaimed. 'You mean really flew? Did it go far?'

'Right over there.' Salih pointed to the islands. 'It's been flying all day long and coming back to me . . .'

The Skipper was beside himself with joy. He picked up the seagull, inspected its wing and cast it up into the air. The bird flew swiftly over the islands and winged back. Again and again the Skipper cast it up, unable to believe his eyes. He clapped his hands like a child and all the fishermen gathered about them, as he told proudly about the ointment he had made and how he had cured the broken wing. And all the time he kept embracing Salih and congratulating him. 'But what's the matter with you, lad?' he said at last. 'Why are you like this?'

'Nothing really, Skipper. It's flown, but . . .'

'Well, aren't you pleased?'

'But nothing, *nothing* happened, Skipper. I mean, when it flew at last . . .'

Skipper Temel took him by the hand and led him up the steps to the lighthouse. They sat down together facing the sunset. The seagull fluttered up and alighted on a rock beside them. Salih looked straight into the Skipper's eyes. 'Nothing happened,' he repeated. 'Imagine Skipper, nothing, nothing at all . . .'

The Skipper gazed at him with love and understanding in his warm sea-blue eyes. He stroked his hair and was about to say something, then thought better of it.

# 21

From that distant garden came again the call of the bird, muffled, dismal . . . The grass and branches rustled and the soughing of the sea sounded from below. Salih was neither in the hollow trunk nor up in the olive tree. Up and down the garden he paced, his hands locked behind his back, his eyes fixed on Metin's front yard, moved by some strange foreboding, a growing certainty, as in a fearful dream, of impending disaster.

Just as the midnight cocks were crowing, he saw the three men. They went straight to the blue truck, where Metin was curled up, asleep, on the driver's seat. Only Salih knew that he had been sleeping there for the past three nights.

'Get out, Metin,' the tall man said, holding his gun to the windowpane. 'We've been looking for you for days.'

The other two men had also drawn their guns. The hunchback's legs were long and thin as a stork's. The long-armed man's left hand swept the ground.

Metin leaped out of the truck. 'Well? What do you want?' he said grimly.

'It's the Colonel,' the tall man said. His voice was trembling. 'He wants to see you.'

'We're only his messengers . . . ' the hunchback said. 'We can't help it.'

'It's between you and the Colonel,' the long-armed one added.

'All right, let's go,' Metin said. 'It's high time I settled accounts with that Colonel. And whose side are you on now?'

The others were silent.

Suddenly Salih's voice tore through the night. 'Don't go!' he shrieked. 'Metin, don't go with them. The Colonel will kill you!'

The dismal hollow cry of the bird sounded again and again. Over the frozen whiteness of the moonlit sea passed the shadows of the moon-drenched clouds above.

Metin turned towards Salih's garden and smiled. He hesitated, as though about to speak, then walked off with the others. Salih followed them from a distance as they descended into the valley. Four men were waiting under the poplars. Salih recognized the Colonel by his broad shoulders.

'Throw down your gun, Metin!' the Colonel shouted.

Instead, Metin levelled his gun and fired five shots in quick succession.

'I'm hit,' the Colonel cried as he fell down.

Shots burst out from right and left, but Metin was already sprinting down the valley towards the wharf, with the intention of getting away in the fast motorboat. Salih was only a hundred yards behind him when he saw the men running across the wharf to block his way. He barely had time to duck behind the rowing-boats, shouting: 'Metin, throw yourself down! They're coming!' And in the same instant there was a volley of shots. Metin rolled to the ground bellowing out curses in the terrible voice of an animal being slaughtered. The next minute the Colonel and his men emerged from the valley. Metin was still floundering about, firing his gun this way and that, but in a little while the gun was silent. Only his wild screams still rang out.

The Colonel strode up to him. 'Take this, Metin,' he said calmly. 'This is the price of treason.' And he fired three times at Metin's head. Metin's body jerked three times, as though he was going to get up, then it slumped back, quite motionless.

'The other one,' the tall man said. 'The one who's been following us all these days, my Colonel . . . He was here too. I saw him. The one with the shrill voice . . . If we don't kill him too . . .'

Salih had slipped into a small rowing-boat drawn up on the beach. He lay low there, stuck to the keel, while the men fanned out over the shore, searching for him.

'It's no use,' the hunchbacked man said. 'He must have got away. I'm sure I saw him running up that path towards the houses.'

241

'Let's go then,' the man they called the Colonel said hoarsely. 'The gendarmes will be here any minute. And I'm losing a lot of blood. He hit me badly . . .' His men had gathered in a circle round the body. 'I wish it had been anyone but Metin,' he went on in a moan. 'I really loved him like a son. He forced me to kill him, but he's killed me too . . .' He shook his head and led the way to the fast motorboat. His men followed, also shaking their heads. The engines throbbed and they were away in an instant, cleaving through the cloud reflections on the moonlit sea, vanishing beyond the moonlight.

Salih remained frozen stiff, stuck to the keel until day dawned, a constant rush in his head, men, footsteps, screams . . . Towards dawn, he felt a fresh little patter on his back and knew at once that it was his seagull. Even then he had difficulty in unlocking his arms from the keel.

The whole town seemed to be gathered around the dead man. The sun was up and the sea smooth and blue and very bright. His eyes dazzled by the light, Salih broke through the crowd. Metin was lying on his right arm. His long moustache, steeped in blood, seemed stuck to the concrete wharf. A bloodstained lock of hair was glued to his forehead. Blood had dried all over his face, even in the wide-open eyes, fixed in a dazed stare. A green fly, lustrous and hard-winged, flashed obstinately about his head and in and out of his nose.

And still more people came swarming onto the wharf . . .

It was well into the afternoon when Salih came home. His mother threw himself at him and clasped him in her arms. 'But where have you been, my darling?' she cried. 'I've been worried sick. Look at you, my poor lamb! You're drenched in blood!'

Salih drew back and stared into the long mirror. Where could all this blood have come from? When? For the life of him, he could not remember.

'Really, Salih, I've been dying every minute since last night. I went down to the wharf and looked for you every-where, even where Metin was lying dead . . . Do you hear that screaming and weeping? Metin's mother and sisters, poor things . . . Metin was such a good brave lad . . . If only he hadn't meddled in that smuggling business . . . This is what it leads to. Poor Metin, dead so young . . . God forbid any mother should suffer such a terrible loss! I went to see her, Salih, she's dried up, dead, finished . . . And I was almost dying too, Salih . . . After I heard the sound of shots and saw that you were not in your bed, I looked for you everywhere, in the garden, in the hollow tree, in those trucks . . . And then, when I couldn't find you, a dreadful fear came over me. I've been all round the town ever since . . .'

Salih wanted to say something, but he simply could not unlock his jaws. They were clamped tight. The sound of his grandmother's shuttle struck his ears suddenly, full of joy the shuttle was, as it came and went in the loom . . . Serve him right, oh serve him right, it crowed. That smuggler, that bandit, that pirate! . . . Salih's gorge rose at what he was hearing . . . Clackety-clack-clack! Triumphant . . . Serve him right, that upstart, flaunting all those trucks in his yard . . . That gypsy . . . Clack-clack-clack! Ask me about that gypsy family of his, how I fed them with leftovers from my table like dogs, in those bad years . . . Clackety-clack! He became so important, twirling his moustache, clack-clack, that he never even came to see me any more . . . Hah-ha! Serve him right . . . Clack-clack!

On and on and on the shuttle sang, joyful, jubilant, and the grandmother's mazy face gloated behind it. Salih fled into the garden, unable to bear it any longer. He must do something, say something to that wicked woman, force his jaws open . . .

He went in, holding his seagull, and planted himself before her. 'I saw it all,' he said, his eyes boring into those dead old sheep's eyes. 'I warned him. Don't go, I shouted. But he wasn't afraid. Metin was never afraid of anything. Then they shot him on the wharf. But before that he brought down six of them . . .'

Clackety-clack! What rubbish . . . One man kill six! Clack!

'But he did kill them, he did! I saw it with my own eyes! Then twenty more men arrived . . . That's how they managed to kill him.' And in one breath he gasped out the whole story

243

of that night. His mother took him by the arm and sat him before the table. A hot soup was steaming in a bowl before him. Salih swallowed a few spoonfuls. Then his head drooped and he fell asleep. His mother carried him to his bed. He slept without a break until the next morning, and the seagull never stirred from his side.

When he woke up he could not collect his wits for a long time. A green fly kept flashing and buzzing before his eyes. Suddenly, it all came back to him. He was about to rush out of the house, when his mother caught his wrist. 'You're not going anywhere without eating first,' she said. 'Look what a nice breakfast I've got for you.'

Salih slumped down and devoured everything that was set before him. Then he flew to the wharf. Metin was still lying in the same spot. Two gendarmes had been posted to guard the corpse. Up and down they paced, with sad faces, and above the body, left uncovered for some reason, the green fly still hovered, but slowly now, as though tired out. A monotonous sound of keening, coming from Metin's house, floated over the whole town as though it would never end.

Metin's body remained on the wharf for three whole days and all during that time Salih stayed huddled out of sight behind a bramble bush in a corner of the garden. His mother and everyone else knew where he was, but they let him be and never once asked him a single question. The sound of the grandmother's gloating shuttle did not reach him there. He would have died of grief if he'd had to listen to that triumphant rattle, mocking Metin in his death. He might even have killed the grandmother . . .

On the afternoon of the day Metin was buried, Salih's father came home, wearing his smartest clothes, his shoes polished bright as a mirror. He entered the house with long firm strides and stood before his mother's loom. 'Mother,' he said in a decided voice. Dilber held her shuttle. Wisps of cotton hovered in the air. 'Mother, I'm going.' Her face changed. It went white as parchment. Her eyes widened in a deathlike gaze. Osman bent down to kiss her hand. A large gun dangled over his hip. 'What can we do, mother, it's a question of making a living. I entrust Hajer and the children to you, mother . . . You'll be father and mother for them until I return.' He embraced her and kissed her on both cheeks, but she only stared at him as though she had not grasped a word of what he was saying. Suddenly, she rose from the loom and went up to Salih's mother.

'Don't let him go, daughter!' she cried in agonized tones. 'Don't send your husband away. Halil had left just like this . . . On just such an afternoon . . . He'll never come back once he goes, never! Don't let him go daughter, don't!'

Salih had been standing by the door, looking on silently. Slowly, he walked up to his grandmother. 'My father will go!' he burst out, all his pent-up anger gathered in his voice. 'And right away too! What business is it of yours? He'll buy a truck. Three trucks . . . He'll go, my father, he'll go . . .' He was beside himself now, shouting madly, waving his arms, whirling this way and that. They all stared at him dumbly. 'My father shall go. He'll go and never come back. He'll go and die . . . Like Halil . . . And I will go too, and I'll never come back . . . Like Halil, like Halil . . .'

The grandmother leaped forward as though propelled from a bow and clamped her hands on Salih's neck. The boy's eyes leaped from their sockets. Rasping noises were already coming from his throat before his father and mother succeeded in wrenching him away from those vice-like fingers. Salih's face was purple.

The grandmother was left there, frustrated, frothing at the mouth. But only for an instant. The next, she had pounced on the seagull on the floor. Salih uttered a shriek, but it was too late. When the grandmother straightened up it was all over. In one hand was the seagull's severed head, in the other its body, blood gushing from its throat.

Still holding the seagull's head and body, her arms outstretched, her dress stained with its blood, she walked out into the garden, whirling round and round frenziedly like some dervish possessed. Round and round she went until she floundered to the ground.

# 22

Ever since morning Salih had been sitting in the shade of the small lighthouse on the tip of the breakwater, waiting for Skipper Temel, drowsing away the time, imagining the nets being pulled out, seeing the flamelike red mullets struggling in their meshes . . . How happy the Skipper would be if the catch was good, how he would laugh, his eyes shining with pleasure . . . The sea was calm, glinting and glancing with tiny pinpoints of light, shedding a play of brightness on the shore, the rocks, the breakwater and the houses up on the cliff. The loud braying of a donkey sounded from a distant field.

The birds had hatched by now, the bees had swarmed. Fazil Bey's pharmacy was thronging with villagers with fresh summer flowers and strange fragrant plants. The town's open market was set up every week now, and on that day the streets overflowed with people. The tourists, too, had started to arrive and Burhan was painting the small sailing boat that would serve him as a restaurant during the season. In every little bay, young fishers cast their nets and hauled them up frisking with heaps of fish. Bahri had been appointed town crier. All day long he went shouting about the streets. The smuggling trade thrived more than ever, with boats putting into solitary little bays every second night or so, all their lights out, and the trucks waiting there to carry the contraband goods to Istanbul. Rumour was rife in the town about clashes between the racketeers, but Salih had not the slightest interest in such things any longer.

Clouds were passing above the sea. In the distance, the returning fishing boats appeared at last.

Closing his eyes, Salih leaned against the lighthouse and did not move until the boats had pulled alongside the wharf. He rose only when he heard Skipper Temel's voice. Slowly he went down the steps and stood very straight in front of the

246

Skipper's boat. The Skipper had not seen him yet. He was bustling up and down, in a great hurry. Suddenly, he caught sight of Salih and stopped. 'Why, Skipper Salih!' he exclaimed. 'What are you doing, standing over there? Come along and let's hear how you are.'

'I'm all right,' Salih said. 'I've come to say something to you.'

'Yes, what is it, lad?'

'When are you leaving town?'

'The day after tomorrow . . .'

'Please take me with you, Skipper Temel,' Salih said, amazed at having been able to bring it out.

'But where?'

'Wherever you're going . . .'

'I'm going to Istanbul, Salih.'

'Well, I can be your apprentice . . .'

'But what will your father say to that?'

'My father's not here. He's gone and won't come back any more. So I thought I might as well be a fisherman like you, and work for you because you're the best person in all the world and you'll teach me.'

Skipper Temel's eyes filled with tears. There was a lump in his throat. 'Well, mate,' he said with a tremulous smile, 'we're setting out the day after tomorrow just at the noonday call to prayer. Don't be late, will you, Skipper Salih?'

'I won't be,' Salih said.

The Skipper sat down on the breakwater steps and began to mend some nets that had been brought out of the boat. Salih helped him until sunset.

'You go home now, lad, and begin to pack. And don't forget to tell your mother you're coming with me.'

'I've already told her,' Salih said. 'Mother said I should go with you because you're the best person that's ever been seen on all this Black Sea coast.'

Skipper Temel stroked his hair.

That night Salih could not sleep and only fitfully the next. The sea had not even whitened when he rose. His suitcase was ready. He had put in it whatever he possessed. He picked it up and slipped out of the house without making a sound. One last glance at Metin's yard, empty now, the trucks gone, and he was away, crossing the deserted market place. The smithy was still closed. Salih went to his old place under the honeysuckle fence and sat down. The blacksmith came walking along the street just as day was dawning. He thrust a key into the padlock and drew up the iron shutters with a loud clatter that resounded through the market place. Salih heard the shutters of the other shops being opened one after the other.

The first thing the blacksmith did was to recite a prayer. Only then did he set fire to the coals and blow them up. The odour of burning coals wafted to Salih's nostrils on the gentle dawn breeze. He felt exhilarated, refreshed. The first sparks fluttered through the dawn light and whirled down ever more quickly as the fire flared up. The blacksmith thrust the iron into the forge and heaved at the bellows, setting the sparks flying madly out of the chimney, the window and the door. The first beat of the hammer made Salih jump. He rose and, with his suitcase in his hand, walked up to the door. Ismail let go of the bellows, laid the pincers on the anvil and turned to face him. 'Welcome, young man,' he said. His voice was very gentle.

'I've come to say goodbye, Master,' Salih said.

The smith was taken aback. 'But where are you going?' he asked.

'To Istanbul . . .'

The smith grasped his beard with both his hands and then scratched his neck. 'Well, go in peace, my child,' he said at last. 'So you've given up the idea of being a smith? Pity . . . After all the time you devoted to this craft . . . I was thinking of you all these days, wondering where you'd disappeared, expecting you to turn up any time to start working at last . . . Well, what can we do, it's fate . . . Goodbye then, my child, and godspeed to you.' He turned back to the anvil, thrust the iron into the coals again and grasped the dusty bellows.

Salih stood watching for a while from the honeysuckle fence. Then, as the smith started beating the red-hot iron, he broke into a run. Never once looking back, he sprinted through the market place and up to the lighthouse. The fishing vessels lay sleepily stern to stern, still moored to the wharf. It was from this very rock, on the edge of the cliff that he had cast his old toys into the sea . . . There was plenty of time before the boats put to sea. He had not said goodbye to Bahri and he should see Doctor Yasef too . . . And Jemil, and Sakip. He was leaving, never to return perhaps . . .

He strayed into the pine wood and down to the little stream. Black Memed's seine was lying in the water. Salih tried to set the wheel turning and to lift the net. A huge fish shot up, its blue fins gleaming in the sun and fell back into the water. Again and again he struggled with the wheel, but it would not turn. He strode back up the hill, past the hotels and found himself before the mosque. The old stork was still there, its long neck strained forward as it took its morning walk. Poor thing, Salih thought, so old and all alone too. Nobody brings it a fish or a frog to eat, and it's too old to forage for itself . . . Oh-ho, there's no hurry. The fishing boats are still there. And anyway, Skipper Temel will wait . . .

He ran down to the rocks where he had hidden the old scoop net and, with the scoop net in one hand and the suitcase in the other, walked along the shore to Kumbaba beach. There was a small pool, formed by the stream just behind the beach. Salih set his suitcase down under a tree, took off his trousers and underpants and began to hunt frogs for that poor hungry old stork . . . He spotted a huge green one dozing on a willow branch over the water, its throat moving up and down as though it were swallowing all the time, its large eyes goggling glass-like. Salih slipped silently into the water and crept up to the frog. With a quick swish, he brought down the scoop net, but when he lifted it there was nothing there. The fat, world-wise frog had gone . . . He sat down on the edge of the pool and waited. The sun was rising in the sky, and still no sign of the fat frog. 'Ah,' he said, 'you're just lucky, old frog! At any other time I'd have waited here three days. I wouldn't have stirred till I'd caught you and fed you to that poor aged stork. But I'm in a hurry. Soon, at the call to noonday prayer I'll have to be on my way . . . The traveller may not tarry . . .'

He rose and cast the scoop net over a tiny frog that had been perched on a stalk all this time. With a bit of string he tied it to a bush. 'You stay here,' he said.

After this he caught ten more frogs, large and small, but try as he might he could not snare that wise fat frog though he caught sight of it five times. Ah, he lamented, if I didn't have to go today I'd show that old frog . . . He was about to have another try, when he heard the noonday call to prayer. At first, he stood frozen in the pool. Then he jumped out, quickly donned his clothes and shoes, and with the frogs in one hand and the suitcase in the other sprinted off towards the town. He ran panting into the yard of the mosque, emptied the frogs in front of the old stork and rushed off to the wharf.

The fishing vessels had weighed anchor. One after the other, they were sailing out of the port. Skipper Temel's three boats were the foremost.

'Skipper Temel!' he yelled. 'Skipper, you've forgotten me! Skipper, you've left me behind . . . You've forgotten . . . Forgotten me . . .'

He sank down wearily and watched as the boats sailed away into the distance. When they were all out of sight, he rose and turned towards the town. The muffled beat of the blacksmith's hammer reached down to the shore and died away over the sea.

Ismail the blacksmith showed no surprise when he saw him standing at the door, the suitcase in his hand. He never said a word. Salih went straight into the back partition of the smithy and set his suitcase on a chair. From the window he could see the whole port, the little islands and the old Genoese fortress. He took the apprentice's apron from its nail on the wall and tied it on as though he had done this all his life. Then he stepped into the forge, picked up a heavy hammer and drove it down over the iron the Master was beating. It was his first stroke. Sparks shot up like stars from the red-hot iron.

The smith's craft is a holy craft and so it has been since the day of the Prophet David, peace be upon him.

Yashar Kemal, Turkey's most influential writer, was born in 1922 in a village in Southern Anatolia, the descendant of feudal lords on his father's side and brigands on his mother's side. When he was five, he witnessed the murder of his father.

Kemal put himself through school, and in 1951 became a reporter for the leading Istanbul newspaper, winning a prize shortly thereafter for the best journalism of the year. His first novel, *Memed My Hawk,* was published in Turkey in 1955 and in America in 1961. He has since written many novels, including *The Wind from the Plain, Anatolian Tales, They Burn the Thistles, Iron Earth, Copper Sky, The Undying Grass,* and *The Lords of Akchasaz.*

Yashar Kemal and his wife, Thilda, who translated *Seagull,* now live in Istanbul, Turkey.